A Backhanded Gift

a novel

Marshall Jon Fisher

New Chapter Press

A Backhanded Gift is published by New Chapter Press (www.NewChapterMedia.com) and is distributed by the Independent Publishers Group (www.IPGBook.com).

The cover photo courtesy of the author. The back cover author's photo is courtesy of Bram Fisher. The book was designed by Jun Ares.

The author wishes to thank Albert LaFarge for encouragement at a critical stage and Sandra Katz for her editorial work.

For more information on this title or New Chapter Press contact:

Randy Walker
Managing Partner
New Chapter Press
1175 York Ave
Suite #3s
New York, NY 10065
Rwalker@NewChapterMedia.com

To Mileta

There he is . . . occupied with God knows what, rushing from lesson to lesson, wasting his youth on a boring and empty task . . . .

Vladimir Nabokov, *The Gift*

1

People will generally assume that what you are doing with your life is what you want to be doing. Ought to write that down. Never will. Robert plucked an excessively fuzzy yellow tennis ball from his left pocket, relinquished it to gravity for a half-second, and then imposed a force of his own, knocking the ball to the other side of the net, where it bounced sluggishly off the orange-red clay.

A woman in her mid-forties, bright orange frizzy hair bursting out of a sixty-mark Fila headband, ran too close to the ball but still managed to intercept its path and return it over the net. After a few apathetic bounces it came to rest in the clay just north of the service line.

How exotic, she'd said. Europe. Tennis. Your novel. All those nymphets in short white skirts clamoring for your sportliche advice. Right.

He stood on one side of the net and fed them ground strokes, five forehands and five backhands each. "Turn your body, Frau Sardovnik," he called. "That's it. Okay, Frau Tzerkovsky, let's see those knees bend." One, two, three, four, five. "Okay, Frau Tägermeier, your turn. Let's go." Sardovnik, Tzerkovsky, Tägermeier. The good ladies of the only Jewish tennis club in Munich. The Mattathias Tennis Club didn't have its own courts yet—that promised construction was the focus of a good two hours of smoky, tumultuous debate once a month at the Munich Jewish Association's meeting—so it rented court time at Sport Scheck, a first-class public facility out on the edge of the farmland near Unterföhring, just inside the Ring. And aside from their religion, their Polish blood (for the most part), and a matter of history, its members fit right in with the other patrons: wealthy, cultured, accustomed to leisure.

"Each gone," Frau Tägermeier was calling from the far baseline. A rich husband and she thought she owned the damn club and everyone in it. Now she was waving her top-of-the-line racket in his direction.

"I'm sorry?"

"I said we've each gone already. That was Ingrid's seventh backhand. Shouldn't we do something else now?"

"Yes." He glanced at his watch. Christ, only fifteen minutes gone. Forty-five to fill.

"I need work on my serve," Frau Tägermeier called out. He looked up. The three women, not many for a Tuesday, were waiting. No, not the serve; save that to kill the last twenty minutes.

"Why don't we work on the volley?" he said.

It was only a few months since he'd stood outside the old Munich-Riem airport, a modest single building only ten kilometers from the center of town, waiting for Max. He could have been in the city in twenty minutes via U-Bahn; instead he waited outside for forty-five, until finally a glistening black Porsche swerved up to the curb.

"You must be Robert," the driver began before he had fully disengaged his long frame from the automobile. "Max Altmann," he strode forward and extended his hand like a prize.

He was about Robert's age, surprisingly, though they couldn't have looked less alike. Robert with his unshaven face, jeans and sweatshirt, lugging a duffel bag like a freight train hobo; Max in his designer Italian suit, hair shined and harnessed perfectly in expensive gel, twirling the keys to his sports car around one finger like a gold-plated yoyo.

"You've been to Munich before?" he asked, once they were on the Tögingerstrasse, passing through rolling farmland heading in to the city.

"Only one night, I'm afraid, on my obligatory whirlwind backpacking tour of Europe, just after I graduated college."

"Which was..."

"Eight years ago, next month."

"Really. Me as well. London School of Economics." That explained his voice, which sounded like an upper-class British English slightly infiltrated by a German accent, rather than the opposite. "Well,

I think you'll like our city. Munich is a small town, really. Everyone seems to know everyone else. Yet you have many of the advantages of the larger metropolis: the symphony, the theaters, the museums..."

They made their way into the city, as the farmland gave way to affluent suburban neighborhoods, then the older elegant buildings of Prinzregentenstrasse, and finally the bustling center of town. Robert knew the apartment Max had arranged for him was centrally located, but he still was a bit surprised when they drove right up to the Hauptbahnhof. Max took a left at the entrance to the station, drove half a block down the street and pulled into a No Parking zone in front of a Turkish bank.

"Welcome to Goethestrasse," he said as he cut the engine. "It's not the most elegant part of Munich, but it's the best I could do for free. My family owns the building, you see. Besides, you don't want to be in the boring suburbs. Here you'll be in perfect position to experience Munich."

He gestured Robert to follow and entered the building, a modest prospect at best. They squeezed into an elevator with a manually operated door painted a sloppy green. It was not a vehicle to inspire confidence, but they managed to ride its squeaks and jolts to the sixth floor. "As you've perhaps noticed, this is mainly a business building. But we do rent out a couple of apartments..." his voice trailed off as they walked down the short hall—concrete floor and pockmarked white plaster walls. He pulled a ring saturated with keys out of his pocket and opened the last room. "After you," he waved him inside.

A single bed in the corner, no sheets. A threadbare brown corduroy sofa against the other wall, and a plain wooden table in between, with a plain wooden chair. Near the door, a small refrigerator and stove. Robert walked to the window and looked out over Goethestrasse. Leaning out, he could look down the street and see the entrance to the Hauptbahnhof.

"Convenient for travel," he said.

"As I said, it's not the most elegant..."

"No, it's fine. Perfect, in fact."

"Perhaps you would have preferred something closer to the tennis courts."

"Not at all. I'll be spending enough time there as it is."

"Well, I hope we can provide you with enough work. I promised the board of the club that enough members would want lessons to justify bringing you over here. And I don't want you to become bored."

"Oh, I won't be bored. I have plenty to do aside from teaching tennis."

"And what would that be?"

Robert stumbled over his answer. He had gotten into the habit over the years of hiding his literary pursuits. "Well, there's a whole city to see, isn't there?" he said. "And my German to work on. And you? You're in real estate?"

"Ya, this and that really. Various business concerns. Well," he began to move toward the door, "you will need to sleep, I'm sure, after your flight. Why don't we rendezvous at the courts tomorrow afternoon? You can meet the fellows at our regular practice.

"Welcome to Munich," Robert heard him say in a normal speaking voice though he was already out of sight, halfway to the elevator.

Slowly, Goethestrasse 10 became home. Robert was the only full-time resident other than the Hausmeister, Karpinsky, who for political reasons had left his Jesuit priesthood training in Russia and come to Munich to study physics at the university, and who took great pleasure in reminding Robert whenever they met that he spoke seven languages— Russian, German, French, Italian, Spanish, Latin, and Serbo-Croatian—but not a word of English. Of course there was also Farakh, the old grey-bearded Turk who had his translation company across the hall (Turkish-German, no English) and apparently slept there too, often stomping through the hallway drunk in the middle of the night and slamming his door shut as though to convince himself he was still alive. But Farakh was not an official boarder; he was supposed to have a home to go home to.

Robert was just as glad that Karpinsky and Farakh spoke no English. Solitude was what he wanted. A place to work. Each morning he'd wake to his watch alarm at seven, take a bath and shave, make a quick run to the *Bäkerei* for pastry and coffee, and be sitting at his table by eight, paper and pen in front of him.

And then nothing. At least in New York he had managed to produce some stories, if not publish them. But Munich, the exotic locale that was supposed to unleash his creativity, had done the opposite. The most he did for months was jot down ideas for future stories and novels in his little brown notebook. He had concocted a tenuous ghost of a plot outline regarding three people meeting in New York City and forming some sort of love triangle. As the characters grew more and more intimate, the sentences would lengthen, grow more integrated, like points on a graph congealing into line segments and finally integrating perfectly into a smooth curve—the final paragraph would be one, thirty-page, rolling, roiling sentence of consummation. *A Calculus of Several Lives*, he would call it.

Ideas he had no shortage of; turning them into actual bundles of prose was another matter. He was no better than the hordes of kibitzers that surfaced anytime one made the irrevocable error of admitting one's literary pretensions. They all had a "great idea" for a bestselling book, usually no more detailed than, say, "It's about a realtor in a little town in New Jersey." "Super idea, Tom," you'd say to Tom, a realtor from New Jersey, and quickly plot your escape from the hors d'oeuvres table. Robert's story ideas were perhaps more ambitious and thought out, but the bottom line was the same as Tom's: all plan and no execution.

At noon he would put down his pen, collect his morning's output of doodles and discarded beginnings and toss them into the wastepaper basket, and carefully arrange the remaining blank pages into a neat pad under the pen.

The hot midday light of Goethestrasse made him wince as he stepped outside with his racket bag slung over one shoulder. One of the countless tour buses had pulled up in front of his building, and it hissed and steamed while its passengers disembarked and lingered in small camps on the sidewalk: families of gesticulating mustached men and fat robed wives and screaming children and bags and suitcases. Businessmen scurried between their shops and their cars, weaving between shoppers, and the corner fruit merchants dealt from their wooden kiosks. Across the street, the porn video theater, The Blue Box, was open for business, and every minute or so another businessman in suit and tie disappeared from the street through the hanging leather straps of its entrance.

He crossed the street and walked by the glass case of photographs advertising the films, glancing at them as if by chance. The brunette, unabashed smile and open blouse distracting passing salesmen and schoolchildren with overflowing breasts. The blonde on the bicycle, not on the seat but with her thighs wrapped around the horizontal bar. The topless twins in cutoff jeans grinning out at the traffic from atop a horse. The two black women making love in a field of daisies, legs crisscrossed like French braids.

On Bayerstrasse, across from the Hauptbahnhof, he caught the Strassenbahn. After transferring to another trolley and then a bus, he arrived forty-five minutes later at Sport Scheck. Thirty-five perfectly manicured red clay courts, a riding stable, clubhouse, and restaurant. He walked five minutes from the bus stop, through the parking lot full of Mercedes and BMWs, and dropped his bag at a table in the outdoor café.

Everyday the same lunch. He barely had time to say "Tortellini" to the dark-haired Italian waitress before she finished it for him, "Gorgonzola," and disappeared. He'd sit back and watch the tennis players, mostly older women at this hour, congregate in the café. Sport Scheck was a public facility but felt more elegant and exclusive than most private tennis clubs back home. Tennis had yet to reach the lower middle class in Germany.

He hit tennis balls to the bourgeoisie. Surely there were worse ways to make a living. Coal mining, dentistry. Don't be an ass. "You're too close to the ball," he cried. Nabokov himself hit tennis balls to ladies like these, just sixty years and three hundred miles away in Berlin. No, what was it? "Like an automaton," something like that, "on hot, dusty courts, shoveling ball after ball over the net to businessmen's tanned, bob-haired daughters." Sirin was his pen name: a fabulous bird of paradise. Held five balls in his left hand all day, just like me. Big difference: for him there was real glory waiting. The poems and early novels his tennis-teaching supported were real. Every day he had more lines, more pages, to prove the worthwhileness of the on-court monotony. Even before he had written them, they existed in his head while he hit white ball after white ball; Sirin probably composed whole poems while Nabokov swung his racket. Whereas my head is filled only with frustration, boredom. "Too close: you're overrunning the ball." Wonder what she's doing now. No, no, forget about that. New York is a past world for you. What's the point of coming here if your head is still there? "Still too close to the ball." When the means to the end becomes the end in itself, and the original goal disappears into mist, what is the end of the means? When will the means end? When will this hour end? "Still too close." He glanced at his watch as he reached into the hopper for more balls. A dim simulacrum of joy rose in his chest. "We only have fifteen more minutes. Why don't we hit some serves?"

When the hour finally ended, a minute and a half early (no matter how many drills or exercises he added, or extra repetitions he insisted on, or how slowly he enunciated his instructions and walked back to his side of the net, he could never seem to quite fill the entire sixty minutes), he retreated back to the café for an Apfelschorle—apple juice and soda water in equal proportions. The men wouldn't be here for another two hours, but that wasn't long enough to go back into town.

"Are you waiting for a date?" Frau Sardovnik approached his table.

"No. Please," he gestured and she took a seat. Of all the women he taught, Frau Sardovnik was the least annoying. No, he even liked her. Located somewhere in middle age—he assumed she only *looked* younger than the others—she seemed content with herself. Content with her looks, not reliant on plastic surgery or expensive accessories. Content with the modest wealth her job (she had some sort of career, he wasn't sure what) afforded her. And content with her slice backhand, which wouldn't win her any club championships but served her well in a pinch—she could always get the ball back in play on ad-out. Most endearing of all, she had a sense of awareness, rare in her milieu, of the shallowness of her society, of its greed and selfishness and collective amnesia.

"So who's your next victim?" she asked.

"The men's team," his voice fell, despite his best efforts.

"Do I detect something less than admiration and respect for our club's macho sportsmen?"

"Not at all, not at all. But I do think they need someone who is more of a...disciplinarian."

"Yes, you're right on the nose. Those boys need someone with a leather whip. Except Max, of course. Max prospers in a more lenient atmosphere."

"Yeah, except he hardly ever shows up for practice. Always off in Italy or France or China or wherever. And when he *is* in town, I'm not sure his day begins before nine p.m."

She sighed. "No, I don't suppose you're the one to run those boys with an iron hand. Still, you're a very good teacher, if one listens carefully enough to hear your whispering. But tell me, Robert, you don't seem the sort who would be here as our tennis trainer. You must have something better to do. What are your plans?"

"I have no plans beyond the summer."

"Surely you're going to do more with your life than teach tennis?"

"There was a time when I was supposed to go to medical school. Then I was going to be a writer. But then I realized I would have to support myself somehow, so I got jobs editing at magazines. But they were not very satisfying: long hours, low pay, trivial work. So I started giving tennis lessons at various clubs and parks. At one club I saw the ad for this job, and Munich sounded like the perfect change of pace."

"Ach! There's a joke."

"You don't like your city."

"No, I like it fine. Then why are we all trying to leave it? But that's a long story. How old are you, Rob?"

"Robert. I'm twenty-nine."

"Then you must stop calling me Frau Sardovnik. My name is Ingrid. I'm only forty-two. Surprised?"

"Of course not."

"I'm much younger than the others in the ladies' clinic, you know. Though I suppose we all look the same to you."

"Not at all." He felt himself blushing. "You're obviously younger than they."

"Well," she sighed again, "Max got me into this tennis thing. He thought I should get more involved in the Jewish community, and I certainly wasn't going to start showing up at Schul."

"You're not religious?"

"No. No, I'm not. And I don't have much patience for the guilt and the suffering they all love to wallow in. Life is too short. Has Max dragged you to temple yet?"

"I've somehow managed to get out of it each week."

"Well, eventually he'll get you there, and you'll see what I mean. Or to the monthly meetings, mein Gott. You could spend your entire life *haken a tschainik* with these people."

"Max seems to have a good time, although he's at every Schul and every meeting."

"Yes, well that's the great talent of Max, isn't it?" She drank her tea and tilted her head back to catch more sun, eyes closed behind her sunglasses. "Max always has a good time."

When Robert made his way out to Courts 25-27, Uschi was there early as usual to stretch out. Uschi, a dentist, was without a doubt the most avid student of the game Robert had ever seen. He was at the courts every day; if he didn't have a game he would hit serves or drill against the backboard, and he would play with anybody—adult or child, male or female— who would give him a chance to hit more tennis balls. Now Uschi stretched his calves by pushing against the net as though preparing for the semifinals at Roland Garros. He had a distinctly nonathletic body, short and still pudgy despite the Nautilus workouts he endured three times a week. Forty years old, he was trying in the arena of men's club tennis to make up for years of being picked last for every team in school. Robert found it hard to respect a grown man's almost ruthless devotion to a recreational game, but Uschi was such a good sort, willing to try whatever drill Robert suggested and to play with whomever he was paired, that Robert could overlook his zeal as a minor eccentricity. (After all, hadn't Robert just a half-hour earlier taken a bucket of balls out onto an empty court and cranked serves as if he were taking on McEnroe the next day? And each morning didn't he waste countless hours at an equally futile task?) You had to deceive yourself, he guessed, if you wanted to get anything done at all.

The next to appear was Emil, a surprise this early. Emil balanced Uschi at the other end of the agreeability scale. A great success in mortgage banking, so they

Marshall Jon Fisher

said, he was in his mid-forties, had a pot belly which proved an estimable impediment to the low backhand volley, and was used to having things his way. He was invariably late, and Robert couldn't imagine why he was early tonight except to complain or lecture.

He walked straight up to Robert and for a second they both watched Uschi, who was now executing ten kangaroo jumps, as Rod Laver had always advocated. "He's going to kill himself," said Emil. "Du, Uschi," he shouted in the middle of the seventh jump, "You're going to kill yourself! Relax, we're just fat old men plodding around the court."

"Speak," Uschi gasped after the tenth. "Foryour. Self."

"If you worked that hard at pulling teeth, you'd be a millionaire." Emil turned to Robert. "So what's up for tonight?"

"Well, I thought we'd start out with stretching, and then...."

"We don't have to," he bellowed from his enormous abdomen, "Uschi has warmed up for all of us."

"Anyway, then I figured we ought to do some serve-and-return drills and then work on our doubles. We lost that last match because our doubles teams had never played together before."

"Well that's what I wanted to talk to you about," he said. "I simply can't play with Bruno again. I mean, the fellow cannot hit a return of serve lower than comfortable overhead height, and that means that I,

21

as his partner, get more tennis balls in my *pupik* than on my strings."

"Well, I guess someone's going to have to be the sacrificial lamb."

"Ya, but not me. Why not Uschi," he gestured to where the dentist was doing sit-ups by the net post. "He likes a challenge. He can work on his return of fuzz sandwich."

"No, I really like the team of Uschi and Dan. But Max isn't here tonight, so why don't we stick Göttel with Bruno and let you play with Saul."

"Fine. Saul is *meshugeh ahf toit*, but he's a good player." Incredible. Emil is satisfied, if only for the moment. Wait until Saul misses a sitter in a tiebreaker, vacillating between crushing it and trying a drop shot. Saul, who was just now entering the court with Dan, was by far the best natural player on the team, had been playing all his life and had groomed flawless strokes on the grass courts of Cambridge during his years abroad at university, but was only the number-two player behind Max. This was because, as Emil had implied, he was a mentally handicapped tennis player. Certifiably insane when trying to play a match. He found ways to lose when it seemed impossible, when his opponent was so inferior that all he needed to do was poke the ball back safely in order to win.

Dan Cohen was his antithesis. Word was that Dan had once been South African squash champion. Whether or not that was true, he was certainly a squash player before a tennis player. His strokes put one in mind of a man trapped underwater in a chained trunk. But his mental game was sublime. Wielding a dirty, weathered old wooden Dunlop Maxply a half dozen years after the last serious player reluctantly gave up his wood, he pushed, sliced, and chopped his opponents into a frenzy. Invariably they were better players than he, but just as invariably they would lose to him, professional men reduced by his spins and lobs to red-faced screaming racket-throwing pre-schoolers. Unfortunately, Dan's mental toughness was a product not only of his purported sporting background, but also of his indifference. He acted as though he'd rather be doing anything than hitting balls across a net.

No one seemed to be able to delineate exactly what it was that Dan *did*. There were references to various business enterprises, though, and it seemed he always had some appointment or other that he had put off for the sake of the team; he checked his watch between points. It was an accomplishment to even get him to show up for Tuesday practice. Saul must have dragged him here; maybe they had been playing earlier. Saul would beat Dan in every practice match, sometimes crushing him with a display of beautiful backhands, spotless serve-and-volley play, and solid overheads. But whenever they played to determine position on the team, as soon as the result *meant* something, the backhands wilted, the double faults sprouted like weeds, and Dan's hideous, perverse shots completely dismantled Saul's elegant but undependable Cambridge strokes.

Afterward, though, everyone would agree that Saul should remain at number two. Though it was never spoken as such, putting Dan at number two would have been like trotting out some deformed, mutant man-beast to ensure victory at a garden croquet party (though in this case the chap *looked* normal enough). It was better to hide him down at number four. Dan never betrayed so much as the slightest discontent at the situation. Play him number one, play him number six, what difference did it make? He had more important things to think about than this silly game.

The last to arrive was Bruno (he had inherited that honor from Max, who was in Italy on business). One of the few Jews whose family had remained in Munich after the war without managing to accrue a fortune in the new Germany, Bruno had a bar/ restaurant on Dachauerstrasse and was never completely comfortable with the country-club crowd. His arms had vein relief instead of *flan* softness. His thick black curls looked tough as Brillo, and he wore seedy sideburns and rarely had a good shave.

With the full team finally assembled, almost fifteen minutes late, Robert began the practice with stretching exercises. The afternoon heat was already fading into another cool Munich evening; the court lights were on, mercury-vapor suns in the darkening vespertine sky, casting a familiar glow on the red clay that reminded him of the same artificial light on the green hard courts of his childhood. Bending forward with one foot crossed in front of the other he looked up to see how they were doing. To his left Saul and Uschi stretched intently, heads hanging loose toward the court as though if they could master this exercise the elusive secrets of the game would be theirs. Next to them Bruno tried to reach his toes, or at least tried to look as though he were trying, but kept looking over to see what the others to his left were doing. Which was more or less nothing. Dan and Göttel, an imperious fiftyish local magistrate, were in the obligatory position, bent slightly at the waist but obviously with no intent of dipping their fingers below knee level. And Emil made no effort at even an ostensible stretch. He stood with his expensive graphite racket tucked under one arm like a riding crop and chatted constantly to Göttel. Every minute or so he would catch Robert's eye and bend at the waist like one of those toy ducks bobbing into a glass of water and then continue his monologue.

"Okay, I think that's enough stretching," Robert said after they had struggled through a few different exercises. "Let's do some serve-and-return drills. Dan and Saul, you take the first court, Uschi and Göttel the middle one, and Emil and Bruno on the end." The players grabbed balls from the bucket and went to their respective courts, except for Emil, who slinked over to Robert.

"What's going on?" he said. Robert looked at him out of the corner of his eye while officially observing the others, and waited. "I thought we had an agreement. I can't possibly play with Bruno again."

"You're not playing doubles with him," Robert said. "I promise. This is just a drill. You're *against* him. If he's so bad, just crush his serves back. And now you can enjoy his high returns." Of course Emil couldn't enjoy Bruno's high returns any more than he could enjoy Tolstoy in the original Russian, possessing no discernible volley or overhead with which to do so. In fact, they always had long, close matches when they played, involving contested line calls on both sides, sweat dripping from oversized guts, and a round of beer afterwards during which their teammates and Robert would try to repair injured psyches. Emil was just one spot above Bruno on the team ladder, five to Bruno's six, but acted as though they belonged in different leagues.

"Why don't you switch and let Uschi play with him? He doesn't mind, and then I could play with Göttel."

"He probably minds just as much as you do, Emil. He just doesn't complain. Anyway, I already announced these pairings, so let's not hurt anyone's feelings."

"Hurt that *Schtarker's* feelings? Impossible."

"Just this once, Emil? I won't put you with him again."

"Okay, okay." He picked up three balls. "For the team." He walked towards the far court, knocking the balls at Bruno on the other side and calling, "Okay,

26

bartender, you start." Bruno flipped Emil the finger as he collected the balls into various pockets in his shorts and got ready to serve. Any point won against the *Mamzer* banker, even in a practice drill, was golden.

Robert noticed after a while that most of the team had stopped serving and were just hitting the ball around lightly or playing out points. Only Uschi and Saul still worked from behind the baseline, dipping into the hopper for more balls to practice with. Emil and Bruno were playing a point as if to the death, running from corner to corner harder than they ever did against other teams.

"Let's get some doubles going," Robert called out. He walked up to Göttel and said, "I was thinking about mixing up our doubles combinations. How would you feel about playing with Bruno?"

"Out of the question. I couldn't possibly play with that madman, and besides, Uschi and I are finally starting to cohere as a team. We just need more practice. Anyway, I wouldn't try to interrupt that singles match right now. They might both attack you with their rackets. Look at the two of them, they look like Roman gladiators."

"Okay," said Robert, "we'll keep the same teams for today. Let me see how Saul and Dan are doing." He walked over to the court where Saul was serving, grimacing, shaking his head, and serving. On the other side Dan appeared bored, hacking back returns completely unconcerned whether or not they landed in the court, which of course they always did. Saul noticed Robert coming towards him and concentrated harder on the ball in his hand. "Toss it higher, Saul," he said to himself loudly in English, his accent similar to Max's—more Oxbridge than German—"by God man, toss it higher." He adjusted the shoulders of his white, collared tennis shirt, took off his round gold-rimmed glasses and wiped them on his shirt, carefully replaced them, and finally executed a serve of flawless form and grace which nonetheless caught the tape of the net and fell back, sparing Dan the effort of another return. "*Scheisse,*" he hissed. "Shit."

"Looks good, Saul," Robert offered. "Just an inch higher toss and you're set."

"Yes, yes, higher, I know. I can't quite get it."

"Anyway, that's probably enough practice for now. It's better to just play some sets."

"I don't know," said Saul. "I just don't know."

"What don't you know, Saul? You're playing well."

"It's just such a difficult game," Saul shook his head and looked up to the sky, now completely dark. "Very difficult."

Once they were into their matches they were more or less content and he didn't need to do much more than watch, though Uschi would probably have liked him to give a running commentary on his performance and work on his serve throughout the match. Luckily this infuriated the others, so Robert could relax and merely pretend to watch with interest. A motion in his periphery distracted him as he watched the doubles and he looked up to see Burkhard, the Sport Scheck teaching pro, over on Court 24 waving his racket to indicate that he wanted to hit some. The last thing Robert felt like doing was hitting tennis balls with his sore shoulder, and he gestured at the men playing as if they were his responsibility, his troublesome children, but Burkhard just kept beckoning. Robert picked up his racket and crossed Emil's court between points. "I can't serve," he said when he reached Burkhard.

"I thought your shoulder was feeling better."

"Yeah, till today. I aggravated it hitting a bucket earlier."

"Sorry to hear that. Let's just practice then." They went to opposite sides of the court and Robert hit a ball out of his hand. With the first hit, Emil and the rest of the team faded away, their noises like the sound of the crowd settling in as he warmed up for a championship match. There was nothing but hitting the ball. His shoulder ached only slightly as long as he didn't raise his arm above his head, and the slight pain felt good, it seemed to add some sort of meaning to what he was doing. They fell into a rhythm, forehand to forehand to backhand to backhand, down the line and crosscourt, like a drill but with the intense consistency of match play. Nothing existed but the ball and his own body, muscles stretching for wide shots and the impact of the hit absorbed in his fingers, sending the ball wherever he wanted, all he had to do was will it there and his body would take care of it, knowing from countless repetitions exactly how to do it, the swing grooved on courts of identical proportions thousands of miles away. Burkhard sliced a backhand deep and came in for some volleys. Robert took it on the rise and sent back a lightly topspinned forehand, initiating a new shorter rhythm like a different musical beat, crack crack thump, crack crack thump.

But the cadence was quickly broken by shouts, men's voices reverberating in the night air, pulling him from somewhere else back to a public tennis complex in suburban Munich. A disturbance had broken out on Court 27. Bruno stood at the net waving his racket and shouting at Emil, who paced in a small circle behind the baseline looking everywhere but at Bruno. "You know that ball was good. Look me in the eye and call it out," Bruno screamed in his guttural street German. Emil refused to even acknowledge him, looking first at the doubles players two courts over who had stopped to watch this confrontation and then at Robert and smiling at his silly partner's tantrum over a game. Bruno appealed to the doubles players, "You guys saw it, didn't you?" but they just shrugged, pleading ignorance, obviously enjoying the argument. "Cheater," cried Bruno. "You're a cheater. Is this how you make your money too, by cheating clients?"

This finally got Emil's attention. He perked up and started toward the net, "You should know more about crooked dealings than me, Mr. Street Corner." He was still smiling, though, apparently getting a kick out of it all. At this Bruno could no longer restrain his temper, and he climbed over the net and walked straight towards Emil, holding his racket in front of him like a switchblade. Emil backed off quickly, his face assuming a serious demeanor for the first time, and the doubles players and Robert rushed over to separate them.

"He cheated me," Bruno complained to Robert. "It was obvious."

"Emil," said Robert, "did you see the ball clearly out?"

"Of course," said Emil. "You think I need to cheat to beat this guy?"

"Now boys, boys," said Saul in English, sounding like a British butler quelling a schoolboy squabble, "come on now, let's forget this and get back to the game. It's been a splendid match so far."

"What's the score," Robert said to no one in particular.

"Five-five," said Bruno. "Five-five and thirty-all, and this guy has to cheat on his own serve."

"It's just a practice match," said Robert.

"The ball was out," said Emil. "It was out. It's not my fault if he can't keep the ball in the court."

"He says it was out," Robert explained patiently to Bruno. Let's just play it from ad-in. I'll watch for a while." He turned and shrugged to Burkhard, who was enjoying the drama from a distance, and took an umpire's position by the net post as the players got ready to continue. The doubles players also got in position on their court but didn't hit a ball, preferring to watch the proceedings.

Emil served the ball, as usual, without bending a knee or turning his shoulders at all. It was all arm, and the ball floated safely into the service box. Bruno charged it like a linebacker and clubbed it past the net, court, and Emil, straight into the fence. He then threw his racket into the net, declared that he was not going to waste any more time playing with an overweight orangutan, collected his things, and left the court.

Robert looked at his watch. "Time's almost up anyway," he said. "You guys can keep playing doubles if you want."

Emil put his expensive racket in its expensive case and pulled his Italian designer warm-up jacket over his sweating belly. "I guess I win," he said, "Six-five."

"Yeah," said Robert, "You win, Emil." He walked back over to Court 24, laughed with Burkhard as they took the court again. *How exotic, she'd said.* He hit the ball out of his hand and fell back into the calming space of the sport.

2

He would sit there on the windowsill sometimes in the evening. Wearing blue jeans, thin lines of bathwater still occasionally leaping from his combed hair and running on tiny lizard's feet down his shoulders, he'd lean against the frame of the large swinging window, one knee bent up on the sill and one arm dangling out above the street. It would be that time when the sky was still blue and the temperature fell through a delicious compromise between the hot summer day and the cold night, and the air soothed his skin, quietly absorbing the heat embedded there in the afternoon on the sunbaked clay courts, cooling without chilling.

Five stories below, the Turkish section of Munich was still alive and active. The tour buses, businessmen, and produce merchants were gone, but in the fading light the restaurateurs had taken the stage, setting up tables and folding chairs on the sidewalk and opening their doors to let in the cool air and out the warm smells of fried dough and doner kebab.

And on the other side of Goethestrasse, the purple neon of The Blue Box lit up, awaiting the night's business. The proprietor, a well groomed man with a thin moustache and a grey jacket and a white shirt with the collar open, stood outside the door enjoying the evening. On either side of the doorway he leaned against, behind glass, were the pictures.

Robert couldn't make out the faded photos from his window perch, but he knew them well. He hated to think that he couldn't raise himself above the base urges that drew men to the door, but still he couldn't help crossing the street before the corner in order to get a quick look before starting the day. He could justify it in that it was easier to cross there than to wait for the long light at the corner, but he knew that the real reason lay in animal instinct, the quickening breath and surge of blood and tightening of denim, the fingerprints of longing.

But he wouldn't succumb so far as to actually go inside. In fact, he took some feeble pride in that drawn line. He headed straight to the Strassenbahn or, later, sat in his window with an Augistinerbräu and actually felt sorry for the loners who wandered off the sidewalk and through the hanging leather strips.

For the most part they looked respectable, no different from those who passed without entering (though almost no one passed without even the most evanescent glance). Some strode to the door purposefully, as though going to buy shoes or have a key copied. Others slowed down at the sudden presence of the photographs, stopped to examine closer, maybe glanced at their watch or looked around to see if they were being noticed, and then finally made their decision and entered with one last sideways look. But most had a plan. They came briskly down the sidewalk, in unison with their fellow pedestrians walking from work to the Hauptbahnhof looking forward to getting home to their houses and apartments, their wives' warm cheeks and their playful children. They divulged not the slightest awareness of the pictures as they grew near. But then, at the last second, as they passed the dark opening, they disappeared, vanished from the maelstrom of civilization, sucked in by the murky delights that waited inside.

He would sit on the sill, shoulder gently throbbing from the day's work, and sip his beer and watch them. Watch the cars and the children looking out their own windows across the street and the thickening sky, until the slight breeze rolling over his chest grew cold and the night began.

When he heard her voice filtered through the telephone earpiece, eight years evaporated, and he thought for a moment that he was still in school, that she probably just wanted to take a study break and get some Steve's ice cream. Why so shocked? He had called her, after all. Her letter had said she was going to be in Europe and might pass through Munich. There was a phone number in Paris, where she would be on this date. A few weeks before, he had tried to imagine her voice, the pitch and inflection and rhythm, and failed.

Now it sounded so familiar again, as though he had never forgotten it. And with the voice feelings which had faded to distant memories ran like electricity from the phone to the bottom of his throat undiminished by time. The familiarity of their four-year post-graduate relationship seemed more distant than the nervous awkwardness of his early infatuation. He could as well have just sighted her coming his way in the campus bookstore junior year, back before he knew her. He breathed adrenaline.

"I didn't think you'd actually be there," he said.

"Why not? Is your offer still good?"

"Of course." He tried to sound as relaxed as she did.

"You're sure I'm not going to be a pain? I mean, if you don't have room just say so."

Pain? You mean by coming or by leaving? You couldn't be an inconvenience if you brought your mother and her Aunt Sara. "Not at all. You can crash here as long as you like. Long as you don't mind a limited hot-water supply. We may be forced to bathe together."

"You're a selfless host. Okay; then I guess I'll take the overnight train. I hope you don't mind—it gets in at seven."

"Tomorrow morning?"

"Is that a problem? Why don't you tell me where you live and then you won't have to get up until I actually get there."

"No, I'll meet you at the station; I'm only a block away."

"That's nice."

They said goodbye and he began to pick bread crumbs off the rug.

As he saw her stepping off the train from a distance, he felt the pain come rushing back down on him from over a year ago. It was almost more than he could take to exchange kisses on the cheek and a light hug and pretend that he too felt no desire.

"What's with the hair?" she said.

"You are referring to the work of Yekül the barber, down the street. He can't understand my German, and I don't speak Turkish, so he just cuts it however he wants, and we're both happy. Only twenty marks, too."

"Oh. Well, 'It looks good,' she said."

"'Thank you,' he replied perspicaciously."

"No, seriously, hair aside, you look good, Robert Cherney." And what could he answer? How could he simply reply that she also looked good, when she looked more beautiful than ever, her skin lightly tanned from summer traveling, her auburn hair even softer and smoother than he'd remembered, her eyes so blue that he wished she were coming to live with him, to share his small plain apartment forever. So he asked how long she could stay.

"Just a few days." They started out of the station and down Goethestrasse. "I want to see Italy, the South of France, and Spain before meeting Chris in London. He said to tell you hi."

The mention of his former rival for her casual affections bluntly reminded him that her visit was not a fantasy come true but simply what it appeared to be. "How's he doing?"

"Fine. He finally finished his novel, and Ted's going to show it to his agent. He also set up a meeting for Chris with his British agent, which is the excuse for the trip to London." Ted Robicheau was the director of the graduate writing program Lexa had briefly attended. The author of one great critical (if not commercial) success at an early age, from then on nothing, Robicheau made his living shepherding literary neophytes through his Master's program, then dispersing them throughout the country to teach at the multiplying swarm of writing programs. Chris, a few years older than Lexa and Robert, had been one of her classmates there. Pompous, self-confident, and not the slightest bit secretive of his intentions, he had practically lectured Robert on several occasions regarding his reasons for pursuing graduate study.

"There's only one reason to go to a writing program," he smiled at Robert knowingly one night as the three of them huddled in a dark tavern on the corner of 101ˢᵗ Street. "The contacts. It's fifty percent of writing, believe me. Sweating in front of the blank page is only the beginning. Take Ted, for instance. Now you may think of him as nothing but an alcoholic has-been, a guy with one good book in the distant past and nothing but empty bourbon glasses since." Actually, Robert had still held far more respect for Ted than that, his "one success" being a pure, beautifully distilled novel that had meant a lot to Robert at one time. "But believe me, the guy still knows everyone in this town. He's already told me he's going to give my novel to his agent as soon as I get it done. And how about Faye?" (An elderly and preeminent British writer, visiting the program for a semester to give a workshop). "You think she can't get someone published if she wants to? Hell, it's only the third week of classes, and I'm having lunch with her tomorrow. Anyone in our workshop can become a published writer within two years from now if they have the desire. We all have enough talent; we need to do only two things. First, write—you have to produce a sufficient quantity of sufficiently good material. Second, you have to make connections. You'll never get anywhere sending in your manuscripts along with a million other faceless names."

Chris represented everything Robert detested about the world of publishing; he was one reason Robert swore never to consider attending a graduate writing program. If it weren't for his blinding desire for Lexa, he wouldn't have remained in Chris's company for five minutes. But she seemed to like him, or at least to want to cultivate that friendship, and Robert wasn't about to voluntarily leave her in what he sensed was Chris's prurient company. What he hated most about Chris was that he was probably right. Robert, working alone nights and weekends on his stories, with utter disdain for "networking" and with no connections in the book-publishing world, would probably never manage to get noticed, while Chris and his ilk, greasing each other at readings and cocktail parties, would be the ones to get published.

They reached Goethestrasse 10, where the elevator, crowded with the two of them and her backpack, took them precariously to the sixth floor. He was used to the slow creaking motion, the shaking of the cable, and the absence of an escape hatch; but he could see apprehension on her face. "Don't worry," he said, "if we get stuck, someone will be in on Monday." He didn't mention that since there was no alarm, whoever came would probably just observe that the elevator was out of order and take the stairs.

"It's nice," she said when they entered his apartment. "Sort of a writer's garret for the lederhosen set." He'd spent the previous evening cleaning, vacuuming, scrubbing the bathroom, and doing laundry. He put her bag down inside the door, she walked in and looked around, he told her she could have the bed and he would sleep on the couch, she just smiled and went to the window.

"Nice part of town you live in," she said. "What in the name of God is The Blue Box?"

"Oh, didn't you notice the advertising in the windows?"

"No, but I can imagine. You ever go inside?"

"Most certainly not."

She laughed. "I just meant out of intellectual curiosity of course." She turned away and sat on the bed. "I'm exhausted. It's impossible to sleep on those train couchettes."

"I'm pretty tired too. I have to work this afternoon, but I can show you some interesting places nearby to walk around. There's the Marienplatz, and you'll probably also like the English Garden. I'm free tomorrow, and we can go see Ludwig's castle at Neuschwanstein if you like. We could also go to the museum at Dachau; I've been meaning to see it again."

"Sounds perfect," she said as she lay back on the bed and closed her eyes. He shut the drapes, but they were diaphanous and not quite large enough to cover the windows; bars of morning light scattered about the room. He watched her, one arm lightly crossed across her stomach, elbow dipped in a stripe of sunshine. "You're sure you want to sleep on the couch?" she said.

"No."

"Well, for the record I don't consider sleeping with exes as infidelity. It's just a matter of timing."

He wasn't about to make her defend her logic. What could he do but laugh and fall onto her, fall back into the falseness of a former life, fall back into her careless, fickle affections. He was at the bed without a sound, and the breasts he had longed for for two years were in his hands again, her taste was in his mouth, her long hair was falling on his shoulders.

The hell with his twelve-step recovery program, the hell with his new life as an artist-in-exile. This was an insufficient gift, an offering that caused as much pain as ecstasy, but a gift nonetheless. And some gifts you took without question.

They had been ruined, he sometimes thought, by early obsession unrequited. He'd wasted his college years yearning for her while she led a normal carefree promiscuous lifestyle. He'd known guys who'd slept with her, heard them talking about it in the cafeteria in the most casual of tones while Robert hid his agony. It wasn't until two years after graduation, when they were both living in New York trying to write, that her careless affections had happened upon him.

It was at the end of one of those evenings spent listening to Chris's endless barroom expatiations on the nature of writing—or rather, on the nature of getting published. Robert had never been faced with such utter fatuousness; he hardly knew how to react, and so remained mainly silent. The man's combination of naiveté and bullheaded determination were implacable; he was sure to succeed.

"How can you stand him?" he asked her as they made their way along the dimly lit beggar's opera of upper Broadway. Couples precipitated from Chinese restaurants onto the street, pulled their coats tight around them, and moved purposefully off down the sidewalk, avoiding the homeless supplicants sitting cross-legged in doorways. Robert had scored a small victory, outlasting his more prolix opponent, refusing to say goodnight before Chris, until at last the older man had given in and disappeared into the ground to catch a downtown train.

"Oh, he's not so bad," said Lexa. Her long black wool coat somehow accentuated the lure of her body; her auburn highlights luminesced under each dim streetlight they passed, a dreamlike beacon in a storm. "He means well. He's actually trying to help us, you know, with all that advice."

"Well, he's just depressing me."

"I think he could be very useful. With all the contacts he's making, he could be an excellent contact himself. You should cultivate it."

"No, thanks. Anyway, I don't think he's looking for quite as much cultivation from me as from you."

"Okay, so he's got the hots for me. Is that a crime?"

"Of course not. Have you slept with him?"

"None of your business. What does it matter, anyway? I like him. He's fun."

"Fun and useful."

"Fun and useful. What are you so lugubrious about?"

"I'm not lugubrious. I'm fun."

She smiled. "Sometimes. Well, here we are. Coming up?" He had been in her apartment many times, so why could he barely breathe as she led him up the ancient stairs of the apartment building? Down the long hallway of her apartment, past her roommate's closed door, and finally into her room. He hardly had time to be nervous before she had removed her coat, shoes, and dress in one blur of movement.

"Surprised?"

"Yes."

"You've wanted this long enough, Robert Cherney." She moved against him and kissed him, hard. He was startled by the force. She seemed to be participating in a hobby that, though she was well practiced at it, still required attention, like windsurfing. Yes, he had wanted this long enough, far too long. For Robert it was a cataclysm of emotion; he was so awed by the naked beauty of the body he'd fantasized about for years that on their first night together he was unable to function. She didn't seem to mind—sex was ordinary enough to her that missing one night made little difference—and they spent the night innocently in each other's arms.

In the morning he failed again. They spent the day together trying to act natural—down to the Strand to browse books, lunch at the Waverly Street Café, rambling walk all the way to Times Square, half-price ticket line, sushi dinner and finally an Off-Broadway play—before taking another stab at it late at night in his Washington Heights room. She still had her dress on, and maybe that's what did it, but he managed to get through the act, and in relief they undressed and fell asleep.

But their relationship never lost its awkwardness. He remained obsessed, physical attainment doing little to lessen her perfection in his mind. She was as close to his physical ideal as he was likely to get in this life. Her mind was sharp, ironic, caustic, as her writing displayed. A writer—above all, this made her his storybook comrade-in-arms. He imagined Henry Miller and Anäis Nin, Nelson Algren and Simone Du Beauvoir; he wanted to have Dorothy Parker, M.F.K. Fisher, and Emily Hahn, all in the body of Brigitte Bardot. Adolescent and unattainable, yes—but he had it! He could hardly believe it; New York had finally offered up to him everything he had dreamed it would.

But Lexa turned out to be more like Lou Salomé. For one thing, she refused to stop seeing other men. Here Robert had thought that the great literary union, the great love of both their lives, had been consummated, and she acted like it was just another casual screw. Meeting for brunch at the Waverly, she would wearily mention that Chris, or Steve, or some other oversexed suitor, had been by the previous evening, and she'd carefully leak the implication that the offending male had been there in the morning as well.

He couldn't decide whether she was somehow oblivious to the pain in his face during these progress reports, or simply cruel. "Chris stopped by last night, and it was so hot that Marina"—tall, dark, voluptuous actress roommate Marina—"and I had been walking around topless. Of course I put something on before answering the door, but you wouldn't believe how long it took Marina to get her shirt on, after I had already let Chris in. Acting so surprised to see him, after I'd already yelled up to her. Not that Chris minded. You would have cracked up, Robert."

I might have at that, he thought. Funny how Marina was never topless when he came over. That might have been enough to cure him of his obsession with Lexa.

He tried to broach the subject of monogamy with her, but was cut short every time with joking ripostes concerning his conventionality. Writers need to sleep around, she'd tease him; where was he going to get his material if he didn't lead a full life like she did? She (and others like her) would get an edge up on him.

But all he could think about was her. Walking through Manhattan with her, though she never held hands, was years of yearning come true. He remembered her in black tights and a dark purple sweater in the fall: the combination of her in that outfit and the crisp weather and the very fact that he was walking around New York, a writer—for every day he wrote—with this beautiful woman, a writer herself, had been enough to make him forget the small cruelties, humiliations, the not infrequent nights alone knowing she was with someone else.

It could be even worse when she was with him. Inconceivable irony: that the object of all his romantic and erotic desires should be, once attained, so pallid. Lexa made love as though riding an exercise bicycle.

(And in fact, as far as he could tell, it was her only exercise aside from city walking.) She seemed to want to do it primarily in order to have done it. She might hold him closely during the act, or even kiss him, but she never betrayed the slightest sign of amorous arousal. It was like sleeping with a prostitute, and he paid with his self-esteem. Sad commentary on male sexuality, he thought one night immediately after ejaculating, that this can remain the subject of my daydreams, of my constant fantasies that drive my mind away from work.

Lying in bed with her on a Sunday morning, his arms full of that body he had lusted after for so long, every hollow tributary of physical, if not emotional, longing inundated by a lazy matinal frolic, long golden triangles of sunlight that had somehow eluded the skyscrapers sliding into her bedroom: paradise for Robert. But she would suddenly look at the clock and jump out of bed, deflating the euphoria, running towards the shower: "I'm late for brunch with Marina." Or worse: "I told Chris I'd meet him to discuss his story." Where had she been trained in such sadism?

One night he called her late. She had declared that she needed to work that evening, and so he had as well. All night he'd spent staring at blank Eaton's Corrasable, trying to clear his mind of the image of her heavy breasts swaying above him, her hips filling the curve of his palms.

"I just called to say good night."

"That's nice, Robert. I'm just getting going here, though. My Russia novel is starting to sizzle." She had spent her junior year of college and two years after graduation in Moscow.

"Wish I could say the same," he said. "It's been a tough night."

"I know what you need," she said.

"You read my mind."

"You should have called earlier. You could have come over and done something to me similar to what you did yesterday morning."

"Ah..."

"But now I'm just getting going with my work."

"Who's that in the background? Rustling the newspaper?"

"You have good ears. That's Marina."

"Reading the newspaper topless?"

"You wish. Now you just do what you have to do and then go to bed. I've got to get back to the great Russian novel."

"I think someone may have beaten you to it. So you don't think I should come over?"

"No, I don't. You know what, Robert? You really should get yourself a girlfriend."

"I thought you were my girlfriend."

"I mean a real one. A steady one. One who's ready for you at midnight, when it's bedtime."

He endured one moment of burning silence while his face filled with blood, then he hung up on her. Swore never to dial her number again. Went to bed furious, satisfied himself, as she'd suggested, but with forced images of Marina in his mind. Slept, unsoundly.

Eleven months passed. Eleven months for the wound to scab over, eleven months for the obsession to wither, eleven months during which he succeeded in arresting the movement of his hand towards the phone each time he was about to fall to the temptation of calling her.

And then, just as he was learning not to torture himself with thoughts of her entwined with various lovers in her Sunday-morning bed, she called. Just as he had concluded a six-week relationship with a woman from his apartment building, a fling that had ended as amicably as it had begun, she called. Just to say hi. She'd finished her novel and was wondering how he was doing.

Forty-five minutes later he was in her bed, submerged once again in her. Like a drunkard fallen off the wagon. He didn't care. He couldn't remember his apartment-building lover's name; he was nestled next to Lexa, falling asleep with his head against Lexa's stomach, his arm resting between Lexa's thighs.

Within days, though, the old pattern was reestablished. Her phone call ending their separation had not signaled the transformation of attitude that he had imagined. It wasn't that she'd realized that he was her true love and banished the other men from her bed. It was simply what she had said: a call from an ex to see how he was doing.

This time he recognized the symptoms of his disease; he saw the pain for what it was. And he didn't allow himself to be toyed with for years as he had been before. Three times they made love, and then like a weight watcher taking one last potato chip before holding out until dinner, he declared no more. He stopped calling her. She got the message and left him alone.

And more months passed. And he left New York, left America, only partly to get away from her. In Munich it was easier not to think about her, although even with the new sights and sounds around him, the hours on the tennis court, and the world of Max and his society, there were still nights when, lying on his furnished bed with the neon light from The Blue Box seeping in his window, that he couldn't get to sleep without conjuring Lexa's image above him. There were still nights when he drifted off with her perfectly remembered breath pulsing in his ear.

Late at night on Goethestrasse, she was again at the window, kept closed after dark to prevent the moths and other insects from finding the overhead fluorescent light. The light was off now, but the room was never very dark: neon light from the street drifted in all night long. He sat slouched back on the sofa and watched her. She had one barefoot leg on the floor and the other knee bent on the bed, denim shorts and white T-shirt, held the drapes with one hand like a young mother looking to see what sort of people are moving in across the street.

"It's really fascinating to see who goes in that place," she said. "And who comes out. Do you ever stand here and watch?"

"Sometimes, when it's nice out."

"Look at this guy come out and look back and forth to see if he's been sighted. Little does he know he's being watched from above. He walks toward his car . . . hey, a Mercedes."

"Half the cars in this town are Mercedes. Anyway, the rich need love too."

"I would hardly call what goes on in there love."

"Don't you think it's sad, though, that these people have to go there to satisfy themselves?"

"I suppose so. They must be very lonely. Here comes someone in a business suit . . . he's stopping, looking at the pictures . . . will he go in? He's thinking about it, he's turning toward the door . . . oh my god."

"What?"

"He looks just like my dad. That is eerie. I swear, from this distance he could just as well be my father."

"Well, your father probably hasn't flown to Munich for a quick turn-on, but this guy is still likely to be somebody's father."

"It's kind of sad. Why can't they be satisfied with their wives? And if they don't have one, you'd think they'd be able to find someone. There are so many single people out there."

"Well, I guess in a perfect world everyone would match up with someone else and there'd be no leftovers. Unfortunately it doesn't work that way."

"Okay, we've all been lonely sometimes, but why do these people have to soothe loneliness by watching rape, degradation, and other people having kinky sex. Human beings can be pretty sick sometimes."

"Yeah, but compared to whom?"

As they sped southwest towards Neuschwanstein, the sun beat down on the Porsche, warming their skin and filling the inside of the car with an orange glow. Max was in London and had insisted that Robert "take care of" his car in his absence. He was relaxed, molded into the leather bucket seat, steering with his left hand on the bottom of the wheel, right hand lightly resting on the stick shift or parking brake. She handled the cassettes, alternating among the small collection he had brought from the States. Dylan to Joni Mitchell to Tom Waits. That was one thing he'd always liked about her—she really listened to music. Didn't feel awkward without constantly chatting, like so many people did, blocking out the best lyrics of a song with small talk.

They left the highway and found themselves winding along a serpentine country road up into the mountains. Cows grazed in fields on either side of them. "I've been following the signs to Fussen like they said to do at the tourist office," he said, "but this doesn't look like the way they described." Eventually he saw some farmers up ahead and stopped to ask them directions. They smiled at his accent and told him in thick Bavarian he barely understood that he was okay, just to keep going straight and he'd get there. The road twisted into tighter and tighter turns, growing steeper until they were crawling in first gear through a notch in the mountain, thick trees darkening their way. They finally pulled out of it and back into the sunshine, now descending, and he was reassured by another sign for Fussen. When they finally neared the town, over an hour later than they were supposed to, they were driving on a flat road by a large calm river. On the other side were mountains, and embedded up in the side was the castle, rising from the countryside like an apparition.

But instead of relief that they had finally found it, he was disappointed that the drive was over and they had to get out and sightsee. He wished that they could just drive for months, gliding by the mountains and hills and coastlines of Europe, slicing through the sunshine like a sailboat through calm waters without ever getting anywhere.

In her summer dress and old-fashioned plastic sunglasses, she looked like a snapshot of a 1962 vacation as they entered the camp at Dachau. Though even a color photograph today would have looked black and white. Behind her loomed the white guard towers, the black barbed wire, and the dead white dust of the courtyard and walkways. Behind the courtyard they could see the long white rectangular barracks, roofs long gone. The sky was a thin gray film of cotton which let the sunlight filter through without revealing its source; the wind blew hard across the open space, and the only other sound was the occasional clicking of a tourist's camera. Nothing lived here.

They entered the first building and looked through the museum of photographs and other artifacts. There were posters from the early thirties warning the German people of the Jewish menace, individual admittance forms from the first prisoners to be sentenced to the camp, and photographs detailing the history of the camp from its erection to the liberation of the victims. In one photograph he could not easily walk away from, prisoners marched in their striped uniforms, perhaps to work or to their barracks or to the gas chambers, shoulder to shoulder and chest to back, filling the picture. All heads were bowed, grim but resigned to their fate, except for one. In the center of the photo one prisoner had raised his eyes to stare directly into the lens of the camera. No matter at what angle you stood from the photo, he stared straight at you.

After leaving the museum they followed a walkway behind the barracks and through an area of bright green trees, over a small brook to the ovens.

Inside one of the three huts a few people stood, looking around. Light crept in through a small window in the corner, throwing long golden prisms across the wooden floors and white plaster walls. Most of the room was taken up by a row of small boxes that opened, revealing long compartments like square torpedo shafts. By each one was a long wooden spatula.

Outside the sun had broken through the haze, an arc of blue sky taking the scene through decades back to the present. Nothing much to say, they walked past the roofless barracks, the guard towers and barbed wire, and back to the neat blacktop parking lot in the quiet suburban neighborhood. It was only twenty minutes back to his apartment.

On the night she was to leave, he took her to dinner at a café near the Karlsplatz. They had lamb and beer, and afterwards iced coffee. It stayed light late, and they watched the traffic around the fountain and the darkening sky behind the buildings.

"Well, here's to middle age," he raised his glass.

"What? Oh, Robert, I can't believe I forgot. It's your birthday."

"Dirty thirty."

"Indeed. Let's get some cake, at least."

"I don't know. I better start watching what I eat."

"Nah. Thirty's not what it used to be. If we were in a Cheever story, we'd be divorced with three kids by now."

"Well, there's no time for cake anyway. Your train."

They walked back to his building and got her backpack from his room. Riding down in the elevator, they were quiet. He didn't know when, if ever, he would see her again, and there didn't seem much point in talking about it. She did speak, "When you're back in the States, we'll get together," but couldn't hide the emptiness of the words. He smiled. "Sure." He picked up her bag and they left the building and walked down the street, the streetlamps now burning, and they entered the station and found her train and exchanged textbook goodbyes and an innocuous hug and then she was going up the steps and disappearing into the car and he walked away from the tracks and back through the crowded station and felt as he always did when he saw the gargantuan departure board raised high off the floor, that he'd like to get on one of those trains and roll anywhere.

Walking back to his room he passed The Blue Box. While she was with him he'd eschewed his habit of staying on that side of the street before crossing right in front of his building, but now that he was alone again he resumed it as though it were the obvious route. This time, though, he actually stopped walking to look, something he had never done before. A fat man in a denim jacket passed through the curtain, and through the resulting aperture he could see lights and a man behind a counter. He walked in.

There was no theater inside as he had expected, just a row of closed doors on each wall. The man behind the counter asked him if he needed change. He didn't. Embarrassed to be standing around looking, he found an open door and went in and locked it. He was in a room big enough for only one person. Against the back wall was a cushioned black stool and a few feet above it a video screen. He wondered how anyone in the chair could see the screen until he sat down and saw the mirror on the inside of the door. But why such an arrangement? A slot to his right called for a two-mark coin. He satisfied it and in the mirror the video began.

A room was filled with naked men and women. Some formed human chains of three or more, head to genitals, male and female mixed randomly. The scene switched to two women servicing each other in a room with mirrored walls and ceiling. A man and woman copulated in an airplane lavatory. The women all appeared to be screaming in lascivious delight.

He felt an impulse to bolt outside and pull fresh evening air into his lungs, but he didn't move. The video was silent. He closed his eyes and heard only a faint mechanical whirring behind his head, and soon he didn't even hear that.

3

"How's the book coming?" Max asked one evening as they sat at a café near the Marienplatz. He had gotten into the habit of stopping by in the evenings, like a benevolent landlord checking up on his tenant's lodgings. Since usually neither of them had eaten yet, they ended up at some fashionable place, Max's treat. Robert wasn't trying to appear poor, he just wasn't trying not to, and Max assumed from his relatively squalid appearance and passive acceptance of the Spartan Goethestrasse apartment that he was a struggling artist.

"Oh, you know," Robert mumbled through his Wiener schnitzel, "coming along, coming along." Can't he see? Isn't it emblazoned all over my face that I am the most miserable of creatures, contorting my face and body into grotesque configurations over a miserable sheet of blank paper for hours every day without a damn thing to show for it?

"What's it about?" Max made the unforgivable error of asking.

"Can't discuss it. Never examine an unborn fetus." Robert felt cheapened invoking Ted Robicheau's pet phrase, which he and Lexa had laughed over, but there were times when it came in handy.

"Fiction or non-fiction?"

"Little of both."

"Well, may I ask are they paying you much for it?"

"Not that much," he said, wiping his mouth conclusively and reaching for the check that Max had almost imperceptibly lifted from the table. "Here, let me get it this time."

"It's all right," Max dismissed his gesture as though the expenditure were too miniscule to be worth the breath of polite argument. "When your secret book hits the bestseller lists, you can buy me dinner."

"Well, in that case I wouldn't count on me for sustenance."

"You're so sure of failure?"

"Well, how many people are going to appreciate my novel? For one thing, they'll have to have at least a working understanding of Newtonian calculus. There, I've told you something about it."

"So you slave away at this book," he gave the waitress a wad of bills and waved her away, "knowing that it isn't going to make you any money, and meanwhile what do you do for a living? You teach tennis to the Mattathians. Like a workman, like their gardener or something. Some of these people should be working for you, not you for them."

"I get by. I don't need much to live on. And of course I do have my hopes."

"Fascinating." He rose, and Robert followed him out the door. "My father would be, how do you say, perplexed? You should come over for dinner sometime."

"Why perplexed?"

"Because for him, you don't do anything until you make a nice living. Then you can devote time to other things, if for some reason you want to. Art does not occupy a high place in his list of concerns."

"And for you?"

"Well," he took one hand out of his thousand-dollar pocket and waved it gently about palm up. "It would be easy for me to say that art is of the greatest importance, but then look at what I do. I go to Italy and convince some eccentric family of scarf makers to sell me an enormous quantity of scarves very cheaply. Then I come back to Germany and sell the merchandise to department stores expensively. They then sell the scarves to the German people even more expensively."

"So that's your mysterious Italian business. You're a schmatte dealer."

"I'm a schmatte dealer. I fiddle around with business concerns all day, and make a lot of money. And yet I'm not necessarily unhappy. So," his free hand, which had been swimming lazily through the air, suddenly pounced upon Robert's, "you'll come over for Friday night dinner."

"Supporting the arts now, Max?"

"Why not?"

Robert declined Max's offer of a ride and walked home slowly, crisscrossing the streets of central Munich as he had grown used to doing as an antidote to his morning literary frustrations. He's not exactly the sort of company I'd had in mind when I imagined the life of a writer-in-exile. Shabbas dinner not the kind of evening I envisioned. Evenings with Lexa, now that would be something. Imagine her staying. Why not? But you didn't even ask her. How could you let her just get onto that train and leave? No, that's what you were getting away from. Don't slip back. Too early to give up the game.

His morning writing sessions grew more and more torturous. He had the basic idea for the novel, but the details escaped him—it nauseated him even to attempt to describe to himself the more intricate workings of his plot. How he detested such nagging concerns! He was a broader thinker; his were vast ideas, structural concepts that loomed high above the fastidious busywork of filling in the spaces. But how to forge a work of respectable weight without the filler? Even the slightest of novels, say *Franny and Zooey*, which Salinger himself referred to as "this pretty skimpy-looking book," was more than just concept. It was concept stuffed with details. What Robert needed was a staff of literary drones to inflate his brilliant ideas to regulation size and weight.

He could not concentrate, that was his problem. His first half hour at the writing table was a daily sacrifice to daydreaming; he didn't even worry about that anymore. But after that prelude it began to annoy him that his mind was unable to focus on the sentence that needed to be constructed. He was filled with grandiose visions of his unprecedented literary output, his consciousness saturated with visions of his completed work—several satisfying pounds of thickly bound ink-filled pages, with a dramatic cover design and provocative black-and-white photo on the back.

And the jacket blurbs, of course:

"Quite unprecedented, structurally. Brilliant idea." *The New York Times Book Review.*

"To think of turning Newton's calculus onto the structure of a novel! Who but Cherney could have done this?" *Times Literary Supplement.*

But in fact, the first well-made sentences that usually found their way into Robert's consciousness each morning were not the opening lines of his novel, but those of his Pulitzer acceptance speech. You schmuck, you write for the wrong reasons, your search is for glory, not truth, not poetry, not art. Not true. But what artist in history, immersed in his scribblings or doodlings or strummings, has never lapsed off into distracting vainglorious fantasy? He forgave himself. But then dropped his head again, realizing that in his case the distraction threatened to preclude any literary production whatsoever.

And of course his fantasizing didn't end with visions of literary grandeur. There were always sufficient concupiscent scenarios dancing across his synapses to obscure any novelistic ones that might have been slouching shyly in the wings. The subject was usually Lexa, though she was often replaced by a host of anonymous sexual partners of various sizes and shapes. Sometimes he even blended his two fantasy genres, and it would be perfectly-endowed literary groupies throwing themselves at his feet *after* his Pulitzer speech who served to aid him in his procrastination. Did Pulitzer winners even give speeches? In any case, the hour of ten-thirty more often than not found him back in bed, answering a call more easily gratified than that of art.

After the conclusive release it was useless to try to write any more. Any buried creative impulse struggling to surface evanesced along with his irksome lust. Resigned to another morning of failure, he would pull on his tennis shoes and step out onto Goethestrasse, choose a direction for the day, and walk the streets of Munich.

Friday night he rode the Strassenbahn on a winding, circuitous route out from the city center. As soon as he got off the tram and walked into the Altmanns' neighborhood, Bogenhausen, he felt he had crossed another border. The bluster and lights of central Munich were far away; here was tranquility and wealth. Robert's footsteps echoed off expensive garden walls. He could hear his pant legs rustle against each other. Suburban mansions, peering out of the leafy darkness, quietly watched him walk among them. This was not Scarsdale or Brookline, however: the mansions required no expansive lawns to mark their rank; they were happy enough to nestle against one another in this Old-World enclave of affluence.

The Altmann residence was one of these behemoths. A buzz from inside opened the wrought iron gate, and a blonde maid opened the front door. Gold-framed paintings cluttered the walls, an enormous chandelier hung in the foyer centering a double staircase, and expensive-looking knickknacks crowded every table and shelf. After ten minutes during which Robert took in the atmosphere and examined his subtly aging face in the ornate mirror, Max appeared on the balustrade.

"Rob," he said as though pleasantly surprised that Robert had dropped by. Absently knotting his tie, he descended the staircase with a carefree, iambic rhythm, slapping his expensive Italian shoes against the marble steps like beach sandals. "We're late," he announced as they shook hands, and he led Robert into an elegant dining room.

Max and his parents, to Robert's dismay, were dressed for dinner the way Robert dressed only for weddings and funerals. He had put on a button-down shirt, but it wasn't going to do the trick.

"When the tennis game?" said Herr Altmann after they were introduced, with a bewildered smile on his face.

"My father's just joking," said Max. "He's not used to seeing tennis shoes at Friday night dinner. It's quite all right, though."

"Come," said Frau Altmann, whose English, though sharply accented, was much better than her husband's. "It's late already."

Robert stood uncomfortably while Herr and Sonn chanted a slew of unrecognizable prayers and Frau lit the sabbath candles. He hadn't so much as witnessed these rites since his Bar Mitzvah, much less participated in them. At one point Herr Altmann gestured at him to Max and mumbled a question in Yiddish. Max answered, and then his father smiled at Robert. "You no know the prayers?"

"I'm afraid not," he shrugged.

"I thought you are Jewish?"

Robert started to explain American reform Judaism and his own nonparticipation in even that dilute institution, but Herr Altmann cut him off.

"Was sug er?" he asked his son. "Nicht versteh."

Max translated into Yiddish and must have gone on to anticipate Robert's full explanation, for he spoke for several minutes, answering several interrogatory interjections along the way. In the meantime the maid had brought out the soup, and Frau Altmann began to eat, motioning Robert to follow her example and ignore the men's discussion.

"Ach," grunted Herr Altmann. "Amerika. Amerika," and he began to eat his soup.

"My father is not a big fan of reform Judaism," said Max.

"I agree," said Robert. He smiled at Herr Altmann and said in German, "I agree. All the way or not at all."

He turned to his son. "Was sug er?"

Max laughed and rattled off some Yiddish. His father shrugged and slurped his soup.

They finished their soup in silence, and the maid cleared the bowls.

"Maximilian says you are a writer," said Frau Altmann.

"Mmm," he wiped his mouth to hide a grimace.

"It is a nice living?" Frau Altmann's appearance was nothing if not stern. Robert was later to discover behind her formal, stony exterior something of a soft side, but at this first meeting he sensed a nascent disapproval. He tried to explain that money wasn't really the point but trailed off after a few words.

"Vas denn is der punkt?" Herr seemed puzzled. Robert said in German that satisfaction, art, and not money, was the punkt. Herr Altmann immediately turned to Max. "Vas?" Max spun a translation in Yiddish, as usual much longer and more thickly-layered than the original. Now Frau joined the discussion, and Robert sat waiting for his salad and listening to a roundtable discussion in Yiddish concerning the legitimacy of his existence. Herr's tone and expression conveyed utter flabbergastedness regarding his son's American friend. Frau's voice betrayed a perfect understanding—eventually he'll grow up and get a job. Max seemed to be having a great time, hunched forward toward his parents with his legs elegantly crossed, explaining in great detail the subtle workings of the Alienated American Jewish Artist's mind. Herr never seemed to quite get it; Frau finally shrugged.

She turned to Robert just as he was switching positions to try to appear more completely at ease with the situation. "You have girlfriend?" she asked.

His first thought was to explain that his girlfriend was traveling at the moment, collecting literary material by sleeping with as many Europeans as was humanly possible, but he was unable to translate properly into German and felt that Frau Altmann might miss some of the idiomatic nuance. "Not at the moment," he said.

"Hmm," she said, eyeing him closely. He nearly squeaked under the oppression of her gaze. He could have kissed the maid when she brought in their salads. The meal continued.

Dinner, with all its attending prayer and ritual, dragged on well past ten o'clock, and soon after the last dishes were cleared by the maid (who conversed with Frau Altmann in a language completely different from the three others that had bounced around the table and even less decipherable to Robert), Max's parents said goodnight and went upstairs.

"So," said Max when they were left alone in the cavernous living room, "shall we meet a friend of mine?"

"On the sabbath?"

"Ya, I believe in moderation in all things. It's important to remember the sabbath and observe it, but at the same time one shouldn't necessarily be a slave to it. But then I remember your motto: Alles oder nichts."

"Just trying to make conversation. Which reminds me—is my German really that bad? Your father didn't seem to understand a word I said, in German or English."

He laughed quietly. "That's because my father's German, though he would never admit it, is hardly better than his English. You could say he has something of a mental block about the language. My mother's German is much better—she handles all the business correspondence. We don't speak German to each other at home. But let's be off; we're already a bit late, I'm afraid."

Fifteen minutes later they pulled up to a modern cement building not far from Robert's apartment. Max drove the Porsche onto the sidewalk in front of the entrance and cut the engine. "The *Filmmuseum*?" Robert asked.

"This is where we're meeting." He led Robert around the back and through a gate, and suddenly

they were in the middle of an outdoor café. "A very
popular place among students and artists and the
like," said Max. "Not really my style, but I thought
you'd like it. Ah, there she is." He waved to a young
woman sitting at a table at the far end of the garden
with two young men. "Véronique," he said after they
had reached the table and he had exchanged double-
kisses with her in the European fashion, "I'd like you
to meet Robert Cherney, a writer from New York who
is going to be living in Munich for the time being."

"Really," said one of the young men. "Would we
know anything you've written?"

"Not likely," he said. "I'm really just a tennis
instructor, but Max hates to think of himself
consorting with a common laborer."

"Rob is modest," said Max. "I won't embarrass
him anymore. And don't ask him what the book is
about that he's writing; he doesn't like to discuss it."

"Oh, but I'd like to hear," said Véronique.
Her hair was shorter than Robert's, a dark cropped
covering that presented her face—her entire head—
without artifice or ornamentation. Was it a pretty
face? he wondered. He supposed so, but there was a
hardness to it, and a hardness to her demeanor that
made him wary: her "I'd like to hear" sounded as
much like a challenge as an invitation.

Mercifully, the conversation turned to other
matters. Véronique and her two friends, both medical
students, were continuing their discussion of the film,
Un Chien Andalou, which they had just come out of.

The med students got caught up in an argument about the meaning of the sliced eye, and Robert turned to Véronique.

"So, are you French?"

"No, no. My parents are Polish, like the rest of the Jews here. But my mother is a great Francophile. She's a French teacher in the Gymnasium."

"And what do you do?"

"I am a translator, as a free lance. I translate for companies mostly at the moment, they pay very well. But I am also studying to become a subtitler for movies."

"You're studying subtitling?"

"Yes. Dubbing as well. There's a program at the university. It's not so easy, you know. When dubbing, not only do you have to translate the meaning, but you have to make it the exact same length. We also learn to use the same vowel sounds so that the words fit the jaw movements of the actors."

"Yes, I guess you'd have to. I never thought much about it before."

"Of course that's not all I plan to do. I also want to translate literature. English and French into German. And also, if I improve my English, perhaps I can translate some German and Yiddish works into English. Of course I'm not a native speaker, but my mother teaches English, as well as French, so I've always spoken it."

"It's hard enough to understand why one would want to be a writer," Max had appeared not to be listening, scanning the other tables with a blasé gaze, but now piped in. "Work like a dog, be paid like an underemployed waiter, and have to sit in your house all day. But a translator seems worse. It's not even your own work you slave over."

"It's literature, Max," said Véronique. "I wouldn't think you'd understand working for low wages, but you at least appreciate literature."

"Reading it, yes. That's why I think it makes sense to make a lot of money without taxing oneself too much, so one has plenty of leisure time to enjoy books, as well as theater and music."

"Now why doesn't everyone do that?" said Robert.

"All right, of course everyone can't do that. But since I can, why shouldn't I? And you, Rob, could certainly find far more appropriate work than teaching tennis for little pay and writing for no pay."

"I've just met him," said Véronique, "but I'd say that Rob would not be happy selling scarves."

"It's not the scarves that matter, it's what they bring you. He's happier teaching tennis? Why not at least be comfortable while you're writing for no pay?"

"Interesting question. Why doesn't everyone make a million a year? One of the mysteries of the universe."

"As you can see, Rob, my old friend Véronique is less than impressed with my lifestyle. So now I see why you live as you do after all."

When they left the café, Robert couldn't help but notice Véronique as she stood: tall thin frame in blue jeans and a thin dark sweater. Her student friends said goodnight and headed one way; she and Robert and Max walked together the other. Véronique and Robert traveled more or less rectilinearly and Max in his own fashion, hands in pockets and veering lazily left and right, occasionally bumping his shoulder into Robert's and leaning like a drunk in need of support. "So," he remarked, "I'm off to Italy on Sunday for a week. What will you do, Rob?"

"I suppose I'll manage, Max. After all, I wasn't counting on your presence when I came to Germany."

"True. It's funny, though, isn't it, how it seems now almost as if we were already friends and you came here specifically to visit me. Aside from writing your book, of course. And your important duties with the tennis club."

"I think Max is pleased to have found his own pet artist to patronize," Robert said to Véronique.

"Ya, very good," said Max. "But seriously, you should let Véronique show you around Munich while I'm gone. She can give you a different perspective on our city."

"I'm sure she has better things to do."

"I'd be happy to show you around," she said. "Have you seen the English Garden?"

"Ya, good idea, he'll like that. See what I mean? I haven't been there in twenty years."

They reached Max's car. There was room for only one passenger, and Robert offered to walk home, but Véronique insisted on taking the Strassenbahn. They walked to the corner, and after making plans to meet Robert on Sunday, she climbed on and the tram took her away. They drove back towards the center of town and Goethestrasse. With the top down, Robert leaned back against the headrest and watched the Munich sky slide past as the cool wind brushed his face. "So you're off to Italy," he said.

"Ya, some business to take care of with a company we deal with there. Also, there's a woman I want to see in Milan."

"Ah-ha."

"An art appraiser for a gallery there. Quite a stylish woman, really. I met her on my last trip to Hong Kong. And if I'm not mistaken, she may have something of a sympathy for me."

"Jewish, I suppose."

"Unfortunately not. Which means a pre-set limit already imposed on the relationship. A pity."

"Still, no reason not to have a good time."

"Ya. As long as everything is understood mutually beforehand."

"Véronique, on the other hand. A nice Jewish girl."

"You think so, too."

"But yet you're not interested."

Max pulled into the tow zone in front of Goethestrasse 10 and cut the engine. Goethestrasse was an empty lot this late at night, the vegetable kiosks locked shut, the Turkish credit unions and bakery closed, even the restaurateurs gone home till morning. "From the point of view of everyone in the Jewish community here, Véronique and I are a perfect match. After all, there aren't that many Jews of the right age to begin with. It would make everyone happy, particularly our parents. Yet she's not really the type that I tend to go for, and…"

"And you're not ready for settling down anyway."

"You don't think so?" He seemed pleased to hear Robert spell out what was obviously true.

"You would only marry a Jew. Therefore, by going out with non-Jewish women, you ensure that nothing too serious will happen. If you became involved with a Jewish woman, you would soon have no excuse for not marrying."

"Very perceptive. You should be a writer."

"So you push her off onto me, in order to get yourself off the hook."

"I wouldn't have made it sound so sordid. She would be good for you to know; I think you'll like her."

"I do like her."

"Excellent. So I'll see you a week from Sunday," he said as Robert got out and shut the door. "Unless I see you at Schul tomorrow morning."

"Right. See you next Sunday."

"*Buona notte*," he called as he hit the gas and whirled around, screeching a right on Bayerstrasse in front of the Hauptbahnhof and disappearing from view.

Instead of praying with the pious the next morning, Robert sat at his table and agonized. Perhaps prayer would have served him better. In his hours of "working time," he did everything but write. He sat on the window sill and watched the busy street-life below, ate, concocted elaborate fantasies of future fame, flipped through a tattered paperback copy of *The Sun Also Rises*. That son of a bitch Hemingway. How did he do it? Younger than I am now. Scribbling in his little notebooks in pencil at his Paris café, pretentious bastard. Robert counted the words on an average page, trying to estimate how many pages of manuscript it would be.

Giving up any hope of composition for the day, he began sifting through the pile of books by his bed, most from the English-language bookstore on Schellingstrasse near the university. He took Philip Roth's *The Ghostwriter* in his hands and grabbed his pen and paper. Two hundred fourteen pages minus four pages worth of blank space between chapters, times twenty-eight lines per page times forty-eight characters in an average line rendered 282,240 characters. This figure divided by sixty-four characters per line on his typewriter back home divided by twenty-six lines per page equaled 169 pages. And so damn *simple*. It had to have practically written itself once the idea had come to him. Only now did he realize that the greatness of this book lay in its very impression of effortlessness.

Malamud's *The Tenants*: very short—only about 185 typewritten pages, by his reckoning. Peter Matthiessen's second novel, *Raditzer*, 131 sheets of manuscript. *Miss Lonelyhearts* by Nathanael West: 91 quick pages. In envy and near disbelief of how they managed to fill even these relatively few pages, he flipped through the books, caught in a murky purgatory between innocence and jadedness. For no sooner had he reread the first chapter of *The Ghostwriter* than he was back at his desk to give it another go, the facile fluency of young Zuckerman fresh in his head, certain that the elusive opening to his Newtonian opus was finally ready to meet its maker.

But nothing. He was sucking a straw stuck in sand. Might as well be in schul, praying. Thanks a lot, God. Thanks for the cruelest of insults upon injury: the miserable and hopeless condition of tangible but insufficient talent. To be good enough to want, to need, to pursue the craft. Enough talent to conceive good work, to feel its pressure against the inside of my skull. But not enough to deliver the goods. Whatever manages to emerge is just not quite good enough. And for the most part, nothing emerges. Talk about a backhanded gift. Cruel insult, indeed: to make one a writer with nothing to say.

Sunday afternoon Robert met Véronique in the Karlsplatz, where they became part of the motley congregation sitting around the large fountain. Shoppers, students, schoolchildren playing in the water, a few backpackers fresh out of the Hauptbahnhof and looking around for a cheap hotel. Then she led him down an U-Bahn escalator where, besides the station, there was an extensive mall underneath the city: markets, newsstands, and other stores, stretching the length of several city blocks. He had shopped there before, but tagging along after Véronique was a completely different experience: she worked the aisles with a domestic fluency that seemed out of character with the hard-edged careerist he had met at the café, and he followed after her like a little boy with his mother. She walked him through one particularly large market, buying fresh bread, fruit, cheeses, and a bottle of wine. They found themselves at another U-Bahn station and got on a train. When they emerged into the sunshine ten minutes later, they walked two blocks more and were at the English Garden.

Large chestnut trees along the street hid whatever lay inside. They started along a path through them and into the heart of the grounds, following a winding brook that curled, twisted, and grew into the *Eisbad*, a wide rushing chute of icy water. The trees gave way and they were on the edge of an enormous open area filled with sunbathers. Many of them were naked, others were completely clothed; most were at some intermediary stage. They were sleeping, reading, throwing Frisbees. Dogs ran between outspread towels, chasing the Frisbees or tennis balls or each other. Some boys were in the water. They had tied a long rope to a slab of wood and fastened the other end to one bank, and were riding the board against the rush of the current as though they were surfing. The field was filling up as the work day ended, the sunset still hours away.

They walked along the water until they found an empty spot in the sun. Véronique produced a small towel from her bag, spread it out and sat, smoothing her dress under her. As she unloaded the makings of a picnic, they sat, like two well-covered Muslims in a land of immodest infidels, on their life-raft blanket in a sea of flesh.

He took off his T-shirt and lay back on it, closing his eyes to the glare. It seemed the thing to do in this arena of nakedness. And he was fatigued from a morning of lessons: several students had had to reschedule from other afternoons, so he had sacrificed a morning of literary wall-staring. Had barely had time to bus-and-Strassenbahn home and shower before meeting Véronique. And now it felt like he were sunbathing on the beach. The rushing Eisbad could almost be the sea....

But suddenly opening his eyes, he noticed that she seemed uncomfortable. He looked around. Bastardized reproductions of renaissance statues, skin and muscle and fat far less perfect than art imitating it, running and jumping and lying and swimming, beautiful in the obliviousness of their own ugliness. They were all well tanned, breasts and buttocks of all qualities floating around the grass, bouncing with athletic movement, absorbing the ultraviolet, radiating away the slowly accreted burden of money earned and money spent.

And Véronique. Véronique so thin and so pale, in her summer dress and her long thin sweater even in the sun. He somehow couldn't imagine her feather-light dress ever coming off, and felt she knew that was what he was thinking.

"How about some of that wine," he said. She smiled and brought out the bottle, as well as the bread and cheese. They ate quietly, self-consciously watching the Frisbees. They found that they had used up most of their small talk Friday night at the café, and would have to work at it today if they wanted to keep a conversation going.

"You're very different from Max," she said, handing him a plum.

"And why not?" he said. "We only just met, you know."

"You seem to get along well, like old friends."

"Well, I think he likes having me around. Shows him what a good life he has. Also, as I said, he seems to have been a patron of the arts in search of an artist."

"Yes, I think he is in search of much."

He bit into the plum. "And you?"

79

She smiled. "I am not in search of him, at least, though he probably thinks so."

"Mmm-hmm."

"Most of the Jewish girls in Munich would find him a perfect match. And certainly my parents would like it. But I think Max and I are quite different. In... compatible." They ate quietly for a while, watching the frolickers around them. "I should have brought a saucer," she said.

He stared at her for a moment. "Oh, you like to play Frisbee?"

"No. Well, I have never done it."

"You speak very good English," he said some time later.

"As I told you, my mother is an English teacher. And then I went to graduate school in England. Just one year."

"I almost stayed," she added after a pause.

"Why didn't you?"

"My parents. They are here, of course. Why they are here is another question entirely."

"What do you mean?"

"You know. Don't you think it's strange that there are still Jews in Germany? Who would stay? They would have to be crazy."

"I hadn't really thought about it. I guess I just figured that home is home—"

"Yes, but it's not even really home. Most of the Jews you meet here are really of Polish blood. They were brought here to be put in the camps. Of course when it was all over and they had somehow survived there was no home left to go back to, but still there are other places. Israel, America."

"Then why?"

"I'll tell you. Well, first of all, most of the Jews did leave. Obviously you're only seeing the ones who didn't. And why didn't they? Uh, in, inertia. That's all. To begin with they had no means to leave. Then they started to make a little money, starting little businesses, plus the war reparations they received, and before you know it they had established a life here. And after that it just becomes more and more difficult to leave, even though they're not happy living here among the Germans. The inertia grows heavy."

"So Herr and Frau Altmann—"

"Brought from Poland, both of them. Haven't you noticed their Polish maid?" That explained the unrecognizable language he'd heard at their table. "And now they're living happily, more or less, only a half hour from their former home—Dachau. Of course the Altmanns have done particularly well in the new Germany. They are millionaires, after starting with absolutely nothing like all the rest. At this point they'd be giving up a brilliantly lucrative business to move away. After forty years it would take a lot anyway to move. It's back at the beginning that I can't understand."

"And you'd like to leave."

"So would most of the young Jews. But as I've explained, our parents are settled in here. Entrenched, you say, right? And we feel perhaps even more obliged than most to stay where our parents are, after what they have been through."

"The locals don't seem so bad here though," He motioned at the happy people around them.

"Mmm." Her smile faded to stone observation. "How innocent they look."

Then she was silent, and he couldn't help but close his eyes again and drift to the sounds of the dogs barking in the distance, the children calling, the icy water rushing by. All morning stretching and bending on the hot dry red clay.... The sound of tennis balls bouncing and ricocheting off rackets was still in his head. He opened his eyes once more and closed them, keeping on his retinas the image of her still sitting upright in the same position as before, her legs folded under her like a unicorn, the few patches of white skin that were exposed starting to turn red, her eyes reaching across the stream.

The sun was gone, slid behind the trees on the western border of the Garden, but the sky was still there, the fading blue which promised darkness and hinted of the end of summer, even in June. The sky between the trees across the water was beginning to blush. The only sound was the water, rushing down the chutes, over the rocks and earth, never stopping.

"Was I asleep?" he pulled himself up and put his shirt on; as the shadows stretched to engulf the fields, the breeze had become cool. The few people left in the park were fully dressed.

"It's all right, I had a book." They sat quietly for a few moments, as he assimilated the change of scene.

"So you don't want to talk about the book you're writing," she said.

"Not particularly." He caught himself frowning. "It's still too early," he added, softening his tone.

"Have you written other books? I suppose it wouldn't be too early to tell me about them."

"Very clever. But no, I haven't. I'm not *that* old, you know."

"Of course not. You're a child."

"Well, I wouldn't say that, either. I *am* thirty."

"And I'm twenty-five. We're just beginning. I'm glad to see you're not like Max, who *is* old at thirty."

They packed up their things, followed the labyrinth of the Eisbad back the way they'd come in, and as they got to where the trees thickened between the bathing area and the street, they realized that it was almost night.

"I had better be getting home," she said. "I have class in the morning, and my parents will be wondering where I am."

"So what part of Munich are you going to show me next?"

She smiled. "Perhaps I could show you some good cafés. Then you could enjoy them yourself when Max and I are busy. You should also hear the symphony. It's a very interesting architecture as well, the building they play in."

They made plans to meet during the week. An awkward moment ensued, during which he was unsure how to end the evening. He felt fifteen years old. Then she leaned forward, and he took this as a cue and aimed a kiss at her lips; but she had apparently only been initiating the standard European double-cheek kiss, and the consequence was an unnerving buss somewhere just east of the mouth, after which she boarded a tram and he waited for one heading in the other direction. Sitting finally in a window seat rumbling towards the Hauptbahnhof, he struggled to shake off the disorientation that comes from an unexpected nap. He hadn't woken up properly in the interval before saying goodbye. What had she thought, watching him sleep rudely before her, leaving her to her book? When had the nudes all disappeared?

4

They sat at a café on Türkenstrasse in the university district, not far from the English-language theater where they had just seen a Marlon Brando double-feature. Véronique had been unable to comprehend many of Brando's best lines, contorted as they had been through his tight-lipped mumble. Robert had tried to repeat them as they walked from the theater, but they'd come out cartoonish in his voice. He'd ordered bourbons and beer chasers at the café anyway, as Brando had for Eva-Marie Saint in "On the Waterfront."

"Max and I really haven't seen much of each other since Gymnasium," said Véronique, "except for occasional functions of the Jewish community. I'm sure he arranged that night at the Filmmuseum just to introduce us."

"Yes, he does seem to have some sort of vested interest in our coupling."

"I know. It's a bit embarrassing."

"I suppose he thinks you'll be able to turn me away from writing and into a good businessman."

"Why would he think that? And why would he want to do that?"

"I don't know. He seems to have appointed himself my guardian angel. Or maybe it just bothers him that there's someone who wouldn't rather be him."

"You don't sound like you like him very much."

"No, that's not the case at all. I never thought I could like a domineering capitalist so much. He has just the right amount of disrespect for what he does. He enjoys the business trips around the world, and he enjoys his money, but he seems to know, as his colleagues don't, how shallow it all is."

"It's true—everyone around here is so proud of their stupid little businesses and the money they are making. Not like you."

"Me?"

"Yes, I think it is so wonderful how you are writing a book—"

"Well, to be pinpoint accurate—"

"You don't have to be so modest. I think it's fantastic. You're doing just what you want to do, that's all that matters."

What was the point of trying to convince her of the reality of the matter? She wanted to believe that she had become friends with an actual artist, an American artist-in-exile at that, just as Max wanted to believe that he was befriending and patronizing a real writer. Robert's pretense at being an object worthy of such veneration was no more ridiculous than their need for such an object.

But what to do about Véronique? Try as he might he could summon no real ardor for her. Desire he felt—mind-spinning, blood-riverrunning, powerfully distracting desire—but it was all for the late, lost, Lexa. This frail sad woman of displaced blood and injured spirit could never arouse the same longing. Too thin, too hard, too angry, too serious. He had taken her to see *Annie Hall*, and she had hardly broken a smile. That was perhaps the moment when he had missed Lexa the most. And this woman was going to be subtitling and dubbing movies? He hoped they'd give the comedies to someone else.

No, I am absolutely not going to enter into a physical relationship I'll regret. No inclination to feel that guilty stress again. Far better to satisfy those base urges alone and suffer a little loneliness than to take the weight of another's damaged psyche on your shoulders. If nothing else, you can take satisfaction in showing a little restraint.

Waiting at the Strassenbahn stop they fell into their normal goodnight double-cheek kiss, and before he knew what he was doing it escalated into a deeper embrace. He pulled her body against him, as thin and light a partner as Fred Astaire's hat rack, and rubbed his fingers under her shoulder blades. "We're practically at my apartment," he said. "Wouldn't you like to see it?"

She shook her head against his chest. "No, I can't. I have to be going home."

He started to protest, but the trolley was approaching, and its rumbling and the screeching brakes scratched away the atmosphere of the movie and the snug café. The doors opened, and Véronique rose a meter into the air, throwing back a wave and a nervous smile from the top of the steps. As the trolley rolled off Robert could see her through the dusty windows finding a seat, a regretful or thankful escapee of his displaced lust.

Tuesday night practice. Mercury lamps throwing clouds of light onto the two-court enclosure. Red dust, kicked up by madly shuffling sneakers, rising into the glow like steam off a cooling lake. Courts 18 and 19 were at the edge of the grounds, pointing away from the city; beyond the green-wire fence lay the darkness of the Bavarian countryside.

Göttel had announced after stretching—well, during stretching—that he and Uschi were going to have a practice doubles match with Max and Saul. Robert considered challenging this breach of authority, but why bother? The four of them agreed they wanted to play doubles. What did he care? That left Dan and two teenagers, Johann and Rafi, who weren't skilled enough to crack the starting lineup but often came to practice.

Robert turned to them. "Okay, we've got three players. Why don't we run some two-on-one drills?"

"Hurrah," Dan mocked with good cheer. Robert started the two boys at net and Dan on the opposite baseline. The idea was for Dan to get a vigorous workout trying to pass them while they hit volleys corner to corner. But Dan had a brilliant knack for avoiding aerobic activity. Instead of giving the boys solid passing shots to volley, he hit deft chops to their ankles, soft angled shots to the sidelines, and his trademark underspin lobs beyond their reach. They lacked the skill to make him run much at all, and when by chance they did send a ball towards the corner, Dan's squash instincts kicked in and he would take one or two steps forward, intercept the ball before it had strayed very far laterally, and send it floating like a shuttlecock to the far baseline. The drill deteriorated into chaos, the boys looking like chickens chasing scattered feed.

Luckily, Bruno showed up. With an excuse to put a merciful end to the drill, Robert sent him on the court for a doubles game. They hadn't hired Robert to watch them play doubles, yet that's what they seemed happiest doing. It was certainly what Robert preferred. Now he could relax, unburdened by the responsibility of uplifting their games. For a while he was able to sit on the bench and drift away, the moths that danced in the halos of the lights and then disappeared into the black sky hypnotizing him into reveries of Lexa. Mid-afternoon in New York. Who was she meeting this evening? Which author, agent, editor would she spend the night with? How could she be so casually prodigal with what I treasure? How can I treasure what apparently has so little value? Of course I should forget her. Best way is to start something new. Véronique the obvious one. Narrow escape for her the other night, you orangutan. Last thing she needs is to be used by you. No, she can't be the one to save you. How can she ever compare?

He was almost glad to see Emil appear in his peripheral vision, opening the gate in the corner of the fence, walking right behind the players in the middle of a point, forcing Robert out of his fruitless meandering.

Göttel missed a backhand and wheeled around. "God damn it, Emil, have you no manners? Wait until the point is over."

"It's only practice, Rosenberg. Save your passion for the matches. Good evening Rob," the banker sauntered over like a prima donna making an entrance at rehearsal. "How are the pupils behaving this evening?" He dropped his bag on the ground next to Robert and surveyed the scene while executing a faux stretch that looked like someone checking his pocket for change for the parking meter. "It looks like they're just playing doubles."

"Well, since we had exactly eight, I figured it was a good opportunity to work on doubles."

"I tell you, Rob, you've got the best job in the world. All you need is a little folding table for tea.

Okay, good, so we'll play doubles. Who should I replace, Johann or Rafi?"

"What do you mean?"

"I mean do you want me to play with Dan or Bruno? Preferably Dan."

"They're in the middle of a set. And you're forty-five minutes late."

"I had business. Listen, you don't expect me to stand here and watch these boys play tennis, do you? Who do you think pays for this court time?" He picked up his racket and walked onto the court. "Thank you, Rafi, I'll step in now."

"What are you doing?" Robert followed him.

"I'm going to practice some tennis."

"You can't do that."

Emil looked at him incredulously. Then he gave the same look to the four from the other court, who had stopped playing and walked over to see what was happening.

"What's the disturbance here, gentlemen?" asked Saul.

"Our trainer is suggesting that I let these boys play instead of me."

Robert waited for Saul to chastise Emil, but instead he turned to Robert. "Rob, don't you think old Emil could use some practice?"

"He's right," Uschi said softly. "We need the starting six to practice."

"Exactly," boomed Emil. "What's the point of working out players who aren't going to play in the matches?"

"But Rafi and Johann were here on time." Robert's argument was starting to sound puerile, though he knew he was in the right.

"Robert, Robert," said Saul, "there is a time for ideology and a time for tennis. We're wasting good practice time here."

Robert couldn't believe how his stalwarts were rallying around the execrable Emil. He looked over to Max for succor, but his friend seemed only to be enjoying the spectacle. Finally Max stepped in. "Jungs, Jungs," he smiled, "luckily, we have an authority here. We'll do whatever the trainer says, right?" All eyes looked to Robert. He had the impression that they would do whatever he said as long as he said what they wanted. He looked at Johann and Rafi, and they both shrugged, as if they couldn't care less.

"Fine," he said. "Emil, take Rafi's place."

Eight players returned to the courts, and Robert and Rafi sat on the bench. Rafi put his racket into his bag, pulled out a pack of Marlboros, and lit one up.

"Sorry about that," said Robert. "He had no right."

"Ah," the boy exhaled a mixture of smoke and fog into the cool night air. "It's normal here. I'm not giving a fuck, you know?"

"Yeah."

"How did you ever come to be working with these guys, anyway?"

"I saw an ad at a club in New York."

"You left New York for here?" Rafi looked incredulous.

"Yeah."

Phew, Rafi blew smoke through his lips, shook his head. He threw his cigarette stub down on the clay and picked up his bag. "I'm going to meet my girlfriend on Leopoldstrasse. I'll see you, Robert."

"See you, Rafi."

Cling of the fence gate. Soft-shoe of sneakers on clay, orange-powdered balls thudding against gut strings, scattered shouts of score and comment. Familiar strains of childhood. Is this the Pinewood Tennis Club, 1970? The sounds of a tennis club to me like sylvan rustles and whippoorwill cries to a country lad, or sirens to a city boy. Fly across the world, a new continent, a new language, same life. Can't escape the 78-by-36-foot rectangle. The percussion of balls and rackets lulled him into a state that he had experienced on random occasions since his early childhood. It started when he could imagine the present as past, when he saw the people around him, the sounds he heard, even his own voice as the memory that it would soon become. Now, sitting by this clay court in the middle of Europe, it seemed as though he were only remembering the scene, just as he remembered driving Lexa around Bavaria or walking home from elementary school. He was feeling the effect of time, feeling it physically distancing him from everyone and everything around him, separating him in fact from himself, his present self. The spells generally lasted only a minute or so, but while he was in one he could imagine it lasting forever, imagine his entire life passing without his being able to experience it as a participant. He was a spectator, his life just a memory.

On the far court, the doubles match ended, and Max, Saul, Uschi, and Göttel shook hands at the net. A faint sense of responsibility brought Robert out of his trance and led him to rise, cross the near court, and join them. "Looked like a good match," he said.

"We were up four-two in the first set," Uschi beamed, "but then Saul burned on fire. He was absolutely brilliant."

"We didn't expect to beat Max and Saul," said Göttel, "but we also didn't expect to be destroyed like that. Six-four, six-love. And we can't even feel bad, because it was simply a case of Saul shining."

"Can you believe this guy?" Max slapped a hand on Saul's back. "He loses to the most ridiculous players from other teams, and then he plays like this. What do you think, Rob?"

"I was loving the volleys. The serves and volleys. That's all you have to do, Saul, to dominate in this league."

"No more pathetic losses, boys," Saul promised. "I think that's finally behind me. I feel like I've passed to a new stage. It's interesting how it works: you struggle and struggle, one step back and two steps forward, and then all of a sudden, like a revelation, you feel a major change. Your body has learned something it will never forget. It's a fascinating process."

"Mazel Tov," said Göttel. "Listen, gentlemen, I have to run. It has been a pleasure. I will see you in church. Ha ha!"

The other match was breaking up too. Robert, Max, Saul, and Uschi walked over.

"Where's Johann," asked Robert.

"He took off," said Emil. "You see? What did I tell you—these boys are not serious about tennis."

"Well, that leaves us with six, so why don't we do two-on-two drills here, and two people can play singles on the other court."

"Brilliant," said Saul. "I'll play singles."

"My old friend," said Max, "you should never play tennis again. You've hit your *ne plus ultra*. You can only go down from here."

"Nonsense. I've got it now. I'm never going back, Max, old man."

"Well, I've certainly had enough doubles," said Dan. "I'll play some singles with Saul."

Oh God no. At least give him one night to savor his fine play before you dismantle his game and turn him into a blabbering madman. But how could he keep Dan away without hurting his feelings? They were already taking sides of the other court. And anyway, he had just seen what havoc Dan could wreak on practice drills. "All right," he sighed, "let's work on our volleys."

He set up Max and Uschi against each other on one half of the court, and Emil and Bruno on the other half. Robert positioned himself by the net post. On the other court, Saul and Dan finished a few warm-up rallies and began a set.

Two contrasting trajectories developed in front of him, like signals from different circuits on an oscillograph. Max and Uschi worked assiduously at the volley drill, Max hitting low ground strokes and Uschi returning crisp deep volleys. When one made an error, he pulled another ball out of his pocket or out of the bucket and began a new rally. The blurred yellow line of their play rarely rose above Robert's eye level. On the far side of the court, however, balls floated by like lazy bumblebees, spun in unlikely rotations, and often bounced several times before meeting an opposing racket. Incredibly, he had paired Bruno against Emil once again, without thinking twice. Already the grumbling was beginning on one end, the haughty obliviousness on the other.

On the other court, Saul served and volleyed his first two points cleanly, continuing his mastery from the doubles match. But then Robert looked up to see Dan return the next serve with a lob—yes, a lob, his typical underspin, just-high-enough, unerring lob off his wooden stick. Saul stopped dead in his approach to the net like a cougar hit with a stun dart. His feet sliding helplessly in the clay, he spun around, managed to retreat towards where the ball had already bounced near the baseline, made a flaying stab at a reverse backhand but missed completely, and with the look of a man whose car won't start watched the ball die on the clay.

"Well lobbed, Dan," he called. He picked the ball up from where it sat in the middle of the court mocking him and served the next point, perhaps just a fraction of a second sooner than he normally would. His serve wasn't quite as hard as usual, his rhythm in getting to the net seemed thrown off just a bit, and Dan's lazy slice return fluttered over the net and right to Saul's feet, where he stiffened up his legs, scraped his racket head across the clay, and succeeded only in preventing the ball from proceeding any farther.

Oh, Jesus. Robert couldn't watch. It was like seeing your alcoholic brother who'd been on the wagon sit down at the kitchen table with a case of Bud and a bottle opener. He concentrated on the two drilling pairs closer to him and actually started spitting out advice: "Bend your knees on those low volleys, Max," "In front of you, in front of you, Uschi," "Stick to the drill, Emil."

It was no use. There was a Eugene O'Neill play over on Court 19, and he couldn't keep his peripheral vision off it. Saul's poise had abandoned the sinking ship. His sweat, which during the doubles match had been the glistening sheen of the sportsman in his prime, was now the stinking dripping effusion of desperation. It clung to his clothes, seemed to weigh him down, slow his gait. He had to stop after every point to wipe his glasses. The balls were a step farther from him, his swings just slightly later, his balance not quite right. "Come on, Saul!" he cried after pushing a backhand so tentatively that it wavered left and out of bounds. "Hit the ball!" Dan had a sad smile on his face as he strolled laterally across the court between points. He knew he was driving his friend to lunacy, but there was little he could do about it. No more than the cat could refrain from batting the half-dead mouse around the basement before finishing it off.

"For God's sakes, not a double fault," Saul murmured after hitting two serves into the net tape. He fetched the balls, returned to the baseline, and pantomimed a practice serve. "That's it, just toss it up there, what could be easier?" But his toss was too low—he seemed not to have the power in him to lift the ball to the proper height—and he cramped another one into the net. "I will hit this one over the net, no matter what," he announced. It barely made it *to* the net, much less over it. "That's it, Dan, I'm sorry," Saul walked somberly to the net. "I'm finished. I can't do it. I've lost my game."

Time was just about up anyway. Robert wrapped up the drills, and the players began collecting balls, slipping rackets into covers. "It's such a goddamn difficult game, Robert." Saul was slumped on the bench. "How do you do it? How do you maintain a level of proper play?"

"You just forget about the bad shots," Robert sat beside him. "Remember the good ones. You'll play fine next time. Just like in the doubles."

"Yes, yes, that's right," Saul spoke with an air of false optimism. "We must move onward and upward. Upward and onward." He slowly untied his Adidas sneakers, slipped them off and replaced them with leather sandals. "I just don't know," he sighed.

They couldn't get to the café fast enough, as far as Robert was concerned. The dim glow of the lamps, the long tables by windows overlooking a sporting ground that was now quite cold in the evening—it felt like a ski lodge. The *Weissbiers* arrived, and soon the atmosphere livened, hearty voices rose and collided like the cigarette smoke that mingled above the tables, and Robert relaxed and shed the anxiety of running practice even as he strained to follow the roiling admixture of German and Yiddish. He knew that whenever they shifted towards more Yiddish they were probably talking about him, but he couldn't say he cared much. At the moment, it was mostly German, and the topic of conversation was utterly banal: could the general club membership be persuaded to allocate funds for indoor tennis practice over the winter? Together with the beer and the noise of plates slapping together and laughter from other tables, the palaver sloshed through Robert's head, causing a pleasant sense of anesthesia.

Too bad about Véronique. Just couldn't muster up the proper enthusiasm. Not right to use her as a way out of his Lexa obsession. But how much of his apathy was due to Lexa? Maybe forcing himself to get involved with someone new would free him. No, Véronique not one to mess with. Too fragile, too angry.

A rise in pitch, a decrease in volume, and an infusion of slurred Yiddish brought him out of his reverie. Emil and Uschi were arguing about tonight's practice. Robert couldn't quite make out their debate— whenever a line of reasoning was about to coagulate in his mind, they would throw in a few lines of Polish, for God's sake—but clearly neither was satisfied with tonight's play. Occasionally Max would jump in, always the cheerful mediator, to defend Robert or make some eloquent point, concerning (Robert hoped) the near impossibility of anyone satisfying this mob of lunatics. Then Saul, in a soft aside, would find some minor inconsistency in Max's peroration, and the two would go off into a side argument in Italian, with Bruno occasionally muttering, "Eh? Eh? Speak German" and winking at Robert.

Eventually the group returned to a general discussion, and it seemed they were all watching Robert out of the corners of their eyes.

"But we're boring Robert," said Max in English. "Even our poor trainer can't possibly maintain this obsessive an interest in our tennis club." Max then managed to steer the conversation toward the upcoming Wimbledon and European soccer championships. German hopes were high on both counts, with Becker and Graf at the height of their games and the West German footballers looking strong. Robert had seen the poster of the 1974 West

German World Cup championship team still hanging on Max's bedroom wall. As in other areas, however, he knew Max and the other Mattathians were ambivalent about their sports allegiances. On the one hand, they found themselves cheering for the German athletes—after all, they had lived their whole lives in this country. But the nationalistic spirit that erupted from the success of those athletes made them wary. Of course, such national pride in sports teams occurred in every country, but here it made one stop and think, and remember. Boris Becker seemed like a decent sort, but still when Robert and Max watched him on television, Robert could feel Max rooting both for and against him.

"So, Rob," Emil spoke softly and gave Max a conspiratorial lift of an eyebrow, "could you understand what we were discussing earlier?"

"I can't say I was trying too hard."

"We were saying what a great job you've been doing."

"Now even I could tell you weren't saying that."

"But you've got to take charge a little more. This group needs discipline. Believe me, if you give them the choice, they'll just play doubles all the time and never improve. But what they really want is for someone to crack the whip and make them work, make them drill. More of those volley and passing-shot exercises."

Robert looked over at Max, who had been listening. "Like the ones you were working so hard at tonight?" Max said.

"Well, listen, what can I do with that *vilde chayea* Bruno? I can't possibly work on my game against him. The balls come back at me with those funny spins. And just looking at his strokes sets me back weeks. I only put up with him for the good of the team."

"But you like discipline, Emil," Max led him on.

"Absolutely. Not that I'm the one who needs it. Bruno, Uschi, even Saul: they're like children, like Johann and Rafi. They need a firm hand over them. That's what we're paying you for, Rob."

"And what about your little Italian *recitative* with Saul?" Robert asked Max. They were in the Porsche now, zipping across the Isar on the Prinzregenten bridge late at night.

"Oh, mainly about what an ass Emil is, and how we can protect you from his idiocy. Saul is your biggest fan, you know. He doesn't want to lose you because you get fed up with Emil and Bruno and others. He gives you all the credit for lifting his game to new heights, as in that doubles match. And then he takes all the blame himself for his disastrous plummets."

"I shouldn't have let him play with Dan tonight. Dan is like a secret weapon, a tool of psychological warfare that only the enemy must be exposed to. I feel like I mustard-gassed my own side. I just hope Saul doesn't quit the game forever."

"Not to worry. He's very philosophical about these episodes. He seems to thrive on his own failure. And anyway, once he hits a few good backhands next time out, he'll forget that he is even capable of playing so badly."

"You know, when I was a kid there was always someone in the junior tournaments who was like that, who had a great-looking game but couldn't beat anyone in a match. He'd be known as a 'head case.' But I never thought I'd see a head case like Saul. I feel like Freud with the Wolf Man. And how do you explain that mutiny against Rafi and Johann? How could they expect me to let Emil, an hour late, replace one of those guys just because they're younger?"

"You have to understand, Rob, in Europe we don't have the same concept of 'fairness' that you have in the States. We have a more practical sensibility. It's like what you call 'cheating' on tests in school. I remember we would sometimes have American exchange students who couldn't believe that we would all help each other during exams."

"You mean actually looking at each other's papers during the test?"

"Of course! See what I mean: you're shocked. We considered it a contest of us against the teacher. If someone were to refuse to show his paper to the guy next to him, he would be completely ostracized. In the U.S., it's the opposite. You even get accolades for turning a 'cheater' in. That would be unthinkable here. As I say, it's practical. The goal is to do well on the test—for everyone to do well on the test. How that is achieved is less important. It's the same in tennis practice. The important thing is for the six regular players to get their practice in. What does it matter that some high American principle of fairness is violated?"

Robert sighed. "I guess I keep making the mistake of acting like I'm coaching a Little League team in New Jersey."

"Exactly. All for one and one for all, right? Everybody carries his own weight. Nobody is bigger than the team. You got to suck it."

"Suck it up, I think you mean. But yes, you've got the idea. You've been studying your Hollywood movies."

"Exactly." Max drove slowly through the quiet late-night streets of Munich. They had no particular destination in mind, though in a secret ballot Robert would have chosen his apartment. It was past two in the morning, and he longed for bed. But after Max had bought him an expensive dinner he felt he had to humor his host's nocturnal wanderlust. How Max managed to stay awake he would never know. Every morning at eight, by Max's own telling, his mother had to force him out of bed to begin the day of business with her and his father. Still, after each long day, he insisted on staying up until all hours, mainly just killing time. Dinner usually dragged on until ten or so, then a drink somewhere to make amends with someone he had stood up five hours earlier, then several long phone calls on his car phone—the only one Robert had ever seen—followed by endless conversation with Robert, until he finally would deposit him on Goethestrasse like an exhausted courtesan.

"So," Max said, "how's Véronique?" Robert could sense him grinning.

"She's just fine."

"You're getting along."

"Of course we're getting along. I get along with everyone."

"I didn't mean getting along like you get along with everyone. I meant are you getting along in any other way?" He stopped for a red light and looked at Robert.

"Jesus, Max, you sound like a yenta, if you'll pardon my Yiddish. Anyway, no, I'm sorry to disappoint your voyeurism, but I don't believe she and I are destined for carnal knowledge of each other."

"That's too bad. Somehow I think that she would not be necessarily dispassionate in bed."

"Well, if you're so tantalized by the thought of it, why use me as your envoy?"

The light changed and Max drove ever so slowly through the empty intersection. "Very good," he laughed. Then in a more serious tone, "Because such a move on my part might be a little dangerous. Munich is a small town, and the Jewish community even smaller. Things get around, and then certain pressures ensue.... There is a lot of pressure for young Jews to marry other Jews and keep the community going. Not without reason...."

"You're just not quite ready to give up your Italian schicksas and take up the responsibility of propagating your race."

"Very good."

"Speaking of which, how was Italy?"

"Very nice. You'd like this woman—"

"Does she have a name?"

"Ya, her name...." his voice trailed off. "I told you she is an art appraiser."

"Yes." Robert gave up on learning her name.

"Very stylish. Sophisticated. I like that, you know. And in bed..." his smile reeked of the memory of untellable pleasures, "a magician."

"You do have a way with words, Max."

"I should introduce you sometime."

"Yes, you should."

"But look, I've already found you a nice woman, and you resist falling into an understanding with her."

"Very funny."

"Listen, you shouldn't mention the Italian to Ingrid. Of course she knows already to some degree, at least she knows that I see other women, and she insists just as I do that we should both be free, but that doesn't necessarily preclude a certain jealousy..."

"Ingrid? Sardovnik?"

"Yes, you know about her and me."

"I do not know about her and you. I suppose I could have guessed, but—"

"Well, Ingrid and I go back several years now. She made a rare appearance at a Jewish community gathering. A sort of picnic; we played tennis together. She was clearly a fish out of water, and that of course piqued my interest."

"Why? You're right at home with the Jewish community."

"Am I?" He seemed genuinely fascinated to hear Robert's evaluation. "I always think of myself as half in the fishbowl, half out. Anyway, we got to talking. She's quite a fascinating woman, you know. Very sharp. She has her own business, selling alarm systems. That must not sound very exciting to you, Rob, no better than my schmatas. Yet she's very good at business. She does well for herself. And in bed..."

"A magician."

"Ya, very funny." He looked obliquely out the windshield as if reliving a particularly delightful moment. "Very passionate, I tell you. You would never guess. Tell me, do you find her attractive?"

"Sure. And the perfect age for you."

"You think forty-two is the perfect age? I'm only thirty-one."

"Perfect for you, if not her. Even though she's Jewish, you don't have to consider marrying her."

"Ah. Well, you may have a point. Of course, there's nothing I can do about her age—I can't make her younger."

"Of course not."

"She can leave me anytime to marry someone her own age."

"Naturally."

"But look: here I've found you someone your own age, and you're not interested. I suppose you still have your old girlfriend on your mind, what was her name?"

"Alexandra."

"Ya. We should give her a call."

"Yeah, right."

They were finally in front of Robert's building. Max pulled up, cut the engine, and picked up the telephone receiver and handed it over. The curlicued cord vibrated expectantly. "What's the number?"

Robert held the phone in his hand as if it were a dumbbell. He'd wanted to call her ever since her visit, but it had all ended in such utter failure as far as he was concerned. To her, he was sure, it was a perfectly pleasant trip, a chance to see Munich and say hello to an old boyfriend. Had she any idea of the turmoil in his brain when he thought of her? She was either stupid, which she wasn't, or she was a callous unfeeling android—which she couldn't be, or how could he be so in love with her? Could he really be one of those love-sopped saps who crawl after their apathetic beloved, begging to be kicked and stepped on? Impossible.

Still, to hear her voice.... He almost could already. And it was only about nine p.m. there. Somehow it was different in Max's car. It wasn't sad sack Robert getting up the nerve and the loose change to make a transcontinental call from a pay booth. It was just Max picking up the receiver and handing it to him. Robert gave him the number.

Max dialed with the look of a young father giving his kid his first bicycle on Christmas Day. The sound of ringing at the other end of the line squeezed thousands of miles into a point and jacked up Robert's heartbeat a few notches.

A woman's voice answered. Not Lexa. Nor Marina.

"Yes, hello, is Alexandra there please."

"No, Alexandra's out right now. May I take a message?"

Out? With whom, god damn it? The quiet tinking of the cooling car engine reverberated with the unsettling uncertainty of where she might be at that moment. "No. Thank you." He replaced the receiver. The Upper West Side shot away at the speed of light, leaving him sitting in a parked car in Munich.

He said a quick goodnight to Max, wrenched his bag from the small back seat, and lugged it into the vestibule of his silent building. Empty mailbox. He pulled open the ancient elevator door and stepped in. Familiar unseen works creaked, and he began to rise. Haven't heard old Farakh for weeks; is he still alive? Would even welcome the voice of Karpinsky once in a while. Like living in a morgue.

Suddenly the building became silent again. The elevator had stopped between the third and fourth floors. For several seconds his mind didn't acknowledge what had occurred. When it did, a tide of panic rose in his chest, ascending waves of nausea and adrenalin. This couldn't happen. Every time he rode the fucking deathbox it occurred to him, but he rode it nonetheless. Because it was NEVER GOING TO HAPPEN. But it has. And on a Saturday night, with no one around, and no one due until Monday morning. He tried to think of something he could do, some action to take, but could think of nothing but the finitude of oxygen in the room. Those doors couldn't be airtight, could they? He tried to wedge his hands between them and pull them apart, but it was futile. He looked up. No trap door, right. Don't they have safety regulations here? There was no way out. He slid to a sitting position against the back wall. I'm not going to die, I'm not going to die. There must be air getting through those old doors, and I can do without food or water for thirty-six hours. I'm not going to die. Thirty-six hours. Panic like a belt tightening around his chest. Already he was having trouble breathing.

Eventually, after what he later realized was just one or two minutes, the car began to drop, silently, ever so slowly, back down to the ground level, where Robert lunged out, gasping for fresh air. He went out to the street and breathed in the open summer night. Thank God, thank God. After he'd calmed down, he felt the weight of his late-night fatigue, and he went back in and walked up the five flights of stairs. Stumbled into his room, to the window, rested his forehead against the cooling glass. Left my bag in the elevator. Get it in the morning. Which will be the last time I'll ever step into that thing. Lexa. Damn. And damn him for pushing me down that slippery slope again. That's the last time I'll try to make that connection.

Sever.

5

Gloaming on Goethestrasse, but only the faintest hint of dying sun. It had rained hard all day. The night before he'd gone to a party with Véronique at the apartment of one of her university friends, and had drunk a bit too much. Today, with an act-of-God day off from tennis, he had slept all morning and begun to work only after lunch. The late start, the oppressive rain, the thunderheads bringing on early twilight so that it felt like the end of fall rather than midsummer, the stubborn white page in front of him mocking the darkness: there was a danger of some serious depression. He riffled through the anemic stack of written pages on the other side of the table. Start something new? What, though, what? Notebook full of good ideas: empty promises.

On this day, however, Robert was saved from the specter of his literary sterility by a knock on the door. He rose from his "work," stumbled to the door, and opened it. After the dingy suffocating cloud that had engulfed him during the afternoon of attempted composition, the sight of Véronique's snowy pale countenance was nearly blinding.

"Mmm," he mumbled. "hey."

"I'm not disturbing you, I hope."

"No no no," he made a protective visor of his hand against the glare of the hall light behind her. "Come in. Work, trying. You know. Need a light on." He hadn't spoken a word out loud the entire day, and these initial attempts proved challenging.

"I think you are well hung over."

"No, no. At this hour? I've just been working and didn't notice it getting dark."

"You were very funny last night at the party."

"Funny?" He didn't remember any particular moments of comedy on his part. More of a quiet semidrunken dignity, really.

"Yes. In your normal cynical way, of course. Don't you remember your impression of Ronald Reagan speaking German?"

He grimaced. "Vaguely."

"And then you gave a magnificent summary of the novel you have been working on."

"I did not."

"You did. Although I could not understand hardly a word of it."

"Oh, God, I remember. But I only gave a brief description of the structural concept of the book. I didn't discuss characters or plot, I'm sure of it."

"I guess not."

"Remind me never to drink in public again. It makes me too…loquacious." They sat together on the bed. It occurred to him that Véronique had been in his apartment only for brief interludes—picking him up to go out somewhere, or to lend or retrieve a book—and had never actually sat down for a true visit. As usual, her clothes belied the season, adding to his impression that months of time had been lost. She wore a black skirt and a sweater that clung tightly to contours he hadn't noticed before. Something was different, a kinetic charge in the atmosphere. Or was it just the enhancement of his lust from sleeping late and working inside all day?

"Then you insisted on seeing me home, when it should have been me seeing you home, considering the state you were in."

"I get very chivalrous when I drink," he said.

"Then you kissed me."

"We always kiss goodnight." Since the Türkenstrasse groping, he had stuck to his vow and restricted their embraces to the friendly double-cheek peck.

"No," she said. "You kissed me."

"Oh yeah." They were very close on the bed. He lifted his hand and did something that had up to that moment always seemed out of the question with Véronique—he put his hand on her sweatered breast. Then he kissed her, breaking his promise for the second time that day.

"You know I have never done this before," she said when all that was left was the skirt.

"Yes," he said and helped her out of that last garment. Her body looked so small and white and impressionable. He was afraid of hurting her. The moment of communion was a completely different act from what he'd used to practice with Lexa. Then it had been like an athletic contest in which he was forever trying to keep up with his opponent. With Véronique he was the leader of an expedition. He felt he was changing her with each surge forward into her body. It didn't last too long; afterward she felt so light lying on his chest.

"I don't regret it at all," she said.

"That's good," said Robert, who did. You certainly are a man of strong will. With the moral compass of a javelina. Where would it all lead? He'd never had a second thought about rushing in head first with Lexa, who was seasoned and tough and in no danger of being hurt by the likes of him. But Véronique was a different bird altogether. She'd been a virgin, apparently waiting for the "right" man to whom to give herself. She probably thought he held strong romantic feelings for her, based on his attempts, however ungainly, to kiss her and his obvious regard for her as a friend. She also considered him a great budding writer, which rendered him all the more deserving of her heretofore protected favors. Both aspects of this assessment were misguided: the only object of his romantic musings was still Lexa, whose face and body had dominated his visual cortex during sex with Véronique; and of course if Véronique ever sneaked into his apartment to find out just what he was writing (or rather wasn't writing) it would certainly be the end of her admiration for him on that score. He was spurious as an artist and a lover. And when the truth came out, as it someday would, she would hate him. Now for the first time he saw the destructive potential of his lust and felt a sense of compunction as he lay beneath her on his bed that evening. The rain had stopped, but the sky remained dark for the early-evening hour. They listened to the dripping of the rain gutters as neon light from the street sifted in through the window and lit her white skin like water in moonlight; his body below remained dark like the land.

A Friday night in July. Véronique at home with her parents. Robert had on two occasions already joined them for Friday night dinner—a much less formal occasion than at the Altmanns' but still somewhat nerve-wracking—but on this night had accepted Max's invitation to his parents'. How ironic that for an infidel such as him the sabbath had taken on such meaning: almost every week an excellent meal at someone's elegant home for the price of a bit of nervous embarrassment over the prayers, putting up with various puzzlements over the employment of his days, and the inconvenience of real shoes and a necktie.

As usual, following a certain prelude of polite English the conversation had lapsed into a bubbling indecipherable cauldron of Yiddish, Polish, and

German. He quietly sipped his soup and occasionally pretended to be following the banter with interest and amusement. Gradually he began to gather that he had become the subject of a colloquy between Herr and Sonn.

Max turned to him with the usual smile. "My father wonders why he never sees you in temple."

"Why you no geh in Schul?" Herr Altmann added directly to Robert, as if to translate his son's English.

Robert tried to think how to explain his skepticism regarding all religions, including his own, without offending his generous hosts, but in the end just shrugged and twiddled his soup spoon in his fingers.

"You are Jewish, nein?" Herr's voice was stern, but his face was lit with a jovial brightness that lent a teasing tone to the conversation.

"Ja," Robert began, and delineated in the best German he could his feelings about organized religion.

"Vas?" His face wrinkled in noncomprehension. "Vas?" He said to Max.

Max winked at Robert and rattled off a few sentences in Yiddish that presumably made clear Robert's position on God and the universe. Robert tried to look intellectual and confident. Herr cocked an ear to his son and watched Robert. When Max was finished he nodded his head once.

"When I vas Jung," He said to Robert, "I vas like you. Then they take me to Dachau. My Frau also, though I no know her then," he gestured to his wife, who had been silently looking at her son. "They not let us pray, but we pray..." He then mumbled something to Max, who mumbled quickly back. "...secretly. We pray secretly. After it is all over, after ich bin frei again, I never again not go to Schul." His eyes sparkled mischievously at Robert.

"Why he is always talking about, uh, the camp," said Frau Altmann to Max. "I don't like it."

"You come to Schul tomorrow?" He said to Robert.

Given the question's prelude, it would have taken a harder man than Robert to say no. "Warum nicht?"

"Vas?" He said to Max.

"Er sug ja," Max laughed.

"Gut," said Herr. "Halb-neun. Uh, acht thirty." He finished his soup.

After dinner, when his parents had gone up to bed, Max and Robert got into the Porsche. "I really should show you more of the Munich nightlife," said Max.

"Take me where you will." Max hit the gas. Robert had grown fond of the feeling of just sitting back in Max's convertible and not caring where it took him. He didn't even pay attention to which streets they traversed, just stared up at the night sky scrolling by.

"So how are things with Véronique?" Max asked.

"Oh, fine. Just fine." He had not yet informed Max of the nature of the recent developments with

Véronique. He hated to give him the satisfaction of knowing he had set them up.

"She's a nice girl," said Max.

"Very nice."

"My parents are jealous. I told them you and she were dating; they were upset. They still want me to marry her. They're afraid I'll wait too long and there won't be any Jewish girls left."

"Great. So I'm the American infidel, come to ruin the few remaining pure fish in the sea."

"So you are 'ruining' her."

"I didn't say that. But yes, I suppose you weren't incorrect in telling them that we are 'dating.'"

"Ah. That's good. I have a feeling about you, you know."

"I'm sorry, but I'm dating Véronique now."

"I have a feeling that despite your professed disdain for religion, you actually want very much to settle down with a Jewish girl."

"You're dreaming, Max. This thing with Véronique is bound to end in disaster anyway."

"Disaster." Max's habit of repeating the key word of a sentence in a half question was becoming annoying. Robert didn't respond. After a while they pulled up in front of a gate on Prinzregentenstrasse, behind which was what looked like a garden party in progress. Outside the gate ten or fifteen people milled about on the sidewalk. "Have you been to P-1?" Max asked.

"No. P-1?"

"It's a club, the name's taken from the address. Very fashionable these days. Why don't you go on in and order a drink while I park the car?"

Robert started to say he'd go with him, but when Max had a plan it was useless to offer amendment. He got out and walked to the entrance of the gate as Max drove off. At the door a young man who would have been a linebacker at Ohio State had he been born in the States sat on a stool. He had spiked hair and a tuxedo. Robert was glad he had worn a jacket and tie to the Altmanns'.

"Ja?" He confronted Robert.

Robert just stared at him. What did he think he wanted, two pounds of mackerel and a carton of potato salad? At a loss for words, he pulled out his wallet to pay the cover charge.

"Your name?" He said in English.

Somehow Robert felt certain this fellow wouldn't be familiar with his name. "Cherney," he said anyway, feeling foolish.

"I'm sorry, but we're at capacity at the moment," he said without expression. "You'll have to wait until people leave and we can let you in." Robert noticed that the people he had thought were congregating idly outside were actually in line. Well, he didn't think Max would want to hang around, but his friend had already disappeared from sight, so he grimaced politely at Big Moose and stood by the curb. After a few minutes Max came walking up, change jingling in his pockets.

"Why are you out here?" he asked. Robert explained the situation, gesturing to the line of people as something they certainly didn't want to be a part of. "Let me just check," Max winked at him. Robert followed him back up to the gate.

"Ah, Herr Altmann, guten Abend," Moose gave Max quite a different reception.

"This is my friend Mister Cherney," Max said in English.

"I'm sorry, Mister Cherney. You didn't say."

"I thought you'd been informed," Robert said generously. Moose opened the gate and let them in to the patio portion of the bar, which was not particularly crowded, as bars go. Max winked at Robert again. He winked back. He'd never been with someone who winked before, aside from his great-uncle Moishe, who thought Robert was a doctor and made him listen to his chest every Passover.

"Sorry about that," said Max. "I thought I'd told you to mention my name. The owner's Jewish. We're good friends. As you can see, it's a very exclusive club."

Most of the people on the patio were dressed as formally as Max and Robert, and a good percentage of them happened to be tall leggy blondes in short black dresses. Max's type. Robert said something to that effect.

"You think so?" He suddenly seemed bored; Robert followed a half-step behind him as he wove around the various sub-groups clustered about. He turned and remarked in confidence, "They're all so German-looking, do you know what I mean?"

"Mmm." Robert knew exactly what he meant. Aryan. The master race. He'd already hypothesized that Max's penchant for seducing these women had, in addition to other motives, an unconscious historical one. The resuscitated son of the Jew fucking the granddaughters. Eventually he'd give them the ultimate kiss-off and marry a nice Jewish girl. If he could break the habit, that is.

"Come on, let's go in," Max said and led him to the door. The inside of the building was one cavernous dance floor, dark with multicolored lights swirling the walls like searchlights. A younger crowd, in more casual and outlandish costumes but still presumably of privileged connection, threw themselves about in solemn fury. A spiral staircase led to a small balcony from where the dancers could be aloofly viewed. The music was loud and formless. After a few minutes Max waved him back outside. He looked bored again.

Suddenly the sound of Max's name turned them both in the direction of one of the leggy blondes, who approached Max with a cocktail and a reproachful smile. They chatted in German, most of it small talk that Robert could make out fairly well: "So you're too important to call me anymore?" "No, as it happens I've been out of the country for some time on business..." "Right, Max." She turned to Robert and spoke English. "Your friend here is such an important man, he has no time for women anymore." "Elke here flatters me, Rob, when she knows all along that I'm simply a pathetically bad correspondent. You would be better off, Elke, with my friend Rob here. He is an artist, a writer, and not a base businessman like myself. I'm sure he would give you the appreciation you deserve." The next few sentences flew by Robert unheard as he concentrated on his nonchalance. Apparently Max had pleaded a lost telephone number, for she was writing something in his little address book, and then she was off to rejoin her friends across the patio.

"This girl likes my money very much." As they watched her stride confidently away wrapped tightly in black, it was almost enough to make Robert give up his literary ambitions and go to business school. But he knew of course that it wasn't just money. Max had style as well; Robert would have to learn to wear the Italian suits and be late everywhere and sit at expensive cafés with mineral water in order to come back and take Elke to bed. "We had quite a passionate affair," Max was saying, "for a few weeks last autumn. She has quite a way about her, don't you think?" Robert grunted appropriately. "But when we really got down to it, there was nothing much to talk about. Still, it's tempting..."

"Now what would your parents think if they knew how you carry on with these German women?"

"They would be horrified. They mustn't know. But then, if they had moved to Israel after the war, their son would certainly have lots of Jewish girlfriends, right? But now, let me invite you to a drink," Max said as a waiter approached. "Beer?"

"Sure." Max ordered a beer and mineral water. He never drank alcohol, and Robert thought he was beginning to see why. Even as he negotiated his way through German society and business, skillfully making his way to the top of both, he kept himself apart. The German Jews were Jews, and the other Germans were Germans; the Germans as a rule drank lots of beer, and so Max drank none.

"I read the books you gave me," Max said. He'd repeatedly expressed a desire for Robert to recommend contemporary American writers he thought were worth reading (implying that it hadn't occurred to him before that any were), and so he'd given him the Roth and Malamud he'd bought, as well as a William Kennedy and an Anne Tyler. "I particularly liked *The Ghost Writer*. What a brilliant way to escape any criticism from his parents and the Jewish community—to marry Anne Frank. I wonder, though, if it's really worth it to him to have incurred so much wrath from his own people simply for writing books. It would have been much easier for him to follow another occupation, one more private."

"It's true. He's been practically pilloried for following his artistic intuition. On the other hand, he's almost as wealthy as you for his efforts. It's hard to pity someone who finds such success and recognition for his art, even if he has to pay the price of misunderstanding and calumny from a few fools."

"Are they necessarily such fools?" Max waved to the waiter to bring another round of drinks.

"Of course," said Robert. "Even when a book serves to provide fodder for the racist enemies of a historically persecuted race?"

"Any religion, or race, that can't survive a few comic novels wouldn't be much to begin with, would it?" He was beginning to feel the two *Weissbiers*.

"But why choose to write something that will enforce racist stereotypes?"

"The artist can't afford to be picky about what subjects he uses." Robert drained his glass, while Max sipped his Perrier with such annoying moderation. "Can you imagine what it's like to sit at a desk day in and day out and rip your own guts out trying to find the right subject? The last thing a writer can afford is to start worrying about who's going to be offended by his work."

Max signaled for another beer for Robert even as he waved him off. Seemingly instantly, the waiter dropped another foaming *Weissbier* in front of Robert with a practiced clink. "I think I've had enough, actually," he said and took just a sip.

"You, though," said Max. "You don't give the appearance of someone tortured by the search for inspiration."

"I," Robert took a longer draft, "happen to be blessed with a virtually bottomless literary reservoir. One cannot assume that poor Roth is so fortunate."

"And whom does *your* book offend, if I may ask?"

"I believe I can say with unabashed honesty and confidence," Robert lifted his glass, "that my writings during my time here in Munich shall offend no one." He drank heartily.

"Well, in that case why do you refuse to show me anything you've written?"

"It's not ready yet. To show it to you would be like coming to a formal party in one's underwear."

"Very good. And now why don't you finish that beer so I can show you another place I occasionally go to."

They drove, in what direction and for how long Robert would have been hard pressed to relate later; after a vague lapse of time they were seated once again, this time in a much smaller bar. Though just as elegant—the cozy room was saturated with long dresses, silky skirts, jackets and ties tailored to look like money. Max smiled hello at a few people they passed on their way to a small table in the back corner.

"You're a regular here," Robert noted.

"I don't really enjoy coming to bars that often. But when I do it might as well be a nice one. And there are certain women that enjoy very much being taken to places like this."

"Have to take them somewhere, I suppose."

"Naturally."

"Can't really invite them over for Friday night dinner."

"Very perceptive." The beer and mineral water appeared on the table. When had he ordered?

Max laughed. "My parents," he said. "They haven't the slightest clue as to what you're doing here. They simply can't fathom what it means that you want to write—as a life's occupation. Why doesn't he have a job, they keep asking me."

"I do have a job."

"To tell you the truth, I'm not so sure I understand much better than they why you don't want to also have a career that makes you a comfortable living. I have many interests outside of importing Italian goods and renting apartments; but I find that I can make a lot of money without too taxing an effort in business, so that I can pursue those other interests. Now, it sounds to me that the business of selling your work to publishers is anything but a secure way of earning money."

"You could say that."

"So why force yourself to depend on such a fickle source of income? You're obviously bright enough to make a good living in other ways."

"It's funny."

"What?"

"You don't *look* like my mother."

"Forgive me for prying. Your glass is empty," he hardly effected the slightest muscle twitch in the direction of the bar and there was the new beer foaming in front of Robert. What the hell, it was too late for an evening of abstinence.

"Max baby," he said. "You know what it's like? My not getting a nice job and all that."

"What."

"Well, you know how you keep going after these gentile women that you know nothing can ever come of, and refuse to settle down with a nice Jewish girl?"

"Ya."

"Well, it's sort of the same thing as that."

"You really think so."

"Well, don't hold me to it. It just sort of came to me, that's all."

"It's not just a matter of not wanting to get married, you know," Max said soberly. "It's the question of having to settle down here in Munich."

"You'd like to leave."

"I have to, eventually. I can't stay here. We don't belong here. We're foreigners in our own country. Everyone we see around us is 'them,' and the 'we' are so few."

"So why don't you move? You could succeed in business elsewhere." With effort Robert was able to somehow keep his mind in the tracks of a somewhat coherent discussion.

"Yes, but my parents are here. It's not so easy to move to a new country at their age. And it's not worth the sadness I would cause them by leaving. It's different for us than it is for you in America. We are bound more closely to the tree."

"Okay, so you stay."

"So I stay. But you see, if I were to marry a Jewish girl from Munich, I would be doubly bound to stay."

"Her parents."

"Exactly. You'd like another beer?" Robert shook his head and waved him off. "So you see, I can't really be satisfied either way."

"You don't want to stay and you don't want to go."

"So it would seem. Shall we make a move?"

Robert nodded assent, but his body was apparently less bold than his mind. Max was halfway to the door before Robert had achieved a posture worthy of *Homo erectus* and begun his way back through the crowd of attractive people. Moments later the lights of Munich were again blurring by through the open top of the convertible and then they were entering another establishment, though this time Robert immediately was stricken with a sense of being overdressed. This was a bar more like what he was used to; He caught snatches of denim and leather in the corner of his eyes as he concentrated on following the exquisitely tailored back of Max's suit to a table.

Music. A horn blowing from somewhere. Somewhere close by apparently, judging from the sonic pressure on his left temple. He looked up and there was the stage, only a few feet from their table. Four black men, a jazz quartet. Wailing saxophone. Where was he, the West Village?

"I thought this might be more the sort of place you enjoy," Max yelled over the music. A young waitress in a tank top placed a beer in front of Robert and a coke before Max. When had he ordered? The man was a cocktail-bar sleight-of-hand master. How many five-foot-ten blondes had he maneuvered into drunken submission in this manner? Robert instinctively thought to protest this assault on his alcohol tolerance; when he got blindly drunk he preferred to do it on his own terms. On the other hand, he decided suddenly not to give in. He'd show him how a miserable failed writer could drink. Besides, if he got drunk enough he'd have a good excuse not to write tomorrow. And the jazz sounded good. He took a long swallow.

"How come we never came here before?" he yelled.

"I didn't realize you liked jazz that much."

The saxophonist finished his solo and received an enthusiastic round from the crowd. "*Ja*," Robert yelled, "*toll!* Who *are* these guys?"

"They're probably Americans," said Max. He seemed less interested in the music itself than in his friend's reaction to it. He looked like a scuba diver in a tie, amused at the various deep sea fish. Robert closed his eyes and felt the music hit him like waves of salt water, pushing him under the surface, light drifting down to him in varying shades of green.

"Man," he said, "these guys have it made. If you're going to be an artist, be a musician, not a writer."

"It's too loud," yelled Max. "I can't hear a word."

"All they have to do is play," Robert spoke no louder. "No wracking your brains looking for the right words. No squirming at the desk, no killing yourself trying to think of fucking details. It's all natural. Just play the music. Look at them; they're actually *enjoying* it. Maybe they're not selling a million records, but at least they can still play. Music is music. But what's an unpublished manuscript?"

Max shook his head and shrugged.

Robert insisted they stay till the end of the last set. "We owe it to these guys," he yelled inaudibly. "They can teach us. They know the secret."

The last note was finally blown. A happy smattering of applause from the thinned-out audience.

"Bravo!" Robert cried. "*Fantastisch! Ausgezeichnet! Gut gemacht!*" A glass half full of beer rested before him on the table. He moved automatically to lift it but immediately, motivated by an ominous tidal flow in the upper portions of his G.I. tract, set it back down. They rose and headed towards the door.

Before they got far, however, he noticed the musicians seated at a table, already with beers in front of them and smoking cigarettes. He stumbled over to them.

"*Guten Abend,*" He began slowly. "*Ich möchtete nur zu sagen,*" He struggled for the right words, "*dass Eure Musik heute nacht war, für mich, etwas wichtig. Etwas höher. Nein, etwas...*" They looked at each other and shrugged.

"I'm afraid my friend here is a bit overcome," said Max. "I'd better take him home." He put his arm around Robert and led him away.

"*Tschuss*, baby," said the drummer.

He woke in a sunny, elegant room, a firm but gentle fatherly hand on his shoulder. "Nahh," he said, delicately prying his tongue from the roof of his mouth.

"You'd better get up," said Max calmly. "We're a bit late for *Schul*."

"I'm sick," he croaked, a reflexive reaction intact from his Hebrew-school days.

"You're all right, Rob. A bit tired, but then so am I. It was well after four when we got home."

"Home?"

"I brought you back to my place instead of bothering to take you to Goethestrasse. I wouldn't have been able to pick you up in the morning, since I don't drive on Shabbas. And you had your jacket and tie with you already. You do remember promising my father you'd attend services this morning?" Through the sticky film covering his eyes Rob detected an annoying twinkle in Max's.

"Wasn't necessarily," he swallowed, trying to kick-start the saliva glands. "A binding contract."

"You wouldn't want to disappoint my father, I'm sure." Was Max laughing at him? "If we leave in ten minutes or so, no one will even notice we were late. I've made coffee downstairs."

"I'll meet you down there."

"I'll help you find your clothes."

"What time is it now?"

"Just after nine. We're late, I'm afraid, although I must admit I rarely get there earlier." Together they managed to prop Robert's corpse up in a vertical position and envelop it with the clothes he'd worn the night before. He was allowed the luxury of half a cup of coffee, a quick micturation, a rinse of the mouth and a combing of the fingers through the hair, and next thing he knew they were strolling along the sidewalk in the bright brisk morning sunshine. Max wore a freshly pressed gray suit and matching fedora. Hands in pockets, he looked like the Polish Jew he was by blood, but in another time, strolling to his Warsaw synagogue in 1909.

Robert walked hunched over, his arms wrapped around his sport coat keeping his stomach inside. "I shouldn't have bought you so many beers last night," said Max in an incomprehensibly cheerful voice. "Not that it was that many. I guess I'm used to being with Germans; I'm afraid they'd drink you right under the table without much effort."

"I was perfectly in control."

"Ya, so I presume you always try to give the bass player a big hug after a performance."

The only sounds in the neighborhood were an occasional bird, a dog barking far off, and the clicking of their shoes on the sidewalk.

"How much farther?" Robert panted.

"Not much more."

"Are you sure you're not supposed to drive on Saturdays? The writers of the Talmud couldn't have considered the existence of automobiles." No answer. "I think my shoes are on the wrong feet."

"So when's the last time you were in temple?" Max asked.

"Ten or twelve years, I'm afraid. But it's gone by like that," he snapped his fingers. Or tried to; all he produced was a slight burning pain on his thumb and forefinger.

"Reform?"

"Yeah."

"Well, this should at least be interesting for you. There's the temple." He pointed to an unremarkable building at the end of the block.

"Holy shit," Robert said. "What's happened?" In front of the building a policeman stood at attention, a sub-machine gun resting ominously in his arms.

"It's nothing," said Max. "Just a precaution, at our request. Nothing's ever happened at our synagogue, but still."

They walked by the sentry, Robert still holding the middle of his coat as if concealing contraband. Outside the side entrance, three or four teenage boys sat on the steps. Except for their suits and kepas, they might have been hoodlums loitering outside the Seven-Eleven. Did we miss the entire service? Robert wondered gleefully.

"Gut Shabbas, Jungs," said Max brightly.

"Shabbas, Max," they rejoined. Each shook Max's hand; his arrival was clearly a welcome respite from the boredom of the morning.

"This is Rob, from New York," said Max in English. Robert exchanged sabbath greetings with the lads. "Don't worry, boys, he'll be fine. Shall we, Rob?"

They entered the synagogue, where it was immediately clear that he was not to be so fortunate as he'd imagined. The sabbath service was in full force. Though it wasn't like any he'd seen before. Twenty or thirty men sat on benches, some with prayer books open in their hands, some without. Those without were chanting to themselves in a low wail, voices rising and falling as though on ocean waves, oblivious to the presence of the other worshippers. Those with books seemed to be following the amorphous lead of the rabbi, who stood in the middle of the room with four or five other men around the Torah. Together or separately they read and chanted; when they paused, one or several of the seated congregation would send up a tremulous howling prayer to fill the space. Collectively it sounded like the desperate ululations of a dying race.

Max led him like a pet to a bench, and they sat. Robert smiled weakly at the old man next to him, who looked him over without expression and went back to his *davening*. Off to his right he noticed Emil and Saul, prayer books open but surreptitiously chatting with each other. No question what they were discussing — doubles combinations for the next match. Robert took a prayer book from the compartment in front of him and opened it randomly. Max reached over and turned to the correct page. Calling upon years of Hebrew education buried deep in his past, Robert tried to match some of the sounds he was hearing from the rabbi's group with the vowelless words on the printed page. It proved fruitless; by the time he found a word he had recognized by sound, they were irrecoverably ahead of him. The mental strain of the task proved too painful. He resolved to turn the page when Max did and otherwise to work towards minimizing physical discomfort.

After a few minutes Max got up, and for one blissful moment Robert thought they were leaving. He made a move to stand, but quickly stifled it and redeposited himself on the bench as he saw that Max was joining the group at the Torah to take his part in the reading. He sat as still as possible to avoid nausea, forsaking at this point even the turning of the pages. At least Véronique wasn't there; he'd feared he might run into her and her parents in his dreadful state. Then he realized that there were no women in the room at all and remembered this curious fact about orthodox services. Paying a measurable price in gastrointestinal sensation, he turned his head and looking up behind him saw the crowd of women in the balcony, watching the proceedings on the floor with an attitude somewhere between casual interest and muted boredom. They weren't even allowed the amorphous chant, an activity he might actually have enjoyed had he not been experiencing the sensation of being idly twirled like ear wax between a very large person's thumb and forefinger. It's like another century, he thought before turning back to his incomprehensible prayer book. He didn't want Véronique to see him this morning, or to be more accurate he didn't want to have to make small talk with her parents after the service. Slowly he began to rock back and forth like the little old fellow next to him. It felt good. It eased his pain.

The wailings of the men around him ebbed and flowed, mixed like warm multicolored sands and filled his ears, blew over him, slowly burying him. The effect was soporific; he drifted slowly away, his rocking motion dampening until he sat perfectly still, head bent forward, eyes closed. By not moving he could shrink his pain into a pinprick deep in the center of the darkness. But then a disturbing sound penetrated his trance, reaching a thin tentacle into the pinpoint of pain and pulling at it, stretching it back to its previous size. His thoughts concretized as though he were coming out of a dream, and he heard the sinuous tones of the chanting forming themselves into a familiar, if distorted, polysyllable.

"Roe-bairt Chairrrrrnay." In his delirium (or was he completely asleep and dreaming?) he heard the rabbi's dulcet voice chanting his name as though a prayer. His surname drifted in two arcing syllables up to the rafters and reverberated back down. He forced his left eye open in order to corroborate that he was hallucinating. The principal image confronting that poor organ, however, was (as in some B-movie nightmare) the sight of Max, by the rabbi's side, smiling demonically and beckoning him up to the pulpit.

It could not be true. Comforted by that tautology, he closed his eye in an effort to recapture his former state of oblivion, but opening it once again a few seconds later he saw the collective gaze of the other Torah readers as well as a few of the congregation following Max's mirthful eyes to his very seat. Like a marionette dangling from the pen of Kafka he rose on unsteady legs and made his way forward. He was living every Bar-Mitzvah boy's nightmare, stepping to the pulpit without a clue, hundreds of pious judging eyes upon him.

He arrived at the hallowed Torah in last night's clothes, his oral cavity exuding an alcoholic halitotic cloud that offended even him. Certain that he was about to be asked to read from the sacred document, his brain had wisely informed his heart to increase its pulse rate by threefold. His epidermis suffered new waves of cold sweat over the dried deposits of the night before. He approached the table, where the men parted (in sardonic parody, he was sure, of their progenitor's famous trick) to let him in closer. He offered Max a weak resigned smile not unlike that of one ascending the steps to the guillotine.

"Et tu, Maximilius?" he whispered.

"The rabbi is asking you to hold the Torah while they put the cover back on," Max smiled back.

Hold the Torah. He breathed for the first time since he'd risen. "Just hold it?" Max nodded back. Well hell, he could do that. He might be hung over, but he wasn't a complete invalid. If these old guys could carry it, it couldn't be *that* tough. He turned to the rabbi and nodded solemnly. The rabbi and another man lifted the holy scroll and handed it to him. Overjoyed at the manageability of his task, he held the Torah upright against his chest while they returned the various sacraments and covers to their place.

After a few minutes, while they carefully arranged each item and said various prayers, his load began to feel heavier. While his initial strength had proved equal to the task, his stamina must have suffered from the events of recent hours. He shifted his load a bit during a prayer to put the bulk of the weight more on his stronger right arm. In doing so, however, he must have slightly miscalculated, for the center of gravity had moved too far to his right. For a moment he thought he was okay and could regain a working balance, but that moment proved transient—before long he had to face the irrefutable fact that he was dropping the most sacred document of the Chosen People.

Luckily he hadn't even the time to plan his escape from the building before the quick-witted gentleman on his right leaped forward and, to everyone's relief, saved the Five Books of Moses from suffering a disastrous meeting with the hard wooden floor. Good God, it's Göttel Rosenberg, that smug bastard. He's finally got me off the tennis court, in a position of moral and physical inferiority. Göttel helped support the Torah, smiling like he'd just hit a lucky drop shot. A few seconds later the now fully attired scroll was taken from Robert's arms, the rabbi shook his hand, and with a sickly glare at Max he returned to his seat.

After a time everyone began to rise and shake each other's hands, and he surmised that the services were over.

"It wasn't my fault," said Max when he saw Robert's look as he joined him. "The rabbi thought it would be nice to have my guest play a small part in the service. Of course I had to agree. That was quite an honor, you know. Not everyone gets to hold the Torah."

Robert was so relieved for it all to be over that the detailed threats of violence to Max he had composed directly following the episode escaped him. "I almost dropped it," was all he could manage to enunciate.

"No one noticed," his friend said. "A slight wavering, that's all. Göttel was there to back you up anyway. Ah, Herr Slotnik," He shook the hand of a small rotund man with a gray moustache. "Good

Shabbas. May I present the American writer Robert Cherney?"

"Good Shabbas," Herr Slotnik took his hand. "You did very nicely."

Robert shook a few hands, and everyone was polite, no one so much as making a jocular reference to the incident. He soon was believing that he had done all right after all.

He caught the eye of Véronique among the people congregated outside the building and had no choice but to join her. He shook the hands of her parents.

"Good Shabbas, Robert," said her mother. "What an honor for you today."

"Yes," said Véronique, "and on his first visit to *Schul* since he's been in Munich. You didn't tell me you were coming."

"A last-minute decision. Quite spontaneous, really."

"You must come and have lunch with us," said Frau.

An afternoon of etiquette and feigned good cheer with the Eisensteins he could not have endured. "I'm afraid the Altmanns are expecting me," he said. "I'll call you," he said to Véronique.

"Okay, Robert," she said as they turned to go. "And congratulations on not smashing our Torah into little bits."

He found Max and literally tugged on his sleeve. Eventually, after countless more handshakes, Max steered him back in the direction of his house.

"Well, Rob, what do you think?" Robert's grim silence was the only retribution he could muster. "At least you got to see what services in Munich are like. You should know what you're forsaking. And you did quite well with the Torah. Our aging congregation needs a little scare now and then."

Robert made it back to the Altmanns' and up to the third-floor guest room where he had spent the early morning hours. Without so much as removing his soiled tie, he fell onto the plush bed and felt fifteen hours of sensation funnel into a black point just behind the bridge of his nose. If he had dreamed he would have dreamed a tumultuous collage: bitter taste of Weissbier, piercing trill of alto sax, blinding blonde women in black, and Max sauntering after them, hands in pockets, nonchalant and lost in space in the Federal Republic, while his parents chased after him, unable to move, their feet stuck in the quagmire of their inconceivable history. As it was he dreamed nothing, simply collapsed into blackness for the rest of the afternoon while Max and his parents observed the sabbath downstairs.

6

Late August, late afternoon, the bed by the window overlooking Goethestrasse. Outside a slight chill ran through the summer air like a cold current in lake water, and already the buildings were throwing burgundy shades across the sidewalks at an autumnal angle. Robert and Véronique were lying in a postcoital torpor, she with her head tilted back to look out the window, her skin so white that his sheets looked old and tainted. Already his desire was a faint memory; it was as if his sexual release purged every trace of longing for this poor pale woman. For hours, sometimes for days if he didn't see her, he could think about nothing but making love to her, but the moment it was over this desire was replaced with a mild repulsion, a longing to be alone. At these times he would resolve once again to stop leading her on; they must return to being only friends. But before he could find the right moment to explain to her, his libido rose again like Lazarus, wiping out any misgivings he might have had. He disgusted himself.

"Sometimes I thought I might never have a lover," she spoke softly to the window behind her, as though she were alone.

"How could you think that," he disengaged himself from her and leaned on one elbow.

"I don't mean I really expected I wouldn't, but sometimes, you know, it seemed that way."

"And now? Do you like having one?"

She laughed, still not looking at him, her neck arched, showing him only her chin and neck. "You know," she said, finally turning to him, "I really have no idea who you are."

"Oh, I'm sorry." He extended a hand for her to shake. "Robert Cherney. American."

"Very funny. That's about all I do know. And a few other facts."

"Facts are all there is to know. What other facts would you like?"

"You never talk about your family. Tell me about them."

"Well, as you know, I'm an only child. My father was a lawyer. He died five years ago. My mother didn't work until I was in college. Then she began working at my father's practice, as a sort of office manager. She still works there, for his partner."

"What made you want to be a writer?"

"Books, I suppose. My father always wanted to write. He always intended to cut back on his work and write. But he never did."

"And what of your romantic past, Mr. Cherney? I'm sure there were many lovers in New York City."

"Only one worth mentioning, and I guess I'd rather not talk about her right now."

"*Ach!* You see what I mean? You never want to tell me anything about yourself."

"True. But enough about me."

"Hah! What do you want to talk about then?"

"Well, how about this?"

"*Mein Gott.* Are all men like this? So often, I mean."

"I wouldn't know. Except from books."

"Me too." Now she was looking away again, back behind her at the window, and smiling. He crawled forward and onto her. Tumescence dispelled all worry about future entanglements (or disentanglements). At least in bed he enjoyed a certain prolificness, as though to make up for the barren hours at the writing table. Perhaps it was one or the other; if he became impotent, maybe he would finally be able to write the book he felt sleeping amorphously in his gut. Or vice versa.

He'd have made the trade in an instant.

Priapus.

He arched his back and Crack, sent a serve ricocheting off the corner of the service box into the backdrop, the ball rolling to a stop as the sound of the hit faded to silence on the empty court. A thundershower, unheard on the indoor court, had darkened the small windows in the corners. When the wind changed he could see the effect on the rivulets flowing down the panes. You've no right to use her like this. You've gotten yourself deep into it, and now you'll have to get out of it. He tossed a ball slightly to his right, silhouetted against the ceiling lights, and rose into it, sending a flat hard one down the T. The hollow sound of racket meeting ball pleased him, reminded him of countless hours since he was ten or so spent practicing this same motion, took him out of his self-loathing and connected him with a familiar and pleasant past devoid of thinking or planning or worrying. Just hit the ball. Toss, bend, crack. The impact of strings on the ball flowed like a neural impulse through the racket into his hand as though they were part of one organism, and then down his arm, pulsing in his shoulder where tendonitis had developed his senior year and dissipating through his back and legs. Everything about it felt good—even the pain still throbbing lightly in his shoulder was a reminder of a happier time when all that mattered was whether they would beat B.U., and he would go out to the courts the morning of the match and hit his serves, pain or no pain, icing before and after to keep the inflammation down. No one cared about the tennis team, there were no fans at matches like for football or basketball, but to him and his teammates it was deadly serious; the aging hard courts by the gym might just as well have been Centre Court at

Wimbledon. They trained, drilled, ran, and when they graduated were expected to forget it all and go to law school or medical school. There was no real shot at the pros for them; this wasn't USC or Stanford, just a place where students complemented their studies with athletics. Now he got the same good feeling from hitting a bucket of balls alone on an empty court, although there was no longer any reason to practice. He tossed to the left and spun an American twist into the backhand corner of the ad court. The shoulder wasn't too bad, just a dull ache. The six months he had taken off last year had done some good. He usually avoided serving hard even when playing doubles with club members or hitting with Burkhard, but he could still go all out once a week or so. It's Lexa you want. Physically, anyway. Better off to have lost her. She was no better for you than you are for Véronique. He threw up the last ball in the bucket, twisted his upper body, and tore into the ball with all his might. In his anger he had tossed the ball too far behind him, which not only made him send it beyond the service line, but also shot a lightning streak of pain through the axis of rotation in his shoulder. He dropped his racket, cursed, and kicked the empty ball hopper, the sound of its wire frame bouncing on the court heard by no one but him. It's no good, no good. For a minute he stood motionless concentrating on the pain and staring at the white court lines that transfixed him in the dim artificial glow and burned their outline into his brain. Then he took the hopper in his left hand and began picking up the balls, connecting the dots and ending up with no picture at all.

One late-summer afternoon he stepped out of his building and began to walk. A long morning of fruitless labor had put him in the usual state of dazed numbness. He would come out of these bouts with blank page like a losing prizefighter, punch drunk and scarred, a little wobbly in the legs. He wondered how much more he could take. Bright sunshine flared through his sunglasses and made him squint. No lessons today; he had several hours to kill before meeting Max for dinner. As usual, he would murder the hours on his feet, wandering through the streets.

He walked over to the Karlsplatz and watched the fountain for a while, then headed through the arch to the long paved walkway, a sort of outdoor mall, new fashionable shops and cafés sprinkled into the ancient architecture. A group of forty or fifty boys, about eighteen years old, approached from the opposite direction. They each wore a white sweatshirt with what looked like handwriting scribbled all over, and a dark fedora with feathers. He'd heard about these guys. In the morning they were going off to begin their mandatory two-year army stint. As was the custom, they spent the twenty-four hours beforehand running around the city in groups, drinking untold amounts of beer and getting as many pretty women as possible to sign their shirts (though by the end of the spree any old lady they sighted was good enough). They looked ridiculous, Bavarian frat boys without a brain cell left between them, and yet he envied them their unquestioning compliance with tradition and law. What joy to be forcefully conscripted into an army! For two years one wouldn't have to think about a damn thing, just do whatever one was told. What a relief: fifty pushups? Yes, sir. Twenty miles? Yes, sir. Bang my head against the wall? Yes, thank you sir. I think I might make a good soldier. Anyone could do fifty pushups if they worked hard enough. As for headbanging, I've been doing that for years now. I'd take the barracks championship in headbanging.

He took a left before he reached the Marienplatz and came to the Frauenkirche. He stood at its base and gazed up to the tops of the twin towers, which he could just see from his apartment window. How on earth did it dodge all the bombs? He continued eastward, zigzagging until he hit Maximilianstrasse, which he took straight over the Isar river. Late afternoon sunlight reflected off the water and off the Deutsches Museum to his south, suspended on its river island like a great temple. He headed northeast, names passing by like a history lesson: Einsteinstrasse, Maria Theresia Strasse, Max Planck Strasse, Kopernikus Strasse, Shakespeareplatz, deep into the wealthy oasis of Bogenhausen, and finally to the doorstep of the Altmanns. Every pedestrian he saw he imagined to be an intellectual worthy of the streets' namesakes. And it still seemed faintly possible that he could one day deserve their company, that he would create something worthwhile, that he would be a true artist-in-exile, deserving of this early summer Munich evening.

As he neared the Altmanns', the postmodern Deutsches Bank tower rose like an anachronism in the distance above the foliage, glinting orange-red in the sunset. Herr Altmann answered the door—the maid must have had the weekend off—and led him into the living room. He motioned to a couch. Robert sat down, but the old man remained standing there as if not sure where to go.

"Maximilian is oben," he said. Herr Altmann gave the impression that he had no idea when he was switching languages, as though words to him were words and all fit together regardless of their original association.

"Ah," Robert nodded his head.

"We are finishing Essen." He nodded back towards the dining room.

"Oh, please don't let me..."

Frau Altmann entered carrying a tray with a tea kettle and cups. "Guten Abend, Rob. Here, we will have tea while Maximilian is finishing working. He's talking to these *shoitim* in Italy we do business with." She placed a tea and saucer in front of each of them (Herr was by now sitting as well) and poured the tea. "So," she looked at Robert, "how you are liking Véronique?"

He started to formulate an explanation that while Véronique and he shared perhaps a certain fondness for each other there remained differences between them that would in all probability preclude a serious lasting relationship, but quickly settled on "She's very nice."

"Yes. We know her all her life, of course. We hoped she and Maximilian might marry, but it is not going to happen. I only hope he should find a Jewish girl before it's too long. We are not so young." Finally she smiled. "I would like some grandchildren, you know?"

"Ja," said Herr Altmann. "I have tell you about during the Krieg?"

"Ach," said his wife, rising with her teacup. "Rob is a young American. He doesn't want to hear..." then she switched to Yiddish for a few sentences and left the room.

"My Frau," he smiled at Robert. "Doesn't like to erinner the Krieg. The, uh, the war, yes? You know we were beide at Dachau?"

"Max told me," Robert said softly.

Herr's eyes lit up as though remembering college days. "You know how I escape from the Russische?"

"From the Russians?"

"Ja. When the Krieg is ending, we are all warting to see wer is going to kom first, the Amerikanische oder the Russische. Everybody say the Russische are worse than the Deutsche. To Dachau came first the Russische. And it is true—they are just as schlecht as the Deutsche. So now have we to escape from the Russische. Mein Freund and I, we escape. Mein Freund is very good artist, you know? He draws pictures of girls, ohne kleider, uh ohne kleider..."

"Naked."

"Ja, nekkid. Und we show this to a guard, and we promise him many pictures if he is going to look the andere way in mittel of the nacht for a minute. And so. We give him a bunch of pictures, and he is not so bad a fellow, like some of them, and he looks the andere way, and we go."

"Just like that."

"Ja. Aber now what? Now we are running through the fields at night, schlafen in the day, try to find the Amerikanische. We steal kleider from a farmhouse and then we can beg food, look like normal Deutsche. Mein Freund, he will not ess Deutsche food, nicht kosher; I have to schlag, hit him, make him ess." He had been smiling throughout the story, as if recalling old school pranks; now the smile faded away. "Endlich we find the Amerikanische." He shrugged. "Many years ago. Ich war zwanzig—twenty years alt."

Max's footsteps came tramping down the long staircase and across the foyer into the living room. "I see my father has been entertaining you," he said. "I'm sorry I was so long. I was trying to explain to our Italian colleagues exactly how they were cheating us." He flosberry-flopped onto the sofa. "They mean no harm, and in fact to them it's not considered cheating. These guys simply don't believe in using exact figures. To be honest, I sympathize with them. Here in Germany, we have to deal with such an other extreme."

"Wo is your mutter?" said Herr Altmann. "She will mir nicht hören. She will nicht von the Krieg hören. Is many years already."

"And what brought up the war?" asked Max.

"Grandchildren." Herr smiled again. "We were sprechen, talking, von grandchildren."

The summer had flickered by like images on a movie screen, quickly fading to memory. Robert was becoming used to the feeling of days flowing by so fast, merging into one long continuum, and he realized that this was how it would be from here on. He could still remember a time when a year, or even a season, was a span so enormous he could not imagine it ever coming to an end. In elementary school the six-week grading period was like a lifetime; six weeks away was as murky a horizon as his eventual old age. It was in high school that he first began to notice the weeks spinning by, that he recognized the sensation of sitting back and watching his life pass like an old silent film in fast motion. Now in Munich the action had become a steady monotonous blur. Mornings flew by in a rush of frustration and inaction, afternoons were taken up by tennis lessons, Véronique would come by in the evenings and they would have dinner or find other entertainments, and after she had gone home at night he would usually end up driving around town with Max listening to tales of his day's business and social intercourse. Finally he would lie down to sleep dreading the moment so soon to come when he would have to rise and address his empty paper once again. Soon the summer was nearly used up; summer—the same period of time that, when he was a child, was a wonderfully interminable season of softball and birthday parties and cookouts and no school but just "what do you want to do?" back and forth all day like a ping pong ball with his friends. Now summer was over before he even took notice of the long days.

On a warm Sunday afternoon in August Véronique suggested they have a picnic at the English Garden. Robert was surprised, as they hadn't been there together since that first time in the spring, but he agreed to meet her by the *Eisbach*.

"You remember the last time we were here," she said as she laid down the blanket and opened a bottle of mineral water.

"But of course. The same verdant summer scene, the same naked people—though not so tan—tossing their little Frisbees and balls and whatnot. "

"I don't think we can make love anymore," she said.

Stunned silence. For weeks he had been uneasily sensing the approach of the day when he would have to do the honorable (if belated) thing and relieve poor Véronique of his specious love. To have the tables turned was unsettling to say the least. And even more shocking, and absurd: he immediately began to feel the pang of loss.

"Something is wrong. You hardly touch me at all, except when we are actually...engaged in the act. Afterwards, you seem almost repulsed by me. Like you'd rather be alone." Of course she's right. Pointless to argue, to try to convince her that she's imagining things. Thought I'd been successfully concealing my mixed feelings, but I guess some things you can't hide. The problem is Lexa. Can't stop thinking about Lexa, even while in bed with Véronique. Lexa, stylishly suicidal emissary of Art, hard-eyed temptress.

"It's not you," he said. "I just have nothing to give these days. I'm empty, in more ways than one." It was true. The writer with nothing to say was also the lover with nothing to give. The two conditions were not necessarily unrelated, either. Has my gradually accruing bitterness rendered me unable to appreciate a perfectly lovely young woman willing to give herself to me freely ("and a Jew at that," comes my grandmother's voice down from the Land of Eternal Guilt)?

The conversation went on. She regretted nothing, nor did he. She hoped they would still be friends. So did he. A nauseating replication of a hundred million other dramas played out between young lovers around the world already. Pure cliché. Must remember never to write this scene. "Abject reality," as the old alcoholic pedagogue Robicheau would have pronounced to his wide-eyed workshoppers.

At last the ordeal was over. They parted amicably, she taking her blanket and bag and heading back to Prinzregentenstrasse and he remaining behind, sitting on the grass and watching the young people of Munich frolic. Clothed or nude, they looked equally absurd.

The air is thick and stagnant, resisting every motion of his body as he apathetically chases balls about the court. On the other side his father sweats, sweat is what Robert senses most about him, rolling down his neck, drenching his shirt (the plain white ripped vee-neck tee shirt that embarrasses the boy), it seems as if the balls that come back to him are weighted down with his father's heavy wetness. And Robert is doing most of the running, retrieving the shots that come randomly off Dad's racket and sending them back smoothly to the center of the court, like a machine absorbing random numbers and arranging them into a recognizable pattern, the graph of which would be as smooth as the trajectory of the ball.

They no longer play sets; it's been several years since they were close in ability, and Robert hates to beat his father easily. They just hit, don't drill or practice anything in particular, just hit aimlessly until Dad's had enough. He wonders how his father can enjoy it at all, this sloshing around in the humidity, and as for himself he gets enough tennis without it.

The heat puts him in a bad mood, and chasing his father's bad shots exacerbates it. The knowledge that his father is doing the best he can does nothing to alleviate Robert's growing anger. "Stop trying to hit winners," he calls out. "I'm not," his father answers. "I can't control it as well as you." He knows this is true, but his head is getting hotter and the erratic shots madden him. He starts hitting balls farther away from his father, making him run a bit, let him see what it's like. And the old man refuses to give in and let any ball get by him. He runs them down. Robert can see his face getting redder, can feel the other's aging knees pounding on the hot asphalt. He sees on his father's face an expression that he has witnessed only a few times before. It is not anger and not embarrassment and certainly not hate, but is somehow related to all three. What it is, he realizes with a sick feeling in his gut, is a letting down of the fatherly facade. His dad is reacting to him not as a son but as he would to any cantankerous son of a bitch who insults him and tries to run him into the ground. And this scares Robert.

He imagines he can see the veins bulging in his father's temples, the heart pounding dangerously in his chest. He could die. His father could die, and he could be the unsuspected murderer, because his father in late middle age will not let a ball go by him.

He wants to stop. He wants to apologize and stop playing, at least for a short break, get some water and see his father look at him like a son again, but instead his father's fading skill and frailty stokes his anger. And he continues to hit the balls back, side to side, forcing his father to run as much as he is being made to. Why won't Dad stop? Why doesn't he say he's tired—they've played long enough, more than usual in fact.

He can hear his father's breath. It's all he can hear, he thinks, the ball has become silent. It caroms off his father's racket, spinning oddly and careening slowly to the far corner. As he runs to intercept it he sees in his peripheral vision his father motionless, resting momentarily between shots. He is exhausted. He could die. Just hit it back to him, Robert thinks for a moment, what are you so angry at? This is what occurs to him, but in the next microsecond his rage sweeps the thought away and he executes a perfect drop shot, watches his father hesitate and then shift his weight wearily towards where the ball has already bounced.

Ambulance sirens break through the summer heat. The rising and falling pitch segregates, breaks up into discrete blasts of sound. The beeping of his watch alarm. It's seven o'clock, Sunday morning in Munich, the day of the summer's final match.

Robert sat up in bed, shook his head like a dog climbing out of a pond. What age was that: fourteen, fifteen? The heart attack was ten years away.

Morning sun already warming the windows. Like any other day, yet the usual blanket of reluctance was missing. He sprang to a sitting position and looked out at the crisp clear sky brightening over Goethestrasse. What joy to rise early on a fine morning for a tennis match, instead of to write! He felt as though he himself were going to play, instead of just coaching his charges. He soaked luxuriantly in the tub, even shaved, and then lay with his cheeks, chin, and lips underwater, letting the warm water soothe the offended skin.

He dressed in tennis clothes and a full warm-up suit—there was a mildly thrilling chill in the air—but left his racket bag and skipped unencumbered down the stairs to the street. The night before Max had had Robert drop him off and drive himself home, and now on Sunday morning the Porsche was the only car on the street. Robert sank into the leather driver's seat and enjoyed cruising through central Munich with no traffic. Part of his sense of well-being, he realized, was due to the sudden absence of the burden of Véronique. Should never have started it; thank God she had the sense to end it. He shrugged off a tremor of guilt and accelerated through the gentle double curve of the Tannstrasse tunnel and sped down Prinzregentenstrasse towards Bogenhausen. He was at Max's in ten minutes, regretted getting there so fast, but parked obediently in the garage.

No answer to his knocks for some time, then Frau Altmann herself, seemingly surprised to see him.

"We have our last match this morning," he explained.

"Ah." she seemed unconvinced. "I'm sorry, our maid does not working today. Come in, come in. I think Max is asleep. On Sundays I *drai ihm nit kein kop*. Let him sleep one day." She walked to the foot of the double staircase. "Maximilian!" she bellowed with a volume belying her slight frame. There was no answer. "Come," she ordered. "Have some breakfast. He sleeps."

Herr Altmann, in a shirt and tie at the head of the table, seemed much amused at the sight of Robert entering the dining room. "You even show up to Frühstück in tennis clothes!" he boomed. The ornate table was set with fine china, a silver coffee carafe, fruit, and some pastries.

"We have our last match this morning."

"Vas? Who is spieling tennis at this clock?"

"Well, I agree, Herr Altmann. It's not Max's or my choice, I can assure you."

"Meshugeners." He stared at Robert, smiling, for two seconds, and then turned his attention back to *Die Süddeutsche Zeitung* and his breakfast. Robert accepted a cup of coffee from Frau Altmann but awkwardly declined the offer of fruit and pastries. He wanted to go up and rouse Max but felt sure this would not be considered proper by the parents. Finally, after he had nervously sipped his way to the bottom of the coffee, he heard the familiar iambic slapping of slippers on the stairs. Bourgeois Bard. Presently Max knocked his way through the swinging doors into the dining room.

"Good morning," he rumbled cheerfully and shuffled over to his mother to kiss her cheek. He was wearing tennis shorts and a warm-up jacket, with slippers on bare feet. "Good morning Rob."

Robert stood up. "We'd better get going."

"You can't do tennis without breakfast," Frau warned.

"She's right," Max admitted, and sat down. "Don't worry, Rob, they'll wait for the trainer."

Robert sat down, secretly ravenous for the croissants, cream cheese, whitefish spread, and smoked salmon he had been reluctant to accept when there was still a chance of being on time. After Max was finished taking each item, Robert accepted the dish from him and filled his own plate.

"So," Max spoke after swallowing an estimable first bite of breakfast. "This morning Rob leads us into our final match of the season."

"Ya," said his mother, munching a croissant in businesslike fashion, eyeing Robert all the while. "Und then what?"

"And then what? Nothing. And then we spend all winter discussing what changes we should make for next summer." He winked at Robert.

"I'm not talking about your *meshugeh* tennis team. I mean what then for Rob?"

"Good question, Mama. What happens to Rob?" He turned to Robert with mock concern. Herr Altmann put down his paper.

Robert looked up from his plate, his mouth full of bread and whitefish. "Of course," said Max, "he still has his students. And his book to work on."

Embarrassed, Robert nodded. "I have no plans to leave. That is, if I may still have the apartment."

"Doch! Of course," Herr Altmann laughed. "Who else is going to live on Goethestrasse?"

"You're still our club trainer, if you give lessons, even if the team season is over," said Max. "So I don't see why we shouldn't continue to provide you with an apartment."

"I'm sure Véronique will be pleased," said his mother.

Robert glanced at Max. He had told his friend about the breakup, of course, but apparently Max hadn't mentioned it to his parents. Robert could guess why.

He glanced at his watch. "I really think we should go now," he said to Max. "They must be wondering where we are."

"What else is new?" said Frau Altmann. "I hope they forfeit your match," she said to Max. "Someday you will have to pay consequence for your tardiness. This son of mine charms his way out of all his missed appointments. He's so *verdemt* charming that I can't teach him any manners." She smiled and slapped him gently a few times on the cheek.

Max had a last sip of tea. "All right. I won't have another croissant. I wouldn't want to hold up the great German tennis-league match. Shall we make a move?"

Max made up some of their tardiness with a mad dash around Munich on the Ring that made even the speedy German motorists around him, taking advantage of the sparse Sunday morning traffic to exercise their Mercedes Benzes, look like Palm Beach seniors. Robert saw 240 on the speedometer and didn't bother doing the math. He held on tightly but didn't have to for long. In six minutes they were at the Olympiapark, just across the highway from the headquarters of BMW, today's opponent. Next to the Olympic Stadium were thirty-two red-clay public tennis courts, every bit as pristine as those at Sport Scheck. At the other end of the vast grounds the Olympiaturm rose like Munich's Eiffel Tower, throwing a monstrous pencil of shade west-northwest, over the wakening highway. Here, on this peaceful lot, in 1972, terrorists kidnapped, and later murdered, eleven Israeli athletes and coaches. Robert never arrived here without thinking of it. But then it was merely a more recent example of atrocity belying Munich's innocuous appearance. The city might be modern, enlightened, even liberal, but it would never again be innocent.

The sun was high enough now in the perfect azure to burn off the morning coolness. Robert slipped on his white cap and pulled it low over his eyes as he and Max walked up from the parking lot. They headed to the back of the tennis complex, where their match would occupy the last row of courts. They were the last to arrive. Saul and Uschi were warming up, and the other four were engaged in some serious discussion on the second court while ostensibly stretching.

"Hey, Coach," said Uschi as he smacked a backhand hard, true, and three feet wide. He bounced on his toes between shots, sucking the crisp air into his lungs. His warm-up jacket covered his upper body with just the right amount of slack, allowing his limbs the freedom to work themselves out, to prepare for battle. No teeth to drill today; this was the morning to use what he had practiced every afternoon to defeat a worthy opponent. Two out of three sets, best man wins. It was clear he loved the moment.

"Okay," Robert called, "let's get together for a minute." He and Max walked over to the others on Court 28 and Uschi and Saul followed. "Hi, everyone. Now, listen, this team isn't supposed to be any good at all. They lost to Messerschmitt nine-oh, and we only lost to them seven-two, so we should clean up today."

"Excellent," said Saul.

The BMW players came into view, making their way down the pathway between courts. The players were introduced, and the six singles matches began.

Robert sat in the shade of the hut by Court 27. Emil and Bruno were on 31 and 32, on the other side of a fence and windbreaker, but he could see the first four matches, and his men all seemed to be doing well except for Uschi, who had perfect form and conditioning but couldn't keep the ball between the lines once a match began. Even Saul seemed to be responding well to the match situation, cracking brilliant ground strokes for winners and rushing the net like a pro. Maybe he'd finally learned to relax and play matches like he practiced. Could Robert's coaching have paid dividends?

Really blew it with Véronique. By starting it at all. He frowned in the sunlight. She was very mature about it all, but it must have hurt her to be used so thoughtlessly. Mixed with his pangs of guilt, however, was a buoyancy in his heart. His familiar old chum, disengagement. He had given up much in his life for the sake of this feeling of possibility. Money, career, family—all forsaken for the fool's gold of potential. Strange how I seem to prefer the possibility of rewards forever unrealized to the achievement of anything.

A smile melted into grimace, then reformed. In a few hours I'll have just what I wanted. Freedom in Europe—no team to coach, no girlfriend, just time and space to work. Lessons too, yes there was that—one had to live—but aside from that, freedom.

Shouts from the other side of the fence interrupted his thoughts. He wanted to ignore them, but he knew he'd better see what it was. If there was a line-call dispute he'd have to act as umpire, since the other team had brought no coach with them. He walked past the first four courts and crossed over on the pathway to the next set of courts. He'd expected Emil and Bruno to get into arguments with their opponents, but instead they were both standing on Emil's court shouting at each other while the BMW players watched in disbelief.

They stopped arguing when they saw Robert standing in the corner with his arms spread in wonder.

"This *Mamzer* won't let me play my match," cried Bruno.

"You want to play, play," countered Emil. "Go ahead and lose. He's choking," he said to Robert, "he refuses to come to the net. He just pushes from the baseline."

"*Schmuck*, at least I'm not too fat to leave the baseline if I *want* to."

"Don't get personal, it's just a game. What's the score?" Emil yelled to his opponent.

Bruno fumed back to his own court. "He doesn't mind his own business, I'll quit."

Robert turned and left the court and walked back to the hut by the other courts. As he passed Court 28 he saw Saul had just switched sides and was by the fence, and he asked him the score.

"Six-one for me," Saul answered, with the voice of a seasoned pro mowing down the new blood on the tour. "Dan's also won the first set, and Göttel is about to. I'm afraid Uschi's down five-two, though. You should talk to him, he needs help."

"Okay, keep it up, put him away," he said. "Concentrate on your own match." He walked back to Court 29 and waited for Uschi to switch sides and come near him. "How're you doing?" he asked.

"Just lost the first set six-three. I'm playing my best, but this guy's just too good."

"Are you kidding me? In a practice match you'd put him away two and two. Don't get psyched out."

"Have you seen his backhand? It's a killer." Sincere, good-hearted admiration.

"Uschi, he's hit two winners on it and about ten unforced errors. Just relax and play like it's practice, okay?"

"Okay, but this guy should be playing number one, don't you think?"

Robert returned to his seat. At least four of them were winning. Maybe only one of his dysfunctional doubles teams would have to win. He sat down and watched Saul continue to blow his man off the court— looked like he'd be the first one finished for once. Maybe I really have helped him.

With luck I'll be home and back asleep by one or two. Starting to feel the effects of the short night. He considered sauntering over to the café for a cappuccino, but that really wouldn't look good. And after all, it was the last match.

Best to keep away from her for a while. Too bad: really prefer her company to Max's. But see, that's why you should have put her friendship above brainless lust.

Saul hit a backhand into the net and walked dejectedly, shaking his head as they switched sides. Impossible—he's been killing him, he can't be in any trouble. Robert jumped down and hurried over behind his court before they began the next game.

"Saul," he hissed. Saul was walking in small circles by the baseline, muttering to himself. Robert called to him again and he finally noticed and walked back to the fence, pulling off his glasses to wipe them.

"What's the score?"

"Six-one, five-two," said Saul. "I had him five-one."

"Oh," Robert said, relieved. "You looked upset. No problem, right?"

"I don't know," his schooled British accent seemed to add grave importance to the situation at hand. "I just don't know."

"You don't know what, Saul? You're serving for the match at five-two."

"Yes, yes, but I just don't know if I can finish it out."

"Saul, you're destroying him."

"Yes, but he's hot. Did you see that last game?"

"He held serve. So what?" Robert made an effort to relax his grip on the fence.

"I've lost the momentum," Saul gave a long sad sigh while adjusting his strings. "I have to go serve now," and he turned back to the court.

"Cheer up, Saul." Robert walked away and headed directly for the café. He felt more like a bourbon but ordered his cappuccino. He was about to bring it back out to the courts when he saw Ingrid waving her fingers at him from an outside table.

"Interesting choice of seat for the big match," he said.

"Ya, I didn't realize they were playing here today. I had a game with a friend this morning. How are the great Mattathians doing?"

"Two imminent victories, a nervous breakdown, a schizophrenic, and one or two assault-and-batteries."

"Keep up the old college spirit," she said. "Isn't that what you say?"

He sighed. "I better get back to the match. My boys need me."

"Good luck. I only saw from a distance, but Max and Saul both looked like they were doing well."

"Max is going to win. Saul won eleven games. Unfortunately for him the rules of the sport call for twelve. On another planet he might have been a champion."

As his doubles teams took the court, he dragged a chair into the sun and sat back in it. Saul's mood was remarkably upbeat after dropping the last twelve games of his singles match; he seemed to feel he had battled well, losing a tough three-setter. Since Uschi and Bruno had also lost, Mattathias had to win two out of the three doubles matches. Robert also had to worry about keeping Emil and Bruno's partners thinking about tennis and not homicide. A victory would be tainted if blood were spilled.

The players hit ground strokes and volleys for just a few minutes and began taking practice serves. The balls traveled in infinity symbols defined by hand to racket, racket to court, picked up by another hand,

and so on, punctuated by hollow thuds and grunts. Robert closed his eyes. The chaotic superimposition of struck tennis balls across three courts became waves crashing in the distance as he drifted towards sleep. Footsteps of beachcombers clopped by him, and then one of them became a presence next to him.

"Wake up, Rob," said Ingrid. "Your team has won again and you've been named the new American Davis Cup captain."

He opened his eyes and sat up straighter. "Last match," he said.

"I know. And you've done an admirable job."

He snorted. "Nothing like knowing you're making a difference in the world."

"Well, how many people make a difference?" she pulled a chair up next to him. "Certainly not me with my home-security systems or Max with his schmattas. Still, if you're going to make no difference, I figure you'd might as well make a nice living making no difference. I'm sure you could do a lot better than being nanny to these babies." She sipped her coffee, leaned back, closed her eyes too. "So I hear you're working on some big book. What sort of book?"

He scowled without opening his eyes. "Ah, you know, stories... Oh, here we go. They're starting their matches. I'd better at least pretend to watch."

Balls flew back and forth across the three courts, graying men watching and pouncing on them as though for survival. On the far court Bruno missed an overhead into the net and bounced his racket off the court and into the back screen.

What strange animals the human beings are, he thought.

As the sun approached its zenith, Ingrid long since fled toward more reasonable pursuits on this fine Sunday, Robert noticed the rickety approach of victory. Granted, Emil and Bruno were going down on the third court in a cloud of red dust roiled up by their thrown rackets and wrong-footed slides, spewing epithets at their opponents and each other. They lost the first set 6-4, and it appeared doubtful whether they would even make it to the end of the match without requiring forceful restraint. However, Max and Saul were winning easily. Robert could swear that Saul actually seemed *buoyed* by his heart-breaking singles loss; he soared across his side of the doubles court, sliding into low volleys and smashing away overheads like a crusader inspired to feats of glory by the sight of his own blood. And on the middle court, Uschi and Dan had their match well in hand. That is, Dan had it well in hand. Uschi was doing his best to drop it—double-faulting at least once each service game, sinking easy volleys into the middle of the net, feeding his opponents mouth-watering overheads. But Dan was imperturbable. He had them practically running into each other going for the same undercut lob and both standing idly by expecting the other to get that chip right between them. And then Uschi wasn't a total loss. He executed enough safe shots so that as a whole things were going quite well.

An incongruous sight distracted Robert: two policemen leaving the pro shop and walking down the walkway between the courts, heading towards the outer courts. Still haven't gotten used to the sight of machine guns held casually to policemen's sides. Seems like such overkill, although I suppose an American cop's revolver in its holster must be equally startling to visitors from England or Japan. Well, this guy's Tommy ought to be more than enough firepower to subdue someone who neglected to sweep their court. What on earth are they doing here?

He watched with an eerie sense of fate as they calmly made their way right up to the last row of courts, looked around, and walked over to Robert. Why am I surprised?

"Excuse me, sir, but could you tell us whether Daniel Cohen is playing here today?"

Oh, Dan. Poor Dan. What could you have done? I thought your schemes sounded too good to be true. But Jesus, do they have to get you now? I need that number-two doubles match. Can't we at least end the season on an upbeat note before they pump you full of lead?

"Uh, entschuldigung, I'm sorry, no German, nein Deutsch. American." He smiled helplessly. They turned away and scanned the courts. One pulled out a photograph—Jesus, they've got a picture of him!— and together they compared each player to the image.

They walked around to the other side of Court 28, waited politely for the point to finish, and then called out, "Daniel Cohen?" to the right man, apparently oblivious of the fact that he had just executed the most absurdist, contorted, inside-out sidespinning and effective drop shot against a player at net in tennis history.

"Scheisse!" yelled the humiliated opponent. "Well hit," called Uschi. "Excuse me, gents," said Dan, and walked, with the aplomb of a tuxedoed dinner host checking on the help, to the side of the court.

"May I help you gentlemen?" he asked the cops in English. Dan spoke his native English to all Germans, and never seemed to quite register those occasions when someone was unable to reciprocate.

"Daniel Cohen?"

"Yes, officers, yes. What can I do for you?"

"I'm afraid you'll have to come with us," the leader said in German. Robert had come over too, compelled by a vague sense of responsibility for his player, but remained a short distance away, due to a less vague respect for machine guns.

"I'm in the middle of an important match here, officer. Surely we can work this out at a later date." At this, Dan stepped closer to them, forming an intimate trio who discussed the matter at great length in low voices. Robert could no longer hear them, nor could Uschi, who had joined Robert by the fence. Soon the rest of the team had abandoned their matches and were huddled together, twenty feet or so from Dan and the policemen. Except for Max, who had joined the principal group and appeared to be acting as Dan's advocate.

"He's a dead man," said Bruno. "He's going straight to prison."

"What'd he do?" asked Uschi.

"I don't know, but these fuckers don't track you down at your tennis club for a parking violation."

"Dan's a shady character," Emil agreed. "Do any of us really know him? He might have done anything."

"Now now, boys," said Saul, "let's not jump to conclusions. And no matter what he's done, you can be sure that Max will have them off his back within five minutes."

"Yes, and he'll have sold them five scarves apiece, as well," laughed Emil.

"Damn, damn," Uschi seemed seriously worried. "It's six-four, four-two. We're about to win!"

"I tell you," said Saul, "these Germans have no respect, no sense of decency. You think they don't know he's Jewish?"

"How on earth did they find him, anyway?" asked Robert.

"Yes, they're very good, aren't they?" Max had just joined them. He raised his eyebrows and smiled ruefully.

"What's going on?" Uschi demanded.

"Well, it seems that a certain creditor to whom Dan owes a considerable sum of money has grown weary of waiting for him to come up with it."

"What? That's all?" said Bruno.

"They wouldn't arrest him for that," said Emil.

"How much is it?"

"No exact figures were mentioned, but the implication was that it was a very large amount of money and a very long time overdue."

"Maybe you others should continue your matches," said Robert. "This must be embarrassing for Dan. We shouldn't stand here watching."

"Are you kidding?" said Bruno. "We have to stand up for our man."

"Ya," Max nodded to Robert, "I agree we should wait and see what happens."

"I agree," said Robert. "We should definitely stand together here and wait." He was embarrassed for Dan, whose face had turned deeper and deeper red as he spoke with the police, glancing occasionally over at his teammates. His facade of composure, his imposture of credibility in this mercantile crowd, were dissolving on Court 28, and how clearly he knew it was there in his sad eyes.

Eventually Dan came over to them. One of the officers had to accompany him, as they were now connected by a pair of handcuffs. "Sorry about this, boys," said Dan, trying to keep up his usual bonhomie. "It's nothing, really. I tried to tell them that we could sort this whole misunderstanding out in five minutes, after the match, but you know how these bastards are." If nothing else, he was confident now that they spoke little English. "It has to be done now. Maybe I can even get back before the end of the match. Guess we'll have to forfeit my doubles, though. Sorry about that, Uschi."

"It's all right. We had them beat, Dan." Uschi shook Dan's free hand. "Your garbage was never better."

"Thanks, mate." Dan turned to follow his already departing consort, a rueful smile on his lips. His teammates called out a few empty wishes of encouragement, and then he was gone. They stood around awkwardly. Nobody seemed to know what to do.

The other team's captain came up to them. "Well, gentlemen, I suppose you are forfeiting the number-two doubles. What about the other two matches?"

"We're playing, of course," said Robert. "Our apologies for the delay." "*Shtarker,*" he heard Bruno mutter as the doubles teams retook their courts. Robert went back to his own position in the wicker chair by Court 27, and Uschi pulled up another. So they would lose another match, and the season would mercifully end. Of course it mattered not at all. It had only seemed to for a few minutes, when it looked as though they would actually win. What makes adult humans want to win at such trivial contests and ignore the important ones? Here he had more or less given up on the great competition of life, which most people sacrificed everything to win, and his heart had been pounding at the prospect of one group of middle-aged mediocre tennis players beating another one. Impressive evolutionary instinct to want to win something, anything.

He settled back to watch. Max and Saul seemed rattled for a game or two by the interruption and expulsion of their friend, but then quickly got back into the spirit of things and finished off their match, six-two, six-four. They packed up their stuff and joined Robert and Uschi. Handshakes all around. The team match was now officially tied. "Well done," said Robert. "You two played like a well-coached team."

"It's no joke, Robert," Saul beamed. "You're absolutely right. To net, to net, to net, as you've said all along. We were ruthless!"

"You see, Rob," Max winked at him, "we have not been paying you in vain after all."

"Too bad you weren't paying the *Polizei* as well. We would have actually won a match."

"Yes, but it's a moral victory," said Saul. "They know as well as we that Dan and Uschi had that match won. It would all be over now. That last doubles match would be meaningless."

"I thought all that mattered over here was the bottom line. Ends justifying the means and all that. Like with cheating on school tests."

"Yes, you're right," he sighed. "Look at those bastards," he gestured at the BMW players close by the other side of the court, loudly cheering on their number-three doubles team, anticipating ultimate victory. "They act as though they deserved that number-two doubles."

And then a funny thing happened. Emil and Bruno, incensed by the partisan cheering and assumption of victory by the onlookers, began to play better. Like Communists and Anarchists in the Spanish Civil War, they instinctively subordinated their mutual repugnance to their hatred of a common enemy. Bruno turned absolutely miserly about giving up a point: he scraped, clawed, dug into the dirt, anything to make sure he got one more ball back over the net. Emil was actually running for balls, oblivious to his apparent impending heart attack. Somehow, against any reasonable expectation, they found themselves in a second-set tiebreaker.

This match was not over. Robert, Max, Saul, and Uschi left their bags behind and went up to the fence to watch from close-at-hand. They shouted out encouragement between points, though Robert did his best to stop them from applauding their opponents' mistakes, as the other side was doing. When Emil transformed a bunny of an overhead into a torturous, anti-orthopedic, shoulders-scrunched, angled volley to win the tiebreaker, the Mattathians erupted in shouts and cheers.

They stayed at the fence for the entire nail-biting third set. It was perhaps the ugliest tennis that Robert had ever seen. The sight of these awful players choking was almost too painful to watch. Even so, Robert found himself caught up in the excitement. He was half laughing, half cheering them on as Emil and Bruno battled into another, third-set, tiebreaker.

Victory. Or rather defeat on the part of the BMW team, who choked even worse than Robert's mental ward. The final point was particularly agonizing for any fan of the game, despite its dramatic tension. Emil and Bruno, as if they'd agreed on the same pathetic strategy, fed the other team a series of short, juicy lobs which they were unable to put away. One after another they would hit weak overheads that merely bounced right back to the Mattathians. "Deeper, for Christ's sake," muttered Robert through clenched teeth, but Emil and Bruno seemed perfectly content to offer up more pastry. Finally the law of averages caught up with the net players, and one of them dumped a particularly anemic overhead into the net. Bruno clenched his right fist, Emil raised his arms, they shouted in unison and hugged each other's sweaty bodies as their teammates cheered. The team celebration continued on Court 29 after the losers had left, and even a sort of camaraderie set in.

"The bartender didn't do so badly," said Emil, patting Bruno on the back. "After he settled down, that is."

Bruno, happy enough in the glow of victory to forget any previous malfeasance on Emil's part, simply said: "I got my serve in to the backhand. That's the key."

"Celebration, boys," cried Saul in English. It couldn't have been he who had just hours before blown a six-one, five-one lead. "Come on, let's go buy our trainer an enormous lunch."

"Gentlemen," said Robert, "I cannot take full credit for today's victory. At least five percent belongs to your own estimable skills."

At the Hirschau Biergarten, in Schwabing, they sat around a big outdoor table with their liter-mugs of Weissbier, except for Max with his lemonade and his damned tea. With the season over, all were friends again. No one would have to face playing with or against Bruno again for a while, or Emil for that matter; there would be no competing for positions until next year. It was almost a pleasure to be in their company now that they were human beings: Saul wasn't a maniac in real life; Uschi was quite easy-going away from the courts; Bruno actually had a good sense of humor.

"Gentlemen," announced Saul. "Congratulations to you all. We are on the way now to a better season next year. All we have to do is somehow keep our trainer in Munich."

"Hear, hear," they shouted, although Robert sensed most of the volume was being generated by Saul and Max.

"I don't think I'm being too overconfident," Saul continued, "when I say that we can realistically work towards a goal of making the first *Kreiseklasse* next year."

Everyone cheered and raised their mugs, while Max leaned over to Robert and said softly, "Ya, perhaps we should first work on winning two matches."

Lunch arrived, with more beer, and Robert felt it difficult to stay attuned to the conversation around him. He drifted into a cloud of alcohol, good food, and fatigue, and the good cheer he always felt at endings of this sort, when he had gotten through something. He didn't have to have gotten through it well; he just had to have gotten through. "Can you believe that comeback in the tiebreaker?" "No, actually, I can't." "It was a triumph of pure determination, I tell you." The summer is over, another summer. The difference this time is that I'm in a place so far from home, somewhere that feels like a place you leave at the end of the summer. Yet I'm not. Nothing to go home to, really. Strange feeling of inertia keeping me here. Would take some force now to knock me out of this path. Will be strange too to see the leaves falling here. "One has to take one's mind out of it. One has to simply hit the ball and not think about it. I was knocking away my volleys without hardly being aware that I was doing it. Do you understand? Hardly aware." "Easy, Saul, you're getting excited." Laughter. Véronique over too. A good thing, a good thing. It was all wrong, what could be more obvious? You were chastising yourself the whole time, for being the lout you were. Should be grateful she had the good sense to end it, because when would you have? Freedom. Freedom like the lifting of a heavy burden. The freedom I came here for. What a mistake it had been to jump into that ill-advised coupling, led once again by atavistic instincts that gave little thought to the consequences.

Lightness now, a feeling of almost weightlessness, ability to go anywhere, do anything. Funny, didn't feel this free before Véronique. Everything in this life is experienced as relative to previous state. "Wonder what happened to Dan." "Mein Gott, forgot about poor Dan." "I'm sure he got out of it somehow." "We should go make sure, don't you think?" "Ya, but go where? Who knows where they took him." "He must be home by now. They weren't going to actually put him in jail, were they?" "Don't think they wouldn't love to, those fuckers. An immigrant Jew. They'd love it." "Old Dan will land on his feet, don't worry. He always does." Late-afternoon, late-summer light was scattering around the garden, bouncing off the limbs and leaves of the chestnut trees, escaping to the patch of blue sky above, refracting through the thick glass of the enormous beer *Steins*. The greens of vegetation, golds of the beer, red-and-white checkered tablecloths all seemed so bright and vivid. Surely this was the last day of summer. Robert felt he would wake in the morning to frost on the windows, maple leaves pirouetting down to earth, and a new life of welcome, foreign, timeless solitude. It was as though this was the last bursting load of warmth and color that the season could hold. He tipped his mug up and drank the delicious cold liquid, watching summer's last light dance about in the golden microcosm of air, glass, and beer.

7

He wished to God that he could go crazy.

Insanity loomed on the misty horizon as salvation, an honorable discharge from his miserable conscription. If only he could lose his marbles big-time, collect every page he'd ever written into a pile on the floor, build an altar around it, and dance a wild dance of literary futility. He wanted to be discovered in the Goethestrasse apartment, sitting on the windowsill staring out at the street, a dozen empty whisky bottles at his feet, defeat and collapse in his blank eyes. There was romance and glory in a nervous breakdown, even if he couldn't write the great novel to go with it. He imagined himself in a white bathrobe sitting in a folding chair by a pond at the bottom of the great sloping lawn of an institution. Occasional visitors would be cheerful to his face and cluck-clucking beyond hearing range, Isn't it a shame, he would have been a great genius had he only not gone mad.

He wanted to go crazy, but he could not. Try as he might, he was unable to lose his clarity of thought, to stir his brain into any respectably bizarre jumble of imaginings. All attempts at alcoholism were equally futile. After two or three bourbons he became as drunk as he was going to be, for at that point he could stomach no more of the stuff. He couldn't even emulate the masters—from Hemingway and Faulkner to Cheever and Carver—in that respect. That malfeasant Manipulator whose plaything was he had had the pernicious vision and skill to create in him a creature incapable of attaining any notable extreme. He was to be neither genius nor maniac, a miserable inhabitant of tepid middle ground. This would not have been the hell it was had He given him the complacency to be satisfied with a normal job, a normal life. But instead He threw in the critical ingredient—the germ of artistic ambition. And here he was, the soul of Rilke in the brain of a yuppie, twisting and writhing through his earthly existence. Unable to attain his vision, unable to lose his mind.

What little prose he was able to conjure had no soul, no guts. It was the result of too painstaking labor. Not that good fiction was supposed to come effortlessly, but he was straining so hard just to put a few sentences on the page that it had the feel of an assigned essay rather than art. He was guilty of the transgression described by Archibald MacLeish: he put in the hours but withheld the spirit. Where was the spark? He searched for it, combing his soul in vain for the diamond in the rough. The frustration that pervaded his existence was unprintable, unspeakable. He had to stop reading, for after witnessing the simple artistry of Kundera or Percy or Matthiessen he could no longer bear to see his own feeble offerings. He flung Emmanuelle Carrere's *The Moustache* against a wall in despair after streaking through it in one long night. Why hadn't he been the one to think of that?

Robert wrote not a page in the pale sad month of September. He went out late nights with Max; he saw Véronique a few times "as friends": after sitting stiffly through another documentary about the Third Reich, they would sit stiffly at a café pretending that they had not recently ended a period of wayward fornication demeaning to both of them; he sat six hours a day at his desk, now usually in a motionless state of near catatonia, worn out by the futile battle; only his duties on the tennis court were able to drag him out of his room in daylight.

He had built up a lugubrious momentum, an unconscious inertia that carried him from one day into the next, through each week; but it was momentum in a circular direction, for he certainly wasn't getting anywhere, and the centrifugal force it created was far too anemic to launch him out of Munich. He might have slunk along like that forever, rising in the morning and falling into bed at night in the same apartment on Goethestrasse. (What a bitter irony for him to be living on the street bearing the name of the great poet. Better for it to be left to the Turkish merchants who, like an indifferent sea, accommodated his presence there but when he one day left would fill the absence and dissolve all trace of his having been there.)

Then, on a crisp early fall day when the first burnt-brown leaves were descending like twirling toy whirlybirds onto the red clay courts at Sport Scheck, Robert gave Ingrid a lesson on the backhand volley.

Her ground strokes were a natural: a strong looping forehand with slight topspin and a steady slice backhand that could always get her out of trouble. But she had never learned the net game. Over the first year of intermittent lessons he had helped her develop a passable forehand volley, certainly good enough for the doubles games she was likely to get into. The backhand, though, was another question. For some reason, her body insisted on always expecting a forehand, so when the ball came to her left side, she would first make a quarter turn to the right, then adjust and turn back left to prepare a backhand, invariably too late.

For most of an hour, Robert hit her backhand volleys. "We're just about there," he said as they convened at the net after picking up all the balls. "You're fine when you know it's a backhand."

"Ya, but when I don't I go neurotic on you. Why do I always turn to the one side?"

"That's a question for a mental health professional. Maybe we need some sort of automatic punishment-reward stimulus system."

"Now that sounds interesting," she said.

"Like an electric shock when you turn the wrong way," he elaborated.

"Ah. Not so interesting."

The air was dry and comfortable, and for one of the only times in his teaching career he wouldn't have minded continuing the hour. Better to be out in this gorgeous fall day hitting balls with Ingrid than sitting alone in some café having dinner with a book. He was comfortable with her in a way that he never was with Véronique; Ingrid, though physically larger, was light and airy, while thin Véronique carried a heaviness about her. Where Ingrid enjoyed a movie, Véronique spoke of *films*; Ingrid read books, but Véronique discussed *literature*. Both their parents had been in the camps, but Ingrid had decided to accept the past and enjoy life in the carefree yuppie Munich of the 1980s, while Véronique, though younger, could not let go. The world had tortured her mother and father and made them old parents. The world had stolen from her.

He also couldn't deny the sexual attraction of Ingrid. She was heavier than Véronique but carried it well; she was comfortable with her body and knew that you knew it. If it weren't for Max, would there be potential for an affair?

"Max is picking me up in half an hour," she said after they had swept the court and collected their belongings and were walking by the riding stables back toward the clubhouse. "Why don't you join us for dinner? Come back to my apartment, since he and I live so close to here, then we'll drive you home so you can shower, and we'll eat somewhere in town, near you."

"I don't want to spoil your romantic dinner."

"Romantic? Max? Don't be absurd. If he could, Max would bring the entire university philosophy faculty along on our dates, so we could have a colloquium while we eat."

"Well, all right." Avoiding the long bus-and-Strassenbahn ride home was as attractive as his friends' company. "But I refuse to get into any epistemological debates."

"Don't worry. We'll keep him spending money on us so fast that he'll have no time to formulate opinions."

Her Mercedes was a low-end model, as differentiated in Munich society from a more expensive Mercedes as a Honda Civic was from any Mercedes in the States. They drove through the suburb of Oberföhring, parallel to the Isar river, parallel to the long thin rectangle of the English Garden where he had picnicked with Véronique, where Max and Ingrid and their like wouldn't be caught dead.

Around the Herkommerplatz rotary and suddenly they turned off onto a quiet side street and were in the oasis of quietude and luxury that was Bogenhausen. Ingrid parked in the wide driveway of a squat three-story modern building on Newtonstrasse. The elevator to the third floor, and she let him through the door.

Her apartment was small but elegant, with marble floors, black leather furniture, and enough emptiness to create the illusion of space. Immaculate as well, not so much as a magazine out of place.

"I'm afraid the maid isn't due until tomorrow," she said as she put her index finger to her answering machine like she were poking a dead snake with a stick. She dropped her tennis bag and while the machine clicked, whirred, rewound, and clicked again repeatedly, she stood looking at him where he stood awkwardly holding his racket bag as if expecting him to speak her phone messages.

He in turn stared at the machine. "Ya, hallo Ingrid," Max's voice came between them, speaking English as he and Ingrid often did with each other. "I hope your tennis lesson has gone superbly, that our friend Rob has treated you well and that you have pried much expertise from him. I would say you should invite him to join us for dinner, but unfortunately I won't be able to make it myself. My Italian colleagues are in town unexpectedly, and as you know if I don't wine and dine them they're liable to give the next big order to the first bidder that comes along, never mind that we have long ago signed the dotted line. So I'm afraid I am an entertainer of single men tonight; too bad you're not home to advise me on where I should take them."

"As though he needs such advice," said Ingrid.

"—but perhaps you can convince Rob to take my place and dine with you tonight. I heartily recommend his company. Let's talk soon. Ciao." The machine proceeded through its conclusive percussion solo of clicks and whirrs and Ingrid stood motionless, still looking at him.

"Well, I've already done that," she said. "Why don't you put down your rackets, Rob? I'm going to take a shower." She disappeared into her bedroom, and he leaned his racket bag against the wall and walked about the living room, examining the few books and CDs on the shelves, the two Klee prints on the wall.

"Very typical of Max," her voice was clearly audible from the other room. "He makes plans with three different parties for every night. You never know if you're going to be the one he sticks with. Often it's other women, I'm well aware of that. Often, though, it's not. He's constantly entertaining business partners, and then his parents are always making plans for him as well. Seems like every other night they're setting him up with some young Jewish woman or other, and he's a good son: he never refuses. They don't know about me, of course. Jewish, yes; but an atheist and much too old. No, no, no," she appeared at the bedroom entrance in the sheerest of silk bathrobes, the dark island below her waist quite visible. "Do you think I'm too old, Robert?"

"No" was about all he could get out.

"I'm going to shower now," she said. "You may join me if you like. If not, that's all right too." And she was gone. A few seconds later, the sound of spraying water.

He stood there for a full minute, and then he took off his clothes. The bathroom was already a tropical cloud when he entered and he thought of a steam bath he had once gone to with his father when he was a child. There was a difference this time, though, which Ingrid saw as soon as he slid open the glass door and entered the shower. "Mmm," she said, "looks like your decision was an easy one. I normally bathe, but the tub's not big enough for two." She began to soap his chest, and he closed his eyes and tipped his head back, surrendering to the onslaught of water jets on his scalp and face, the strange lack of privacy in such a private chamber, the invisible hands exploring his body. Soon they were well into it, and hot water rolled in rivulets down her back and formed evanescent pools where their bodies touched. He had never felt so free in sex, so unconcerned with matters of responsibility and consequence. This was her great gift, he realized: the ability to make lovemaking into something pure and uncomplicated.

She wanted to take him to dinner at Reitschule, the exclusive restaurant overlooking the English Garden stables. It was just over the river from Bogenhausen, but they had to detour to his apartment so he could change—it wouldn't do to be seen at Reitschule in sneakers, much less a tennis outfit. Their dinner was delayed further when Ingrid intercepted him between tennis shorts and jeans. They began where she had intervened, on the floor by his dresser, and finished somehow on the bed without ever having interrupted their methodical rhythm. They arrived at the restaurant a half-hour before midnight and started groping each other again in her car before realizing that the restaurant would close soon and forcing themselves to go in and eat.

"Well," she said, "I hope Max had as nice an evening with his business friends."

"Not quite as nice, I hope."

But his nonchalant air must have poorly hid his misgivings, for she said, "Don't worry, Rob, about Max. I assure you he never turns down an opportunity on his travels for a good roll in the hay. He and I are not going steady, as you say. I'm tired of being left alone when he finds that he's, uh, overbooked for the evening. Plus, I'm forty-two years old and maybe I want to find someone to marry. It certainly won't be Max. He is a child, an absolute child. Playing with his toy Porsche, riding in his toy airplanes all over the world, playing his big Monopoly game, importing, selling, buying, watching his pot of money grow. Schtupping his blowup girls from Italy and America — but he doesn't realize they're not blowup girls. A child, I tell you — " she paused to take another bite and swallow, " — with not a care in the world. Mama and Papa wake him in the morning, make sure he keeps all his appointments. Except with me, of course."

"Still, he does all right for himself..."

"Don't get me wrong—the child is a genius. He's smarter than everybody else, a brilliant conversationalist, and very business savvy. The last— only the last—he learned well from Papa. There are those in the community—less successful, of course— who say that Max was born with the silver spoon in his mouth, and that's true. But it's what you do with the silver spoon that matters. Max took over the business from Papa and made it twice as profitable. And Papa wasn't doing so badly: a millionaire."

"A rather eligible bachelor."

"You said it. There's not a Jewish mother in Munich—or Berlin, for that matter—who doesn't go to bed at night dreaming up ways to bring Max and her little *Mädela* together."

"Must be quite a strain on him."

"Mmm. He avoids young Jewish women like they had social disease."

"Like Véronique, for instance."

"Ha—Véronique. Now there's one Jewish girl he couldn't have if he wanted. Poor Frau Eisenstein would give her teeth for it, but Véronique is not so easily controlled. She doesn't stand for Max's nonsense, doesn't care for his Italian suits and expensive dinners. To be honest, she's not a very high-class girl. But I like her. Why did you break up?"

"I don't know, there was just nothing there. Why did we get started is the question. I like her fine as a friend—she's smart and interesting. But she's so damn serious. If I say something ironic or facetious she always takes it literally and is offended."

"You know why she is so serious."

"Sure—her parents were in the camps. But so were yours and Max's."

"Everyone handles it differently. Véronique is unable to let go of it. But tell me, how was it sexually between you?"

"Awful—and it was my fault. I simply felt no love toward her, and no great lust either. It's impossible to fake it, so I just went through the motions and made her feel bad. You can see why it had to end."

"Yes. Too bad, though. Lucky for me, I suppose."

"And for me."

"Yes, but not for poor Véronique. Oh well, she's young. She'll find many new men. And I suspect she'll also lose some of that seriousness in time."

"And maybe Max will find some."

"Ach, Max. The hell with Max. Let me tell you, Max will be fine. Am I supposed to wait around while he shows his customers the whorehouses of Munich, until he finally knocks on my door at four in the morning? Or not at all? Listen, I'm very sexual."

"You don't say."

"I do say. Now why don't you let me pay for this, since I don't pay you nearly enough for tennis lessons—you could charge these Jews twice as much and they'd probably feel they were getting an even better bargain—and then we'll go back to my place for a drink? I have to work tomorrow, but what the hell."

"This was work, too," said Max a few nights later as he drove Robert home from Sport Scheck, where they had had another Italian dinner after tennis. "You know, you can't stop at five o'clock—you have to make the customers happy. When they're your best friend they can hardly sell to your competitor instead. The other night is a perfect example. You remember the Italians—" Robert nodded but he explained anyway, "—family-owned textile business north of Florence. Make the best mass-produced scarves in Italy and charge very reasonably for them. We had a deal months ago that this particular new shipment—new colors, new design, very fashionable, to be honest—that this new shipment was ours. I made an advance payment and thought it was settled."

He paused to swerve two lanes to the left just before the Tannstrasse tunnel and passed a couple of teetering Volkswagens. *Licht,* ordered the sign at the tunnel entrance, and every car around them clicked on their lights on cue except for Max, who took advantage of their slight reduction in velocity to accelerate and pass the BMWs of strudel-filled mustachioed Germans who honked in protest of this impropriety. "If there were a painted sign by the side of the road saying, 'Sit parked here until further notice,'" Max's face lit up as though he were pointing out a favorite zoo animal, "these people would starve to death in their cars.

"Anyway, you can't be too trusting in this business, although trust in a sense is what it's all about. So last month I make a little surprise visit to Florence.

Fantastic city, by the way. I have a great affinity for the Italians, as you know: so much more open, more relaxed. If it weren't for my parents I would move there in a day. You should see the woman I met in a restaurant there this time. Very stylish, I must say. We exchanged cards. Perhaps when I go back...." He screeched to a halt unnecessarily to let a young couple cross in front of him, then floored the accelerator to make up for the delay.

"So you stopped by the factory," Robert prompted.

"So I stop by the factory, unannounced, just passing through, I say, and the brothers greet me with great hugs and the mother insists I come for dinner that night, and while I'm there I take a quick look at the new merchandise, and the entire stock has the label of a different company, not mine. I couldn't believe it. So Enrico, one of the brothers, runs up to explain: 'No no no, pay no attention, we were just placating these other people, the stuff is yours of course,' and he proceeds, with the help of his extended family, to replace all these labels with Altmann labels.

"So fine, we go to their house and have an enormous meal—a five-course pasta meal you cannot *comprehend*—with many bottles of wine—"

"Though you of course stick to mineral water."

"Ya. Very good. And we all embrace, the brothers are embracing, the mother is embracing me, and we bid each other *arrividerci*, and I head home to Munich. Two weeks later I really am just passing through—

you remember Saul and I drove down to that Italian spa for a week—and I stop by to say hello and have a cappuccino. What do I see? The other guy's labels are back on the merchandise! I stood there practically laughing, and Enrico says 'No no no, not to worry,' and he switches the labels again! I mean, these guys are truly amazing."

"I wonder if I could go down there and get *my* labels on those scarves."

"So this week the brothers are in Munich, God knows why, and they call me up unexpectedly the other night. So naturally I have to entertain them."

"And just hope the other guys aren't the last to entertain them."

"No, I don't believe other customers entertain as I do."

"What'd you do, take them to a whorehouse?"

"Would you think that was immoral?"

"Jesus, Max, I don't know. I was joking."

"I understand. But do you think it's wrong?"

"I don't know. I guess not. Victimless crime and all that."

"Have you heard of 1,001 Nights? The Munich establishment?"

"No."

He quickly hung a right on Briennerstrasse, circumnavigated the Karolinenplatz obelisk, and headed northwest. "Well, what can I tell you? The brothers were looking for, shall we say, more base entertainment than you or I might choose. And they wanted me to show them what Munich has to offer. I bought them a number of drinks, hoping that would suffice, but they made me take them into several nude dancing places we passed. Finally I gave up on an early evening and took them to 1,001 Nights. Ostensibly another 'dance club,' but here you can get more than dancing."

"Ah—a full late-night kitchen."

"I thought I told you about my 1,001 Nights experience."

"I'm not sure I want to hear."

"When I turned eighteen, I was given quite a considerable sum of money, as you might imagine."

"I might."

"Well, in my rather limited dealings with members of the opposite sex—Jewish girls from the schul, friends from school—I had of course not yet had my initiation experience. And I had heard about 1,001 Nights: it was a subject of much conversation and fantasy among the boys at school, none of whom had ever gotten near the door.

"Well, now I had so much money suddenly that a night of pleasure wouldn't so much as make an impression on it—before I had always been given sufficient spending money, but let me tell you a night at 1,001 is not cheap. So I decided that I would invest some of my windfall in losing my innocence, and I drove out here." They were now parked on the side of the road, and Max pointed to the other side where a white sandstone building with Arabian domes was the only one with lights on. In the full parking lot, ninety percent of the cars were Mercedes or BMWs.

"Well, I start buying drinks for all the women around me in the bar, Mister Big Spender you know, until I start taking a special interest in this one woman. She was extremely dark, African I thought until she started speaking Italian, and then I was just beginning my Italophilia, so that decided that. She took me up to a room with a fine big bed and a wonderful expansive shower. Then she takes off all her clothes, and I am in ecstasy. Let me tell you, what a body. Do you like large breasts?"

"Go on with the story."

"It was all I could do to take off my clothes without climaxing. Then there we were, standing there naked, and I must say I was quite ready to cross the threshold, so to speak, when she says something to me in Italian. My Italian was getting fairly proficient, but I didn't catch what she said, so she switched to German, to my disappointment. 'Willst du Nasspiele spielen?'"

"Oh God."

"You know what this means."

"I have a pretty good idea."

"Well, it sounded good to me, with that lovely shower in the other room, and I grin yes. But she tells me to lie down on the bed, which I'm afraid I do. And then—"

"Don't say it—"

" —she's pissing all over me. I have to tell you, I have never been so disgusted in my life. I ran into the shower, cleaned off, dressed, gave her all the money I had, and drove around town for an hour before going home."

"Well, at least you got to use the fancy shower. And I suppose this turned you away from a life of vice."

"Ya, look, I wasn't going to become a pimp or anything anyway, but to tell you the truth I did try 'professional service' once or twice more."

"You went back?" Robert was incredulous.

"No, of course not back to 1,001. It was in Italy, on a business trip. And several years later, after the bad, uh, taste had worn off."

"I hope the experience was more routine this time."

"It was excellent, in fact. It made me wonder what all the terrible stigma was about it. It's perfectly acceptable to pay for a good massage, and after all massage is a fairly intimate act as well. And a skilled prostitute can really make you feel good. Where I went she was quite well paid for her skills, too."

"I'm sure. So this is what you do on your 'business trips.'"

"Not at all. It's been some time, in fact. I found that seduction can be much more exciting, even if the act itself is less...expert."

"It's amazing to me, Max, how you can say such sleazy things and sound like you're discussing Spinoza."

"Would you like to go in?"

"What? In there?" He looked to where Max was gesturing: the blue and green neon lights, the palm trees around the entrance. "No. Thank you. Though your recommendation as a former customer is tempting."

"No, I didn't think so. I'll treat you sometime if you like. But I suppose you don't need professional assistance in this area."

"Now what do you mean by that?"

"Well, I hear you had dinner with Ingrid the other night."

"Well sure. Why not?"

"No reason, of course. I'm glad—I felt bad about having to stand her up. It seems to happen more and more often lately, as the business grows. So how was dinner?" His eyes lit up like he was questioning a small child.

"Fine. Reitschule. Exquisite cuisine."

"Ya, I know," he said under his voice as he started the engine again and pulled out onto the road. Max had a way of ignoring or treating with utter disregard anything anyone said that strayed from his own line of conversation or thinking. "I suppose I wasn't actually asking about the food."

"Then I don't know what you mean."

"I'm afraid I'm being misunderstood, Rob. Ingrid and I, as you must know, have a very liberal relationship. She is quite aware that I occasionally have a dalliance with another woman, and in the same way it's very clear that she is free to meet other men. For her sake, I hoped that she might meet a man who is more of a candidate for a permanent alliance—let's face it, she's no baby—but if—and I speak hypothetically now—she and you were to come to a certain understanding, and hit it off, that would be fine with me."

"I see. It would confirm your freedom, I suppose. Don't want to allow even a thread of commitment to slow you down."

"And why should I? Or you? We're still young, Rob."

"And what would happen to you and Ingrid? If this hypothetical situation should occur?"

"What would happen? Nothing, I would assume. Why would this change the situation?" They had reached Goethestrasse, and he pulled up to Robert's building in a wide swath, parallel to the curb, and cut the engine. Hardly anyone was on the street, save for the occasional visitor to The Blue Box, whose lewd ladies watched them from the display cases. Max had put down the convertible top as they slowed near the city center, as he was wont to do, fiddling with the roof like someone idly bending a paper clip, up and down, up and down, sometimes several times in a single short trip. Robert felt cold in the open air but said nothing. He wanted to get out of the car and go to his room but instead sat there looking at the sky. The moon drifted behind parallel ripples of clouds, a stone sinking in a deep dark lake.

"So how's your writing coming along?" asked Max.

"Fine, fine." The ripples drifted; he could never match this.

"Anyway, I still think it's a shame it didn't work out with you and Véronique."

"I know you do," said Robert. "But it just wasn't right."

"Too bad. You know, she's a lot more interesting than I had thought before. Maybe you were a good influence."

"I doubt it. How do you know?"

"We've been chatting lately. You know, her French is superb—she spent several years in Paris. And I do regret that my own French is lapsing terribly. We've decided she's going to give me conversation lessons. We'll get together once a week and talk for an hour or so in French, and she'll correct my errors. Terrible to get out of practice."

"Terrible." Robert finally got out of the car and closed the door. "We'll have our regular lesson on Thursday?" he said through the roof.

"Absolutely. And say hello to Ingrid for me."

"Sure. And you say hello for me."

Max took off in a wild swinging arc, brand new tires on the asphalt sounding like Saran

Wrap, and was gone. Suddenly averse to the idea of his room, Robert began walking aimlessly down Goethestrasse. Why does the idea of Max and Véronique alone in a room, sipping tea and speaking French, rub me so? Wouldn't understand a word. No excuse: you're an ass to even consider jealousy. He reached the Hauptbahnhof and entered. It was late, and there were only a few people milling about. A single train was preparing to depart for Vienna. He bought a half-liter Weissbier from the only kiosk still open and sat on a bench watching porters loading luggage and two final passengers boarding, and he watched until the train pulled out of the station.

8

In mid October tennis in Munich moved indoors, regardless of the weather. Even into November Robert would look out of the Strassenbahn windows with longing at the gorgeous autumn: the crisp blue air, the last few leaves spiraling down. It reminded him of his favorite days in college, practicing after the fall season was over, cherishing those last few days of outdoor play, when after ten minutes his rising body heat would turn a cold November day into perfect playing weather. But at the Mattathias club they paid no attention to the temperature; October 15 they went indoors.

There were no fall or winter leagues. Robert gave lessons, two or three each afternoon, as much as he could endure. At the beginning of each the fifty minutes seemed like a prison sentence that could never expire. How could one spend five-sixths of an hour generating verbiage about someone's tennis game? Every five-minute interval was an interminable trial. He felt the same hollowness in his chest at the beginning of a lesson that he did each morning as he sat down to write. Nothing to give. The difference was that the tennis lesson got done. There was no choice but to teach, no alternative to hitting the balls, one inexorably after the other out of his hand toward the imperfect forehand or backhand. If he weren't expected to speak he might even have enjoyed the monotony of it, the soothing rhythm, the familiar resistance in his muscles as the ball impeded the racket's accelerating arc. But he must pontificate, there was the problem. If he refrained too long, his students would not hesitate to elicit advice, get their money's worth. It wasn't difficult: they weren't turning enough, they weren't keeping their shoulders down on the follow-through, they weren't stepping into the shot, they were swinging on their volleys, they were standing in one place, they were tossing too high on the serve. But it pained him to have to regurgitate these advices again and again. He held no disdain for his students; some of them he liked quite a bit. He just felt they deserved better.

After his lessons he repaired, as in summer, to the club's Italian restaurant for his tortellini gorgonzola. Several times a week he would follow dinner with either a couple of sets with Max (easy recreation for Robert, a consummate challenge for his friend) or a hard practice session with Burkhard. Lessons were given on the dark green indoor Har-Tru courts, the kind they called clay in the States. But when he played with Burkhard they often used the single artificial-grass court, housed in its own room. The ball skidded fast and low off the rug, providing a welcome contrast from the slow pace of the day's work. Robert could no longer serve hard enough to have a serious match—the summer had been enough to put the finishing touches on his degenerating shoulder—but they would drill their ground strokes and volleys. For Robert it was like karate *kata*: pure form and exercise. It cleared his mind of the platitudes he forced out all day and his body of teaching's bad habits.

Tuesday, though, held Ingrid. Her lesson was the last of the day, after which he rode in her Mercedes—soft warm contrast to the bus and Strassenbahn—to her apartment. Sex in the shower was followed by sex on the bed, sofa, or plush rug, and another, more pragmatic, shower, after which they sped to some fine restaurant in Bogenhausen or Schwabing or Nymphenburg. Then she would drop him back at Goethestrasse. She never invited him to spend the night, and he never asked, though he would have relished the opportunity to waste a morning languishing in Ingrid's expansive bed after she'd gone to work, and take the trolley home: a fine excuse for not writing. Charles Willeford, wasn't it, who had said Haiti was his favorite place to write? Beautiful beaches, comfortable weather, plenty of nightlife: he'd hardly had to write at all.

Far better Ingrid's queenly bedroom would have been to rise to than his cold bare room (with no thermostat) where he faced another futile morning at the table. He'd once thought of writer's block as a disease reserved for others, like cancer and claustrophobia; it would never happen to him. There was so much to say about life, so much to pour out! But after two novels written in New York which lay sunken in the lightless depths of a trunk in his parents' Westchester basement, the germ of uninventiveness had taken hold in him. The best he could do was to jot down in his journal notes of his daily life in Munich, notes that he knew would never see the light of fiction. No, the block had seized him in its icy grip, a reminder of his weakness, his fallibility, his mortality. Like the claustrophobia, which had begun in the Goethestrasse elevator a few months earlier. Not only had he not stepped inside an elevator since then, he also avoided the U-Bahn, as well as the underground mall, and he didn't even like to get in the back seat of a car. And the claustrophobia, he felt, was just one symptom. It was as though a switch had been flipped in him, opening the floodgates to a river of fears, weaknesses, infirmities that once seemed powerless to affect him. Now sitting at his desk he felt the same sort of panic about his lack of inspiration. There was a time when he didn't understand or fear writer's block. That was for others; he would always have something to draw on. After all, what's so difficult? You have all the time in the world; all you have to do is *write*. But now, at thirty, he sat there in shell-shocked discomfiture, stifled by the fear of rejection and the impending specter of mediocrity.

It was part of getting older. The impregnable fortress of youth was cracking, weak points opening in the armor. A bad shoulder, claustrophobia, writer's block.... Barbaric human frailty, digging at the cracks, scratching to get in.

And what would it matter, were you able to conjure your vision, make it materialize on the paper? Would it make you happy? Remember Ted. Remember a cold New York night, accompanying Lexa and Chris to meet some of their classmates and the master at the Green Torch, a dark Irish pub on West Eleventh Street. The waitress, red-haired, middle-aged, whom Ted called B.J., seemed to know him (or at least to expect him) and piloted the group through a nearly empty room to a large round wooden table at the back. They weren't seated two minutes before B.J. deposited a bourbon and water into the curve of Ted's right hand and looked around for the other orders. Chris asked for bourbon as well, the rest of them beers.

Before long two men of about Ted's age showed up. He introduced them: writers whose names Robert had heard since he'd been in the city; they taught at other writing programs, gave occasional readings around town. Gary seemed a normal sort of guy, dressed in chinos and tweed sports jacket, a pleasant half-smile settled into his face, and he even occasionally spoke. Aaron, on the other hand, sat silently sunken into his chair, both hands fondling his drink while his dark features passionlessly followed the conversation or, more often, stared out across the bar.

Soon Ted was off on one of his verbose diatribes: "They hate us, I tell you, whether I'm paranoid or not, they still hate us. Damn paper-pushers. The so-called

'Literature' side of the English department. Because we do what they wish they could do instead of just writing about others doing it. They're just voyeurs, we're the real McCoy, yet they've got their Ph.D.s and their publishing credits—if you call that publishing—and they try to act like they're the only ones in the building doing any real work, while we putz around at home in the mornings writing about our last marriages."

"But Ted, darling," drawled Blythe, a fortyish woman who'd left her restaurant-tycoon husband back in Mobile to follow her literary dreams to the city, "I thought you *were* writing about your last marriage."

"Hell yes, and I promise you it's a hell of a lot more interesting than another paper on symbolism in Melville. A lot more fucking and much less whale oil. That's what I was trying to tell you," he pointed his glass at Jack, a callow Midwesterner newly arrived in the big city, clearly the youngest in the class, before taking a swallow. "Your prose is marvelous. Spotless, clean. Those scenes of kids riding around in the middle of nowhere are fantastic. Great nostalgic stuff. But where's the fucking? I mean, whether they actually did it or not, we all know they were thinking about it, but where is it in the story? More fucking."

"Hear, hear," Lexa raised her beer.

Ted swallowed the last of his drink. "I'm half kidding."

"Now what would Sally think of all that?" laughed Chris.

"Sal? Old Sal, our fearless chairman?"

"Chairperson," said Blythe.

"Chairman," said Ted. "I'd be a chairperson; she's a chairman if I ever saw one. Sally would put it all down as the ravings of a drunken writer. She hates writers even more than the rest of them do. Living writers, that is. As long as they're cold in the grave she likes them fine. Where would she be on those lonely Saturday nights without her dear old Henry James? I mean if I have to congratulate her in the halls on another article about James' mother I may not make it to the men's room before puking." Chris laughed a little too hard. "But if he were alive, he'd be just another sap taking away some Ph.D.'s spot in the department, right?" Ted sighed and waved to B.J. "Christ, I can't stand the paper-pushers."

"What the hell," he'd said a little later in the evening. "I suppose I'm happy. I have a good job I enjoy. My book will be published next year. Already at work on another."

"You enjoy teaching writing?" said Gary.

"Absolutely. And what a life-saver! Instead of waiting tables, or selling insurance like Wallace Stevens, I have a respectable academic position— and without having to publish articles about Henry James."

"Yes," said Gary, "I guess it's a pretty good deal. Though sometimes I wonder if it's all worthwhile. If there's any point to it. I mean, good writers have always found a way to develop their talent. And what's the point of encouraging the mediocre ones in a field that offers them little or no success?"

"Who are we to say who has no talent? I encourage everyone, to some degree. And maybe there's a potential great writer out there who would never discover his talent if our writing programs didn't encourage him. Who knows?"

"I do." All heads jerked together towards Aaron, whose deep throaty voice had finally broken its silence. It was as if the family dog had spoken. "You do too, Ted. We all know the point of our precious writing programs. To give paying jobs to all of us earnest, talented, dedicated writers who can't make a living with our fiction and don't have the humility to get real jobs. And what are we accomplishing, except to train hordes of young people, as well as middle-aged people who've left their spouses, to become teachers of more workshops? If we truly cared one whit about them we'd send the whole lot off to law school. They'd thank us later, the slush-pile readers at the magazines would thank us now, and maybe we'd even sleep better at night."

Aaron drank. The younger crowd examined their drinks.

"Thank you, Ed McMahon," said Ted. He put his arm around Aaron's hunched shoulders, gave him a big squeeze, and looked at the others. "Aaron is actually the sweetest guy you'll ever meet. Not to mention a phenomenal writer. I love this man." He placed a firm kiss on Aaron's head, which had remained motionless even as he spoke. He was still hunched over his drink, looking past us.

"I have to get going," he said, rising to his feet. "I'll call you tomorrow, Ted. Goodnight, everyone." He dropped a few bills on the table and quietly left the bar.

Chris matched Ted bourbon for bourbon (Robert was surprised he hadn't grown an identical gray moustache by now) while the rest nursed their three-dollar beers until B.J., evidently deciding Ted had reached his limit (thank God for poor Chris), threw down the check without prompting. "We'll see you tomorrow, Ted. Night, kids."

Outside Ted and Blythe agreed to share a cab to the upper West Side, leaving the others standing on Eleventh Street.

"What a fortunate coincidence, that they were able to share a cab," said Lexa.

"Not all they'll be sharing tonight, I'd bet," said Chris. You'd think they'd at least make it less obvious."

"What's the point?" Jack was catching on to the jaded flippancy the subject merited. "It's like Ted said: more fucking. It's all material."

"I can't believe about Ted and Blythe," said Robert an hour later, blissfully in bed with Lexa.

"Why not? It's no secret that Ted beds down with just about every good-looking acolyte who comes his way. I hear that at Breadloaf they call him the Erection in Residence."

The literary hero. The man who'd written, somewhere, what was it? *Writing is about logic, grace, and precision of thought. It is a lifelong study of the exceptional in human existence.* Great.

"Well, I hope you're at least resisting the temptation."

"What, to screw myself into print? I wouldn't be the first. Or the thousandth. But no, I haven't had any special tutoring sessions with the master. Yet. I'm joking, Robert, don't give me that look. Come one, let's generate some literary material of our own."

Hmm. Wonder if she did. Who cares, now? He placed the mint-white sheet atop his stack of paper, snapped his pen down on top, and walked to the window. It was late November, the day after Thanksgiving back home. The first snowflakes of the fall sprinkled lightly from an opalescent sky and melted on Goethestrasse. And who cares if I can't compose one fucking sentence for my life? He had tennis lessons to give, information of recreational import to impart, followed by a couple of sets with Max in exchange for the dinner to which his friend would almost certainly treat him. And then they would meet Ingrid for a concert of Beethoven string quartets at Schloss Nymphenburg. If he couldn't write he could at least live.

Max's tennis game was built on the same cornerstones as his business game: cheerful pragmatism and unflagging confidence. Unlike his business acumen, though, his tennis skills were far from expert: his elbow bent weakly on both the forehand and backhand, his back slouched on the serve to accommodate an overcautious low toss, and he sat on his heels at the net, often seeming to fall backward as he hit an inevitable drop volley instead of punching it deep. But where his opponent got tight on the big points, Max became steady as a rock; where the other man would go for a big serve, miss, and then double fault, Max would slice it in prudently to the backhand; where Saul, for example, would use his perfect form to strike a brilliant backhand two inches long, Max would chop a high and safe one that died in the red clay.

And, up to a certain level of competition anyway, there was no doubt in his mind who would claim victory. An opponent would have to be several levels of play better than Max to beat him. Often the match seemed over before it began, as Max shook his man's hand like an Oxford squire welcoming a guest to his backyard grass court, no matter that they were playing at the other fellow's club.

Robert had enjoyed a similar sangfroid in his college days, and a confidence more grounded in the reality of his game. Max seemed fascinated by this American who was so much better than he, and so confident of that fact, who beat Max every time, convincingly, without apparent effort. Every week Max insisted they play a match; he clearly had set a goal of someday taking a set off Robert. Yet he also appeared pleased to be put away so perfunctorily: it reaffirmed the proper order of things. Robert's perceived greatness was a source of pleasure for not only Max but the other club members as well. They had no idea of the levels above him in amateur tennis alone. How the top college players from UCLA or Stanford would crush him and in turn be crushed by lower-level pros who had no chance themselves against top pros. Levels upon levels, burying him in oblivion. They had no idea here. Herr Altmann had asked him how he'd fare against Becker. He could only laugh.

Robert was far enough removed from serious competition to need reminding sometimes of his own skill. Warming up with Max today, it seemed perfectly reasonable that this would be the day Max's fantasy came true. Max was in good form, hitting the ball back with the same pace with which he received it; he was looser than normal, his arm extended properly. Maybe Robert's tips, his informal instruction, had actually had some effect. There was no reason that Robert must inevitably win this match.

Yet after a couple of close games at the beginning, he began to take control despite himself. It didn't matter that his serve was enfeebled with tendinitis; his ground strokes were strong and solid and dictated the tenor of every point. Max's inexpert game was futile in the face of such practiced onslaught; he simply wasn't used to hard topspin sweeping him from corner to corner and sidespin approach shots that backed him up on his heels, and his own attempts to rush the net were met with passing shots that were as easy for Robert as hitting a pond with a pebble. Before Max could get used to his surprisingly competitive beginning, it was over: 6-2, 6-1.

"Remarkable," said Max as they sat in the club restaurant drinking Apfelschorles. "I thought I had you today, Rob. But once again, without looking like you're even moving, you took over."

"I don't believe you were ever actually ahead."

"No, but it was 1-1. It felt like it would be a tight match. You looked listless, and I must say I felt quite... in *synch*, you know?"

They drove to Max's house, and Robert waited in Max's room while the young master took his bath. Max, thirty years old, something of a Valentino and effective head of a prosperous international business, not only still lived with his parents but slept and dressed in a room unchanged since his adolescence. On the wall was the photograph of the 1974 World Cup team. In the dresser, left open, stacks of cleaned and pressed dress shirts, folded around cardboard by Hilda, the Polish maid. Rummaging through the desk drawers, Robert found dried-up old pens, letters, yellowed photographs, tests and reports from Gymnasium, and, buried under all that, several well worn copies of Italian Playboy. So that's how he achieved fluency, thought Robert, unable to resist flipping through and culling a few guilty throbs of desire from the impossible shower-glistening breasts and dewy black tufts before Max came strolling down the hall talking to him even before he arrived, then entered and threw towels and cardboard around the room as he dressed in one of his usual Italian suits, all the while rattling off insights into the superiority of Robert's tennis game. His detritus would be laundered and neatly stored in his absence.

"I'm afraid we have to stop by the airport," said Max as they zigzagged through Bogenhausen in the Porsche.

"If we're leaving Europe I should shower first."

"Shall we take a trip? Not tonight, though. I have to pick up a business associate. Mr. Chang from Beijing. I've told you about Mr. Chang."

"No, as a matter of fact."

"But you know all about my trip to China last month."

"Nothing except that it was 'quite productive.'"

"Well, it all began on the plane. I was sitting in first class next to a rather ordinary looking Chinese woman. Now *you* would have had your nose in your book and never spoken with her."

"I do try to avoid conversation on airplanes."

"It could be Catherine Deneuve next to you, and you'd never even notice."

"But this was no Catherine Deneuve."

"No. But I always strike up a conversation; one never knows whom one will meet. So I chat her up, and it turns out she's a concert promoter, and has organized some big rock concert that week in Beijing. I tell her how I'm visiting China for the first time in the hopes of striking up some business relationships and perhaps beginning to import goods from China to Germany."

"You have no appointments there."

"Nothing. I'm just going to go and see what's up, see who I meet. So she invites me to stay in one of the VIP rooms she's reserved at Beijing's best hotel. Apparently she's overbooked and there are plenty of empty rooms. There are many important businesspeople attending the concert as her guest, and I should come to the VIP dinner and the concert as well."

"You are truly amazing."

"What's amazing? I'm just friendly to people. Though I do, if I may say so, have a knack for ingratiating myself to strangers. For instance, you know about the Lufthansa stewardess—"

"I know all about the Lufthansa stewardess, thank you. So who's Mr. Chang?"

"One of the dignitaries at the concert. I sat next to him at the banquet, and we came to a business understanding by dessert. I'm going to be selling his pocketbooks to stores all over Germany. It should be very profitable."

"You also got a free concert in the deal."

"Ridiculous music; I could hardly sit through it. Mr. Chang enjoyed it quite a bit, though. And he invited me for an alarming number of drinks afterward, most of which I poured into the water glass and the plant behind me when he wasn't looking."

"And now you're going to reciprocate."

"Yes. It's all part of the business."

"I hope you're not going to suggest 1,001 Nights."

"No, no, not for Mr. Chang. I may have to buy quite a bit of alcohol, though."

Mr. Chang was waiting for them outside as they pulled up at the terminal. Not much older than they, short and stocky, in a dark suit and tie, he looked relieved to see Max.

"Mr. Chang! You're early," said Max as he hopped out of the car.

"Not early, Mr. Altmann. Land right on time. I have waited almost an hour. Very happy to see you."

"My apologies. Mr. Cherney here," he waved to Robert in introduction, "and I had some unexpected business come up..."

"Pleased to meet you." Mr. Chang offered a rock-solid handshake. "You are playing tennis."

"Yes," said Robert, then looked down at his tennis warm-ups and sneakers. "Oh no, we were just..."

"Rob is a well known American writer," said Max. "Perhaps you know of him."

"No, I am afraid not," Mr. Chang seemed ashamed. "I am afraid I do not have much time for reading these days."

Embarrassed to admit his claustrophobia, Robert folded himself up into the luggage space that doubled as a back seat and gave Mr. Chang the passenger seat. He felt like a child in his tennis clothes, unshowered, while the expensively clad businessmen luxuriated in the front. Knees against his chest, roof up against the November cold pushing down on his head, he braced one hand against each side of the car to stabilize himself during Max's wild ride through the streets of Munich. For once he was grateful for Max's motoring style, as fear for his life deprived him of the luxury of mere anxiety.

"So you'll join us at the concert," Max was saying. "I think you'll find the Schloss Nymphenburg quite impressive."

"No, no, not tonight. Tonight I must sleep. Jet lag. Tomorrow you will show me Munich, Mr. Altmann."

They left Mr. Chang at his hotel with the not entirely inaccurate impression that Americans wore tennis clothes to concerts at palaces, and they continued on to Goethestrasse. There was no longer time for dinner; Robert barely had time for a quick bath and to change to his only jacket and tie.

"I went down and called the ladies while you were bathing," Max said as they pulled out of Goethestrasse. "They'll meet us at the concert."

"Ladies?"

"Ingrid and Véronique. I can't say Ingrid was too pleased that we hadn't left yet."

"Véronique? You didn't say Véronique was coming."

"I must have. We had our French lesson today; I invited her to join us. You don't object, do you?"

"Of course not. I just didn't realize." He hadn't seen Véronique in two months, since three or four uncomfortable outings following their breakup in the English Garden. He'd wanted them to remain friends, but she hadn't returned some calls, and he soon stopped trying. He was surprised she would come, knowing that he would be there. How was it that he, a pleasant and reputable fellow by all accounts, had managed to become an object of animosity for such a nice young woman? Was it the lingering lust for Lexa, the like of whose ample body he was unlikely to encounter again? Was it discomfort with Véronique's seriousness? Or was it merely the fruit of his surrender to his own baseness, a pathetic grab for sex wherever it offers itself, with little concern for the consequences? If only she weren't so damn serious about everything, they could have had their little affair and moved on amicably. But he should have known from the start that Véronique was not one for casual affairs. When you kissed her you entered into a contract that could only be broken with pain.

They arrived at Nymphenburg a minute or two after nine. The only legitimate parking left was a good quarter mile away. Max drove right up to the castle grounds and bumped the right two tires of the Porsche over a curb and onto the finely manicured lawn in front of a marble fountain, and they walked the length of the long rectangular reflecting pool. Max seemed neither surprised nor disturbed to find the grounds empty already. He led Robert through the courtyard—how does he make $200 shoes sound like flip-flops?—and turned a corner where suddenly they saw a mass of humanity packed silently into an enormous drawing room. At the other end, a hundred yards away, the quartet tuned their instruments. Ignoring the disapproving gazes of the Germans, Max strode through the crowd, Robert in tow, looking for Ingrid and Véronique, who must certainly have saved them seats.

Of course, they had—a third of the way from the stage, in the center. Why be punctual when you had others to be punctual for you? The nervous rush of blood to Robert's head at the sight of Véronique was compounded by the embarrassment of slithering through a row of well-dressed Münchners, stepping on high-heeled feet, causing corpulent old men to stand, drawing a palpable wave of disapproval. At last they reached the women. Max dove into the usual series of bilateral kisses as though they were meeting at a cocktail party. Robert felt that with the string quartet and an audience of hundreds waiting for them such formalities might be waived without opprobrium, and he took a seat without even removing his coat. Véronique too looked ready to settle down, but the force of Max's greetings had spun them all around so that Véronique was closest to Robert, and Max and

Ingrid were still half locked in embrace and chatting. Véronique sat down next to Robert and they exchanged awkward glances of greeting. Finally Ingrid and Max sat down, Ingrid next to Véronique. Ingrid leaned forward and caught Robert's eye, smiled, winked. The lights came down, and the music began.

Véronique's hair had grown. It reached down now to her neck; the cropped look was gone. He hadn't realized how much he'd missed her company. The sexual thrill he felt, though, was propagated from the next seat, from Ingrid's barely concealed breasts and thighs.

They were playing the Opus 18, Number 6 in B-flat major. Some years later, Robert would receive it as a gift and, on playing it, would immediately remember this night. During the concert, however, he perceived little about the music. The interweaving folds of sound were but a single wave, a high-tide swell that filled every cranial crevice, producing a trancelike state focused on the women beside him.

Véronique sat stiffly watching the musicians, black-jeaned legs crossed, thick-wool-sweatered arms in her lap, concentrating on the music as though at a physics lecture. He could hardly believe he had made love to this woman. She seemed as strange to him as if they had just met. Had he really lain between her thighs, nestled inside her, stupefied by carnal release? It was inconceivable. He felt a great friendliness towards her—he suddenly wished they could be the best of friends, enjoying the cafés, films, and concerts of Munich without the awkwardness and bitterness of recent meetings—but no lust. Who was he, that he could have abused her thus, misled her, polluted her? He had always had faith in his own harmlessness, in a basic decency which he assumed others saw in him as well. But no one could see decency in the way he had treated Véronique. Like any beer-swilling frat boy, he had followed his erections into miscreant behavior.

After the concert, they flowed with the crowd out into the courtyard. Ingrid and Véronique were talking about the music, but Max began speaking about their tennis match as if the concert had been but an interruption of their discussion.

"Ya, I really thought this was the day. But no. You are quite amazing, Rob. Even without your serve, you had no doubt that you would win. And that's why you do win, in part."

Robert heard hardly a word. As he had slowed down to keep pace with Max's swaying, unfocussed perambulation, Ingrid and Véronique were now ten feet in front of them, deep in conversation. About what? Don't be such an egotist, he told himself. They have better things to discuss than your sexual mannerisms. Or your caddishness.

"So Véronique seems to have forgiven you," Max was saying. He had stopped walking completely, although his body still listed to one side as though caught in motion.

"Well, she agreed to come to the concert," Robert conceded.

"Ya," Max began, ever so gradually, to resume locomotion, "I'm not sure whether I mentioned you would be here or not. But certainly there is no resentment in her attitude."

"And Ingrid has forgiven you, too."

"What's to forgive? I am who I am. Perhaps I should be forgiving her. But then I don't believe she has done anything wrong. So: what shall we do?" They had caught up with the women, who had stopped at Max's car. Their fellow concertgoers gave them suspicious glances as they strolled past, either at the egregiously parked vehicle or because they remembered Max and Robert's rude entrance. "Shall we go for a drink?"

"I think there is a transportation problem," said Ingrid, gesturing at the two-seater. "We're not all going to fit into your passenger seat. Véronique took the Strassenbahn and I came in a taxi."

Max looked at his car as if for the first time. "I suppose not. So. Why don't two of us split a taxi and two drive?"

"I need to go home anyway," said Véronique. "I'll just take the tram again."

"We can't just let you ride the tram alone," said Max.

"I'll ride with her," said Robert. "I need to get up and work in the morning anyway, and the Strassenbahn goes right by my place."

"I'm perfectly fine alone," said Véronique. "I travel all over Munich by public transportation, as do all sorts of other people," she glared at Max. "But if you want to come with me, that's fine too, Robert."

"It's decided, then," said Max, and he opened his car door.

"You're sure, Véronique?" said Ingrid.

"Of course. Maybe I'll pick up some tennis instruction."

Then the Porsche was screeching away—how often had he watched Max rocket off into the Munich night?—and he and Véronique were walking out to Notburgastrasse to catch the tram.

They stood on the corner waiting in the cold breeze, she in her thick wool sweater and jacket, he wrapping his arms around the tattered black overcoat he'd found at the enormous thrift shop near the Marienplatz. A few months ago he would have wrapped them around her, and it almost seemed natural to do so now, but he stifled the instinct. They were less than strangers.

"So," he exhaled.

"So, Mr. Cherney." He noted, with relief, that something had given; the edge of contempt was gone from her voice.

"So how's the subtitling business?"

"Same old, same old." In her voice, with the accents on the "old"s, the expression sounded doomful. "I finish my courses in the spring. Then I'll have to find work."

"Here in Munich?"

"Well, that's the problem. If I stay here, I'll probably have to do dubbing. There is not much subtitling in Germany. To subtitle, I'd probably have to go to Paris or London. And to do London I'd really have to work on my English idioms."

"Then there's New York. Or Hollywood, or wherever they do the subtitling."

"Ha—can you imagine me in Hollywood? New York maybe. But I don't think I'm interested in living in the U.S."

"Not intellectual enough?" he kidded her.

"Correct. And besides, it's too far from my parents. Why should I cause them such sadness? We can't go zipping back and forth on the Concorde like the Altmanns. Ach, I'll probably end up teaching like you, Robert."

"Not like me, I hope." The somber blue-and-white tram approached, hissed to a halt, and swept them into its warm belly. She sat by the window and looked out for a moment. He sat beside her, careful not to let his leg touch hers.

"How have you been, though?" he asked.

She continued looking out the window. Clean streets, sided by stucco houses and granite apartment buildings, slid by them. "Fine, Robert." Finally she turned around to look at him. "I was very angry for a while, you know."

"I know."

"You had no right to take me like that when you knew that you had no deeper feelings for me. It should have been obvious to you, someone with experience, a novelist no less, that I was not used to such dalliances."

"I know," he said, wincing at "novelist" as though she were deliberately exposing him for a charlatan. He felt like a prisoner in the pillory, forced to listen to his crimes, not only convicted of literary fraud but also exposed for the lout that he was.

"But I ... got over it. I'm not really so fragile as you think. And I know now that you didn't mean any harm."

"That's true, Véronique."

"That doesn't mean you didn't do any harm," a touch of the victim's pain clouded her face, then dissipated. "But perhaps you also did me a favor. I suppose I have been too sheltered in my life here. Living with my parents at my age..."

"Well, I wouldn't go that far. I didn't do you any favors. But I certainly never meant to hurt you. I just wasn't all there."

"You still have Alexandra in your mind."

"I guess so," he said but knew even as he spoke that his erotic-romantic obsession for his old girlfriend had somewhere along the line evolved into a faded excuse. It was easier to use that than to try to explain, or even understand, why he had been unable to be a proper lover to Véronique.

"I have to tell you the truth," she said, "I had no idea that you would be here tonight. Ingrid just called me to say that Max had an extra ticket. And I don't know if I would have accepted if I knew you were coming. But I'm glad that I did. Now I know that I am truly over you."

"I'm glad too." He wished he could be over on her side, with the family of the victim, straining over the crowd to get a glimpse of the guilty defendant—the perpetrator. He deserved this, he knew, and tightened his face muscles in resignation, waiting for it to be over.

And eventually it was. The streetcar squeaked, turned, fragmented into a serpentine vessel, felt like a submarine roaming submerged through the Munich night. Their legs even touched on several sharp turns, and they talked of movies they might see together, concerts upcoming, Max's French solecisms, Ingrid's backhand volley. He rode with her into Schwabing, walked her to her parents' house, exchanged the double-cheek embrace of their first days together, and then he took the long walk home to Goethestrasse feeling like a convict released from prison, as free as if he were wearing the only clothes he owned.

9

Dirty snow now lines the curbs of Goethestrasse, swept aside for the cars and food vendors and busy pedestrians to continue their daily evolutions from morning into evening. Robert stands inside his closed window to watch the terrestrial activity below, sipping mouth-deterging Turkish coffee, the cheapest brand he can find. It is December, and most of his clients have replaced tennis with winter activities. He has retained just enough weekly lessons to keep him solvent, and that suits him fine. He is like a wild hamster, holed up in his winter burrow, subsiding on rarefied portions of cereal grains through the meager months. A couple of free dinners a week courtesy of Max don't hurt. Mornings he sits at his desk with white paper, white mind, white frost on the windows. Afternoons he makes his way to Sport Scheck to hold forth on the dark indoor courts. Evenings there is entertainment of some sort: a film with Véronique and her friends; a late rendezvous with Ingrid, less and less frequent it seems; dispatching of time at Ludwigstrasse cafés; waiting hours on end in his single-lamped room for

Max to show up and lead him on a desultory neon-whipped tour of the city.

On the shortest day of the year, a Friday with no lessons, he sat rapping his pen against the corner of his table, watching the last embers of scant daylight loiter in the window frost. He had not written a word all day; the only sound his pen had made was the tap-tapping against the table as he promenaded the ship's deck of his frustrations, tap-tapping in ironic imitation of a more prolific man's typewriter. And yet Robert did not feel unhappy. Something about the early darkness of winter and the cloistering space of the small room and the late sleep and stupefaction of working inside all afternoon—the same elements that normally would depress him—paradoxically gave him a pleasant feeling despite the day's lack of production. Only an ephemeral flash of doubt—How long can I persevere like this? How long convince myself that what I do is worthwhile?—burst once like lightning through his cloud cover. But his sense of shelter quickly returned, the atmosphere of his room allowing him once again to convince himself that he was *working*, and that one day, out of this coal mine, a canary would emerge.

By four-thirty the light scattering through the window had turned from sunset red to streetlamp gold; the sky was dark. He rose, that familiar punch-drunk pugilist after the final round, and staggered to the window. His tenuous euphoria evanesced like the last sunlight. He sighed into the cold glass, fog meeting frost. He almost wished he had a lesson or two to give tonight. Max was in Israel with his family. Ingrid was off somewhere, probably selling security, not answering her phone anyway. He would have liked to call Véronique, but they had met for a movie on Wednesday, and he felt that, considering the past, he shouldn't call her too often.

The radiator had turned silent; someone must have shut off the heat early. He pulled on an extra sweater and shuffled out to the hallway, went down to check the mail, using the stairs for exercise and to warm up, among other reasons. In the foyer a couple of employees from the Turkish bank, leaving for the weekend, looked him over suspiciously. I suppose a bath and a shave might be in order, he conceded.

Several circulars from local businesses and a ravaged thin blue international envelope with a Soviet stamp, addressed to him in a familiar hand. Right, he had heard she'd gone back in the fall—stringer work, more novel research. Even after all this time the thin-spired loops of her l's, the blue-black fountain-pen ink she preferred, the thought of her tendons stretching and pulling to direct the nib along the paper he now held was enough to make him dizzy. Like the hamster hoarding his acorn, he jogged upstairs with his letter unopened. In his room, he made more coffee and settled on the couch.

At last he took the pale blue envelope and turned it over in his hands like a master woodworker lovingly fingering a piece of pristine maple that he was about to turn into a hummingbird. Six months had passed, two women had filled the chasm of that absence, and still he could feel her breasts cupped in his hands, the small of her back had left a permanent imprint on his belly, it was her skin that he smelled in his deepest dreams. It's just sex; you're obsessed with her sexually. Well, all right, but anything that can hold such a power over me deserves some respect. Knowing I was a fool, I'd still "barter life for love," trade a year of emptiness for one night in her bed.

Dear Robert C.,

How's the exiled-writer's business in Deutschland? Things have been hopping along here in the CCCP: my book's almost done, just need to get some distance in order to wrap it up and then it'll be ready for my agent's hungry hands. To that end I'm leaving Moscow and heading back to good ol' NYC for final stage. You know: cold sesame noodles at House O' Szechuan, toasted bagels at the Waverly, late-night coffee at Lee's, the sound of those fucking garbage trucks at two in the morning while I browbeat my typewriter. (Never one of those word processors for me!)

Anyway, I thought I'd make a sort of farewell voyage through Europe, first stop being old Münchentown, where famous infamous writer-in-weltschmerz Robert Cherney tends to his pencil, entertains traveling women, and reportedly earns his living by teaching Germans to swat fuzzy balls with sticks.

Actually, old Münchentown may be the last European stop as well. Len has fled London (some sort of scandal involving the Prime Minister's daughter or something), and in any case he and I were a bit on the out and out lately. So maybe I'll just fly out of Munich (you could join me—haven't you had enough wienerschnitzel?).

I'm arriving on the 20th, 8pm—though the Soviet train to E. Berlin should be predictably late, fouling the W. Germans' beloved timetable by several hours at least. Mind having a Yuletide guest? I promise to be gone by New Year's: need to be hard at work on Jan. 2.

Hope you get this, or I may be barging in on a romantic candlelight dinner (or worse!) on 12/20. You really ought to get a telephone one of these days—this starving writer thing has gone far enough.

love

A

Who the fuck is Len? He sighed, looked at his watch. The 3 was effaced by a simple black-and-white 20, like pica strokes on 10-pound white paper. For several seconds he stared at the numerals, the concept of December 20 as abstract to him as Heisenberg's Uncertainty Principle. Could the date scraped in her desiccated ink correspond to his current reality? Could those strokes of her pen (stretching tendon, nib-caressing finger) signify his morning slumber, his wretched afternoon of impotence, and the inexplicable euphoria of the gloaming?

He picked up the envelope again. It looked like it'd been run over by a train. Yes, time had passed while this folded rectangle of paper and glue had been misplaced, forgotten, abused, rediscovered, and finally hurried on its way like a child being scolded for the school bus breaking down. Weeks had evaporated, December had nearly slipped by. Another few hours and she'd have appeared at his door like the ghost of Christmas past. The letter was enough of a shock.

As though in a negative movie reel of six months before, summer light turned to winter darkness, he bustled about the room, organizing his sloth into compartments, clearing, cleaning, compiling. In the bath, idly drawing on his chest with the handheld spray, he mused on life's unexpected windfalls: a night promising nothing but loneliness, self-doubt, and confusion suddenly turned into an adrenalin-pumping visitation from the object of his life's greatest longing. The hell with his well-disciplined resolve to forget: he'd be well disciplined after she'd come and gone. Until then, he would enjoy the random bounty. It was all he could do to restrict his bathing activity to hygiene.

At eight o'clock at the München Hauptbahnhof a male figure appeared on Platform 12. Wet hair combed back, face freshly shaven, body ensconced in a threadbare black coat. As she'd predicted, the train was late. For the first half-hour he stood, fidgeted, paced along the platform. Then, remembering he'd had no dinner, he bought a Weissbier and bratwurst at one of the circular indoor kiosks. Halfway through the bratwurst it occurred to him what it was doing to his breath. He considered running home to brush his teeth, but she could arrive at any moment. He finished eating, then bought another beer to use as an antiseptic mouthwash, scouring his teeth with his tongue before swishing the beer violently and swallowing.

Another hour passed, as he made a series of ever-widening concentric semicircles around the track's terminus, watching the faces of the cheerful Münchners greeting holiday guests. From time to time he felt in his overcoat pocket for the blue envelope as if to reassure himself that it was real, that it was not idle lust that had led him into the train station on a twisted fantasy. Could he really have received a letter informing him that his old love was arriving imminently by train?

He had just taken the letter out one last time, to look for hidden meanings in the text—perhaps a friendly joke at his expense?—when at last the train slid up in an audiovisual cloud of brake friction and engine steam, pulled up at the end of the track like a running back just barely dragging the defender across the goal line.

And then she was there, appearing out of the letter he had just read as though summoned by language. They hugged like old buddies. Her smile was warmer than in the past; it seemed to remember some good deed he had done or else a trial he had undergone and passed. "Welcome back to Goethestrasse," he said.

"How's the Blue Box?"

"Open for business." He shouldered her backpack. Eleven minutes later they were in bed.

"That was fast," she said, after another eleven minutes.

"Sorry. Your letter kind of got me riled up. I'll do better the second time."

"That's all right. I'm glad you're happy to see me. Or was that a ten-gallon hat?"

"I suppose you've been starved for sex too, over there in the People's Republic."

"Not really. I was going out with an oboe player, and then a *Pravda* journalist. If you can call that journalism. Nothing serious, though."

He knew his disappointment was unwarranted, obnoxious even. "Good God," he tried to joke. "Don't you ever have dry spells?"

"It was a dry spell, believe me. All that was just fooling around. Just sex and a few drunk laughs. I was there to work. It wasn't like this, Robert."

And she held him tighter, in a way he had longed for in New York but always been denied. He held her naked body against his, felt how perfectly it fit, ran his fingers down her back, and tried to feel the way he'd felt in her New York bed on Sunday mornings, before she jumped out of bed prematurely to begin the day. He was unable to recapture that sense of bliss, but the pang of jealousy from her flippant revelations of casual sex with others was reincarnated with no effort at all. After seeing her twice in two years.

Christmas week in Munich was not what he'd expected. He'd imagined himself walking the streets alone while his students spent the holidays with family, eating by himself in dim restaurants and cafés with Max away. Instead, as he walked the streets he had by his side the woman he'd once thought was the answer to all his yearnings. And she was *there* in a way that she hadn't been in the past, even when they'd supposedly been "dating" in New York. Her grip on his arm was tighter, she leaned into him as she never had before. He tried to recreate the joy of walking with her that he'd had in New York. This time, he was more successful. The physical memory was strong enough that the very act of holding hands could produce the ecstasy of the past. And yet he felt he was promenading along a Hollywood sound stage, and behind the backdrop lurked the real world, in which his ability to love this woman had long faded. The scene they were playing was historical. Five years ago it would have been the happy ending; now it felt like a forced attempt to go back in time and undo the infidelities, the cruelties, the hurts.

He also found himself suddenly busy with lessons. In the States, Christmas week was a vacation time for everyone, Jews and Christians alike. Even if people didn't have the week off from work, there was a general feeling of holiday; people traveled, or were just busy with family. In Munich, though, his club members seemed to want to take advantage of all the empty court time at the goyische Sport Scheck. Each time he showed up there to give a lesson, there were two or three messages waiting for him on the Mattathias bulletin board: courts already reserved, was he available?

Robert and Lexa arrived home one afternoon after touring some museums. "Touring" indeed: Lexa was a gallery-sprinter, the fastest purveyor of fine art he had ever seen. She dashed through the ornate rooms of the Neue Pinakothek like a buyer for Carpet World, taking in whole rooms at a glance; he, dull enough to spend several minutes staring at one Kokoschka, soon lost her completely and only found her on reaching the exit, where she sat reading pamphlets about the art she had just fast-forwarded.

Back on Goethestrasse, taped to his mailbox was a folded sheet of notepaper. "Just a student canceling a lesson," he told her in the elevator, but while she was in the bathroom he pulled the crumpled paper out of his pocket and read again.

Dear Mr. Tennis Trainer,

Are you still in the street of the poet? You haven't called, and of course there's no way to reach you. I would have mailed a letter, but I was "in the area."

You're finally going to see Munich in bridal gown, I hear.

Véronique

He crumpled it back up and started to toss it in the wastepaper basket but stopped, and almost without thinking he smoothed it out a bit, and slid it into the middle of a book. He had bought a new paperback edition of *At Swim-Two-Birds*, and he needed a bookmark.

It was Christmas Eve. Lexa, in the first display of sentimentalism he had ever witnessed in her, wanted to go see the enormous lighted Christmas tree at the Marienplatz. He happily indulged, content to take in more of the late-year atmosphere, that secular mood-lifting thinness in the air, the effect of the short days, imminent festivities, and electric lights that was the same here as back home. On their way home earlier, the air had suddenly become enhanced by the barely perceptible presence of snowflakes. Having no television or radio, Robert had lost all interest in weather reports, and so this sudden precipitation came like a gift without occasion, all the more thrilling for its unexpectedness. He found it nearly impossible to imagine the city covered by snow. He had known

Munich only in summertime, and then in fall, when it felt so different but retained the same basic visual status. When they went back outside, though, the city presented him with its wintertime visage: Bayerstrasse's normal maelstrom of tram lines and hotels and traffic was muted by a soft white covering; the Karlsplatz fountain was a sugary doughnut; the pedestrian mall stretching to the Marienplatz was pockmarked by the boots of a thousand shoppers, and at the Marienplatz the Rathouse rose like a moonlit mountain in a winter squall. They gazed at the gargantuan tree, drank hot spiced Glühwein from the Christkindlmarkt, and stood under the twin towers of the Frauenkirche, heads tipped back, letting the torrent of flakes melt deliciously on their cheeks and tongues.

As they walked home, the storm picked up, and they huddled together against the wind and the parabolic onslaught of snow against their faces. With almost a foot of snow on the ground, near midnight on Christmas Eve, the streets were empty. They walked down the middle of Bayerstrasse towards the Hauptbahnhof, veering serpentine several padded inches over train tracks, curbs, medians, navigating by the hulking vision of the station in the distance. Goethestrasse was one blank corridor of the labyrinth. And there was Number Ten, startlingly noble in its white mantle, like a bum in tails.

In the elevator—Robert had been embarrassed to admit he was scared to take it, and in fact had discovered this week that, after six months, he was able to ride the rickety conveyance once again without panic—they separated from the jolt of the chamber's precarious takeoff and leaned against opposite walls watching each other. "Why don't you come home with me?" she asked.

"But you've already come home with me, my dear."

"You know what I mean. Come back to New York. There's nothing holding you here. Or is there?"

"Nothing like what you're thinking of. I've had my evenings quite free for you, haven't I?"

"You could get a cheap last-minute fare and join me tomorrow. Nobody's traveling on Christmas Day. Come on, who am I going to have two-p.m. brunch with? And how am I going to afford an apartment by myself? I'm too old for strange new roommates."

It did sound inviting. Her characteristic flippancy was now but a cover for a new side of her. Emotional neediness was not something he had ever seen her reveal; he had always been the one longing for her. Just six months earlier he would have been dancing in the streets at this sea change: to have the love of your life suddenly come round! But somewhere between dropping her at the Hauptbahnhof and picking her up again he had lost his passion. Not the physical infatuation—just waiting at the station, picturing her in her compartment speeding across Europe towards him, had been enough to bring back the sexual urgency of a nineteen-year-old. There was something in that woman, some genetic spark across a synapse between her DNA and his, a voltage set somewhere in their ancestors' time, that he doubted would ever cease to stun him. But the romantic component, he now found to his surprise, had dissipated, lost somewhere under the wheels of the Strassenbahn, in the tall grass of the English Garden, buried in the red clay of the tennis courts. Was it the cumulative effect of callousness in New York—not just sleeping around but doing it and then relating it to him as if it were a golf game; canceling dates at the last minute in order to meet women friends for coffee; in short, treating their relationship like the least important of a series of casual friendships, when for him it was the most passionate event of his life? Or was it simply a gradual realization that she was not his fate, that it was not for him to be forever wounded by her, forever crowded out by her own obsession (journalistic, yes, but a rapids of composition next to his own trickling brook), eternally pricked by her caustic mocking of that which he held most dear: the theater, art, the beauty of nature? The most convenient and well-worn excuse for the severing of romantic ties was in this case conversely true: he was still in love with her, perhaps would always be, but he did not love her.

"I don't know," he said as they moved down the dark hallway, speaking softer so as not to disturb, or rouse interest from, Herr Farakh. "I don't think I've reached the end of my Munich period."

"I suppose you don't want to leave your imaginary friend Max, who never seems to be here when I visit."

"Can't you see him? He's right there in the corner, cleaning his paws."

They kicked the thick snow off their shoes, flopped onto the brown corduroy sofa, and pulled the quilt from the bed over them. They sat, not touching each other. Though not warm, the room was a shelter, a shell closed off from the white storm outside. Bells began to ring from somewhere far off.

"So it would seem," she began slowly, "that you've lost your passion for me."

"Not the passion, Alexandra. I just can't come and live with you."

"You wanted to two years ago."

"Yes, and you didn't want to stop sleeping with John and Chris, if I recall."

"Look, I'm sorry about that. I had this thing about wanting to be like a man, wanting to sow my wild oats just for the sake of doing it. It had nothing to do with my feelings for you."

"If only I'd known that, I'd have felt so much better."

"I'm sorry I hurt you, Rob. But I never broke up with you. We still had good times, even through this period. We still made love."

"Well, you let me sleep with you. You never seemed fully engaged in the activity."

"Part of my wanting to be like a man, I suppose."

"Was telling me to get a girlfriend also a manly act of yours? Right when I was ready to propose that we move in together?"

"I'm sorry, I'm sorry, I'm sorry. Can't you let me forget that? Now *I'm* asking you to live with me, and you want to stay in this icebox and teach tennis. I think you have a love interest."

"I really don't. I'm quite alone, apart from imaginary Max. I have some friends, of course. And I was seeing someone briefly, I told you, but that's long over."

"So it's just that you don't like me. You love me—or at least you like making love to me—but you don't like me."

"Of course I like you." Neither was looking at the other, just staring into the quilt.

Had this room ever been so quiet? Not a horn from the street, not a voice or footstep rising from the sidewalk, no squeak of a streetcar from the corner. Not the slightest cough or television static from Farakh across the hall. Even the fluorescent bulb in the hall had quit its buzzing. It was as though the snow had thrown a soundproof blanket over everything inside as well as out. Their voices too, surprisingly in this quietude, sounded muted.

"I'm not a happy person, you know, Robert. You think I'm having a great time waltzing around the world, spinning off glorious dispatches, screwing whomever I see fit. Great way to see the world, I suppose. It's miserable. I'm never going to finish my book. All I do is compile more and more notes. And more and more acquaintances. I have nobody to really talk to. My parents, as you know, are divorced egomaniacal former intellectuals; I can barely stand to visit either of them. I have no real friends in New York, or elsewhere. I'm going back to face those awful parties full of frustrated lonely artists who really want to be married and living in Scarsdale but won't admit it. To face Sunday mornings again, and Sunday afternoons. God, I can't stand it."

He had never seen tears in her eyes before. Never thought that he could hurt her like this. How could he possibly wound The Great Bohemian? Surely she could take it as well as dish it out. This vulnerability was like a fruit's fleshy essence uncovered beneath a barbed shell. It was almost enough to make him want her again in the old way, to make that flight back home. But not.

"So I guess that's it." She threw off her half of the quilt and in a few strangely quiet steps was in the bathroom. The bathtub faucet turned on, a somehow incongruous sound in the snow-muffled apartment. He sighed and stood up slowly, like an old man. What was the point of all this? Four days of traipsing all over Munich, arm in arm like real lovers, four nights of lovemaking that you knew was a lie. It was all just work, manual labor of passing time, and slaking of your own sexual thirst. You're like a stray mutt, surviving from sunrise to sunrise, scratching your itches and moving your heavy bones. In a stupor he made up the sofa; that is, he took a pillow from the bed and switched the quilt with the blanket on the bed. It would be an awful night, but he would sleep soundly through it nonetheless. He could sleep for weeks. Would she fume at his smug snoring from her insomniac perch on the bed? It wouldn't matter; all he had to contend with were his dreams.

The water continued to pour. Could it take that long to fill the bath? Or has she taken a bottle of sleeping pills, and in a minute I'll see the placid waters flowing out the door? She's always had that suicidal Weltanschauung, that artistic psyche always perched on the precipice, hanging on with a mixture of writer's bravado and a nothing-particularly-better-to-do-than-go-on-living attitude.

The waterfall ceased. He undressed and lay under the blanket on the couch, leaving only the bedside lamp on for her. Sounds of ripplings came to him, fingertips thighs and knees breaking the liquid-air limen as on a midnight lake. The silences between lengthened—as, he imagined, she checkmarked her way down the hygienic agenda—and then became one. Cool late-summer moonlight on the warm lake water, face and breasts protruding the surface, reflecting. He could see the shimmer on her skin. Silence, utter pacific calm with the flakes dropping by the window as in a silent film. Was she asleep? Could one drown that way? Or was it a purposeful ending via his razor blades found by the sink: was the moonlit summer lake swirling in crimson?

No. The lake had turned river: water was moving. He could see it orbiting the rusted drain like a whirlpool of nebulae around a black hole. The entire universe in her offscourings. Footstep, then another, on the linoleum floor. Friction of towel on skin disturbs the air, slightly but unmistakably. Water was still swirling, trapped between the inexorable pull of the drain and its own centrifugal force, when she stepped from the bathroom, wrapped chest to thighs in one of his two drab brown towels from the Hertie department store. She walked in the dim orange light to the table, where her handbag was, and stood while she combed her wet hair. After all we've been through here I am again, lying like a kid in a sleeping bag wondering what the hell I'm doing. All you want in the world right now is to join her in the bed like you were last night, and yet you've made a decision not to. Are you sure you have any idea where your happiness lies?

He expected not a word from her, just an awkward night and a torturous goodbye in the morning leaving him mercifully past the Alexandra chapter. Their conversation of a half-hour ago would have been more judiciously scripted for the walk to the train station; they were like vaudevillians caught on stage with five minutes left to kill before the next act was ready.

Her grooming done, she replaced the comb in her bag, turned out the lamp by the bed, and stood for several moments looking out at the snow falling in a never-ending pattern through the frame of the window like an Escher print on a wooden roll. Then, instead of getting into the bed, she stepped to the couch, stood by him, and let the damp towel fall to the carpet. The snow, interrupting the passage of light from the streetlamp, played kaleidoscope games across her body; dark flakes cascaded from her face down across her breasts and belly and either fell to her feet or were lost in her dark bush. "Make love to me," he could barely hear her say, and he moved against the back of the sofa to make room, and she lay next to him, and the last few hours were as distant as a vague memory of youth, and the morning's goodbye simply did not exist, as it had not yet occurred. Now he was in her, wondering how to save this moment: how could what he had longed for for so long not only be true but already have occurred many times and now be occurring for the last time? How could he have purposely decreed that it shall not happen again? She was holding him tighter than ever before; for the first time she seemed truly engaged in their physical engagement. Her legs were wrapped around him, squeezing his thighs. He fought to hold off, to make the moment last, to fix it in his memory. It was a vain attempt, he knew by now. In a year, a month, a week, how could he ever recreate this sensation? It would be as lost as a smell from childhood that you can almost but not quite summon. Giving up the struggle on all fronts, he groaned and wilted on top of her, his face against her neck collecting the precipitation of her tears.

A few hours later, Christmas morning, they walked the one block down Goethestrasse. It was as quiet as the night before, though now bright sunshine avalanched off the two-foot-thick virgin snow. Bridal gown, indeed. So that was what she'd meant. But the sun, where it collected in wind-formed dimples in the whiteness, looked like tears. It was the morning after, and the groom had not showed.

They had spoken not a word since waking. The night was an unmentionable covenant; now they faced the exposure of bright reality. He had insisted on accompanying her on the U-Bahn out to the airport in Riem. She refused. Wouldn't even let him carry her bag. His tennis shoes and her Russian boots crushed the snow crystals into dough.

They stopped at the entrance to the subway. It looked like a nuclear missile facility in Siberia.

"I'll wait for the train with you."

"No, I'd rather wait alone."

"It's confusing which way to go."

"I think I can figure it out by now."

"It's Riem. Remember, Richtung Riem."

"Jawohl."

"Here, take a U-Bahn ticket. I have plenty."

"I can buy one."

"Please. I have plenty."

"Goodbye." She finally broke the détente and came close, and they hugged each other in a desperate grasp. Then he watched her descend into the underground, a relinquished paradise that he didn't understand.

That morning he walked the snowy plains of Munich in his tennis shoes, seeing the frozen city through real tears. It had been years since he had cried like that, and it brought back the memory of being four years old and weeping for no good reason, a tantrum brought on by some parental slight. He didn't even try to stem the flow; the few Münchners he passed would assume his red eyes and wet face were a reaction to the cold. If they didn't, he couldn't care less.

By afternoon he apparently was his old self again: composed, emotionlessly returning ill-struck tennis balls to their perpetrators. When Bernd called out to him over the net, "Hallo, Robert! What on earth is going wrong with my forehand?" it was nothing so unusual: his students were forever pleading with him to be more demonstrative. He really hadn't been paying any attention to Bernd's forehand, which also wasn't so unusual, but he shouted for him to turn his body, get sideways—Bernd stubbornly faced the net at all times, as if defending himself from a hoodlum— and as he'd suspected Bernd's returns suddenly focused into sharper trajectories.

The dark green dust of the Har-Tru court seemed fake, a dismal attempt to simulate the outdoor red clay of summer. It didn't kick up as much as the red and infiltrate his shoes, socks, and shorts; but still it somehow insinuated itself onto his person. He could feel it there, even if he couldn't see it, it was dissolved into the dried sweat on his skin, he could sense it in his lungs, could smell it even as he rode home on the Strassenbahn—a canoe over a midnight lake in a negative. He felt it on his fingertips every time he picked up his racket at home and gripped it, swinging imaginary ground strokes in his apartment instead of composing paragraphs. At least swinging the racket warmed him up a bit, for this was the coldest winter he'd known. He'd thought a Munich winter would be similar to a New York one, but it was more like Canada, and living in his apartment was only marginally better than homelessness. Being cold in the apartment was worse than when he was out on the street, where, wrapped in his long coat, he was no worse off than anyone else. He took long walks all week, like polar explorations in his mind, and slowly the ache of having denied himself the exquisite torture of a continued relationship with Lexa was growing numb. Up through the frozen pleasure fields of the English Garden, down to the hibernating zoo of Thalkirchen, across the barren wastes of the Theresienwiese, that great field not far from Goethestrasse, where in summer the carnival simmered and snorted. Once, he took the bus all the way out to Dachau and visited the camp for a third time. With her it had been a summertime specter; her sunglasses had made him think of Jackie Kennedy and the color-movie nightmare of the assassination on TV. Now, with bare trees and a coat of snow, the camp had fallen back into the pit of the more distant past. The wintry black and white made it seem more real, easier to imagine the horror. He took one slow walk around the courtyard, half expecting to see a guard in high boots and long coat taking a cigarette break, machine gun hanging from his shoulder, and a black early-model Mercedes come lumbering through the gate. But nothing disturbed his solitude; he was the only visitor.

New Year's Eve he walked up to the Hauptbahnhof and descended the same staircase into the earth that Lexa had taken to leave him. He was not headed for the U-Bahn, but rather for the great subterranean market. He noticed with satisfaction that his claustrophobia, though it might return, he knew, at any time, incited by another elevator breakdown or other such incident, was indeed for the moment in remission. Ostensibly he needed a wrist support (*Handgelenkstütze, Handgelenkstütze,* he kept repeating in his head) to keep him returning balls to his students. The minimally heated air of the indoor courts and the unexpected surge in lessons had conspired to inflame the tendon in his wrist. His expectations, though, for finding a quality orthopedic device in the underground mall were low. Preprandial warmth was his real goal.

It was early enough that the stores were still open, and the shop-lined tunnels were busy with the traffic of imminent revelers. The general quality of dress was a bit sharper than usual, people walked slightly quicker, there was an extra charge in the Doppler shift of their voices as they approached and then sank back into the void behind him: *He was joking, of course . . . Monday or Tuesday, Monday or Tuesday . . . I have no idea at all . . . Ha! I love it, I love it! . . .* Only he seemed unhurried, browsing as it were, swaying through the crowds as if strolling through a public garden, hypnotized by the heated air, the fluorescent lights, the pinball arcade of humanity.

Like a bass tone penetrating from the core of a symphony, a familiar voice broke through the din. At first he couldn't place it, for the disconnectedness of its words: *That's it, look at juice. . . fresh like new. . . so much juice. . . Gesundheit! Gesundheit!* Just as he was about to recognize the bad German, the speaker interjected some South African English: *There's nothing like it, I tell you. One glass every morning, and you won't believe how much better you'll feel. No more of that Valensina crap for you.* "Ah, Robert! What a coincidence!" Before Robert had decided if Dan Cohen was a welcome feature of his New Year's Eve promenade, he was captured by their mutual recognition.

Dan's back was to one wall, and in front of him was a folding card table. On it were a dozen or so oranges next to what looked like an impressionistic metal sculpture of a squirrel poised on a branch with its head down low and its tail in the air. Scotch-taped and hanging from the front edge of the table was a sign, in English: *FRESH ORANGE JUICE! FEEL BETTER!*

"How are you, my friend?" Dan's handshake looked jovial but felt desperate; Robert waited out the painful embrace. "Frau Klausmeyer here is just sampling the best orange juice in Munich." But Frau K., a suspicious-looking medicine ball of a woman who was obviously in this for the free sample, was already slipping away into the current of shoppers without so much as an apologetic glance thrown behind her.

"These damn Germans," Dan said with a sigh, finally releasing Robert's hand. "But how are you, Robert? Coach? Getting a wintertime rest from your students, I hope?"

"I'm afraid not. They're all trying to get a jump on the competition. I need the money, or I'd give my shoulder and wrist a winter break."

"Bad news, bad news. Your own game's going to go down the shoots, old boy. My squash career ended when I started giving too many lessons. You'll start playing more and more like your students. It's inescapable. Worse yet, you'll start playing like me. Ha ha."

"Could be worse. You were the only one I could count on for a win. More likely I'll start playing like Saul. Look as good as ever, but unable to hit the court with the ball when it counts."

"True enough. Ah, Saul. There's my dream opponent. Can you imagine—a head case like that against my junk? Remember that practice match? After fifteen minutes the old boy was ready to sit on a loaded shotgun. Look, do me a favor, drink some damn orange juice while you're here." He took an orange, sliced it in two, lifted the squirrel's tail, and dropped a half-orange in. A bit of elbow grease applied to reconstituting the rodent's lower abdomen produced a stream of juice into a waiting cup. "Isn't that delicious?" he said loudly while Robert enjoyed his first fresh juice in months. "The best orange juice in Munich! Fresh oranges flown directly from Africa, squeezed in the special Müller machine! Müller's OJ Café, opening soon near you!" Then, much softer, "Cohen isn't exactly the best name for selling here." Most people marched by without the slightest indication of noticing Dan; a few turned their heads as they strode by, interest piqued by the spectacle of a man trying to sell fruit juice in winter by shouting English at a German crowd.

"What do you think?" he asked Robert.

"It's everything you say. I haven't had fresh OJ since I've been here."

"Exactly! This is a guaranteed fortune. What do you think of my squeezer?" He worked the mechanism a few times. Having expressed its function, it had lost all semblance to a squirrel; it was now simply a stainless-steel juicer.

"Did you design it?" Robert asked.

"More or less. Well, found it anyway, but that's art of a sort, isn't it. Duchamp, right? I discovered it in a small shop in Johannesburg. I'm going to be the official European importer. I'll sell it all over the continent, in department stores, specialty stores, and of course in my cafés. I'm opening my first one right here under the Hauptbahnhof, as soon as I can raise the initial capital. I'm telling you, Robert, fresh orange juice is going to be the new cappuccino, the new Löwenbräu. The beer gardens are passé. I'm going to start a whole new fad. It's time these Germans started thinking about healthy living."

"I hope you're not going to ask them to stop smoking."

"Of course not. They'll be sitting at my tables, enjoying a cigarette, reading the *Süddeutsche Zeitung*, over a few OJ's."

"I'll be there," Robert promised. "Right at the bar."

"Never a charge for you, Coach."

Robert sipped his orange juice, and they watched the passers-by for a minute. He tried to look invigorated, but his example lured no more customers than had Dan's chatter.

"You should have been here earlier in the day," said Dan. "The free samples pulled them in—and they call *us* cheap—and I sold quite a number of take-home liters. It was enough to make my old squash elbow act up."

"OJ elbow can be disabling."

"Anyway, I've only got a few months to get this off the ground and under a manager's stewardship before my new tour begins. Did I tell you—no? I must have—I'm running the new women's professional squash tour. It's going to be first-class, let me tell you, the first tour of this quality for the gals. I've got dates set up already in Joburg and here in Munich—at the Olympiapark, beautiful world-class facility—and we're all but signed in Berlin, London, Paris, and Rome. You should see these girls play. I'm telling you, Robert, squash is going to be the next big sport. It'll be the biggest racket sport in the nineties, for certain. Tennis is on the decline—it's already a dead game. Sure, it's big here right now with Becker and Graf, but everywhere else: who cares? They never should have allowed the big rackets. Who wants to watch these weightlifters blast a-hundred-and-thirty-miles-an-hour aces for five sets? But squash is the same pure sport it always was, and big rackets will never make it in squash. Because it's a finesse game by design. And once people see what a natural spectator sport it really is—contrary to popular belief—it's going to take off. We just need to bring a few people in at the outset, and word of mouth will do the rest. These girls are appealing, too, and that doesn't hurt. I'm working on a deal with Fila to design sexy new outfits, revealing in an athletic sort of way, in exchange for free sponsorship. We're talking to SAT1 TV about coverage. Of course I won't be available to play on the Mattathias team next summer," he took a breath.

"We'll miss you. It's nice to have someone who knows how to win."

"Oh well, always glad to help out. But it's really not my sport. Listen, I'm sorry about that disruption at the last match."

"No, no..." Robert tried to hide his embarrassment.

"A minor financial misunderstanding. You know how bad my German is. And my business rests on oral agreements, of course. A little confusion regarding deadlines, and these Germans have the Gestapo out after you. In any case, it was all cleared up practically by the time we reached the station.... Still, it's a shame they couldn't have waited fifteen minutes, let me finish my match like in a civilized country. You'd never see that happen in England, I tell you. They allow one a little dignity there. I bet my opponent was pleased, anyway."

"Yes, he looked like a tortured kitten rescued from a sadistic little boy."

"Ten minutes and I could have finished him off like a gentleman. These Germans, I tell you. Goons with machine guns: nothing's changed."

They watched the pedestrian traffic, which had already thinned a bit.

"Well," said Robert.

"Yes, time to carry on. I bet you've got a party tonight."

"I do, but I'm not expecting much. Probably just stick it out till midnight, you know."

"Yes. New Year's Eve parties. What a bore."

"Would you care to join me? We could be bored together."

"Not for me, my friend. Too much work to do. Plenty of paperwork to take care of. I want to get the café lease settled by next week."

"I'll be looking for it."

"That's right. Tell all the boys."

"I will."

"Happy New Year, Robert."

"And to you, Dan. Watch that OJ elbow." Robert left him there, his spiel starting up again and then fading with distance, alone among the Germans with his oranges.

Robert walked by the shops, thoughts of *Handgelenkstützen* gone from his mind. He was glad Dan had turned down his invitation. His desire for warmth was gone, too—he needed some cold fresh air. It was too hot down here: didn't they realize everyone would be wearing heavy coats? He found the nearest exit and climbed to the street. He walked up Barerstrasse toward Schwabing, where the party would be. Véronique had said she would be there at nine.

The Christmas snow was completely driven from the streets and sidewalks by now, meticulously swept onto nonessential surfaces. Dirt from street, tires, and shoes swirled through it, transforming it into frozen muddy rivers running alongside the thoroughfares. He walked around the obelisk at Karolinenplatz; the spire too had shed its white sheath and was as clean as the sidewalk. Past the art museums and into Schwabing, where he found a café at which to have dinner.

Eight fifty-five found him at Schnorrstrasse, early as usual. He paced up and down the quiet residential street a few times, then crossed a busier street and walked the well-shoveled rectilinear pathways of the Old North Cemetery. He forced himself to wait until nine-fifteen, then strode purposefully back to Schnorrstrasse and up the steps of No. 15, a typical three-story stucco apartment house, two apartments to a floor. He followed the sounds of rock music and intertwined conversations to the second floor and pushed open the unlocked door.

The unpleasant shock of walking into a party of strangers was a feeling familiar to him since his high-school days. For several minutes he wandered the living room and kitchen, enduring the turning of heads, the blank smiles, the turning back of heads. He took a Spatenbräu from an ice bucket in the kitchen and maneuvered his way into the hallway, where he finally saw her, leaning against the wall in conversation with a couple in their forties, old for this crowd. He was struck by the length of her hair. It was only two weeks or so since he had seen her, but in that time it had crossed a border somewhere along her neck and, as if suddenly, had attained a new stage, in the way children one day suddenly become teenagers. It framed her ear so differently, he hadn't realized how pretty.... Any such wrongheaded impulse, however, was immediately squelched by the relief of finding a friend among the cacophony of strangers.

"Congratulations," she said as they descended the stairs a few hours later. "Thank you." They pushed open the heavy wooden door and leaned into the cold blast of air, stepped out onto the neatly manicured frozen sidewalk.

"Aren't you going to ask me why I congratulate you?"

"No," he said. "I assume it's for my haircut. I finally learned the Turkish word for stop."

"You would be better off cutting your own hair. I congratulated you for your self-control. The last party I was with you, you made a more lasting impression."

"Yes, well I try not to drink too much anymore. Dropping a Torah in Schul is more effective than a twelve-step program."

They walked down the near-silent street. The coldness was like amber, fixing everything in a motionless, permanent state. Only they moved, ants slowly tramping across the specimen.

"How was your holiday week, Robert?"

"What holiday? Lessons, lessons. I need a *Handgelenkstütze*."

"What?" She burst out laughing.

"A *Handgelenkstütze*. What's so funny? My wrist is killing me."

"I have no idea what you're talking about." She persisted in giggling. Just as well he hadn't made it to the store. He wanted to tell her about Lexa's visit, how he had finally ended it all, but somehow he couldn't get started. A reflexive protectiveness of his newfound freedom from complications, and fear of giving her the wrong idea, prevented him. "So how was your week, anyway?" he asked.

"Fine, fine. No school of course. I did work," she hesitated, "on an application. To a program in New York City, of all places."

"New York? You're kidding."

"No. A teacher of mine told me about this program at the New York University film school, intended specifically for people from other countries, from programs like mine. It would be exciting, but I would never go, even if they accepted me. I just filled out the application for the sake of it."

"You should do it. You'd love New York. Not all Americans are boorish tennis players, you know. There's quite a thriving intellectual life in New York."

"No, no, I could never leave my parents. It's different here, you don't understand."

"You've told me."

"But still you can't understand. I'm all they have left. They've lost enough in their lives."

They stood between the Alte and Neue Pinakotheks. Not a soul walked the streets. Not surprising, considering the deep freeze. "Ah, I suppose I'll just marry Max and bear many rich babies."

"I doubt it."

"I doubt it too."

It was the first time they had been alone together late at night since they had broken up. He had been dreading a moment like this. No, idiot, how can you even think that?

"I'll walk you home."

"No, you don't have to. It's only two blocks. And the neighborhood couldn't be safer."

"No, I really should. What would Max say?"

"He would insist on it. But I really don't want you to. Good night, Robert." She moved toward him and gave him a big hug in place of the old double-kiss. He hugged back, and they held it for several seconds. Then she half-ran the first few steps, waving back to him.

So much better this way. This was what he had really wanted from her. A real friendship. Of course, it was easy to say tonight, so nearly removed from the sinful Lexaweek and its cathartic conclusion. He walked south towards the Hauptbahnhof. The cold was absolute, merciless in its strength. Little promise of relief on Goethestrasse. Only refuge his own body underneath three layers of blankets. Enough, though, enough.

10

One January night, when the cold seemed like an ice age that had settled upon Munich for a thousand years, Robert returned to Goethestrasse. After a few afternoon lessons, he had prolonged his dinner as long as possible in order to minimize the time in his cold apartment before which he could submerge under his blankets. Racket bag slung over his shoulder, he slammed shut the front door, opened and shut his empty mailbox, and chose the staircase to keep his body warm a few minutes longer.

Voices stopped him between the third and fourth floors. Who could that be, in this dark icy cavern of an office building? He resumed his ascent, and the voices grew louder with each step. As he approached the sixth-floor landing, he recognized Herr Farakh's Turkish-accented German; but to whom could he be complaining so vociferously at this hour? He stepped lightly into the hallway, and indeed there was Farakh, in pajamas, robe, and furry slippers, a thick afghan pulled around his shoulders. Talking to him now, as congenially as could be, was none other than Max, dressed impeccably as always in one of his Italian double-breasted suits. "Herr Farakh, Herr Farakh," he was saying, "have pity on me. You know there's nothing I can do. This is supposed to be a place of business only, that's why you get such a good deal on the rent. If I were to ask the gas company to give you more heat at night, I would be in big trouble and you would be out on the street. Do you not have enough blankets?"

"Ja, ja, I have blankets. But an old man should not have to be so cold. You *should* be in big trouble to do this to such an old man."

"Herr Farakh, I thought I was doing you a favor letting you live here. I only wanted to help. What can I do if the gas company— Ah, Rob!" he switched to English. "My God, where have you been? Look at what you got me into."

"You're going to jail, slumlord," Robert said. "What can we do?" he said in German to Farakh. "It's a cold building."

"You're his friend! You're his friend!" Farakh shouted.

"Exactly," said Robert. "I'm his friend, and I have to freeze too. There's just no good heat here."

Farakh retreated to his apartment in a flurry of obviously unflattering Turkish. His door slammed. "I really should get you a telephone," said Max as Robert let them into his apartment. "It's like we're back in the shtetl, how I have to come to your apartment just to chat. So how's it going? Did you have a good vacation?"

"Some vacation. I've never worked so hard. Lillian is determined to hit a backhand over the net, Uschi has escalated to three lessons a week, and Bernd has committed himself to possessing the semblance of a serve by springtime."

"I see. Congratulations: you seem to be making a real name for yourself as a tennis trainer."

"Very funny. My students seem as dissatisfied as ever. I keep asking myself: Why do they keep coming back for more?"

"You're very modest, Rob," Max toyed with him. "And what about your erotic life?"

"You speak as though I'm your science experiment. Checking up on the mice again? How's *your* erotic life?"

"Not so bad." He threw himself and his thousand-dollar suit onto Robert's sofa like a frat boy in Bermuda shorts. "You know, it's cold in here. You live like a pauper." He pulled the blanket over him. "Ya, I tell you, Israel is a dangerous place for me. I'm always meeting one woman or another there—you know, some of those Israeli girls are quite sexy—I must say I find their post-military forward behavior and lean fashions somewhat refreshing—and of course they're all Jewish."

"And you were warm there, of course."

"Ya, quite hot and dry. Not unpleasant, though one wouldn't want to live there year round. You should have seen this woman I met at a Hanukkah party. Daughter of my parents' friends. We escaped the party, and she drove me to the beach at midnight. Quite a setting."

"Name?"

"Sasha. A minerals engineer. I tell you, you don't see women like that here. They learn judo in the army. Very provocative. She gave me a demonstration on the beach. Nearly broke my back. But come on Rob, you must have had some sort of romantic intrigue while I was gone."

"Well, you did miss the visit of one Alexandra."

"You're joking. I listen to tales of this goddess all these months, and then she comes while I'm gone. "

"Don't look so distraught."

"I can't help it. You can imagine the expectations I've developed, hearing about this woman of your dreams. And now I've missed her for the second time. I'm starting to think she may be one of your fictions. Next time give me some advance warning, and I'll arrange my travel plans accordingly."

"I'm afraid there won't be a next time."

"Ah, I'm sorry. Things didn't go so well."

"Things didn't go so well."

"She was on the bed and you were here on the sofa."

"No, we slept together."

"Ah, but you didn't..."

"Oh yes, we really *slept* together."

"So things didn't go so badly after all."

"It was paradise for a week, at least on the surface. Then everything fell apart when she was about to leave."

"She dropped the bomb."

"Well, in a sense. She asked me to come live with her in New York."

"So!" Max's face lit up with surprise. "Congratulations are in order. That's what you mean that she's not coming back to Munich. Neither are you."

"No no, I'm staying right here. I told her no."

"You told her no."

"Yes."

"You're telling me you told the girl of your dreams that you didn't want to live with her. All the time you've been here I've been listening to your lamentations for this woman, how she is the only one for you, et cetera et cetera, and now that you get the chance to have her, you turn it down."

Robert cleared his throat. "Changed my mind."

"I'm quite stunned." Max was lying flat on his back now, one leg folded knee up and the other on the floor, his head resting on one ear as he faced Robert. He did indeed look stunned, but also mischievously pleased. "So there must be someone else."

"No, no, it wasn't that."

"Our friend Véronique is back in the picture."

"Not at all. I mean, I've seen her, but nothing romantic. That's over for good. She invited me to a New Year's party."

"And?"

"And and. And nothing. Look, you pushed me into going out with her in the first place, I made a mess of the whole thing, I'm lucky she doesn't hate my guts, and I'm happy to still be friends with her. But there's nothing romantic or sexual between us. Sorry to disappoint."

"That reminds me, I must schedule more frequent French lessons with her. I'm going to Paris in March for a week or so. I'm hoping to cement a deal with one of the major French chains to sell our scarves. You like Paris?"

"Sure."

"You should come with me. I'd like to take you to my haircutter's. You'd like this place. On the Rue George Sinc, a very fashionable street. It's for men only, women aren't even allowed in the place. A chance to completely relax from the stresses of both work and home life. From the time you walk in, you wear nothing but one of their robes. You start with lunch, listen to music, maybe watch a soccer game. Then the girl comes to take you in for your massage. She rubs oil into your hair, massages your neck and shoulders: I tell you, these women are wizards. By the time she's done with you, you don't care if the barber shaves your entire body. But Francois gives you the finest of haircuts, I assure you. And the shave, and the skin lotions, of course. By the time you're all done, you've spent six or seven hours."

"All day inside, instead of strolling the streets of Paris."

"Ya. It's not cheap, either. Twelve hundred francs just for the haircut."

"Then there's lunch, the massage..."

"Ya, and occasionally one opts for the special massage."

"The special massage."

"Let's just say that she applies her technique to more than just the scalp and shoulders."

"And I've been going to Yckül the barber."

"I tell you Rob, there's something about a woman who is a professional at satisfying your sexual needs. If she is able to give you such pleasure, and you are able to pay her handsomely for it, what's wrong with that? What this girl can do with her hands, most women cannot achieve that effect with their sex."

Robert sighed. "It's like being friends with an Edwardian pornographic novelist." He was lying on the bed under the covers, still wearing his tennis warm-up suit, overcoat, and sneakers.

"By God, it's freezing in here," said Max. "Let's make a move, shall we? I'll invite you to dinner."

Robert had eaten at Sport Scheck, but any excuse to get back into a warm restaurant was welcome. And if they stayed out long enough, he'd have an excuse to sleep late and avoid writing. He took a quick bath— might have left Max shivering out on the sofa for hours if there'd been enough hot water —and they headed back down to the street.

"And Ingrid?" Max said, leading the witness as usual, once they were seated at Mövenpick. It was an enormous, gaudy, overpriced family restaurant, the sort at which Véronique and her friends would never be caught. Robert couldn't understand why Max went there. It certainly wasn't a high-class establishment, and the food was mediocre at best. It was a place his parents went.

"I think you should marry her," said Robert.

"I should." Max pronounced this, in his way, as a statement of fact that he was half surprised to hear. He seemed highly amused at the proposition. "You really think so."

"Why not? What more do you want in a woman? She's smart, good-looking, makes a lot of money, and is Jewish."

"Interesting." Max took a bite of pasta and weighed over the question as if tackling a good chess problem. "You're certainly right about the first two points. But the money is not a factor. I think I might manage to support a family on my own income. In fact, her career might be a disadvantage to me. I suppose it's old-fashioned of me, but I might prefer a wife who is interested in looking after our children."

"But you've always said you'll have servants to do that."

"Ya, to do the menial tasks: changing diapers, preparing food, et cetera. But don't you think it's important to have a real parent around?"

"Of course I do. I didn't realize you did."

"I do. It just can't be me. Imagine how much money my family would be losing if I took part of my day away from doing business and devoted it to child-raising. Don't be offended, but I think it's economically more feasible for you to be a modern father than it is for me."

"Well, Ingrid might be willing to stay at home for a few years. You never know."

"I don't think so. She's too good a business-woman; she enjoys it too much. What one needs is a woman who's smart enough to be interesting but who also is not tied to her own business."

"Your requirements get more restrictive every day."

"Ya, unfortunately. But you: you have the time to take care of the kids. You're the perfect mate for Ingrid."

"Come on," Robert worked on his sandwich. They both knew that they both knew about Robert and Ingrid, but neither would admit it. Now that it was over, it hardly seemed worth the effort.

Ingrid hadn't taken any tennis lessons during the holidays, and she didn't schedule any once January was under way either. Robert thought she must be angry, but she dropped him a line saying he should call her, and when he did she suggested dinner. No post-lesson shower together, no ferrying together back to his place before dinner. He bathed alone, shaved sitting in the bath, bristle-specked clouds of shaving cream floating around his knees like icebergs, and dressed quickly in the cold. Too late to walk, he jumped on the U-Bahn for the few stops up to Schwabing and the restaurant she'd suggested.

"So how is everything," she said cheerfully after he'd found her at her table and exchanged cheek kisses. "How are you managing all your women?"

"My women?"

"Well, I hear you're still seeing our Véronique, and there was the visit from your old flame. And then there was me for a while, wasn't there."

"I see you've been chatting with Max."

"What else is there to do with Max? He chats about everyone but himself. Try to get him to talk seriously about his own future, and what do you get?"

"A vague wave of the hand, a change of subject. I keep telling him to marry you, but there's always some excuse."

"Ha. Do me a favor, Mac, don't do me any favors, right? Can you see me married to Max? No, what that boy wants is a nursemaid of a wife, not a partner. He'll find one, too. When he's forty, he'll marry one of the twenty-year-old Jewish girls whose parents will push her at him. And where will I be?"

"Happily married, in contrast?"

"Perhaps. If not, so be it. I'm right at that line where one begins to consider that one will never have children. Another couple years, and I'm on the other side of the fence." She took her first bite of food. "I met an Israeli man in Paris last month."

"Really." Robert chewed cheerfully. Now that he and Ingrid were no longer erotically involved, he felt strangely paternal toward her. He wanted to see her happily paired off with someone who would take good care of her.

"Yes, he sells Uzis in Europe. Israeli machine guns, you know. I may go there for Pesach."

"Uzis? Good God."

"It's a business. When you're in business it really doesn't matter what you sell. You think Max cares about scarves?"

"This is what I've never understood."

"Business, it's business. It's just a game. You join in where you see an opportunity, try to get your numbers to add up higher than the other guy's. We can't all be great writers, great artists."

"Mmm. Anyway, you should know that I am *not* seeing Véronique, at least not in that way. And my 'old flame' is come and gone, for good. I am completely unencumbered. Who told you Véronique and I were back together, anyway? Oh, right. Never mind."

"Munich is a small town. The Jewish community is a small community. Watch yourself, my boy. You're not in New York anymore. Here, try one of these."

That was the last time he saw Ingrid alone. He would still occasionally dine with her and Max, when serendipity or a confluence in Max's date book brought them together, and once or twice she was playing doubles at Sport Scheck while he was teaching — filling in for someone on a Saturday morning was one of her few remaining connections to the Munich Jewish community. On these occasions, they would greet each other warmly, if only at a distance of two or three court-widths. But she no longer invited him to dinner, nor whisked him across town in her Mercedes; he certainly never again knew the illicit warmth, the sinful pleasures of her apartment. Their affair, it seemed, hadn't had the energy to last the winter.

His friendship with Véronique was the converse of that with Ingrid. He and Véronique remained friends, and managed to get together at least once a week, but their relations remained tense, tentative. He sensed that she had never really been able to forgive him for the way he had treated her. For his part, he wondered if it was such a good idea to see her so frequently; there was always the chance of opening up that gate once again, leading them down the same misleading path of lust. But he *wanted* to see her. He was growing comfortable with her presence even as the tension between them resisted lifting. And it was only with her that he really felt himself. In Max's presence he was always playing a part: the writer declining to reveal details of his magnum opus; the sophisticated playboy-philosopher, his host's counterpart, discussing the finer points of women, wine, and the meaning of life for the upper classes; the American Reform Jew at the Altmanns', defending an entire nation and movement to which he belonged only marginally. It was the same with the rest of his Munich acquaintances: since they could not fathom what he was doing there, and he could not stand talking about his true goals, he played the role of the devoted tennis professional, or of the young man at a crossroads in his career, about to make a move into a burgeoning and no doubt lucrative field. Even with Ingrid he wasn't quite comfortable; she understood that he was trying to be a writer, but that seemed to make sense to her only for a limited period of time. After six months, wasn't it time to actually *do* something? Only with Véronique could he be himself: comically dismissive of his tennis job, insecure regarding his tenuous future, contemptuous of their mutual acquaintances' tendresse for capital.

As winter wore on, and he began to sympathize with Ingrid's attitude towards him—what on earth *was* he doing here month after month?—he valued Véronique's friendship more and more. At times he even found himself thinking of her with a romantic nostalgia for the time of their more intimate relationship. But then he would catch himself. That's where it all went wrong. Sex was what was all wrong between you. You confused lust with Platonic sympathy, and nearly made a fine woman hate you. Do it again, and you really are the grade-A schmuck she thought you were.

Véronique, for her part, betrayed no romantic feeling for him, if in fact she felt any. She seemed finally to have put her anger behind her and accepted him as a friend—a friend she should never have gone to bed with. Yet there was still the tension—even if she had been able to forgive him and herself, there was still the fact of their unwarranted copulations, a history that stood between them as an embarrassment and a still-open wound.

One night she joined him and Max for a movie at the English-language theater on Türkenstrasse. Afterwards they got a drink across the street. The movie was *Prizzi's Honor*, with Jack Nicholson's already normally slurred speech swallowed by a Brooklyn Italian accent. Robert had never before seen the erudite polyglot Max flummoxed by language problems. Max seemed exasperated. "I mean, what on earth were they saying? I couldn't make out a word."

"I have to say, I was without a clue myself," said Véronique. "Kathleen Turner was no problem, but everyone else was speaking some other language."

"Now you know," Robert said to Max, "how I feel when your family starts throwing Yiddish into their German."

"I've been to New York," said Max, "and I never had a problem understanding people."

"I suppose you stayed pretty clear of the Mafia."

"Ya, though I was arrested several times by the police when I drove up to Boston."

"Pulled over."

"Ah, then you know what I mean! Unbelievable. He asks me if I know how fast I was going. As if I were driving dangerously or something. I was only doing maybe 220 kilometers. Of course, I replied only in German, as if I didn't understand."

"You deserved to be arrested," said Véronique. "You shouldn't drive that fast even here."

"Here they wouldn't even notice. One of them, near Boston, kept saying, 'Get outta the cah,' 'Get outta the cah.' But at least I could understand him, though I pretended I didn't. Not like in this movie."

"I had a friend," said Robert, "a woman who had just moved to Boston. Her phone rang, and when she picked it up, a man said to her, 'I got a hat on.' 'I'm sorry?' she said. 'I got a hat on.' So she hung up. Then it rang again. 'I got a hat on, baby.' She didn't figure it out until long after she'd hung up." Max and Véronique looked at him, waiting for the punch line. "It doesn't matter. Anyway, it's refreshing for a change to be the only one who's able to pick up the nuances of conversation."

"Listen," said Max. "You know about the tennis meeting tomorrow, right?"

"What?"

"The tennis meeting. All the boys are meeting at Bruno's bar at eight o'clock. If you don't know, then perhaps I was the one who was supposed to tell you."

"Oh come on Max, I don't have to go to that."

"You're expected. You're our trainer!" He reached out, a toothy grin on his face, and patted Robert on the back, a little too heartily. "It's not far from you. I'd pick you up, but it wouldn't look good. They already think we're too intimate for the team's good. Ya, like I beat Emil because I'm friends with you. Anyway, I may be a few minutes late. I have a business appointment."

"Ah, meaning we'll see you for the final round of coffee. I have to sit through that crap while you have a pleasant dinner somewhere."

"I suppose you could find some similar reason to miss it..."

"No, no, I'll go. I'm an irresponsible enough coach as it is."

"Listen, I'll cheer you up with some other news. We're going to Buenos Aires."

"We?"

"Ya, well I'm going to pay a long overdue visit to my cousins, and you should come with me."

"You have a cousin in Argentina?"

"The daughter of my father's cousin. He took his wife to South America after the war, they were still quite young, had no children for twenty years, and then suddenly Ana. He died a few years ago, and I believe the mother has remarried. The daughter, though, Ana, is a fashion model. Already quite successful at twenty-one."

"A twenty-one-year-old fashion model," Véronique spoke to Robert. "You should go. I'm sure there will be fascinating company."

"I don't know, Max, it doesn't sound like my sort of scene."

"What do you mean? You need a vacation, some warm weather to break up the Munich winter. I've already bought your ticket."

"What? It's refundable, right?"

"Ya, it's refundable. Listen, we leave in ten days. You should come. Think about it."

"I'll think about it."

"Sounds like a wonderful intellectual journey," said Véronique.

"Very good," said Max. "And, speaking of intellectual destinations, Véronique, you and I should discuss Paris."

"Paris? What on earth are you talking about?"

"I mean that I have some very important meetings coming up in Paris, and we need to accelerate my French lessons."

"He's meeting with his hairdresser," said Robert.

"He's going to Paris for a haircut?"

"And other personal services."

"So why not mix a business trip with pleasure?" said Max. "You should come with me, Véronique. As my translator and assistant. It's good to get out of Munich in the winter. My prospective clients have already promised me the best tickets to the opera while I'm there."

"I didn't realize you were such a music appreciator," said Véronique.

"I'm not. Still, it's what one does. I was in the third row for Pavarotti's last concert here in Munich. It's something to hear him from such close range. My ears were vibrating. I tell you, the man has the most enormous organ."

Robert cleared his nose of beer. "Now, you see," he told Véronique, "that's the sort of thing you need to help him avoid in French. Or he'll be buying more than scarves."

Véronique was still laughing. "I'm always afraid I'll do something like that in a subtitle," she said at last.

"So, my friends," Max said. He seemed not to have noticed his gaffe, scanning the café as though he had arranged to meet someone there. "The night is young. Shall we make a move?"

A couple of hours later Robert and Véronique walked up her street, Arctic trekkers through a late-night glacial wilderness. They couldn't all fit in Max's car, so he had left Robert to walk her home.

"So, are you going to the Rue Georges Sinc with him?" asked Robert.

"I don't know. He only just told me about it. You know, he tried to get me to come to Israel with him, so he wouldn't miss any French lessons. I found it easy to say no then."

"But this is Paris."

"Yes, Paris."

"And how is the Marquis progressing with his studies?"

"Quite well. The Marquis des Écharpes is supremely confident, and that is half the battle in conversation. Most people let their mistakes freeze them up, but not Max. It's remarkable how he manages to convey the same strong personality in a different language."

"Are you going to go to Paris with him?"

"I don't know. Should I?"

"I don't know. Should I go to Buenos Aires with him?"

"Well, it's different with you. Why not? A free trip halfway around the world."

"Yeah, a free trip."

"And summertime there. You look like you need some sun, Robert."

"I suppose a tennis pro should follow the good weather, like a surfer chasing the perfect wave."

"Sure. Why not have a good time? But in my case, I'm afraid the Marquis might expect more than French lessons. On the other hand, why should I be so suspicious? I deserve a good time, too. And it might be fun to see Paris from a different point of view."

He contorted his face like Nicholson the Mafioso. "Do I come running along like a boy toy? Do I stay and freeze to death on Guddastrassee? Which wunna dese things?"

"That's right, Mr. Cherney," she laughed. "Which wunna dese things?"

The next evening at 8:15, after a nearly hour-long walk west from Goethestrasse to the Laim neighborhood, where he'd never been before, Robert entered Bruno's bar, *42nd Street*. It suggested nothing so little as Times Square. It was a typical German pub, with long wooden tables, dim lighting, and empty glass liter *Steins* all over waiting to be refilled. Bruno,

Uschi, Saul, and Emil were already huddled over a table, typically deep in debate.

"Hey, my good friend," Bruno said in English as Robert approached. They all welcomed him. Bruno stood up and insisted Robert take his place. He put his arm around him. Bruno was a different man here. No longer the outsider infringing on the tennis club of the wealthy—this was his bar, his business, his castle. He looked into Robert's eyes with a friendly sensitivity Robert had never noticed. "What are you drinking, my friend? Weissbier? Of course." He left to fetch it.

"The Committee is considering giving us the money to build our own courts," Uschi jumped right back to business as usual.

"My God, Uschi," Saul was flabbergasted. "How many years will they have to disappoint you before it sinks in? They'll approve our tennis courts as soon as they get around to building a sauna bathhouse at Schul."

Uschi drew on his cigarette, nodding his head gravely. He had the look of an espionage officer who had just been pulled off the biggest case of the Cold War. Robert knew this was not the first time they had discussed the new courts, nor the fiftieth.

"Believe me," said Saul, "we're at Sport Scheck for the rest of our playing lives."

"Could be worse," said Robert. "As public courts go, it's quite nice. Better than anything in the States."

"We need our own courts," said Uschi quietly. "I'm tired of being bumped off the court by those people. And you know they come a few minutes early when it's us playing."

"Listen, don't be paranoid," Emil burst in. "You've got enough problems. Yes, they do hate us, but you're still paranoid. Ha ha!"

"Motherfuckers," said Bruno, using the English word with relish as he placed an oversized beer before Robert. "I tell you, some of those German tennis fairies I'd really like to meet in the alley behind my bar sometime. They think they're members of Iphitos instead of just public-court hackers."

"Okay, boys," said Saul, "let's move on to more pressing issues."

"Like kicking Altmann off the team for being late to so many meetings?" Robert offered.

Emil laughed. "You don't kick a dog for having spots."

"No, I disagree," said Uschi. "No one likes Max more than I, but there's no reason he can't be on time for meetings. It's disrespectful."

"He's a child," sighed Saul, "a child. There's nothing to be done with him. We must take him as he is. And of course, no one has done more for the team, vis-à-vis the Committee, as Max. Why do you think they're even considering our new courts? But listen, let's stick to the issues. We have to decide whether to move up to the first *Kreiseklasse*."

"Absolutely," said Uschi. "I say absolutely."

"It costs more," warned Emil. "Will the Committee approve the higher fee?"

"Uh, excuse me," said Robert. "I don't want to be a spoiler, but wasn't our record in the second *Kreiseklasse* one and twelve? I thought you have to be in the top two of your division to move up."

"Yes," said Saul, "but in Kreiseklasse One you're allowed to have one professional play for you. In the *Bundesliga* it can even be a touring pro. I hear Stich is going to play for Iphitos next year. In our case, you could play number one for us. And if so they would probably allow us to jump leagues despite our record. After all, having a first-rate player at number one, and everyone else playing down one spot, makes an enormous difference."

"I see. But I hate to tell you, my shoulder is in no shape to be playing matches."

"Nonsense. You'll be fine by the summer. You've been resting it for months."

"We could also perhaps hire some other American player," said Uschi quietly, "just to play the matches. Keep Rob, of course, as trainer."

"Yes," said Saul, "but in that case we should pay Rob extra to play, if he plays."

"The Committee, gentlemen, the Committee," Emil interjected. "We don't even know if they'll approve the higher entry fee."

The claustrophobia rose in Robert's chest. He had thought he was over it, aside from the occasional aftershock on the U-Bahn, during a slight delay between stations. Now the beast had struck right here in an open, albeit "cozy," bar. Would it find a way into his apartment? Then what? He envisioned himself walking the streets all night to avoid the encroaching walls of his room. He could subdue his panic now only by concentrating on his beer, on the drops of condensation sliding down the glass like rain on a window. Suddenly the thought of coaching these guys through another summer season, which he had gradually come to accept as his short-term destiny, felt like an emetic. How long could he prolong the masquerade? How long pretend to himself to be a writer-in-exile sustaining himself temporarily as a tennis instructor? How long pose as Nabokov in Berlin, with no totalitarian regime back home to keep him away and no inspiration to lead him onward? It was absurd and sickening. At some point he would have to accept the fact that he was simply a tennis pro, and not a very good one at that. The ridiculous episodes he had to endure as coach of the Mattathias team were not a comical backdrop to the real drama of his morning literary work: they were the main action. They were *his life*.

"Well, look who's here," shouted Emil, and Max appeared at the table. "Guten Abend, Jungs," he smiled and pulled up a chair next to Robert. "Sorry to be late. Business, you know." He shrugged his shoulders and held up his palms.

"Yes, we know what kind of business you have in the evenings," said Bruno with a lascivious grin.

"Now, now. One of my Italian buyers is in town, and I had to take him to dinner."

"Yes, yes, of course," said Saul. "Now, Max, we were discussing the possibility of moving up to the first *Kreiseklasse*."

The debate resumed, with an apparently endless source of energy yet never a higher level of argument or any approach to resolution. Max threw in his two cents, and more, but of course took neither side. It seemed to Robert that he was caught in a painting, or an endless loop of film, and that he might never leave this bar or this conversation. The old feeling returned: he saw himself sitting at a rustic table in a Munich bar, with a vociferous group of drinking friends. But who was that young man, turning his head to each speaker in feigned interest but seemingly apart from the flow of debate, in that scene of long ago? Twice Max jolted him back into the present, slapping a hand onto his back and holding it there for a minute before turning towards him conspiratorially and murmuring, "Buenos Aires." Robert ignored him the first time, but finally he nodded and without moving his gaze from his mug of beer, he murmured himself, "Si, si, *esa mala costumbre, that bad habit, Buenos Aires*...." Was that the Borges line? Yes, why not? Might as well make one more bad habit before you start breaking them.

11

They flew all night, extending the darkness by four hours and falling nearly ninety degrees of latitude from winter into summer. Robert felt like a high-class whore letting Max fly him around the world like this, but on the other hand he wouldn't have wanted to make that flight in coach. Free bourbon had eased him into sleep, a condition he normally found difficult to attain on airplanes, and the wide plush first-class seat kept him in that state for at least a few of the fourteen hours from Frankfurt to Buenos Aires. The comfort and service and the elegant dress of his fellow bourgeoisie—even he had worn his jacket and tie in order to minimize the contrast between himself and his companion—gave him a taste of what air travel must have been like before capitalism had brought it to the masses. Even so, an airplane seat was no bed, and as they stood hangjawed around the baggage carousel at Ezeiza airport, they felt like they'd spent the night roped and tied and under interrogation. Even Max, for once, had lost his patina of expensive grooming and easy living. He was unshaven, his Italian suit was crumpled like a used Kleenex, his hair was in bad need of a visit to the Rue George Sinc. It was eight in the morning and Max was awake, and that would have been bad enough in Munich, without the eighteen hours of travel.

While they waited for their bags, Robert found a men's room and leaned over a urinal, resting his forehead against the wall. When he returned, Max was looking much refreshed. Robert saw him from a distance talking to a young blonde woman in a short black skirt and black leather jacket. The wrinkles were gone from Max's face, the curtain of fatigue miraculously lifted from his eyes. Unbelievable: this guy never lets up. We haven't even left the airport and he's making moves.

"Rob, there you are. Let me introduce Helena. Fourteen hours on the same airplane and we didn't meet her."

"Well, we cannot all be sleeping like baby up in first class," said Helena. "I am thinking they will arrest me if I try to use the toilet up there." As usual, he's picked the best of the lot. I'd no idea our plane held such a sexy woman. Leave it to Max.

"Helena is Czech, Rob. Living in Berlin. She's an actress." He sounded as if he were introducing an old friend.

"So what are you doing in Argentina," asked Robert.

"I love travel. Any chance I get I am in an airplane going somewhere. Lufthansa is offering special youth rate to Buenos Aires, so I am immediately jumping on it."

"Are you visiting anyone?"

"No, no, I know no one. I am just traveling. Some days in Buenos Aires, then perhaps over to Uruguay, up to Brazil. I would kill someone to be naked on a beach. Ach, the Berlin winter is full of pain. Hey, there is my luggage."

Robert jumped a few steps ahead and retrieved her duffel bag, brought it back to where they were standing. Helena stayed with them while they waited for theirs.

"So how are you getting in to the city," she asked. "There must be some public transport."

Robert was about to explain about the bus line he had read about in the guidebook, but Max cut in, "We're taking a cab. Would you like a ride?"

"You're so nice! I accept."

They stuck together through customs, and outside, in the warm sunshine, they climbed into an old black-and-yellow Volkswagen taxi. A half an hour later, they were in the downtown area, crawling in traffic between great concrete monoliths that reminded Robert of Manhattan.

"So where can we drop you?" Max asked Helena.

"Oh, I don't know. You can just go to your hotel. I am finding my way from there."

"But you must have had some idea of where you were going to go," said Robert.

"Oh, I always find some place. There must be a youth hostel or something. I am only so tired. I would kill someone for a chance to lie down and sleep."

"Look," said Max. "We can't just leave you on the street. It's difficult to look for a place to stay when you haven't slept all night. Why don't you be our guest for the morning while we all try to get some sleep? You can look for a hotel in the afternoon."

"Ach! Du bist so süss! You boys are so sweet. I really should not accept, but I am so tired that I accept! It's a deal!" They pulled up in front of the Jockey Club, and a uniformed valet opened their door. "Mein Gott," said Helena, "you boys really know how to do it."

The desk clerk looked at them suspiciously, particularly so at Helena, who, though a normal enough student or artsy type on the street, looked like a cheap prostitute in the cavernous ornate lobby where everyone dressed like the millionaires they were. Max and Robert were ragged, but Max's suit showed its cost even in wrinkles, and Robert got the benefit of the doubt.

In the room they realized why the clerk had given them such looks. The room was large and elegant; the bathroom was the size of a good hotel room itself, with copper plated faucets and bathtub; but there was only one bed. King-sized, but alone.

"What is this?" said Max.

"Perhaps I shouldn't have intruded," said Helena as she collapsed onto the easy chair in the corner.

Max picked up the telephone and spoke Spanish with an Italian accent for some time. "Ya, unbelievable," he said when he got off. "They thought I was with my wife, and now there are no rooms with two beds. Perhaps we should look elsewhere."

"I don't care," said Robert. "It's a big enough bed, and I'm exhausted."

There was an uncomfortable pause, before Helena said, "Don't worry about me. You won't even know that I am in there with you."

"A pity," said Max. Robert frowned at him.

"Ha ha," said Helena, "Ich glaube *du* bist der Schauspieler."

"So," said Max, "it's settled. We stay."

"I would absolutely *kill* someone for a shower," said Helena and disappeared into the bathroom. Robert began to unpack, and Max flopped onto the bed in his full suit and tie as if in his pajamas. "So you see," he said, his hands behind his head, "this is how it happens."

"Yes, but who chats up strangers at the baggage claim? Especially after an all-night flight."

"Who chatted up whom? She came up to me and asked if this was the right luggage station. I simply continued the conversation. How can you even avoid such interactions?"

"Easy. I don't believe I've ever conversed with a fellow passenger for more than a minute."

"That I don't understand. It's half the fun of traveling."

"Well, for me half the fun of this trip is going to be jumping into that bed right now and sleeping." Robert removed his shoes and dress pants and closed the curtains on the window just as the bathroom door opened letting out a cloud of steam like a stage set for *Die Walküre* and Helena still fully dressed. Embarrassed, Robert rushed to the bed and slid under the covers.

"I'm having the hot water on completely for a time to let the room full up with the smoke," said Helena, pulling off her shoes. "It will be fantastic." In the dim light they watched her remove and fold her clothes item by item until she stood up completely naked and walked back into the bathroom.

"No wonder you're a travel enthusiast," said Robert.

"It's not always this easy, but as I say things do tend to happen. Shall we join her?"

"We?"

"Ya, well, I would say she just invited us to a steam bath party."

Robert was honest with himself: he very much wanted to see Helena in the steam bath. He also very much did not want to see Max in the steam bath. The thought of sharing a small shower with Max *and* Helena was enough to overcome his concupiscence. "You go ahead," he said.

"Well, if you like." Max rose and began to undress. "I must say, she turns out to have quite a body, doesn't she?" Naked, he walked to the bathroom door and turned the handle. He looked back at Robert, stunned. "It's locked." He knocked on the door. No answer. They could hear her humming in the shower. "What the hell..." He tried the door again, knocked again, waited, and finally came back and got into bed. "Can you believe this?" he said, sounding strangely amused. "This is a funny girl."

Robert couldn't sleep. Plane rides always made him horny, so did hotel rooms, so did celibate periods like the past month, and then it didn't help having a beautiful naked woman in the shower. Max, on the other hand, was snoring on the other side of the boat-sized bed within minutes. The shower water eventually stopped and Helena emerged wrapped in a towel. Robert didn't make a sound. She dried her hair with a second towel, then dropped both of them on a chair. She pulled the end of the covers out from under the edge of the mattress and crawled under the sheets up to the pillow, situating herself in the center between them.

Max woke like a bear roused by the smell of camp food and turned to face her. He's got to be kidding—I'm right here. From the other side of the bed, rustlings and whispers ensued. "Schauspieler," she giggled once or twice. In hushed German tones, she was explaining to Max why it was impossible for her to allow his advances. Robert could make out only the general tone of the debate. Her argument, he felt, couldn't help but be compromised by the fact that she was butt naked. In conclusion, she turned onto her other side. It was a strategy whose wisdom Robert doubted. Sure enough, within seconds she was inching closer and closer to Robert as if prodded with a stick. Finally, she turned back away from Robert, with no more than an inch between them. He couldn't slide away to give her more room without betraying the fact that he had been awake witnessing the little *pas de deux* under the sheets.

Max apparently gave up—the jabs and ripostes, verbal and physical, grew less frequent and faded away—and heavy breathing ensued from the far end. I should turn around. There's not much room, but just enough to turn my back to her and try to get some sleep. He didn't move. Now and then a coincidence of heavy inhalation on her part and exhalation on his would bring his thinly clothed erection in contact with her backside, still warm from her steam bath. He found himself timing his breathing to maximize such friction. You're nothing but a dumb animal. Intelligence, civilization, manners, philosophy, what are they all when your cock comes up against an ass? You're just another dog humping a leg, a toad sloshing around in the mud. Stop degrading yourself, turn around, get some sleep or you're going to ruin your entire week.

But the respiration-sex continued, and gradually it became clear that Helena was not asleep, that she was in fact doing her bit to maximize the counter directional motion of their parts. Slowly, though, slowly enough to maintain utter silence beneath the three rhythms of breath. It took a long time, so long that at times he thought he had been asleep, even though the motion continued uninterrupted, like a delicate silk piston apparatus. Then he slipped through the fly and felt a new rush of warmth and friction against her skin. He tried to push between her thighs, desperate to cross the threshold of sensation, but she firmly closed them and worked him back up against her buttocks. Finally she took his hand and filled it with her breast, which he squeezed gratefully, and they both sped up their rubbing just a bit and at last he arrived, flooding the safe cavity between his belly and the small of her back. They both remained silent and became motionless, his hand still on her breast. Within seconds, it seemed, they were asleep.

He woke from a void black as death, revived by the pristine click of a hotel door closing. The room was empty. Who cares what's going on, he thought, and dropped back into the abyss, only to be yanked back up seemingly seconds later by the same door click. Max was there, alone, dressed in what looked vaguely like the suit he had worn on the plane. It was as if the plane had crashed and he had survived and hiked for days through the bush to get to the hotel. He straggled to the bed and flopped onto it. "Can you *believe* this girl?" he grinned at Robert. "Okay, I don't mind being played the fool and used for a place to sleep. But then she insists I walk her to the lobby, find her a cab, and even give her cab fare. I mean, it's unbelievable." He began to laugh into the pillow. "My God, I am fatigued."

"What time is it?"

"Dinner time. About eight, I think."

"Shit," Robert sat up and rubbed his forehead. "We've got to get up or our schedule's going to be all off." He stumbled into the bathroom and had a little steam bath of his own, standing under the hot spray washing off the lingering exhaustion from the trip and the embarrassing memory of his late-morning encounter in bed. What the hell was he doing? He felt like a high-schooler after a prom-night grapple with a last-minute date. He thought of Véronique and winced. What do I care what she would think?

"We missed Ana for the night, apparently," said Max, hanging up the phone as Robert emerged from the bathroom. "Her mother was quite pleased to hear from me, though. I tell you, they're going to try to marry me off. I'm going to have to be careful in Buenos Aires."

"Just show up with Helena."

"Ya, that would do it. The great actress."

They got dressed and walked up Corrientes past the theatres and bookshops looking for a place to eat. At every corner, buses came hurtling down the narrow cross streets, beat-up jalopies spewing black smoke and barely slowing down for the pedestrians who strolled, oblivious, across their paths. The noise, smoke, and general commotion overwhelmed the senses; this was like New York City on speed. They reached the Avenido 9 de Julio, modeled after Paris's Champs Elysses but even bigger—the widest boulevard in the world. Every restaurant seemed to have the same menu in its window, so they picked one and found a table by a window overlooking the boulevard. The prices were astronomical—Robert felt like a Wisconsin tourist stumbling into a Times Square steakhouse—but Max didn't seem to care, so Robert went ahead and had a ten-dollar Manhattan and ordered a steak. When it came, he had to explain to the waiter that he hadn't realized just how rare *jugoso* meant, and the waiter, with no more than a haughty glance, took the raw slab back to the kitchen to have it ruined for the gringo.

It was too late for the theaters after dinner, so after Max tried calling Ana one more time they began to meander along the streets. They visited one café after another, too wide awake to go back to the hotel. At two in the morning the streets felt like early evening; the Porteños were showing no sign of heading home. Robert and Max found themselves on the Avenida de Mayo, another major boulevard, which led down to the Casa Rosada, the elegant government building from whose balcony Evita had galvanized the people. They stopped in at the Café Tortoni, which Robert had read was once a meeting place for the city's literary heroes and intellectuals. It had apparently been renovated, though. It looked more like a fancy tourist trap—which it probably was—than a dive where artists could afford to eat. They had a drink there nevertheless. Robert caught sight of a room in the back with pool tables, and he urged Max to play. "Not the sort of thing I normally do," said Max, puzzled at the invitation, but he acquiesced. Robert inquired about how one went about getting balls to play, but the waiter seemed amused and just smiled. They took their drinks back to the room, where a teenaged couple occupied one of the four tables, and Robert asked them how one might play. They too seemed amused, but the boy told him that you have to pay the waiter. Confused, Robert walked back into the dining room and found another waiter, who pointed out yet another waiter. This man finally accepted some cash in exchange for a cue ball, and the tourists were in business.

Max played pool with utter apathy. Robert would knock in a few balls before missing, then Max would take a swipe at the cue ball hardly even taking time to take aim, talking the whole time, and then relinquish the turn again to his friend.

"Quite an episode with this Helena," he said.

"Quite," Robert sent a slow cue ball, with underspin, all the way across the table, where it ever so gently nudged the two ball away from the bumper's felt and into the corner pocket. It was a shot he made once out of twenty tries, but he acted nonchalant.

Max didn't notice the shot at all. "I tell you, I don't get it. What was she doing getting naked and coming to bed like that?"

"Maybe she's a nudist. Your turn."

Max bent for a second, gave the cue ball a solid thwack with his cue, sending it ricocheting back and forth against two side bumpers. The closest candidate for a target was the six ball, to which the cue ball's iterative motion brought it closer and closer without ever touching. "You'll be meeting a very different sort of woman once we manage to hook up with my cousins. You know, they can be very stylish in Buenos Aires, I hear."

They got back to the Jockey Club around six in the morning and slept most of the day again. By the time they emerged, a low sun was threading sienna rays between the buildings, and it was time to plan the evening. They caught a quick snack and managed to get tickets to the ballet at the Teatro Colon, a majestic old theater that rivaled any in the world. Robert was mesmerized by the program, which featured one act of a nineteenth-century Russian ballet by Glazunov followed by the contemporary *Porteña Suite*, a sort of *Rhapsody in Blue* for Buenos Aires. But he could sense Max's wandering attention; at times he seemed to be looking everywhere but at the stage, as if he could possibly sight friends or acquaintances in a theater audience seven thousand miles from home.

"Not much of a ballet enthusiast, are you?" Robert said as they walked in search of a restaurant.

"Ya, I understand that it's supposed to be a great art form—or even that it *is* a great art form— but it simply does not *move* me the way a great book does. The same goes for the theater. I can never really believe that the characters in a play are real and not just actors. A great novel, though, becomes absolutely real in my mind."

"But you go to plays and ballets all the time."

"Ya, I suppose one should support the arts. And of course it's a social activity."

"You don't go to many movies, though, do you?"

Max shrugged. "The movies. It's not really the same sort of...atmosphere, is it?" Robert smiled. It was true: Max was as out of place in his designer suits at the Türkenstrasse cinema as Robert was at Shabbas dinner at the Altmanns'. "Now, where shall we eat?"

The inverted schedule they were on proved hard to break. They woke in the late afternoon, barely had time to catch a play or concert after showering, dressing, and eating; then they were wide awake until dawn, at which point they slunk back to the hotel to sleep away the better part of the day. One night after dinner they determined to play tennis; after all, they had dragged their rackets all the way down there, and it appeared that if they waited to play in sunlight it would be in vain. They arrived at the Palermo Lawn Tennis Club around eleven. This may have been a reasonable hour for dinner or dancing, but it was unusual for tennis even in Buenos Aires. Still, the club was open—there was a restaurant and bar for members—even if the courts were all dark. The fact that it was a private club, which would have dissuaded Robert from even entering the gates, did not throw so much as a sliver of doubt into Max's resolve. After all, he was related to the Weinribs, who were members. They were supposed to have met Señor Weinrib, Ana's stepfather, for a doubles game, but of course they were never able to wake up in time. Why shouldn't they be allowed to play now, even if Señor Weinrib was not there? The courts were empty. No no, Señor, for one thing guests may play only in the company of a member; for another the lights can not be turned on after eleven at night, by local ordinance— this is a residential neighborhood, after all. It is really impossible. Well, I'm sure no one will mind if a few minor rules are bent a bit late at night, when no one is around to be bothered. After all, my cousin Señor Weinrib *would* be here with us, if only we could have managed to get here at the same time. Here, let us pay our guest fees, plus a little extra surcharge considering the late hour.... Oh, and by the way, I forgot to pack proper tennis shoes and socks. Could you sell me some—and some balls, of course—from the pro shop?

They walked onto the red clay of Court One in the dark; the six mercury-vapor lights were just lit and would take five or ten minutes to reach full strength. They started to hit in what felt like twilight: only the yellow balls and white lines were visible, along with the tape of the net cord and the clothes of the other man. It was close to midnight before they could start playing for real, and they played for a couple of hours, in full view of those diners in the restaurant with window seats.

Inspired by the pristine court, the excitement he had felt since childhood when playing under lights, and the presence of spectators, however otherwise engaged, Robert played like his old self and beat Max three sets in a row, giving up only a few games. He was hardly aware of his friend on the other side of the net. There was only the cool night air rustling through the hair on his arms, the clay giving way to his sneakered slides, the familiar inertia of the ball against the force of his muscles. So often these days he couldn't stand to be on a tennis court: a hot sun beating on him made his limbs as heavy as sandbags, or, when forced to play or teach in cold weather, four or five aches would erupt in various joints and he could barely rouse himself to lumber after balls just a few feet away from him. But occasionally, as now, his body would feel right again, and the good feeling of hitting tennis balls, the satisfaction of the practiced rhythm and motion, would return. It was just such a revisitation of form that he waited for in vain at his writing table. But there it never came, because composition required more than form, more than muscle memory. It required inspiration, and inspiration came from talent, and talent required more than intelligence and skill and practice. What a joy it was to play tennis! One didn't have to think; one merely relied on instinct and let one's body free to follow its memories back to thousands of happy days spent in the mindless pursuit of knocking tennis balls across a net. But even as he thrilled in the act he was pursuing on this earthen court on an Argentine summer night, his heart sank at the thought of that other, mental, incapability, that frustration in the little room across the world. The pang didn't ruin his mood, however; it served as a stimulant to his palate, sweetening the effect of this familiar yet otherworldly corporeal thrill.

Ana had wanted to meet them for lunch, but Max convinced her to have dinner instead. They rolled out of bed, shaved, showered, and caught a cab to Recolleto just in time to pick her up in the palatial apartment she shared with her parents not far from the famous Recolleto cemetery. Max and Robert were met by Señor and Señora Weinrib, who greeted Max like a prince come home from the wars. Robert they regarded with some puzzlement: they seemed mildly bewildered at his clothes—how could a good friend of Max's wear such a cheap suit—and not certain what he was doing there at all. It was obvious, at least to Robert, that to the Weinribs Max's visit was intended to end in a state of betrothal. Why, then, had he brought along this ill-clad American sidekick? Young people these days…. Still, they treated Robert with some friendliness, however distanced. After all, he was a Jew, albeit a poor one, and apparently quite a tennis player.

"I hear you boys broke into the club," boomed Señor in English. Max and Robert had started speaking in Spanish but were immediately answered in English. Max didn't like this—he was used to his friends around the world admiringly accepting him as a colingual—and for a few minutes he persisted in his florid Spanish, but eventually he gave in like any tourist and complied in English. He probably guessed it was due to the presence of Robert. And at least he could show off his Oxbridge accent and erudite vocabulary.

"Ya, it was rather amusing. I tell you, you'd think we were asking to go horseback riding on their courts, the way the fellow looked when I asked for a court."

"At midnight! Ha ha, I love it. You boys are true Porteños. You out-Porteño the Porteños, in fact. And then you try to play without being with a member! And you manage it. That's some feat. You don't just walk into the PLTC and ask for a court."

"I don't see why not. The courts were empty, and after all I'm related to a member."

"Because of the rules, my friend. The rules!"

"You sound like a German," laughed Max.

"Not me. I'm as Polish as your parents. But *they're*"—he gestured out the window—"the ones who sound like Germans, and that's not just a joke," he winked. "They're not so crazy about their Jewish members, if you ask me. That makes it twice as much of a coup that you got yourselves in. Anyway, I love it. The barbarians are at the gates! Ha ha!"

"For God's sake, Leon," said Señora Weinrib, "you haven't even offered them a drink, and already you're talking about the tennis club. What would you like, boys? Some good Argentinian wine? Whiskey?"

"Tea would be nice," said Max. "With sugar."

The whiskey had sounded good to Robert. He didn't relish the thought of playing the third wheel for the rest of the evening, much less the rest of the trip. Might as well get buzzed if he was going to survive as an inconsequential witness to the Weinribs' courting of Max. "Yes, tea is fine, thank you," he said.

"Did you see Sabatini at the club?" foghorned Weinrib. "She practices there sometimes. No, I guess at midnight you didn't see her. Vilas too. They say he's going to start playing on the seniors' tour. Say, why don't I set up a doubles match for next week? You two boys against me and Vilas! No, don't worry how I'll manage it. I'll make it worth his while, believe me. How much dough can he have if he's dragging his old bones out on that seniors' circuit?"

"Max," Señora Weinrib spoke in a gentle liltingly accented English as if purposely to cleanse the air of her husband's boorish tones. "Tell me about your parents. It's been so long since I've seen them."

"They're very well, thank you. They send their love, of course."

Leon couldn't help himself: "Is your father raking in as much as they say? I don't blame him for staying in Munich! Who could have predicted it? Of course, we left as soon as we could—Leah with her first husband, me with what was left of my family. Who wants to live in the same country with those *paskudnyaks*? On the other hand, if I'd known how much gelt there was to be squeezed out of the *mamzers*, maybe I'd have stayed. Not that I've done so poorly here, as you can see."

"For God's sake, Leon, do stop talking," Leah Weinrib said to him quietly in Spanish.

"Max," she continued, "I think your Bar Mitzvah was the last occasion we saw you." But at that moment Ana appeared in the sitting room. She did not go long unnoticed. Her mother cut off the conversation and stood, as did the others. "Darling," she went to her daughter and put one hand on each shoulder, taking her in with obvious pleasure, "Max and, uh, Robert are here." Simultaneously Leon was crowing, "Well here she is at last. What have you been doing up there, plastic surgery?"

They had known she was a model, but Robert was not quite prepared for the visual onslaught of a fashion model in the flesh. Ana was tall, of course, about six feet in her high heels. Her black hair was fashioned into an impossibly perfect trapezoid around her shoulders. She wore a shiny silver cocktail dress which her body had stretched taut as a tent. She looked like a Christo landscape sculpture. She was beautiful by any contemporary standard, but Robert felt oppressed by her person. Her head was too big, her lips too full, her body seemed twice as expansive as it was. He had no doubt that she was a black belt in Tae Kwon Do.

Max, on the other hand, appeared to feel no such apprehensions. After all, Robert figured, Max's head was too big also. Ana was just his sort of woman: physically extreme, led by money and breeding towards overconfidence, socially trained, appreciative of a fine Italian suit. And he was eating her up. Chatting about music, theater, Argentine wines, evaluating Buenos Aires in comparison to European capitals (similar quality in architecture and theater, lacking somewhat in restaurants; Oh you simply haven't been to the right ones, she told him, we'll have to correct that), tending conversationally to the parents at just the right moments—Your daughter seems to have strong opinions about Europeans. You're telling me! (from Leon) Strong opinions: there's an understatement!—working the hour like a master of ceremonies, telling all the right jokes, massaging the egos of each person present (even Robert: he managed to squeeze in a succinct but complete retelling of their one-sided tennis match at Palermo, with obvious pleasure at his friend's skill), leaving everyone feeling like social adepts.

"Well, you certainly have seduced my parents," said Ana in the cab.

"Very interesting couple," said Max, trying out his Spanish again.

"My mother's a darling," Ana stuck to English, "but my stepfather is an ass."

"What was your father like?"

310

"The opposite. Sophisticated, intelligent, urbane. Tactful. He would have hated my being a model as much as Leon loves it. He gets to come to functions with my mother and rub against all those fake breasts."

"But your mother is in favor of your profession..."

"My mother is seduced by the glamour of it. Yes, love her as I do, I must admit that she is too impressed by skin-deep beauty. I suppose because she had it once, and I have it now."

"So why do you work in a profession you loathe? You could be in university."

"I make a lot of money, Max. Why do you do what you do? If my father were alive I *would* be in university. But he's not, and I'm not. Modeling is just what I do. Look, I have a good time too. It's not all so bad. In fact, tonight there's a party you two should come to. Inko has rented out the Colonial Theatre for one of his bashes."

"Inko?" Robert made his first sally into the conversation.

"The designer. Don't you know him? He's just as big in Paris as here. Oh, well. Believe me, if he weren't already world famous as a designer, he would be famous for his parties. It's invitation only, of course, but you can get in with me."

"Will we have time for dinner?" asked Robert.

Ana laughed. "It's not even ten! The party begins officially at midnight, but no one will show up before one. We have to eat very slowly."

Three hours later, there was a small crowd outside the Colonial. It wasn't clear whether the people were trying to get in or just enjoying glimpses of the beautiful people who entered. Ana strode through them, Max and Robert in tow, and kissed the bouncer, who looked like a gay professional wrestler, on both cheeks. He waved the three of them in without so much as glancing into the men's faces. They were simply Ana's entourage.

The lobby appeared as it might during intermission at the opera. Except that in place of the overweight bankers indulging their wives' social calendar, the white-haired philanthropists who had to show up once in a while, and the poorly dressed music students who actually loved the opera, were what might have been the cast of a Hollywood portrayal of a South Beach nightclub. Everyone was beautiful and dressed as if for impossible hedonism. Robert and Max stood out like accountants in their conservative suits. They *should* have been at the opera. Not that Max seemed to notice or mind in the least.

Ana was immediately busy sweeping her lips past a swarming ganglion of powdered cheeks, exchanging overzealous greetings. Max seemed half drawn in to the scene and even merited a few introductions. Robert, a step behind, a yard or so further removed from the center of activity, was just outside its gravitational field. A free radical, to be generous. In the corner of his eye, against a far wall, he sighted what appeared to be an open bar, and he headed off purposefully in that direction.

The bartender, a heavyset man about Robert's age, with long thin sideburns and slicked-back dark hair, was talking with several guests at one end of the bar. Robert took a standing position near the center of the bar and waited. He tried to make eye contact, but the conversation must have been highly entertaining, for the laughs never ceased and the bartender's attention never wavered. Then it did: he moved away from them and fixed a new round of drinks, brought it back and reentered the conversation, never once glancing up at Robert. How does one go about getting a bartender's attention? What is the protocol practiced by saloon denizens, the sort that never get stuck in this position, leaning on the bar trying to look unhurried, pretending to be waiting for drinks already ordered while at the same time desperately seeking to alert someone to the fact of their existence? Does one shout out "Bartender!" like a leader of men or a party guy? Wave one hand nonchalantly, the blasé barfly confident of receiving his beverage in due time? Call out your order? Sit or stand? How to distinguish yourself from the other bar patrons already enjoying their drinks? How to distinguish yourself from the air?

This situation, though, was different for Robert from the countless other times he had been shipwrecked at a bar. Here he actually *was* unhurried, in fact needed to kill time, and wasn't even particularly thirsty. And standing at the bar gave him a chance to survey the scene without appearing to be a wallflower.

The atmosphere was beginning to sizzle like a buttered frying pan. A critical mass of hipness, beauty, and flesh seemed to be accumulating, the music was growing louder, and a tangible electric buzz was flowing through the crowd. Ana and Max were lost from view.

The bartender suddenly came up to Robert, as though the latter had only just arrived at the bar. Robert ordered in Spanish, and to his surprise, the bartender answered in kind. Things were looking up.

He took his Manhattan and ventured bravely away from the bar. Saw someone disappear up a staircase and followed. The balcony was almost as crowded as the main floor. Robert walked along the side until he found an empty space by the railing and perched there. He had a perfect view of the main floor, packed now with the pulchritudinous throng, and the stage, where a line of chorus girls was forming. The lights suddenly went out, stage lights came up, Abba's "Dancing Queen" came blasting out of the speakers, and the performers began kicking up the most licentious disco moves he'd ever seen. After a few minutes, a woman came up next to him and assumed a monumentally bored pose against the rail. A few peripheral glances assured him that an actual fashion model had planted herself next to him. Things were looking up indeed.

"Quite a floor show," he shouted in Spanish over the din.

"I suppose you haven't been to Inko's parties before," she shouted back in English.

"No, as a matter of fact."

"It's always the same."

"Why do you come, then?"

"What else is there to do?"

"Tell me something: why does everyone speak English to me here? I thought my Spanish was pretty good. The bartender was the only one who would speak to me in Spanish, and our conversation didn't go much beyond bourbon brand names."

"You're American, eh?"

"Yes."

"Well, I can't speak for anyone else. Your Spanish seems fine. I just prefer to speak Spanish only with Argentinians. Even other Latin Americans botch the language, you know?"

This was impressive snobbery. Talk about stylish: where was Max? Here was a girl for him. How disgusted Véronique would be. With this entire evening. He felt embarrassed suddenly, as though she were watching him.

"Inko hire these dancers?" he asked.

She shook her head. "A bunch of his models arranged it, as a surprise for him."

"Well, they sure can dance." She made no reply. At the climax of the song, all ten dancing girls in synch whipped off their dresses to reveal ten well-buffed male bodies wearing only black jockstraps. Robert watched in stunned silence.

"I would have preferred real women for a change," his companion sighed.

"So what's the occasion for this party, anyway," he tried to recover from his naiveté.

"Occasion?" She finished her drink and tossed the plastic cup onto an ash receptacle. "It's Tuesday. Ciao ciao." And she disappeared into the balcony crowd.

The next afternoon at five, Robert and Max stood on a noisy, dirty street corner waiting for a bus. Robert had roused his friend out of bed a half-hour earlier—it had felt like dawn—and dragged him outside. The party had thinned out around four or five a.m., but as Weinrib had said, they out-Porteñoed the Porteños; they had dropped Ana off at home and squandered the rest of their wakefulness at an all-night restaurant. Today, after the night's indulgence in the fashion world's extravagant debauchery, Robert was determined to see some *real* Buenos Aires. They were going to La Boca, the old port section, and they were going to get there by public transportation.

"My God," mumbled Max, squinting at the sun, still high in the western sky, "this is highly uncivilized. It's one thing to pull me out of bed like that, but at least we could take a cab."

"This is precisely forty times cheaper than a cab. That's good business sense, right?"

"Ya, but the whole point of being in business is so one doesn't have to live like this. There's a time to be price-savvy and a time to spend."

Robert wore jeans, a t-shirt, and sneakers, and he had convinced Max to leave his jacket and tie behind. He wore slacks, a dress shirt open at the collar, and loafers. The air on Avenida Eduardo Madero, the main thoroughfare running along the harbor, was warm, and the constant exhaust fumes of cars and the procession of buses made it warmer.

Finally, a battered old vehicle that looked like an American school bus painted blue, with the number 42 in front, came barreling down the road. Robert waved at it, and the driver reluctantly swerved over a half block past them. They ran to the door and climbed on. They paid their fifty centavos, the bus lurched back into the lane, and they swayed and stumbled rearward and found two seats near the back. As the bus bumped and slalomed down the street, Robert smiled at the sight of Max looking like Louis XVI in the custody of the proletariat.

A wizened old passenger in the front seat got up and made his way back to them, a disarming grin seeping through his overgrown gray beard. He held out two small pieces of paper and slurred a sentence that neither Robert nor Max could decipher. "No, gracias," said Robert. Max fixed him with his most ingratiating smile, compadre to compadre. The man didn't leave, just held out the papers again and repeated his mumble. "No, gracias," Robert repeated, and looked away. Max sighed and took out his wallet, bursting with bills. He pulled one out and handed it to the man, nodding with an encouraging smile. The man just shook his head in disgust and dropped the papers at their feet, walked back up to his seat, and said something to the driver that made him laugh.

Robert picked up the papers and looked at them. "Ah, *boletos*, he was saying," he told Max. "We were supposed to take these from that machine up there." Max looked so discomfited that Robert added, "It's all part of traveling. Learning the local customs."

"Ya, there are other local customs I would prefer to be assimilating."

She should be here instead. She wouldn't be so dismissive, would appreciate the experience. Someone you could ride a city bus with, see a city or countryside on foot, sleep in a tent. Also probably would have understood about the *boletos*.

Robert watched the cross-street signs assiduously, waved madly at the driver at the appropriate moment, and they jumped off the bus. Following Robert's map, they found their way to an open square surrounded by a gaudy mosaic of brightly colored wooden buildings. Primary colors along with oranges, aquas, and greens assaulted their senses. Artists sat by easels, offering their works for sale. A smattering of tourists made the rounds. Robert felt suddenly depressed. So this was La Boca. In trying to escape from Max's travel world of exclusive clubs and expensive delights, he had succeeded only in exchanging them for tourist tchachkas.

Max seemed oblivious to Robert's disappointment and to the surroundings. He had regained his composure, as evidenced by the return of his Brownian-motion saunter, and he maintained a constant chatter as they put in an obligatory circumambulation of the square.

"So what do you think of Ana?"

"Very fine. Hard to believe she's your cousin. Actually, it's hard to believe she's anyone's cousin."

"I know. One never knows where one will find the best chicken, right?"

"Uh, right. So, can Señor and Señora Weinrib begin their wedding plans?"

"Ya..." one hand left a pocket to cantilever palm-up as though checking for rain, "one could do worse."

"One could do worse," Robert agreed.

"We don't need to review her attractions, which are obvious. Am I right? But certain questions do arise, even if things were to progress to a point where I might be inclined to pursue the issue. One: would she be amenable to moving to Munich?"

"But you're dying to get out of Munich."

"Someday, someday. But who knows when that will be feasible. In the meantime, my business is in Munich, my parents are in Munich. Two: would she be amenable to giving up a high-profile career to settle down and raise children?"

"No."

"I'm not so sure. Modeling I don't think exerts too much of a pull on her. The settling down and raising children part is another matter. Three: is she perhaps too young right now to provide the right sort of companionship, to assume the role vis-à-vis the business, entertaining and so on. I think perhaps in a few years I could imagine some sort of understanding arising between us...."

"Four: would she want to marry you?"

"But what about you, Rob? Perhaps you're the one who should step in and save the day. Her father loves tennis."

"Stepfather. And she hates him. No, I think your cousin is a bit out of my league. I was treading deep water at that party last night."

"Ya, that was something, wasn't it? Not your usual fare back home, or in Munich."

She would have been disgusted, he couldn't help but keep thinking. Keep feeling like I let her down. Ridiculous. Come back with her someday, ride decrepit railroads, stay in old Patagonian motels, see the gauchos. Even more ridiculous. A couple more days and it's back to frigid Munich, back to the icebox apartment, back to the barren table in the middle of the room. How much longer can you take it? When do you give up? What were those lines I underlined in the Piglia book? "In Buenos Aires, aleph of the native land, by some inconsiderate privilege of the port city, young writers are young even after having crossed

the infernal wilderness of their thirty-third birthday."
Should settle here, maybe. No: that quote outdated.
Even back home, now, thirty-three is adolescence.
Used to be middle age; now if you publish before
thirty you're a *wunderkind*. But see, that's the trap. You
used to be able to quit in time to begin a new career.
Now, by the time you grow out of your youthful
artistic "phase," you're ready for Social Security.

"Look, Rob, I'm glad to see you're amusing
yourself. What's so funny? But shall we make a move?
I think it's time for a good steak. And I see some
taxis over there." A line of cabs had formed near the
water, ready to take the tourists back to their hotels.
Behind them, a flotilla of ancient, rotting ships floated,
stern to hull and side to side. They seemed to have
been left there to decompose. Robert walked over
to them, leaned against the railing and looked onto
the abandoned decks, rocking slightly in the breeze.
Fishing boats, tug boats, tankers from another age. He
turned at the call of a voice, and saw Max already
inside the cab, beckoning through the open door.
Rare meat.

12

Munich was still frozen in time, March's icy armor unchallenged. Two days back and one couldn't imagine that it was really summertime in Buenos Aires. The sidewalks of Goethestrasse had been reduced to thin wavering passages between banks of dirty snow. Robert walked these paths like a gulag worker, his racket bag weighing on his shoulder like a sack of shovels and ice picks. His clientele was down to a core group of five. He had ceased to solicit new students, and he had even been surprised to find himself turning down some requests, on the grounds that he had no time.

Time, however, was all he had. Mornings he spent hopelessly at his desk, like a man who gets fired from his job after thirty years but shows up at work every day anyway, as though force of habit could deny his destiny. He no longer had a real hope of producing anything of worth, but if he didn't put in his three hours every morning, then who was he? Certainly not a tennis pro. What was he doing in Munich, if not being a writer?

One thing he was doing was sitting in his window watching the street life. It was from that perch one late morning—late enough to have left his desk with at least the pretense of a morning's work behind him—that he observed Max's black Porsche perform its familiar curlicue from Bayerstrasse to Goethestrasse and into a vaguely parked position in front of #10. Max leaped out of the car, his wool overcoat, tie, suit jacket all flapping about in the cold interstice between warm car and building.

A minute later the familiar Italian-loafer shuffle down the hallway. "Hello, Rob," in a rising pitch as he pushed open the door, which Robert had left ajar.

"Hola, señor."

"Back to work, I see. Very good."

"Mmm."

"Writing down all our adventures in South America? I think there's a story in there."

"Well, as your official biographer, it's important that I document everything."

"Very good." Max flopped himself onto the sofa. "So it's back to life in cold Munich. How are your lessons?"

"No one's complaining. Yet."

"No one complaining is good. Soon it will be time to get the team going, you know. The season begins next month."

Robert said nothing. The thought of getting back on the court with that group of warring neurotics was an appropriately caustic tonic to cap his wasted morning.

"I saw Emil and Bruno last night, and they're very eager to get started."

"They're speaking to each other?"

"The best of friends. The approach of a fresh season has them chirping like lovebirds. And speaking of love, I'm off to the City of Love. See you in ten days."

"Paris?"

"Paris. I'm meeting with the big boys from one of the major French chains."

"So you told me. You were going to take me for a haircut."

"Ah, that's right. I forgot. So, you should come with us."

"Us?"

"Véronique and me. She's coming as my French-language consultant. Not that I really need it, for the sort of business conversations I'm having. If I say so myself, I've done quite all right in Paris in the past. But I figured she deserved a perq for being my French tutor. Perq?"

Robert nodded. "I wonder if she realizes just how much of a perq she's getting. Have you discussed sleeping arrangements?"

"Naturally. As you know, our Véronique is not exactly inclined towards, how shall I say, free love? So I have assured her that it will be a perfectly platonic arrangement. Separate rooms, of course. All she has to do is accompany me to my meetings as my assistant and speak some eloquent French to my prospective partners. In return she gets a free trip to Paris, some unparalleled French meals courtesy of Altmann Apparel, and even some new French clothes. Her current Bohemian wardrobe would not quite work at these business meetings."

"How could she refuse?"

"She couldn't. And neither can you. Why don't you come along? You look like you need a haircut."

"I think I'll pass on Paris, however. Thank you. I'd like to get some work done before the summer hits."

"As you wish. We can always do Paris some other time."

Buenos Aires was still too near in his memory, and Robert felt he needed some time alone in Munich, to try to figure out just what he was doing. Paris would have been fun, but he had had enough freeloading decadence for a while. On the other hand—why this sudden pang?—Max had been just a tad too quick to accept his refusal. Normally he would have put in an admirable effort to persuade Robert to join him. It had to be Véronique. So she had caved in. Max had been avoiding being set up with her for years, but Robert was sure that he had been developing a thing for her of late. And why not? She wasn't the same person she had been for years. It was more than that her hair had grown in just enough to give her face the framing it deserved. A layer of hardness had been stripped off, a veneer of anger and impenetrability, revealing a woman who was still smart and tough, who had not completely jettisoned her sadness and regret of the past, but who was somehow brighter, more chipper, and undeniably more attractive.

Véronique urged him to come. "It will be more fun with the three of us," she said as they sipped coffee at the Filmmuseum café. It was an unusually warm evening for late March, early harbinger of spring, and they sat outside for the first time in months, warming their hands against their coffee mugs.

"It *would* be fun. But I've just had my fun in Buenos Aires, and I feel I have to try to get some work done. If I just go from one jaunt to another with Max, I may turn into a gigolo."

"Yes," she sighed. "I suppose I am just his tart to go on this trip. Not that I would sleep with him— God forbid—but let's face it, he has no need of me to be there. But what the hell, I want to have some fun for a change. When I'm in Paris I stay in the youth hostel. For once I want to see what it's like on the Rue Georges Sinc."

"I don't blame you. But you should heed this bit of advice: Don't let him talk to strangers at the airport."

The conversation shifted, the evening ended, as they tended to now, with a double-cheek buss and ever more affectionate hug, he didn't see her for a few days, and then one morning as he tried to summon an original phrase to describe a certain feeling upon waking in the morning that had no doubt been adequately delineated by some five hundred other writers, he realized that Max and Véronique must be in Paris.

It struck him how his entire social life depended on these two friends. Through them he saw a number of other people, but there was no one else in Munich he would call up for dinner or who would stop by to see what he was doing. For a week he tried to work in the mornings, gave the occasional lesson (less and less frequent) in the afternoon, and in the evenings sought dinner, sometimes a movie, or perhaps just a long walk.

One morning he quit "working" early, around eleven. The emptiness of his mind's production room was one thing. That he had gotten used to. But the long hours afterward, from lunch through the evening, with no one to talk to, were becoming unbearable. No Max to meet for lunch, to drag him along on his afternoon ramblings through the city, to arrange dinner and social events. No Véronique to call and meet for coffee and movies. He had fooled himself into thinking that he merely put up with Max's imperious commandeering of his hours, but in fact he had come to depend on it. And Véronique. *How strange that I should miss her now, after having pushed her away. Would I miss her if I were engaged with other friends? Probably not. After all, hardly thought of her in Buenos Aires. No, not true. But I didn't* miss *her. No time.*

The vacuity of his prospective afternoon was too much for him this day. He could weather the waves of frustration in his chest, so long as the quitting bell brought some relief in the form of his friends. But solitary fruitless work followed by solitary leisure was too much. He grabbed a book and headed out to get a cup of coffee.

In the café on Türkenstrasse, he sat by the window and opened his book. He had long since had to rescind his self-imposed ban on books. He could no more give up reading than he could eating. He'd found an old paperback copy of *Glory* and was rereading it. Each time it offered up new morsels of brilliance. He'd never even conquer this book as a reader, let alone as a writer. Setting his sights too high, of course. No need to outhit Ted Williams in order to justify a career in baseball. Still, it could be discouraging.

Martin saw through the window what he had seen as a child—a necklace of lights, far away, among dark hills. Someone seemed to put them from one hand into the other, and pocket them. Must remember that, so that I won't use it. How will I ever be able to describe in a unique manner a town seen at night from a train, now that I've read this? It's as if this is the only way to say it, as if Nabokov's words are now the proprietary caption of the scene, its scientific classification. I'll be writing a scene taking place on a train, and when I imagine the train passing a town in the night I'll automatically describe it in these terms, as naturally as saying, *the sky was blue, the clouds were white*. I'll have no idea that I've appropriated the metaphor. In fact, almost no one would recognize it, unless they happened to have just read *Glory*. My novel could be published, full of such stolen phrases, my agent, publisher, and editors oblivious to the crime, until one reviewer, literary denizen at some small paper in Idaho, raises his eyebrow at a particular formulation of words pertaining to a certain stretch of sky. Plagiarizer! he cries, and sets out to unearth the countless other misdemeanors in my meager text. Within weeks I'm the laughingstock of the literary community.

You wish! For one thing, the odds of your manuscript getting written, multiplied by the odds of it ever being published, are so infinitesimal that you might as well steal every word from your canon of favorite writers. It will never make a difference. Secondly, you must admit that whenever you arrive at such a junction in your compositional journey, and are in need of such a natural description, the well is bone dry. None of those domineering passages from Vladimir and his ilk come to mind at all, much less any original offerings.

That very morning he had wanted to recreate the feeling of early springtime, when the trees have just begun to bud. The damn phenomenon was happening right outside his window. All he could summon, though, were pat clichés involving the renewal of life and the direction in which a young man's fancy turns. Even if he had wanted to borrow them, the intellectual properties of Nabokov, Hemingway, Woolf, even Updike and Roth, were lost in the caverns of his memory.

No, it was only when reading such brilliant phrasings, or for a few minutes afterwards, that the danger of misappropriating them lurked. Just as it was only then that he could be deluded into believing he might compose similar original notations himself. A sentence from Nabokov would suggest a sentence he himself would create the next morning, and he would momentarily be elated, before realizing that this beauty, supposedly to spring from his mind at an undisclosed moment in the future, like Athena from Zeus, was not in fact his own offspring but merely that of Nabokov, a slight variation on the very sentence he had just read. The elation was an artificially induced high, and lasted barely longer than the ingestion of the lexical drug.

With a painful gasp he recognized that he was no better than the fools who remarked offhandedly to him that they were thinking of writing a novel, whenever they got the time. Like them, he had been deluded by the apparent simplicity of good writing into thinking that he could accomplish it himself. Reading great writers made him *feel* like a writer, in the same way that, when he was a kid, watching Rod Laver and Ken Rosewall had made him feel he could play tennis just like them. The difference was that it was fun to go out on the court after watching Wimbledon and pretend he was Laver or Rosewall, whereas pretending to be Hemingway or Nabokov was both pointless and torturous.

Masquerader. So disorienting that I should turn out in the end to be a phony. How could I have known? Certainly felt like the real thing, for years. Just a bit callow yet, wanting some years and experience. But there comes a point, whether at the toll booth of thirty, or while crossing Piglia's infernal wilderness, when you have to stop and admit that you just don't have what it takes.

He wasn't untalented. That was the whole problem. He was good enough to write better than most people, even better than most people who want to be writers. But that wasn't enough. In order for the endeavor to be worthwhile, you had to have the real gift: not just the calling, but also the ability and the inspiration to produce work that *must* be read.

His gift, however, was a pale simulacrum of that, a backhanded offering at best. If it had had a Giver, Robert would have blasphemed Him for eternity. But no, this insufficient endowment was merely a random amalgam of chromosomes evolved from molecules originating a billion light-years out in the cosmos. What insignificance was his frustration, his tortured soul!

No, you didn't need to be Williams or DiMaggio, but what was the point if you didn't even have major-league stuff? If only he'd lived through some extraordinary times, perhaps his limited skill might be enough. For even if you didn't have Joyce's pen, the talent for absorbing experiences might set you apart, so that even if you related them in a merely competent manner, you made your mark. But Germany in the 1980s had proved the wrong place. Berlin in the 1920s had been a goldmine for Isherwood, but today's West Germany seemed not much different from Westchester. Of course, if you had the gift you could make literature from any material. But Robert needed something of historical proportions.

He suddenly remembered something and reached into his jacket pocket, where he always kept a notebook. Back in his parents' basement, he had a stack of these 6 1/8 x 3 3/4-inch ruled memo books in a secure box: his journals of the past decade. Now he rifled through the worn pages of this one, looking for a quotation he had copied many months ago. There it was, from *Joe Gould's Secret*, by Joseph Mitchell.

> ....*reminded me of a novel I had once intended to write. I had thought of this novel for over a year. Whenever I had nothing else to do, I would automatically start writing it in my mind.... For several years I frequently daydreamed about it, and in those daydreams I had finished writing it and it had been published and I could see it. I could see its title page. I could see its binding, which was green with gold lettering. Those recollections filled me with almost unbearable embarrassment....*

Robert's face flushed, reading these incriminating words here in a public café. He couldn't even be original in his misery. Mitchell had never written his novel and had eventually disappeared into his *New Yorker* office, sunken in terminal writer's block, until he died.

But at least he had written several great books. For *Joe Gould* alone his life's work had been worthwhile. What accomplishments would Robert have in which to find solace, when his novel had vanished into the mist of murdered years? For surely his Newtonian opus, his *Calculus of Several Lives,* was destined to come no closer to fruition than Joe Mitchell's *Bildungsroman.* He acknowledged this for the first time. He was never going to write it.

It was like a Joycean epiphany. He knew what needed to be done. It was as though he emerged from years of dense fog into a clearing where his destiny was so sharply visible that its obviousness stunned him. Whereas Joyce's epiphanies drew him to his desk to compose coruscating gems of prose, Robert's did the opposite. He was not a writer! He didn't have to do this. Didn't have to spend his mornings in squalid isolation, his afternoons in rambling ambulatory worry about whether he was wasting his life. He could give up the mantle, throw off these chains and become a normal person. Get a real job, one that didn't involve exhorting people to bend their knees and watch the ball.

He turned back to *Glory*. It was enough to be a reader. In fact, it was more glorious, more valuable, to be merely a reader. Better to spend one's time appreciating the great novels that have been written, numerous enough already to fill one's entire reading life, than to waste time struggling to put out one more mediocre one.

He read a couple pages with fervid joy, almost as if he'd written them himself. He felt suddenly free. He left the café and walked up Türkenstrasse. The decision to write no more detonated a chain reaction of liberating revelations. If he wasn't a writer, he wouldn't have to teach tennis anymore. He was going to get a job he could excel at and for which he would be properly recompensed for his abilities. How long had his parents preached the religion of law school? He had fought against that destiny like the last defender of Rome holding up the city walls. What for? Had he really been so blinded by common puerile resistance to parental advice that he had been unable properly to evaluate the option? Now it seemed so innocuous, even salutary. He had had it all backwards. It was artistic ambition that was the debilitating force, the dismal fate that had threatened to usurp his life. Life as a lawyer was the rewarding one, the choice that would allow him to excel, to take advantage of his natural talents and not torture him by demanding a gift he did not sufficiently possess. There was no shame in performing a task well for handsome compensation.

He unconsciously paced a maze of side streets until he found himself entering the English Garden from a new vantage point, halfway up its western border. In a few minutes he stood on the bank of a large lake. From off beyond the trees, he could hear the faint roar of the highway. He would leave Munich. Return home and begin a new life. Munich, which had at first been such an exotic escape—he'd had visions of Weimar cafés, himself an Isherwoodian figure at a corner table—had turned into a bourgeois flytrap. He might as well be in Scarsdale. Tennis, Chinese food, movies. And where was the art, the gradually thickening sheaf of prose-splattered paper, the talented coterie of expats, the sense of living in a momentous moment, a Zeitgeist for his generation? The experiment was a failure, and it was time to clean out the lab and go home.

He wouldn't miss much. Not the Spartan room with the efficiency stove, the brown corduroy sofa, and the makeshift desk. Not his students or team members, with their pathetic quest to master a game of rackets and balls. Not even Max, maddening jester, Prince Hal of the Mattathians—but Robert was no Falstaff!—would exert any pull on him. Max had been a good friend—aside from wining and dining and generally showing him a good time, he had done his best to rescue Robert from the artist's fate even while enjoying his proximity to a supposed creative spirit—but would fade easily enough into the *Munich* compartment of Robert's past. He doubted they would keep in touch. There would be a series of overseas calls from east to west, and letters in the other direction, but they would gradually die out over the months and years. Before long Max would outgrow this youthful phase of indulgence in the world of semi-impoverished yearning and settle into the gilded circle of wealthy middle age. He would glide in a milieu of self-satisfied moneyed businesspeople and would barely remember that he had ever had anything to do with failing writers and perpetual students.

And Véronique? Would pale, dark-haired Véronique ever creep into his consciousness as he labored over court briefs on late winter afternoons? An unexpected tightness settled on his gut as he considered the prospect of never seeing her again. Well, you make friends throughout your life, and sometimes you have to move on. You think Hemingway worried about missing friends as he moved from Paris to Key West to Cuba to Idaho? (No, you're through with those comparisons, remember?) She should come with me. She really needs to get out of Munich, as she's always saying. New York would suit her. What are you saying? If you'd wanted her, you could have had her. But you didn't. Let her be. The last thing she needs is you stringing her along.

A clean, well lighted break.

A few days later, he returned from Sport Scheck to Goethestrasse to find Max in conversation on the sidewalk with a man from the Turkish bank. They were both gesticulating wildly, with forced grins on their faces to show their good humor.

"Hello Rob! I'm sorry, Mr. Ahmeti, but I have an important meeting with Mr. Cherney here." Mr. Ahmeti glanced at Robert. Though they'd never spoken, he was used to seeing the unkempt American coming and going. Probably had a suspicion that he was a friend of Altmann's and paid no rent.

"We'll discuss this later, Mr. Ahmeti," Max led Robert quickly into the elevator. "So, my friend."

"Bonjour. How was the Rue Georges Sinc?"

"Very nice, actually. You should have come."

"You're probably right."

"Yes, I think it's safe to say that Véronique enjoyed herself too. Listen, why don't you come over for dinner tonight, and I'll tell you all about it?"

Robert was tempted to say Yes, and I have some news of my own to tell you about. But no, it was too soon. His decision to quit his impersonation of an artist was still too fresh to share. He didn't want to see the satisfaction in Max's eyes as he told him how he was going to join him in the pursuit of income. Instead, he took a quick bath while Max lounged on the couch, he put on his tie and sport jacket, and he accompanied his friend out to Bogenhausen.

"*Gottenu*, Max," Frau Altmann greeted them as they entered the foyer, "Kurt Freier has been waiting for you since two o'clock." It was now after six.

"Our Austrian connection," Max explained as they rushed down the hallway, Robert beginning to wonder about dinner. "He's going to sell millions of our scarves in Vienna alone."

Max burst into the living room, dragging Robert behind him in his jet stream. A man in his mid-thirties, wearing jeans, black boots, a jacket and tie, and a fashionable five-day beard, rose from the sofa.

"Kurt, Kurt," called Max in English as he strode across the Oriental rug, arm outstretched, "where have you been?"

"I was going to ask you," Kurt responded.

"I was working on our deal. I've secured the first hundred thousand scarves for you."

"I thought that was already settled last month."

"Ya, you know there are sometimes last-minute details... Have you met the novelist Robert Cherney?"

"No..." Kurt was obviously impressed, but also apparently used to being impressed by Max. Robert shook his hand with a meek smile. He no longer bothered protesting Max's claims for him.

Frau Altmann bustled in, holding open Max's coat, which he had tossed onto a chair in the foyer. "Bist shpet zum Schul. Kom."

Max allowed her to help him into his coat without hardly noticing. "So, Kurt, I must go to Friday night services. Why don't you relax here, the cook will bring you in some good food, you have the television and the phone, and I'll be back in an hour."

"I drove all the way up here this morning," Kurt protested. "I really need to get back. My wife expects me..."

"What's the hurry? At this point, the children will already be asleep before you can get there. Please feel free to call them from here for as long as you like. You can sleep in the guest room. You shouldn't drive that far at night anyway. You must let me make up for my tardiness with some hospitality. That way we can discuss things in a leisurely manner, when I get back from Schul."

Kurt shrugged. This was obviously not his first experience with the Way of Max. There was little point in arguing.

"Rob, why don't you walk me to Schul? We can catch up on our news."

Robert was hungry, but he had given up hope of a timely dinner long ago. "Sure," he sighed.

"We'll be back in an hour, then," Max announced again to Kurt. "You'll be glad you stayed. I have some very good news about the Pereglini scarves." He and Robert exited the living room. In the foyer Robert put his jacket back on, and Max grabbed his fedora from a hat rack.

"You shouldn't have keep him waiting," his mother appeared from the kitchen. "He has wife and children waiting for him, something you don't understand." She mock-frowned at him.

"It's all right. I'll make it up to him. He'll leave happy in the morning."

"'Back in an hour.'" She frowned. "You are lucky to get out of there in three hours."

"I'll explain when I get home. Don't worry." He grabbed her and gave her an excessive kiss on the cheek.

"Geh! Go on. You're late already, not that that will surprise the rabbi. Or your poor father."

They stepped outside and pulled their coats tight. Their shoes on the marble steps, the metal gate snapping shut, even their steps on the clean sidewalk in the lamplight, all sounded crisp like the sounds in a cavernous skyscraper lobby. They strolled down small side streets through Bogenhausen, and Robert was struck by the preternaturally cold (to him) spring evening. White tugboats of breath pulled their faces along the route. Walking by the large old family homes, he felt strangely thrilled by the combination of flowering trees and cold moonless air.

"So why Friday night services?" Robert asked.

"It's the Jahrzeit for my uncle. My father's brother Isaac."

"Oh, I'm sorry. When did he die?"

"Nineteen forty-four."

They clicked along the empty sidewalk in silence. Once again the walk to Schul. Once again the time travel to prewar Poland, the transformation of his companion from jet-set businessman to Polish Jew clopping on cobblestones.

"So," Max merged lanes, rubbing his shoulder against Robert's like a cat. "You haven't asked me about Véronique."

"Why don't you tell me?"

"So you're eager. I must say, she was quite engaging. And quite comely. She's really come into her own under your influence."

"What are you talking about?"

"I tell you, she's a different woman. For years, when everyone was trying to get me to marry her—"

"Except her."

"—except her—she held no interest for me whatsoever. She was too skinny, she had no hair, she was a military feminist,—"

"Militant." Robert snorted.

"Militant. Now I'm all for liberated women, strong women, as you know. I find them far more stimulating, don't you? Also, if I'm going to be involved with someone, I would prefer that she have a life of her own. I don't like to feel that I must provide her with one. Although fascinatingly enough they don't always tend to be better in the sack, it's interesting. I must admit I always imagined that Véronique fell into that category. You know, she was so full of anger. There is another sort of modern woman who is strong and independent, but who also likes men, if you know what I mean, who is tender in matters sexual."

"Like Ingrid."

"Like Ingrid. And it seems to me that Véronique has been making a ... metamorphosis in that direction.

Ah, here we are. It appears that they have begun without me. Shall we go in?"

"Uh, I think I'll wait for you out here. I wasn't mentally prepared for Schul tonight."

"But it's cold."

"I'm fine. I'll wait here in the park."

"As you wish. But the rabbi will be disappointed."

"I'm sure. You can tell him his Torah is safe."

"All right. I'll be quick. And then we can chat some more. And have dinner."

"Oh yeah—dinner." Robert was starving. Max crossed the quiet street and entered the side door of the synagogue. The only other people on the street were the obligatory policeman with his machine gun and a tall stocky young man talking with him, with a kepah on his head, who looked like the bouncer of this holy bar. Robert was standing across the street where Max had left him, on the edge of a small one-block city park. The bouncer caught his eye and they nodded to each other. The bouncer said a few words to the cop, probably assuring him that this guy in the park was okay, he was with Altmann.

Robert turned and walked into the park, found a bench. The chestnut trees were in bloom. Petals rained down through the dark air, illuminated by a street lamp, throwing a silky blanket on the grass, the pathways, the bench, him. He noticed a plaque just a few feet from him: *Shakespeareplatz*.

The irony deflated him. What humiliation, to have to sit in the Bard's own haven and wait like a valet for the master to return.

It was too cold to remain motionless on the bench. He sat for a few minutes, stood and paced up and down the path, rubbing his hands together or warming them in his pockets. Every now and then he'd glance up at the policeman and bouncer, who always seemed immediately to catch his eye.

What the hell was he doing here, paying for a meal with his obeisance, slave once again to the whim of his eccentric patron. This was just the sort of thing he was giving up, one of the degradations of the writing life—at least of *his* writing life. He should just leave now. Max would figure out what had happened. Certainly people had gotten tired of waiting for him before.

He sat down. Consulted his watch for the thirteenth time. In two and a half minutes, at ten-thirty, he would leave, walk to Prinzregentenstrasse and catch a trolley home. Just then, however, the side door of the synagogue opened and the men began sifting out.

Max had said he'd sneak out early, but he wasn't even one of the first to appear. The men and boys poured out in a single line, congregated again briefly on the sidewalk, dispersed in every direction through the lamplit suburb. Another service without anti-Semitic vandalism or violence: the policeman shook hands with the bouncer, got into his cruiser, and took off down the street, the only running automobile in sight. The bouncer, with one last glance at the shadowy figure in the park, went inside the temple. Not a soul was left.

What the hell? Had he sneaked out the back door with some young cleaning woman? Robert walked across the street, thinking what a fool he'd been to wait.

He heard voices from inside the building. They grew louder, and just before they threatened to become bodies in the doorway he recognized Max's expansive conversational tenor. Then his friend appeared, waltzing out with two older men in beards. They struck Robert as three drunken revelers stumbling out of a New Year's party, their kepahs silly party hats that they'd forgotten to remove from their heads. As they slowly half-stepped towards and then down the steps, Max characteristically bumping into the closer of the men as he walked, draping one arm around his shoulder to get in a gibe then pulling away to drive home his point with a serious gesticulation, they were debating, in half Yiddish and half German, something to do with whether or not a particular prayer book was appropriate for the upcoming Pesach services. The future of Judaism apparently hung on their decision.

Robert waited politely. It was a skill he had honed during his time at Max's side; he wondered suddenly if it might not be a marketable talent. Finally Max managed to bring the conversation to a temporarily sufficient understanding and bid his co-congregants goodnight.

"Manage to sneak out early, did you?"

"These guys are really unbelievable, I tell you. Did you get the gist?"

"I think so. "

"This one guy thinks we should adopt a new, modernized, prayer book. And the other guy seems to think that's tantamount to us all converting to Christianity. Naturally they bring me into the middle of it."

"And you mediated a satisfactory conclusion?"

"Ya, so we'll try it out once and let the congregation vote. Not such a difficult compromise to formulate. But it was tough getting Rosenbach to agree. It doesn't matter what the people want, you see. Even if they vote for the new book, it's wrong. The people need to be told what is proper, he says. So we'll vote, and then the argument will start up again from the beginning. But at least I can go home for dinner tonight."

They retraced their path back towards the Altmann home. If Max, like Robert, longed for a meal now several hours overdue, he didn't allow it even so much manifestation as a quickened gait.

"So where were we?" he asked.

"Véronique's metamorphosis," Robert sighed.

"Ah—you're eager for details?"

"Not particularly."

As usual, Max ignored any remark that did not lead the conversation directly down the path of his choosing. "I must say, she looked...ravishing the night we dined with the big cheeses."

"The big French cheeses. That's very good."

"But perhaps it would be insensitive of me to tell you everything. Maybe you still harbor some feelings for Véronique?"

"What are you trying to say?"

"I'm just wondering if perhaps it would upset you, were you to hear that another man had succumbed to charms you seem so able to resist."

"I don't suppose we're talking about anyone we know?"

"So you would be upset."

"I didn't say that. Véronique and I broke up, we're just friends now. I certainly would have no right to object to her seeing someone, even if I did object."

"Which you don't."

"Of course not."

"Good. I'm relieved."

"What do you mean?"

"Well, let's just say that Véronique's long indifference towards me may have finally begun to dissolve."

"And yours toward her?"

"Would it be so surprising?" Their shoes tapped on the cold sidewalk. Robert's temples were flushed, as hot as the rest of him was chilled from the long wait. He wanted to hear it all, out with it in one swollen lump, but he refused to indulge Max's narcissistic prurience by prodding him for information. He would wait for it to come out in excruciatingly slow morsels.

"Ya, I have to say I was torn a bit. I was harnessed by the thought that perhaps you were still attached to her. There was one time I almost rang you up quite late at night to get your...well, not your permission exactly, but your...reassurance." He rubbed up against Robert and it was all Robert could do not to shove him back to his own side of the sidewalk. "But then it was quite late, as I said, and hardly a good moment to run to a telephone. I hope I was not misguided in assuming that your breaking up with her was a sign of genuine indifference."

"As I said, Max, I have no right...."

"Exactly. Good. Our friendship is not compromised, then."

"Of course not." Of course not. I may kill you, but that won't compromise our friendship, will it? How could you? How could she? With him? With the "Marquis des Écharpes." *Not that I'm going to sleep with him—God forbid.* Had she gone mad? Cavorting around Paris with him, wearing the skimpy French gowns he bought her, then screwing him, drunk on an Olympic-pool-sized bed in the Four Seasons George V? The hell with her, then. Let her become an Altmann and bring up his Orthodox children and never leave this city where they tortured her parents and murdered the rest of her family. Let her grow fat on the profits made off the children and grandchildren of the culprits. Well, why not? He was selling out, why shouldn't she? He was unable to keep his compact with himself, to live the life he most admired, most desired. Why should he expect her to pursue the life of the mind, live like a student her whole life, while he went home and raked in a solid suburban income?

The hell with her. May she be as comfortably compromised as he.

They opened the gate of the Altmann property. It was almost eleven o'clock. Kurt rose from the living-room sofa as they entered, Frau Altmann from her gilded chair, both with the weariness of people subjected to hours of late-night small talk. Herr Altmann, who must have been in the crowd of men in hats who had left the service promptly, could be heard talking to the maid in the next room.

"Gut Shabbas, everyone," Max called out in highest humor, striding toward his mother to give her a kiss. Kurt returned his jovial handshake, stifling a yawn. "Shall we dine?"

Half past midnight the sabbath dinner finally ended. Herr and Frau Altmann pushed back their plates, stood, and wished all a good Shabbas. The three young men were left at the table.

"Rob, why don't you stick around while Kurt and I have a short business meeting?"

"I don't know," Robert glanced at his watch. "I think I'd better go."

"It'll take forever to catch a tram at this hour. I'll give you a ride. Just wait fifteen or twenty minutes. We should finish our conversation."

Robert gave his usual shrugging assent, and Max and Kurt disappeared up the stairs. Alone at the ornate table, an infidel billy goat in a garden of fine china. How had the day led to this bathetic outcome? How had it started? In a familiar pose, alone at my desk. The usual dull agony. Then the sudden flight into the city. And the revelation. Was it only this morning that life changed, at last, forever? There had been a flash of lightness, a slight giddiness in place of the overbearing weight of desiccated ambition. The knowledge that it would soon all be history—all the pain, the frustration, the excruciating elusiveness of the goal. Had spent the afternoon half imagining a new life, a simple life with a given task to accomplish each day and a family to come home to.

Then Max had reappeared. I'd thought that he no longer had any power over me. He was part of my Munich interlude, an entr'acte necessary to deliver me from the tortures of the artistic life into the warm haven of a normal, humble adulthood. Yet now Robert simmered in a stew of loathing. His pretty new future had somehow been tarnished. He stood and moved to the living room, collapsed on the deep soft sofa. Could sleep right here. Heard the maid suddenly in the dining room cleaning the table. Shouldn't have made her wait for me. Bad enough she has to outlast the Altmanns. How could she do it? How could she sleep with him? And why does it bother me so? After all, she is poised to dive away, along with him, out of my life forever. Why shouldn't they do it arm in arm?

One o'clock is my limit. Midnight is one thing, but *no one* keeps Robert Cherney waiting until one o'clock in the morning to tell me he's been screwing my ex-girlfriend. At 0100 I am exiting this palace of decorum, this monument to Jewish perseverance, I am stepping back out onto the silent sidewalks of Bogenhausen, and I am *walking* back to Goethestrasse if I have to.

At 12:55 the familiar slapping of Max's loafers came caroming down the marble staircase. Too bad. Robert had been genuinely curious to find out whether he was going to make good on his threat. Goethestrasse was a long walk in the cold.

"You look comfortable." Max sounded like it was three in the afternoon and Robert had dropped by unexpectedly during office hours.

"How are you supposed to look uncomfortable on this sofa? I would have left, but I need a hand to get off this thing. Where's Kurt?"

"Going to sleep in the guest room."

"How was his business trip to Munich?"

"Satisfactory, I believe. He got a nice meal, a hundred thousand units of merchandise, and a good night's sleep in a comfortable bed, without having to get up and change his baby's diaper in the morning."

"You do take care of everyone, don't you?"

"That's business. Some people do business with their head in an account ledger. I find I get more enjoyment—and more lucrative results—by pursuing personal relationships."

Robert mumbled something vaguely concerning Max and personal relationships.

"So." Max fell onto the sofa next to Robert, his leg dangled over his friend's. Robert extricated his limb. "So I notice you have refrained from actually giving me your blessing."

"I chirped right in at dinner with the fruit of the vine."

"I mean with regard to Véronique."

"Doesn't sound like you needed my blessing."

"Need? No. But still one would hope not to hurt the feelings of one's friends."

Don't be so sure who your friends are. Robert sat in silence, his anger diluted by fatigue.

"Extraordinary. That I could go for years without the slightest desire to settle down, without even a very strong feeling for any of the women I see, and then all of a sudden to discover such a connection in the very woman I avoided for years. Do you think it's possible?"

With every intention of noble, mature, affected disinterest, of bestowing the disclaimer, the blessing that Max was soliciting, all Robert could muster was a protracted sigh that came out more as a grumble.

"You're tired," said Max. "Must be working hard in my absence. Lessons?"

"A few."

"Writing."

"Mmm."

"We should get you home. I'd put you in the guest room, but Kurt is there. Shall we?"

Once more in Max's car, in a daze he watched the lights of the city streaking by. He was as drunk with fatigue as if he'd had three liters of Weissbier. No more shall I rocket through the Munich metropolis in this luxury ship, vassal to the wealth of others, indolent hanger-on. No more play the captive audience to his late-night ramblings, no more cull vicarious thrills from his tales of international promiscuity. She can have him. (Forget about letting *him* have *her*.) I have not been a camera, I have been a camcorder, endlessly looping my tape through, recording and erasing, recording and erasing. I am a pinball. I am a crash-test dummy, the way this guy drives.

Max rounded the corner of Goethestrasse, leaving a fair portion of his tires on Bayerstrasse, whirled around and came to a rest half on the sidewalk, and turned off the engine. Even with the heater off, the air inside remained warm, apposite to the scene framed in Robert's window: a cherry tree in full blossom, illuminated by a streetlight. The cooling engine crackled in the quiet night.

"So," Max turned to him with barely restrained glee. "You refuse to react one way or the other."

"To what?"

"To what. Very good. After all, it isn't so long since you and she were on intimate terms. I expected either hurt indignation or else perhaps relief. There's no better way to end a story than to start a new one."

"Sorry, Max, but you get neither extreme. I think it's fine, of course. Why wouldn't I?"

"Why wouldn't you?"

"If you want me to be angry, just keep repeating my fucking questions! But I'm sorry, I'm not going play the jilted lover. Véronique is completely free to be with whomever she chooses. And after goading her with my lack of enthusiasm into breaking up with me, I'm certainly not going to be jealous."

"You're not jealous. Interesting. Then, I have to say, it's almost too bad."

"What? What's too bad?"

"That Véronique and I never did reach an intimate understanding."

"You didn't."

"No, of course there were moments when such matters approached the surface, you know. After all, we were in Paris. But she made it clear that nothing was going to happen between us. One might even have detected a slightly submerged affection for someone else, holding her back. It's funny, after all the years I avoided being brought together with her, and now I wouldn't have necessarily withstood the approach of an amorous moment...."

Max went on unheard. Puppeteer. Nothing. There had been nothing. How many hours—since I

came back from my walk, to now, that's nine hours—
of bitterness he force-fed me. Nine hours of my trying
to tear the last vestiges of an attachment from my gut.
Never could have predicted the pain of it. Thought
that was all over, and glad of it. Of course she wouldn't
have, how could you have believed it? He wanted to
call her immediately, to hear her side of it, to laugh
about the absurdity of such a coupling. Too late to
call, of course. And he wasn't going to run over and
toss stones at her window. Though she'd enjoy that.
He'd probably guess the wrong window and wake
some Bavarian shopkeeper. She'd enjoy that too. No,
nothing to do but wait for morning.

He woke before eight and without a thought of
sleeping off the morning rose, bathed, shaved, was
out on Goethestrasse before the sun had risen above
the Blue Box. Too impatient to wait for a Saturday
morning tram, he found himself practically running
towards Schwabing. *Manhattan.* Slow down, you're
living a cliché. Can't even be original in this. What
am I doing? What am I going to do, say when I get
there? Like a salmon fighting its way upstream, with
no more thought in its head than a vague evolutionary
whisper, he raced urgently up a river of sidewalks.

"Robert?" Her voice sleepy and stunned through
the intercom, she buzzed him in. He ran up the three
flights to find her framed in a thin rectangle of open
door, in a tattered nightgown and a thin black sweater
pulled around her, pale skin dark against morning
sun backlight.

Finally he stopped. Strange, only now I realize I didn't really expect her to be here. "You're not at Schul."

"No," she screened a yawn. "I called in sick, let them go without me."

"Your parents are at Schul."

"Of course, Robert. What's going on?"

He kissed her, for the first time. She cupped the back of his neck and one shoulder as if wondering where he had been all morning. In her room, she still had her sweater on as they began to make love. Nestled between her thighs, his face buried in her neck, he suddenly remembered the words of Freud's patient, upon experiencing coitus for the first time: "One might almost kill one's father for this." He laughed, she took it for a reflexive response to joy, and indeed it was. This couldn't be more different from their past encounters. Whom had he seen back then, when he looked at her? How had his vision been wrecked by solipsistic longing, bitter experience?

They came to rest, he luxuriated in her, she held him tight. "And to think I could be in Schul," she said.

"The rabbi would understand."

"So I am guessing you missed me while I was in Paris."

"Running around with Max. Controlling, lecherous bastard."

"No, no, he was a perfect gentleman. He never once made an improper advance. He certainly talks about you a lot, though. Seems to think you and I belong together."

"We do."

"I know. I certainly didn't think so a couple of months ago, but now it's so obvious."

"Come to New York with me."

"New York? You're leaving Munich?"

"If you will. The thought of beginning another season as coach of the Mattathians is unbearable. I can't even stand to step on a tennis court with a student. I'm canceling all my lessons. Listen: I'm going to get a job."

"Robert Cherney. You're mad."

"I know. A decade dedicated to avoiding gainful employment, and now I'm giving in. And I've never felt so relieved. I'm just not good enough, Véronique. Good enough to feel the need, but not good enough to make it worthwhile."

"I don't believe you."

"You've never read anything I've written."

"I know, but I still don't believe you."

"It doesn't matter. Everything will be fine in New York. I bet you'll get that fellowship..."

"Oh, don't move. As a matter of fact, I did get it. The letter came just a few days ago. I almost mailed my decline letter back already, but now..."

"Now you'll accept."

"Maybe. Okay, yes. Now I'll accept. I don't know. Incredible. How could everything change so abruptly?"

"That's how everything happens. One moment it's before, the next moment it's after. That's it, turn like that."

"Yes."

Soon they dozed for a short while, awoke, made love again, slept again, woke and got out of the apartment just before her parents would return. They spent the entire day together, planning, recounting, trying to make sense of the past eleven months, trying to create a story that seemed credible, that would have meaning for them. The awkwardness of the summer before, the sheer incompatibility, seemed to have no place in their history. Eventually they would have to write it out.

In the late afternoon, they found themselves in the English Garden once again. Véronique had rarely gone there before meeting Robert, and none of his other Munich acquaintances ever went there, yet for them it was the most natural place to take their picnic. The fact that it was the site of both their awkward first date and the conclusion of their ill-executed first stage, rather than keep them away actually made them gravitate towards it. Sprawled on their blanket in the season's nascent warmth, the sound of the Eisbad rushing by, they felt a humble victory over their past.

Also a joyful concupiscence. At one point, aroused by the touch of each other's sun-warmed skin, they followed a twisting narrow path into the woods to find a trysting spot. Before they could manage any kind of consummation, however, an unshaven drunk appeared out of the bushes, spewing barroom Bavarian, sending them laughing running back out into the sunshine.

They made their plans. There was no point in delaying now. As soon as arrangements could be made, within a month, they would leave for America. After years of doubt regarding what he should do with his life, he suddenly felt completely confident in his decision. A mantle of assuredness had settled over him. She professed the same. Her parents would accept it—they would have to. If this was not the right moment, then there never would be one.

At last, exhausted by the long day of ardor and future-gazing, they gathered their things and headed towards the forested perimeter. She would go home but not tell her parents yet. They would not tell anyone for a few days, would enjoy their secret. There was plenty of time for all that.

The pale sky had darkened to a deeper blue. As they walked, Robert gazed above the fingerlike tops of the barely budding oaks and watched a pair of hawks gliding effortlessly through the gloaming. Adjusting their wing positions and their stabilizing tails to maintain flawless flight without the slightest thought, they described perfect circles around the evening's first star. Once again the impossibility of doing it justice. No matter, though; certainly someone has already written it better than I ever could. The yoke is gone, no more must I torture myself to describe this scene. Enough just to enjoy it. There it all was, in a bird dwarfing a star: the immeasurable smallness of earthly life, the undeniable meaninglessness, and also the unimaginable beauty that might just suffice.

13

April was an avalanche of time. The citizens of Munich emerged from the winter like survivors after the war, trying out the parks and sidewalks again, rediscovering their old favorite spots. As one final, spring snowfall melted, Robert felt that a covering of another sort was being lifted from his life. Now that he felt no compulsion to produce prose every day, he began, in his final weeks, finally to appreciate Munich. The museums he revisited while Véronique was busy finishing up school and making arrangements to leave seemed brighter, more beautiful, less foreboding than when he had roamed them in a fitful state after yet another wasted morning. What a contrast, too, from frustrating afternoons spent hurtling through museums and galleries chasing after Lexa. Véronique would never give art such short shrift. Was it my misbegotten literary obsession that made it impossible for me to see her? Or was I just a chump? How could I have misplayed it so? He sat on a bench in the Neue Pinakothek staring at old Kokoschka. Each day brought new beauty he had been blind to, as if the world were a developing Polaroid.

He had written letters to everyone he knew in magazines and book publishing back in New York. He would accept any position, from entry-level on up. The mail room would be fine. What a relief it would be to spend his days sorting mail, the radio in the corner humming golden oldies. Not that he would do that forever. He had also written to law schools, asking that applications be mailed to him at his mother's house. He would fall happily into the role of long-toothed classmate, "old man" of the intramural teams, butt of gentle jokes. Perhaps he would even become a father while still a student. Then work: the comforting security of thirty years or more of a daily task to do and the ability to do it.

How could what now seemed so obvious have been so obscure?

He told Max of his decision after trouncing him 6-1, 6-1 their first time back outdoors at Sport Scheck.

"Remarkable," said Max with a grin as they sat outside the café, culling the most warmth they could from the May sun. "You hardly hit a serious tennis ball all winter, and then you step out here and make a toy of me."

"Well, you haven't exactly been training all winter yourself."

"Correct. But then for me there is less polish to lose. The Volkswagen suffers less from neglect than the Mercedes. It would stand to reason that after a long break we would play a little closer to each other.

It looks as though perhaps we should have moved up to the first *Kreiseklasse* after all."

"Maybe not. I'm leaving, Max. Moving back to New York."

"You're joking."

"I'm not. I'm sorry for the late notice. But I just can't face another summer of teaching tennis."

Max stared at him. "I can't say I'm surprised at that. But leaving so soon? What about your book?"

"There's no fucking book, Max. I've hardly written a page the entire time I've been here. I'm going home and getting a real job, just like you. Well, not just like you."

"There's no book."

"There's no book."

"Helena down in Buenos Aires was wrong: *you're* the Schauspieler."

"I guess so."

"So. What other surprises do you have for me today?"

"Véronique is moving to New York with me."

For the first time since Robert had known him, Max displayed actual discomfiture. "She's going with you."

"Yes."

"Unbelievable." His shock passed and assimilated, a smile of mere interest settled onto his face. "I must say, this is quite a *coup de theatre*. I thought it was all over between you."

"I did too."

"You wanted her all along but didn't know it."

"Apparently."

"Just as you didn't want to be a writer but didn't know that."

"Yes."

"Fascinating. All this soul-searching is so foreign to my experience. Not that I haven't engaged in my share of the philosophical quest, but as regards the particulars of what I'm doing with my life, it all seems so clear cut."

"Except for your love life."

"Ya, but even that I don't wring my hands about. Someday the moment will come, and until then I'm having a good time."

"Still sorry you didn't make a play for Véronique in Paris?"

"I must admit, in the last few months, Véronique has taken on an entirely new image for me. I almost found myself becoming obsessed with her, in a way I never am with the women I see. But then perhaps I could see something between you and her this winter that even you couldn't. Clearly any move on my part would have been futile. And to be honest, I'm happier to see you and her together. I'm not quite ready to be moored."

"Well put."

"So. Rob. You're really going to leave us. The boys will be disappointed. I hope this won't mean the end of the tennis team. There was so much argument this winter about which league they should play in, whether they should try to fund two teams, who should get to play in the higher level, etc. It was all I could do to keep them from each other's throats. And then, you know, several of them have been bitten by the golf bug."

"What?"

"Golf is becoming very big. Saul and Emil, even Uschi, have been taking lessons. They started indoors at this special facility out in Riem, and now they've been playing. I've even played a few rounds. To be honest, I think the main attraction for most of them is how outrageously expensive it is. Three hundred marks, minimum, for one round. It sets them apart even more from the lower classes. But you know, it's not a bad game. Why are you shaking your head?"

"I'm just not sure it's a good idea for Saul to be taking up golf. It's the most mental sport of all. It drives stable men insane. What will it do to him?"

"Ya, I did see him the other day tossing a club into the woods. Listen, you'll have to come by the practice range one day when we're all there. Maybe you can convince him to stick to tennis. At the very least, you should say goodbye."

Surprisingly, as May progressed, time seemed to slow back down, so that his final fortnight in Munich passed at the same rate as any two weeks. With everything decided, and this period already a part of his past, the time should have kaleidoscoped by in a flash, or else have slowed to an excruciating crawl. Instead, the days seemed like days, the weeks like weeks. He could pack up in ten minutes on the final day, but for Véronique there was much to do, and he helped where he could. Otherwise, he toured the last parts of the city he had not yet seen, saw Max a few times in the evening, and read. Read, for the first time in memory without thinking of writing, without feeling he was apprenticing for a greater task. He chose Walker Percy's last novel, *The Thanatos Syndrome*, and it seemed oddly fitting. For as he had read Percy's other novels like an intern seeking to learn from a master, he consumed this one like anyone lying on the beach; and in fact the book was a page-turner. It was as though Percy, in his final effort, had given him a transitional text to complete his transformation from writer to reader.

As the time remaining compressed into a few days, only two items were left to be addressed. The first and more monumental was slated for the Friday evening before their Sunday morning flight. He arrived at the Eisensteins' around eight. With the summer equinox only a month away, summer's late sunsets—and late Shabbas dinners—had arrived in advance of summer weather. Their three-bedroom

Schwabing apartment was far more modest than the Altmanns' mansion but had a similar continental elegance. Robert's one jacket and tie were a Friday-night requirement here as well.

Véronique, sitting at the dining-room table in a black skirt and white sweater, was exquisite. Blindness, the blindness. Was I mad before? He felt slightly vertiginous with joy, as though emerging from a long illness, moving from his hospital bed to the sunshine and windswirled petals of a spring day.

"Véronique tells me that you have decided to go to law school," said Frau Eisenstein. Why did she sound so suspicious? She had waited patiently, exchanging trivial pleasantries before dinner and all during the grapefruit appetizer. Véronique's parents knew that she and Robert were seeing each other again, but she hadn't told them that they would be living together in New York. The NYU fellowship was given as the reason for her (temporary) move across the ocean.

"Yes," Robert cleared his throat. "I had never really intended to stay here teaching tennis for more than a year."

"I hardly thought so," said Frau Eisenstein. "But your writing..." Véronique had clearly fed her the same delusion he had been passing around for years.

"I'm afraid it hasn't been as productive as I'd hoped. But I really am looking forward to doing some more useful work."

"Hear, hear," piped in Herr Eisenstein. Like Herr Altmann, he had always assumed a somewhat bemused attitude towards Robert and his quixotic station in life. He looked positively confident that Robert had made the right decision. But his wife seemed oddly disappointed.

"You'll look after our Véronique," she said.

"I won't let her out of my sight. And really, New York is not such a dangerous place. You should come visit and see."

"I think I am a bit old to go and visit New York," said Herr Eisenstein.

"My husband finds it difficult to sit on airplanes for long. And in any case I'm sure Véronique will be very busy. We won't bother her."

"Don't be ridiculous, Mama. I would love for you to come. You should come."

"Well, perhaps, perhaps. We will see. This is a funny country to want to stay in, anyway, isn't it."

"Your parents seem perfectly reconciled to your leaving," Robert said, his lips brushing the nape of her neck, in her bedroom after dinner.

"Yes." She nuzzled him back like a cat. "I dreaded telling them, got all worked up about it, and when I finally did they acted as though they'd expected it. Hey, James Dean, not here."

"I know, I know. Come to Goethestrasse. We'll say we're going to a movie."

"Yes. Yes. Won't New York be grand?"

As they were preparing to leave, Véronique's mother took her aside to show her some clothes she had bought for her travels, and Herr Eisenstein cornered Robert by the hat stand in the foyer. They smiled awkwardly at each other for a minute.

"Cherney. What sort of name is that?"

"It was shortened by the authorities at Ellis Island when my grandparents emigrated. Chernyshevsky was their name."

"Not Jewish."

"Sure. It must be. Believe me, Zadic and Bubbie...."

"You are going to marry my Véronique?"

"Yes." His own voice took him by surprise. Véronique and he had not even uttered the word. It was comforting to learn that his mind was so well made up on such an important matter. "Yes, Herr Eisenstein, I am."

"Gut. We are glad with you. You are good man, you are Jewish, even if you no go to Schul, and in fact we are glad you take her away from here. It will be a great pain for us not to have our little Véronique with us, but she needs to be away. This is no place for a Jewish person to live."

"But you..."

"Ach. We are like heavy stones, difficult to move."

"You could move to America too. After we're settled. We would be happy to have you. Véronique would be thrilled."

"No, we could never do that. Someday, perhaps. No, I think no."

"Well, then, we will visit often."

"Ja, okay, you visit. You just protect my little Véronique. She is thinking she is tough and doesn't need anybody, but you protect her. God protect you if you don't protect her."

"I will protect her." Robert forced away a smile. If she could hear him swearing to keep her under his wing, how she'd bristle. He could hear the women approaching from the other room.

"Listen," Véronique's father moved close to him, so close Robert could smell his aftershave and the sabbath wine on his breath. "This is the marriage. You leave with her, this is the marriage."

"This is the marriage," Robert repeated. Véronique and her mother entered the foyer. Véronique took her denim jacket from the hat stand and put it on. Frau Eisenstein came up to Robert, put her hand on his cheek. "Good Shabbas, Robert," she said. "I knew you were a mensch. I'm a very good judge of character, you know."

"Good Shabbas, Frau Eisenstein. I hope you're right."

"I know I am." She finally removed her hand. "Listen, you'll come to Schul tomorrow, all right? Just this one last time."

"Of course."

"And then it will be Sunday, and your flight. Time goes so fast, one can barely say it exists. Enjoy the movie, you two."

"Good Shabbas, Mama." Véronique kissed her mother, and she and Robert were out in the burgeoning spring night, running down the sidewalk, as well as two people can run without letting go of each other.

Saturday was the first hot day, deep blue skies and uncompromised sunshine a startling preview of summer's best. It had been hard to believe that such weather would ever return, impossible to imagine the thermal absorption on the skin; now suddenly you could close your eyes and convince yourself it was July.

In the afternoon, Robert rode with Max out to Riem, where the Paragon golf club rubbed verdant shoulders with the Munich Horse Race Course. The Mattathians had been meeting there every Saturday, Max had said, and it would be a good chance for Robert to say goodbye to them all at once. Only ten minutes from downtown, they parked in a lot cut out of a bucolic setting and walked towards a well manicured garden where a smattering of smartly dressed patrons sat sipping coffee at white tables. Robert saw Göttel and his wife Lise sitting with Bernd and Uschi and their wives. He followed Max over to them and sat down.

"Rob," cried Göttel, "can it be true? You're leaving?"

"I'm afraid so."

"But how can you bear to leave this group of self-important nincompoops?"

"And I hear you're taking our Véronique with you," said Lise with a wry smile. Robert didn't know they were acquainted. "I know her since she was a baby. Congratulations. A marvelous girl."

"Listen," Uschi drained his beer and stood up. "It's time for my lesson." He walked over to Robert and laid a heavy hand on his shoulder. "We're going to miss you," he said somberly. "You were making real progress with my game. This golf," he gestured vaguely at the line of well-dressed hackers on the range and the far off clusters of golfers on the rolling green hills behind, "is for fat rich people. But I can't get these guys to hit tennis balls with me anymore."

"Come on," Max stood up. "We'll walk over with you and have a look. You should meet Ken, the golf trainer," he said to Robert. The three of them headed towards the range.

"Don't tell me Bruno is a golfer now too," said Robert.

"No, no," Uschi laughed. "Not his style, which is to his credit. Can you see him here? No, he is my only ally in trying to keep the tennis team going. But Bruno has little influence. And you know, he of course wants to play tennis with me, but what's the point? Better for my game not to play at all."

"It's not as destructive as playing against Dan," Max offered.

"Or even watching Dan," said Robert. "What's he up to, anyway?"

"Gone," said Uschi. "I tried calling him just a few weeks ago. His phone was discontinued, so I stopped by his flat, and there was no sign of anyone living there. His name was gone from the placard. I've asked around, but no one seems to know where he's gone."

"I didn't know this," said Max. "But then he wasn't very socially connected, aside from tennis."

"Even Bruno didn't know. Perhaps he's gone back to Johannesburg."

"We'll have to keep a watch for news about a new women's squash tour," said Robert without conviction. Poor Dan. I suppose orange juice didn't become Munich's cappuccino after all. Wonder how far he had to go to escape his creditors. Or his reputation. Where would he land? Probably run into him in New York, at the Racquet and Tennis Club.

They reached the range and promenaded down the lineup of struggling acolytes whacking little white balls off rubber tees. Trying to, anyway. Hitting anywhere but straight. Fat man in peach slacks and button-down white shirt slices one into a perfect hyperbola, attaining a path parallel to the line of hitters just as it enters the woods. Young woman dressed in old money swings big, just skims top of ball, sends it tottering forward five yards. Same with next ball.

And next. Older man who ought to have something better to do trying desperately to make any kind of contact at all, swing after swing producing nothing but his curses. Same pathetic quest for meaningless improvement, but at least on the tennis court one gets some exercise.

Near the end of the line was Saul, in crisp khakis, white golf shirt, and his round spectacles, bent over the tee, sedulously adjusting the position of the ball so as to maximize the range of its imminent flight. Robert immediately picked out the instructor, a portly man of thirty-five or forty in well-worn beige slacks and black golf shirt, with dark curly hair and a thick black mustache. He waited with head down, massaging the bridge of his nose with one hand, for Saul to complete his ball placement. Next to Saul, Emil sprayed ten or twelve balls across the lawn like fertilizer while Saul prepared for one shot. The pro paid him no attention whatsoever. "That's Ken," Max whispered. They had pulled up ten yards short and waited for Saul to swing. "Emil took a lesson from him during a business trip in England. Convinced him to move here for a while and be our trainer. He's been a big hit so far."

Finally satisfied with the ball's posture, Saul straightened up and began a series of maneuvers involving his own. He spaced his feet meticulously, stiffened his legs, tentatively fingered the grip of his driver, placed the club head just so on the ground behind the ball, repositioned his feet, adjusted his glasses, regripped the club, wiggled his hips slightly, lifted the club head and replaced it on the same spot behind the ball, slipped Ken (whose head was still down, not watching at all) a surreptitious glance as if hoping for an approving nod, then repeated the entire procedure. Finally, just as his friends were about to abandon their politesse, an event that had begun to seem inconceivable occurred: he began his backswing.

The swing looked good to Robert. Saul was a fine athlete, after all, and he brought the club up behind his head and then back down in a smooth acceleration towards the ball. The club head, however, grazed the ground just before reaching the tee, took out a delicate divot, and bounced up and hit only the top of the ball, sending it dribbling forward a few feet. Saul shook his head hopelessly. Ken, who appeared not to have lifted his head to see the shot at all, spoke through his hand, which stroked his mustache. "We're here to hit the ball, love. Keep your head down and watch that little white ball, or you're going to ruin your shoulder, the club, and that patch of ground. Try it again."

Saul saw his friends, shook his head at them. "This game is torture, boys. Pure torture." Resigned to failure, he turned, picked another ball out of the bucket, and began to arrange it on the tee. Ken inched over towards Emil and watched him hit a few with an expression of mild disgust. Emil was at least making contact with the ball, and seemed pleased with the results, as though hitting the five-acre lawn anywhere was the goal.

"Hopeless, love, you're hopeless," said Ken. Emil's smile fell from his face. "Listen, love: what I'm asking you to do, a cripple could do. Take that bloody five-iron and hit the ball somewhere within shouting range of that hundred-and-fifty-yard marker. And do it without jumping into the air in the middle of your bloody swing. Make some show at swinging as I've showed you."

Emil frowned and placed another ball on his tee. This time he took a few seconds to prepare, set his feet and club in proper position. He pulled the club up high and let it come swinging down with a jerky motion that displaced his feet from their starting position. The club head bore through the rubber tee, lifting the ball high into the air, a dark star against the bright blue sky. It fell to earth a few seconds later, twenty yards away.

"You've got no hint, love. No hint." Ken moved back to Saul, who was just beginning his next swing. It was a thing of beauty, fluid and powerful, and this time he struck the ball square and sent it soaring in a glorious trajectory, low and rising with underspin, straight away. It came to earth just short of the two-hundred-yard marker, bounded forward, and disappeared into the grass. Saul held his follow-through position for a few seconds, then turned back to his onlookers with a grin.

"You call that a bloody golf swing?" Ken was shaking his head. "You'll never get off the range with that thing. I don't give a crock where the ball goes.

Your right leg's all wobbly, your left arm's bent, your entire swing's as wild as a madman's. This is golf, love, not cricket."

Robert and Max and Uschi left Saul standing there in absolute puzzlement and retreated to the café. Poor Saul. Tennis was enough of an emotional trial for him; golf could double his psychoanalysis bills. He's bitten, however, and the bug will not rest until it's sucked away a good portion of his fortune.

"I have to get my equipment and begin stretching," said Uschi. "Bon voyage, Rob. It has been a pleasure."

"Good-bye, Uschi. I'm sorry I couldn't keep the guys interested in tennis."

"It's not you. They always need something new. Something more expensive. But hey—what a great win against BMW, eh?"

"That was something," Robert agreed. They shook hands, and Uschi walked off to the locker room. Robert and Max took seats and ordered coffee and tea.

"So that was Ken," said Robert. "He's a big hit?"

"I've been telling you all along, Rob," Max laughed, "these people want discipline. They want to be told what they're doing wrong."

"If that sort of debasement is what they want, they could get it at 1001 Nights. Probably cheaper."

"That's true. But here they can bring their wives."

"Well, I can see the sort of tennis pro I should have been. Sort of a dominatrix in tennis shorts."

"You were fine, Rob. It was good for these people to meet someone like you, who's not so . . ."

"Goal-oriented?"

"Very good. But in fact I always was the one who thought you *were* goal-oriented. I thought you were working towards the completion of your magnum opus. Yet in fact you had no goal!"

"Oh, but I did. And I've achieved it. My goal was to give up. To quit. For years I thought I couldn't, I thought that I was doomed to a lifetime of pursuing the unattainable. I was unable to quit. And then suddenly I was able."

"At least for the moment. I have the feeling that such 'callings' are not so easily abandoned."

"And what about you, Max? Where will your 'philosophical quest' end? Or will it simply fade away behind the daily race for profit?"

"Ya, I'd like to say that I'm going to give up my business and move to California to live on the beach and search for truth, but we know that's not going to happen. In fact, I wouldn't even want to do that, as you must know. Business will always be my life, but one hopes that the deeper search doesn't have to fade away."

"Or the search for that perfect companion."

"Or that. Not that there's any rush. We're still very young, for men anyway. Why not enjoy ourselves for a while longer?"

He sipped his tea, Robert his coffee. The distant pop-gun retorts of golf balls being struck pleasantly perforated the glorious spring day.

"So," Max smiled, "you're off tomorrow."

"Into the wild blue yonder."

"I'll have to plan my next New York trip soon."

"We would love to see you."

"You can show *me* around for a change."

"I'll introduce you to the subway. I bet you've never tried it."

"You're correct. Why would one want to travel underground? I'd rather see where I'm going."

"Well, Rob," he said after a brief sun-poached silence, "at least you managed to last an entire year with the Mattathians."

May 20. Today was, Robert realized, exactly one year. Too bad; flying out tomorrow ruins the perfect symmetry. Max turned to answer the call of a friend who had just sighted him from a distance, and Robert watched him execute his perfectly mannered banter. He would never regret having known Max, though he knew their friendship would fade relatively quickly. Where would Max be in ten years? Would he ever manage to wrench himself, and his business, away from the place he both loathed and was so comfortable in? Perhaps when his parents were gone he would be able to leave, finally to carry what was left of the Altmann line—himself—away from the locus of their tragedy. Probably not. It was far easier to picture Max growing old right here in Munich, amassing his millions, squiring his fancy women around the world. A true character. No, not in that sense; that's gone forever. Robert tipped his head back to catch the full sun, let the energy diffuse through his sunglasses and into his cranium, his mind one deep red glow. Surrendered to a pleasant sense of vertigo, the sounds of the people around him merging into a crickety chorus and the heat on his arms seeming to spin him gently like a solar pinwheel. Twenty-four hours left, and then he would be sailing through the ether in a metal tube, his so recently discovered love at his side. Twenty-four hours so evanescent that they might as well be lifting off the German soil already, racing westward over the city, where they could see the Frauenkirche still standing as it had stood five hundred years ago, as it had stood on his first day in Munich, as it would stand for who knows how long. Westward, over the Bavarian farmland that reminded him of the countryside along the Connecticut River. Westward, and higher, until Europe was just the Earth far below, distant land appearing sporadically between clouds. Westward, as her parents should have done but could not when they were younger than we. If they had, we would have met as suburban children, at recess, in high-school English class, or on rolling New England university lawns. Instead, she had become a consequence of history's epilepsy, marked forever by Europe's seizure. Still, though a half-century late, she was finally heading West. And indeed they were immigrants, headed for a new life.

"What on earth are we going to do in America?" she said suddenly, without much concern. He turned from the small oval window, which had been giving his forehead a hint of the barren frigid air four inches away.

"I'm going to get a job for a year," he said. "And you're going to school, remember? Afterward, I suppose you'll get a job too. You can always find translation work—you'll be a hot commodity."

"And you really want to go to law school?"

"Well, we'll see. Maybe I'll like working so much I'll just stick with it."

"Hmm. You can teach all those enormous athletic Americans to become tennis champions."

"No, no, no more tennis. I've given what I have to the world of recreation. There's plenty of other work I can do."

"You can write."

"No, I wasn't joking before. I think it's time to give up that particular dream, don't you think? At some point you have to recognize that you just don't have the talent. When you no longer have the excuse of having no time to write, and you're over thirty and have been writing for years, and haven't produced the book you imagined you would. No, I think I'll just concentrate on getting a job and working well at it."

"All right, Rückhandmann."

"We'll have good jobs. No frustrations, no worries. A nice house somewhere in the country. The American dream for you, Véronique."

"That's nice. But I think you'll always be a writer, Mr. Cherney."

"There's nothing there, Véronique. I tried, but there's just nothing there."

"I could say 'That's okay, darling, I just want you to be happy and it doesn't matter to me if you're a writer or a tennis trainer or a plumber, as long as you're happy.' But I know that's the last thing in the world you'd want me to say."

He looked at her, but her eyes were closed. On the other side of her, a newspaper lay on the aisle seat. WITH HUNGARIAN BARBED WIRE GONE, EAST GERMAN REFUGEES FLOW TO WEST. Hmm, remarkable times on the way? No, leave it to a new Isherwood. Feel like my own barbed wire has been clipped.

"I would like to have a baby with you someday," she said.

"Of course we will."

"Maybe we already have one."

"That would be perfect, Véronique. Maybe we do."

"I doubt it, but it's possible at this point. We were a little careless."

"I hope we do."

"So do I. But then we would have to get married, you know. I'm very old-fashioned."

"Of course we're getting married, Véronique. Didn't you know that?"

She smiled. "Perhaps."

"Véronique."

"Yes?"

"Véronique."

"What is it, Mister?"

"I'm just saying your name."

She smiled again. Her eyes still closed, she turned toward him and laid her head against his shoulder.

She woke suddenly with ocher sunlight pouring onto her face from the west. At first she seemed surprised to find herself on an airplane but immediately adjusted her consciousness to her new situation: mid-flight to a new continent and a new life. "Where are we?" she asked.

He looked out the window and saw nothing but blue, couldn't tell if it was ocean or sky. The plane was banked, and the sun, in a disorienting position, flooded the window with a burnt yellow scattering of light and heat. So it was sky: an endless canopy arcing over them. Suddenly, as though seeing the flash of the northern lights, he was struck by a vision: Max, his parents, the tennis players, Lexa, Ingrid, Véronique, (Véronique, Véronique), the Goethestrasse apartment, the Altmanns' gilded home, the Eisbad of the English Garden, all laid out in perfect arrangement. For the briefest moment, before he forced it back down like bile, he was visited by the apparition of all these elements transformed into the crystalline structure of art. The real thing? Unlikely. Still, one never knows. What cruel irony, what a devilish trickery, that it should all come to him now, present itself like a contrite lover, just when he had finally turned away. To burn the image out of his mind, he stared at the reflection of the sun on the wingtip. Soon all that remained of the vision was her. "The stratosphere," he answered, but when he looked back at her she was fast asleep.

ALSO FROM
NEW CHAPTER PRESS

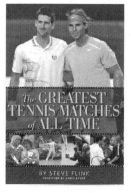

The Greatest Tennis Matches of All Time
By Steve Flink

Author and tennis historian Steve Flink profiles and ranks the greatest tennis matches in the history of the sport. Roger Federer, Billie Jean King, Rafael Nadal, Bjorn Borg, John McEnroe, Martina Navratilova, Rod Laver, Don Budge and Chris Evert are all featured in this book that breaks down, analyzes, and puts into historical context the most memorable matches ever played.

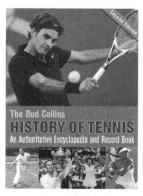

The Bud Collins History of Tennis
By Bud Collins

Compiled by the most famous tennis journalist and historian in the world, this book is the ultimate compilation of historical tennis information, including year-by-year recaps of every tennis season, biographical sketches of every major tennis personality, as well as stats, records, and championship rolls for all the major events.

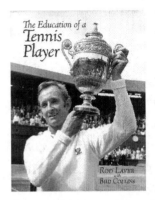

The Education of a Tennis Player

By Rod Laver with Bud Collins

Depicting the monumental achievements of a world-class athlete, this firsthand account documents Rod Laver's historic 1969 Grand Slam sweep of all four major tennis titles. This frank memoir details Laver's childhood, early career, and his most important matches. Each chapter also contains a companion tennis lesson, providing tips on how players of all levels can improve their own game and sharing strategies that garnered unparalleled success on the courts. Fully updated on the 40th anniversary of the author's most prominent triumph, this revised edition contains brand new content, including the story of Laver's courageous recovery from a near-fatal stroke in 1998.

TITANIC: The Tennis Story
By Lindsay Gibbs

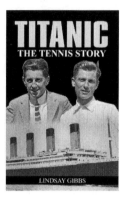

A stirring and remarkable story, this novel tells the tale of the intertwined life of Dick Williams and Karl Behr who survived the sinking of the *Titanic* and went on to have Hall of Fame tennis careers. Two years before they faced each other in the quarterfinals of the U.S. Nationals – the modern-day U.S. Open - the two men boarded the infamous ship as strangers. Dick, shy and gangly, was moving to America to pursue a tennis career and attend Harvard. Karl, a dashing tennis veteran, was chasing after Helen, the love of his life. The two men remarkably survived the sinking of the great vessel and met aboard the rescue ship *Carpathia*. But as they reached the shores of the United States, both men did all they could to distance themselves from the disaster. An emotional and touching work, this novel brings one of the most extraordinary sports stories to life in literary form. This real-life account – with an ending seemingly plucked out of a Hollywood screenplay - weaves the themes of love, tragedy, history, sport and perseverance.

www.NewChapterMedia.com

ALSO FROM
MARSHALL JON FISHER

A Terrible Splendor

Before Federer versus Nadal, before Borg versus McEnroe, the greatest tennis match ever played pitted the dominant Don Budge against the seductively handsome Baron Gottfried von Cramm. This deciding 1937 Davis Cup match, played on the hallowed grounds of Wimbledon, was a battle of titans: the world's number one tennis player against the number two; America against Germany; democracy against fascism. For five superhuman sets, the duo's brilliant shotmaking kept the Centre Court crowd–and the world–spellbound.

But the match's significance extended well beyond the immaculate grass courts of Wimbledon. Against the backdrop of the Great Depression and the brink of World War II, one man played for the pride of his country while the other played for his life. Budge, the humble hard-working American who would soon become the first man to win all four Grand Slam titles in the same year, vied to keep the Davis Cup out of the hands of the Nazi regime. On the other side of the net, the immensely popular and elegant von Cramm fought Budge point for point knowing that a loss might precipitate his descent into the living hell being constructed behind barbed wire back home.

Born into an aristocratic family, von Cramm was admired for his devastating good looks as well as his unparalleled sportsmanship. But he harbored a dark secret, one that put him under increasing Gestapo surveillance. And his situation was made even more perilous by his refusal to join the Nazi Party or defend Hitler. Desperately relying on his athletic achievements and the global spotlight to keep him out of the Gestapo's clutches, his strategy was to keep traveling and keep winning. A Davis Cup victory would make him the toast of Germany. A loss might be catastrophic.

Watching the mesmerizingly intense match from the stands was von Cramm's mentor and all-time tennis superstar Bill Tilden—a consummate showman whose double life would run in ironic counterpoint to that of his German pupil.

Set at a time when sports and politics were inextricably linked, *A Terrible Splendor* gives readers a courtside seat on that fateful day, moving gracefully between the tennis match for the ages and the dramatic events leading Germany, Britain, and America into global war. A book like no other in its weaving of social significance and athletic spectacle, this soul-stirring account is ultimately a tribute to the strength of the human spirit.